the desplazados

a novel

martin zehr

First Printing, April, 2017

ISBN: 978-0-9987583-0-5

Library of Congress Catalog Number: 2017903532

ZenRider Press, LLC
5607 Rockhill Road, Suite 100
Kansas City, Missouri 64110-2741

Cover and interior design by
Graphikitchen, LLC
219 South Main, Suite 300
Ann Arbor, MI 48104
www.graphikitchen.com

For Susan, co-rider

A Day's Work

Habit and inertia are the first principles of thought and action for ninety-nine percent of humanity. — GUSTAV FLEISSHAUER

D riving at the speed of the interstate herd, in the monotonous pattern governing these trips and those of the faceless commuters surrounding him, Gregory Barth's thoughts drifted back to the conversation with his friend. In his rolling metal and plastic cocoon, music ordinarily inducing singing, Otis Redding's "The Dock of the Bay," had become background, his present thoughts intruding, assuming centerstage. He'd lost awareness of driving and surroundings, preoccupied with a gnawing upset forcing his focus on important, if not eagerly confronted issues. His unease demanded attention, and got it.

The monthly Nelson Gallery lunches with Dave Maxwell were reliable respites from the pressures of their respective life routines. Their friendship, forged years ago in the crucible of graduate school, was the foundation for these meetings, surviving as habit through upheavals in their professional and personal lives, including Dave's divorce. In the wake of his split, Dave had weathered fits of depression, but, with much still unresolved, he exhibited a calm that Barth found disconcerting.

After a hiatus of twenty years, Dave had taken up motorcycling, an attempt, Barth assumed, to fill a void during this turbulent period. Mostly a social thing, Dave dubbed the riders he hung out with the "Latte Loiterers," after the hangout where these "wild and crazy guys" gathered, an upscale coffee shop in the Plaza, the swank, Spanish-motifed shopping area south of downtown Kansas City.

He'd mentioned the woman before, Barth recalled, not the prototypical biker babe. The riders called her the Duchess—not for her demeanor, but as a tribute to her bike, a bright red Ducati. The kind of ride, according to Dave, that looked fast and sensuous, even parked curbside.

Today, he had shocked Barth into his reflective mode.

"We started dating two weeks ago. She's one of the regular riders, works in the downtown public library and has two teenage daughters."

"Are you sure it's smart getting into something like this? I mean, it seems like a lot to handle so soon..."

Barth's voice trailed off. It wasn't necessary to complete the thought, but he continued, attempting a brotherly, cautionary exhortation.

"Dave, I just hope you know what you're doing."

"Hell no, I don't know what I'm doing, you old fool, and I couldn't care less. If I waited until I knew what I was doing, I'd never get moving. I'd just rot. I'm not going to be another geezer rocking my life away in a nursing home, wishing I'd tried things. No way! Time to move on, even if it's in the wrong direction... I'm feeling alive again, for the first time in months, and I don't give a damn. I'm going with this, whatever it is. No offense, old man, but you could use a taste of living for a change."

Barth smiled at the reference—he was two years younger than his friend. Dave's decisive tone was a foreign commodity to him, but a quality he nevertheless admired. The last jibe contained no hint of malice, but it stung. He decided not to respond. Dave's energy was real, and he knew better than to put a damper on it.

"Yeah, you might be right about that, maybe your ignorance is bliss, kid."

They laughed.

"Hey, our lives aren't getting any longer. Better to burn out than rust out and all that crap."

His friend's optimism was astonishing, considering his situation. Barth realized that his reaction to Dave's newfound dynamism was based on envy—plain, unadorned envy. Dave's aliveness in the midst of the chaos and uncertainty in his life was the mirror image of the dull repetition in his own. His friend's turmoil and adaptation underscored a nagging dissatisfaction in his own life, a notion that his middle-aged automaton existence had provided a degree of comfort, the value of which he was starting to question.

Whether this was the ordinary musing of someone in his settled life pattern or not was, to Gregory Barth, irrelevant. If this was his "mid-life crisis," the sense of alarm he felt was undeniably real, and, just as undeniably, demanded his attention.

If not for this gut feeling, he might have been satisfied with a detached, perfunctory analysis of the "problem," but that was no longer possible. The stirring within that had emerged during lunch was now the entire foreground of his being, absorbing him like nothing in recent memory. The conversation was only the immediate cause, the "tipping point," forcing awareness of a constellation of thoughts needing only the push of Dave's remarks. What had been a dormant, vague malaise was now a nagging irritation, prodding Gregory Barth into recognition, gnawing at him, grabbing his attention, with a clenched-fist grasp that wouldn't let go.

His friend's calm, in the midst of the state of flux defining his life, struck Barth with the force of a hammer blow, awakening him to the fact of his own growing dissatisfaction. How could it be that his own existence, with its routine, control and predictability, was acquiring a frame of existential angst, while Dave, who couldn't see the end of his struggles, seemed at perfect peace? The contrast was disconcerting, and this feeling must surely, he thought, push him, pull him, or point the direction to somewhere, an as yet unknown but suddenly desired destination of the soul …his soul.

Some neuronal connection urged to consciousness an image that seemed relevant to these musings. The patient he'd seen this morning, Mabel Cavanaugh, very different from what Barth expected. He'd received a routine referral from a local nursing home to see a new resident with a common malady—probable depression following her admission, which was voluntary. Or at least nominally voluntary. Her daughter, concerned about her mother's increasingly frail health, had urged her to move into what was designated as an "assisted living apartment," for reasons of safety. Mrs. Cavanaugh, the dutiful mother, reluctantly agreed to a three-month trial stay, on the condition that she have her own room, with a window, at the end of a hall, and that she be left alone.

Reviewing her medical chart at the nursing station, Barth noted little out of the ordinary. She was eighty-eight years old, twice widowed, and had been living with her daughter, whose concerns regarding her mother's osteoporosis had prompted the admission. It was a bit odd that, aside from calcium supplements, there was no medication regimen, and she smoked, requiring staff time to wheel her out to the patio after dinner, apart from the other residents, to indulge her habit. She had isolated herself from staff and residents, according to her chart notes, and the staff was appropriately concerned about the new resident's "withdrawal," precipitating the call to Dr. Barth.

Barth knocked on the open door, waiting a few seconds before the invitation to enter, a curt, irritated "What do you want now?"

"I'm Dr. Barth, I'd like to talk with you a few minutes."

"You're the shrink. They said I had to see you, so I can't tell you to go to hell."

Barth entered the room, surveying the space. His first surprise was the sight of its occupant, sitting at a desk abutting the window, staring intently at a computer screen. In his experience, it was still atypical for octogenarians to be computer literate. She didn't turn immediately toward him, but began furiously tapping on the keyboard. Her hands, moving with the speed and vitality of youth, were betrayed by their bony appearance and a smattering of brown age spots. She paused, and turned, facing the intruder.

"What do you want from me? I'm busy and don't have time to waste, so let's get this over with."

This was the type of response Barth expected in conjunction with a court-ordered evaluation, not with a nursing home resident. In these cases, it was common for the conversation-starved individuals to welcome him.

"The staff thought it would be a good idea for me to check and see how you're doing after your first week here."

"So they think I'm crazy, do they? You want a little privacy, some peace and quiet so you can work, and all they can think is that you must be nuts because you don't want to abide by their rules and play happy."

"No, I don't think you're crazy. Listen, if you'll just talk to me, answer some questions, I'll be able to learn something about you and leave you in peace. A few minutes, that's all I'm asking."

Responding in something other than a rude, impatient manner, the woman shifted in her chair, fixing her gaze in Barth's direction, meeting his eyes, examining her examiner.

"What are you working on?"

"If I tell you anything private you can't tell anyone or write about it so the staff can read it for their amusement, isn't that right?"

"Basically that's correct, unless it's directly related to your health."

Barth wasn't used to being the first to answer probing questions in a professional encounter, but he had to acknowledge that her concerns were legitimate and that, indeed, she was within her rights to question him.

"Well, Doc, I guess it's okay, I just need to know where I stand. If you must know, I'm writing an e-mail to my agent. He's always in a rush and doesn't understand that it's not as easy for me to do research here as it was when I could get out."

"Research?"

"Yeah, didn't they tell you? I write romance novels. It keeps me going, it's different from the writing and reading I could do when I was working."

"What kind of work did you do?"

"I taught English for forty-two years at Southeast High School. Then I had to make sure we read the classics, you know, no junk, although I had my share of complaints from parents who thought *Huckleberry Finn* was 'the *veriest* trash.'"

The significance of the latter allusion eluded Barth, but already he knew this lady was a character, someone who would obviously appear, at first glance, to be eccentric, or worse.

"So why do you write romance novels?"

Barth thought the question might help break the ice.

"Because it's fun. I try to entertain and do good, solid writing."

"Have you ever published anything?"

"You've probably never heard of Ellen Foster Hoolihan, or you don't look at the paperbacks in airports and grocery stores. Yeah, I've had a few printed, enough to pay bills and keep me busy answering readers' mail."

Barth sized up this lady—feisty, independent, energetic, somewhat of a workaholic, direct and to the point in her social interactions, and, of course, eccentric. No wonder the staff was concerned. Depressed, however, she was not, at

least not on the basis of her desire for privacy. He decided to take the biographi-
cal approach, if she'd allow it.

"I don't want to take more of your time than I have to, Mrs. Cavanaugh. I
just want to get some idea about what you need here besides being left alone. I
get that."

"You can call me Mabel."

She smiled, for the first time, sensing that Barth was empathetic. At least he
didn't count her odd behavior as a source of particular concern. She had no idea
whether his interest in her was genuine, but accepted his commitment to keep
her private life private and trusted his respectful attitude, so far at least.

From that point the conversation became just that. Barth was intrigued and
entertained by Mrs. Cavanaugh's story. A well-educated woman, she was twice
widowed and had two children, a son in California and her daughter, a widow
herself, living in a small house in Grandview, just south of Kansas City. Life
with her daughter had worked out well until her osteoporosis progressed to a
point that precluded driving, reinforcing her daughter's concerns regarding her
safety. Mrs. Cavanaugh reluctantly agreed to the trial stay here in the city, where
public transportation made access to the university library reasonably reliable.
The combined income from her pension and royalties from her hobby could
have financed a comfortable living in a Plaza condo, with available assistance,
but Mabel's lifelong frugality and an ingrown disdain for those who relied on
servants rendered such a choice impossible. Never mind that the staff could
have been regarded similarly. Mabel rationalized her presence here as vital for
her health, while simultaneously encouraging as little interaction as possible.

Had he limited his observation to her thin, stooped frame and wrinkled,
pale visage, Barth would have been able to guess this woman's age, certainly
within five years, he thought, especially seeing her in these surroundings. By
this point in their meeting, however, he noted other aspects of her appearance
suggesting an unorthodox approach to living. The long, thin cotton dress, plain
in its cut and faded blue color, certainly did nothing to contradict the picture
he had formed prior to this meeting, but other outward anomalies hinted at the
woman he had observed since then. The digital watch, the small, elegant silver
and turquoise ring on the little finger of her right hand, and the stockingless feet,

comfortably encased in a pair of worn handcrafted leather sandals, all raised questions about this remarkable woman.

By far the most compelling aspects of this encounter, of course, had nothing to do with her visual presence. This woman's energy, her enthusiasm, her "impertinent" questioning of and lack of automatic deference to his professional role—these facets of her behavior, with which he had been taken aback, were the source of intense interest. Mabel, the "recluse" who was, within a few minutes' time, more open in her personal dialogue than many of Barth's regular patients, was alive and engaged in the world she had constructed for herself, one she didn't feel obligated to share with the nursing home staff.

I should be so depressed, thought Barth, feeling somewhat inadequate at the realization that this lady had more to offer him than any "insight" he could hope to provide within the context of "therapy".

Scanning the room, his view was filled with awkwardly stacked books and papers, arranged in an order he could not divine. Two cartons of unfiltered Pall Malls lay in wait next to the keyboard. No plants or knick-knacks adorned the windowsill, giving the room a more utilitarian, spartan look than he'd come to expect in nursing home settings. There was a conspicuous absence of personal photos, no clues suggesting that Mrs. Cavanaugh was part of a family network. More surprising, in Barth's experience, was the missing television, the universal pacifier for young and old alike, including himself. He couldn't recall entering a resident's room in a nursing facility that wasn't furnished with this appliance.

"Not much of an interior decorator," he suggested, as much an inquiry as a comment.

"No time," she replied, as if that was explanation enough for her visitor. Then, sensing the deeper implications of Barth's remark, she elaborated.

"I don't want to get the feeling that this is home, like I'm here for the duration or anything like that. As far as I'm concerned, this is a place to get some work done in peace until I decide what comes next. Just passing through."

"I noticed you don't have any photographs."

"Not true. I just want to stay private. The staff thinks it's their God-given right to come in any time they damn well please, poking around and talking when I'm not interested in chit-chat. I'm not giving them a chance to start one of their 'Oh, that's so nice, she looks so beautiful, who's that, where was that taken' talks, especially since not one of them is really interested. They just need to fill their time until the shift's over."

"That seems kind of harsh, Mabel, I'm sure you're exaggerating."

He wasn't actually sure, but felt an obligation to mute her criticism, keeping in mind the fact that this facility wasn't designed to meet this woman's particular needs.

"Here, Doc, if you're really interested, I'll show you some memories. Pull out the box over there by the bed."

Barth complied without comment, accepting what he interpreted as an invitation to her inner sanctum. He hadn't noticed the crudely-fashioned wooden crate resting against the bed. Mabel pulled back the lid and began sorting through bunches of photos, letters and postcards tied together with colored ribbons. She produced photos depicting travels with her daughter, Veronica, from birth to middle age, photos of family scenes with her daughter and both husbands, laughing as she extracted selections for their story value. Barth couldn't help noting the compliment in her willingness to share her stories.

Mabel picked up a manila envelope with a reverence that piqued Barth's interest, carefully removing an oversize black-and-white image and smiling as she fondled the paper memory in her hands. After pausing for her own reflections she offered it for Barth's study.

"Take a look at every woman's fantasy."

Barth took the photo he'd been handed with an appropriate degree of respect, careful not to let his fingers come in contact with the glossy surface. Mabel did not exaggerate—the photo was that of a young Elvis, circa 1960, at the controls of a well-chromed Harley-Davidson, with an older, prim-looking woman wearing a long, pale, cotton summer dress, sitting behind, her arms around the King's waist and a wide, white-toothed smile aimed directly at the camera. Presley was dressed in black slacks and shoes, with an inch of white sock showing, a dark casual shirt with rolled up sleeves and open collar, and a slightly cocked captain's hat, *a la* Brando, adorned with a gold braid band above the visor.

"After he took Veronica for a ride, he asked me to get on." She laughed, recalling the incident.

"You must have been excited."

"Not really, not at first anyway. Veronica made me promise to stop at Graceland, and, you know, I wasn't really a fan. Knew who he was, of course, you couldn't help that.

I have to say, he really had a magic about him. I couldn't help myself, when he asked me to get on, I was thrilled. I didn't think it showed and, honestly, I was worried about what Veronica might think, her mother going ga-ga like a teenager, but something told me I couldn't refuse an invitation like that, even though I probably should have been scared. I'd never been on a motorcycle in my life. You know, he was so polite, so nice. He made me feel I was doing him a favor by riding with him, not the other way around. I can still remember thinking, my arms are holding Elvis, this is something else!"

Mabel was blushing, lost for the moment in vivid recollection. Barth guessed there was a hint of an erotic aspect in her experience, then and now, but decided not to intrude on her privacy any more than he had thus far.

"That's a great memory" was the only comment he could muster.

"Hey, I'm not dead yet, Doc," she replied, grinning directly at Barth, seeming to acknowledge the implicit sexual feelings in her recollection.

"I felt like a kid when it happened, like a giddy teenager, but I didn't care. Veronica was embarrassed, her mother behaving like some floozy, even though it was nothing but an innocent ride, but I think she started realizing that her mother was a person too, with desires just like hers—submerged, of course, but not so different. After that, the trip to New Orleans was just two girls having fun, and things between us changed."

Barth felt a twinge of regret at this last observation. As a boy, he'd never shared such an experience with his father, and his relationship with his mother was formal and distant. This woman, in the confines of her room at the end of the hall, was more alive than many lonely beings "outside in the world."

By this time Barth had seen and heard enough to establish, to his satisfaction, this woman's status as an interesting character, to be sure, but not someone requiring psychiatric attention. His first impulse was to remain seated and entertained by Mabel's stories, but he knew he'd observed enough to fulfill his professional obligations. Any longer and he could justly be accused of voyeurism, no matter that she was obviously comfortable with him.

"I have to say you're one interesting lady, Mabel, although I suppose you know that already, but I've got to get going, and you've got to get back to your agent." He rose and turned to the door, looking back, meeting her unflinching gaze and sly grin.

"You aren't going to rat on me now, are ya Doc?" Her playful smile betrayed her confidence that the question was unnecessary.

"Mabel, consider it our dirty little secret. I'll stop by sometime next month. Good-bye."

Barth left the room and its busy occupant, re-entering the hallway with its antiseptic smell. He stopped at the nursing station, taking possession of Mrs. Cavanaugh's chart. In the section labeled "Progress Notes," he scribbled "No observed evidence of depression."

In the next instant, Gregory Barth reasserted control over this train of thought and the flood of vaguely disturbing feelings. His workaday reality forcefully displaced these meanderings as he made the turn into the office lot. He could put these feelings aside, he assured himself, shelve them for the time being, while assuming his professional persona. Surely he could muster them out for inspection and further analysis at a time of his choosing. In the meantime, he managed to submerge them, by sheer force of will, as he began the process of reintegration necessary to impart an air of competency for at least another hour.

While walking through the lot to the south entrance and up the stairs to the office suite, Dr. Barth reviewed last week's session with Karen Leffler, his one o'clock. She was his only appointment this Friday afternoon, the prelude to a transition to another weekend. This one was the beginning of his annual two weeks of summer vacation, for which, as usual, he'd made no plans.

Mrs. Leffler was a client without a crisis, without an acute trauma. In their long, joint history, she'd presented (or was it concocted?) an unending catalog of obstacles to her well-being for which Barth served, at best, as a sounding board. It had become obvious that there was no solution. Hell, there wasn't even a distinct problem forming the basis for their sessions. Rather, series of successively-displaced subjects became the targets of their discourse, each "crisis" disappearing with hardly a mention and no evidence of relief. Try as he might, he'd been unsuccessful in his exhausting campaigns with Mrs. Leffler. Attempts to shift the focus to her overriding need for attention were quickly acknowledged while in transit to other forms of self-absorption.

Gregory Barth alternately viewed this situation with exasperation and a desire to meet the challenge to his stamina and clinical abilities. He occasionally broached the subject of therapy termination, based on feelings of guilt for maintaining the relationship absent evidence of a real need or noticeable impact of his efforts. Each time he did, however, she flatly rejected the idea of even a temporary hiatus, asserting that their explorations were vital to her sense of competence and well-being. Barth would retreat in the face of her insistence, choosing to indulge himself in the unconvincing self-delusion of the importance of his role as catalyst in her eventual self-realization.

Standing by his desk, staring out the window, Barth heard a low, throaty rumbling originating in the parking lot, growing louder. Seconds later a motorcycle and its rider came into view, rolling toward the boulevard exit. He wasn't an outlaw biker, but one of the brokers who worked in the investment firm occupying the first floor. He'd seen this rider before, attaching and undoing the bungee cords securing his leather briefcase to the seat, dressed in an outfit advertising no club affiliation, his face partly hidden in the shell of a plain, unadorned silver helmet. The red tie peeking out above the collar of his leather riding jacket was an incongruity, at least for Barth, watching the rider turn into the stream of traffic, accelerating and disappearing as he headed west.

Barth wondered if the lone rider's feeling of freedom compensated for his day-to-day grind in the world of finance.

Is this his fix, his minute of escape?

He was aware of his own literal and figurative immobility, underscored by the knowledge that the biker could, if he chose, head off in limitless directions. The idea of the freedom of the road, the untethered nomadic existence of the mythical biker outlaw, was trite, but no less compelling or attractive for this realization. He recalled celluloid images of Peter Fonda and Dennis Hopper cruising through adventure-laden landscapes, blissfully, perhaps deliberately, with few set destinations. But, after all, he was projecting a sense of well-being and personal satisfaction in his perception of the anonymous rider, just as he had with Dave an hour earlier.

The contrast between these imaginings and his stationary existence was beginning to induce in Barth a building tension that was abruptly ripped away by a disembodied wailing from the phone intercom.

"Mrs. Leffler is here for her appointment."

The brief excursion outside his present existence ended, requiring a change in focus and a transition to his professional role. The bout of self-created anxiety quickly abated as he resumed life as he knew it, responding with his automatic, reflexive, "Send her back."

In the next few seconds he directed his attention to his internalized file summary of the client whose presence necessitated the switch from his reflective interlude—Karen Leffler, middle-aged, well-educated suburban housewife, who he'd been seeing on a weekly basis for a year—*or was it two?* Barth wasn't aware of conspicuous temporal signposts that would serve to answer this question but, just as he was dismissing it, he realized, not for the first time, a significance that couldn't be denied. Mrs. Leffler had been meeting with him for an unquestionably long period now, and he couldn't immediately conjure up any landmarks of the relationship that could be remotely characterized as "progress" or breakthrough "insights." Only after a few milliseconds in this train of thought did his client's initial presenting complaints, expressed so long ago, come to consciousness. Barth recalled that, during their first sessions, she laid out for him her deepest, alarming concerns regarding her then-existential crisis. The source of her distress, as she expressed it, was her determination to "find herself," to excavate the core of her being that lay beneath the alluvial layers of misguided, dysfunctional parentage and unrelenting societal demands and strictures which certainly bound her primal self, to her continuing detriment. That is, the search for her "hangups."

As she entered his office they exchanged introductory niceties, while assuming their seats, an automatic repetition of ritual behavior. Karen Leffler was a woman whose lack of distinguishing characteristics would have presented a challenge for someone attempting to provide a description to a veteran police artist. Attractive, her short, dirty-blond hair contrasted with her dark gray coarse wool business suit and modest, unadorned black pumps. She could have been a ten-year associate at a business law firm, a clerk in an upscale clothing store, or the mistress of the manor in a gated community, which she was, without looking out of place. Her dress and demeanor conveyed a sense of deliberate cultivation of understated success and confidence. She displayed all the outward trappings of the well-tended upper middle-class madam—not ostentatiously, but in a manner which readily and unequivocally obviated the need to communicate her status in any other medium. Indeed, her therapy sessions, sandwiched between weekly yoga workouts and exploratory outings in the mall, constituted one of the more prominent prerequisites, an insignia of subsidized indulgence. There was no stigma attached—on the contrary, for the segment of the community in which she lived, her deliberate attempts at self-disclosure and psychological exploration were regarded as something akin to an admission requirement, post-graduate studies in class maintenance.

Today's crisis, today's worry, was Karen Leffler's chronic inability to attain visible progress in her chosen aspiration, becoming an interior decorator. She had yet to produce her first designs; not even a draft had appeared in all this time. As she put it, "I just can't get started, nothing comes to me, the well's all dried up." Hardly a new complaint—she'd mentioned this problem numerous times during recent sessions, but had quickly been diverted, with no discernible resistance, to other pressing concerns in her litany of crises. Today, however, she brought up the subject with an insistence that wouldn't be denied. Barth quickly sensed the emphasis, if not its source, and decided this was the time to make a frontal assault.

"All right, Karen, today this is important to you. When you've talked about this problem before, we discussed possibilities for dealing with it. The way I see it, you've never followed up on suggestions you yourself thought worth trying, so why is this bothering you *now*?"

Karen Leffler paused, folding her hands over her knees, then, leaning forward, parried the opening gambit.

"I think that might be it, I just didn't think it was so important, now I do, now I'm starting to think I'll never get started. I really did try the things we talked about, copying drawings and sketches, just to get going, but nothing worth anything comes to me."

She paused briefly, then, realizing that Dr. Barth was not going to take a turn, resumed talking, thinking aloud.

"Now I'm thinking the problems I've been having with Ted aren't really so bad... I kept going over them because I thought you wanted to hear them. I think maybe they're just normal problems, you know, not so bad, really, but the designs don't come, no ideas come into my head, and Ted's as good an excuse as any to talk about something else."

Barth reflected on this spontaneous bit of self-analysis that, uncharacteristically for his client, sounded right on the mark. For weeks they'd been hashing out the couple's recurring sources of friction until it became apparent that these were "ordinary" grievances, none of them particularly aggravating, none of them new or surprising. He had held back, hoping against hope that Karen, who spoke of these difficulties with no evident frustration, in a matter-of-fact tone underscoring their unimportance, would gradually lose interest. Now that it had actually happened, however, she was redirecting her energies to the problem of her "drawing block."

Barth was at his wit's end, trying to achieve some balance between an outright rejection of the supposed importance of this problem and a gentle push toward the recognition, if not acceptance, of other possibilities.

"What if you couldn't become a designer, what would you do then?"

"What do you mean, if I couldn't design?"

"I mean, you're the one who keeps insisting this is so important, yet you don't make much of an attempt to get yourself going, you drop the subject without missing a beat and decide it's your relationship with Ted that's keeping you from making progress... Now you think that wasn't really such a major problem after all, and you're back to this. Karen, can you tell me what it means for you to think of yourself as an interior designer, or what you'd think of yourself if you ever concluded that you *weren't*, or didn't *want* to be one?"

"Didn't want to be one, WHAT ARE YOU TALKING ABOUT? I'm just stuck for awhile and need your help, and you try to tell me I should give up."

"Whoa, who said anything about giving up? Unless my hearing is messed up, those words came from your mouth. I'm asking for your thoughts about yourself if YOU decided you didn't want to, or if YOU could see yourself in a life that doesn't include it."

Karen Leffler sat there, struggling with the question, sensing she wasn't getting off the hook, not just yet. She felt cornered, experiencing a rush of anxiety at the realization that the question, one she hadn't bothered to ask herself, couldn't be avoided. She resisted an initial impulse to lash out at her tormentor, to protect herself with an accusation of his insensitivity.

Against his usual instincts, Barth did not immediately insist on a response, taking the opportunity to expand on what he thought was his point.

"Look, Karen, in all the time we've spent on this subject, one fact is crystal clear. You haven't actually been drawing, or taking courses, no matter what the reason. You haven't demonstrated enough interest to even sit down and put a few sketches together, and now, suddenly, it's the most important thing you can think about to *talk* about. Just go along with me for a second, if you will, indulge me and tell me who you are without this goal in your life."

He would have to be appeased, after all.

"Well," she started, tentatively, "I'm Karen Leffler, adult woman, mother, housewife, community volunteer, running the house, trying to take care of my-self too, enjoying my friends, things like that."

"Okay, let's stop right there. Is your description so bad?"

"No, of course not. That's really a lot, you know, these days, it's a lot of energy, but you know, if you're not into something else, everyone thinks you're bland, stupid, uninteresting."

"Everyone?"

"I don't know. I want to be fulfilled, that's all."

"Fulfilled, what's that?"

Despite the trace of sarcasm, Barth knew he was onto something, a raw nerve, and he would not be distracted.

"Well, you know, hell, you're the psychologist."

"Yes, I know who I am, but the question is, who is the 'fulfilled' Karen Leffler? Is she sitting in front of me now?"

She'd been shifting her internal compass during these minutes, cautiously at-tempting to see herself through a new, untried frame of reference. It was like de-liberately trying on an outfit in a color or style completely outside her acquired tastes, an action occasionally resulting in the alteration or expansion of her ho-rizons. Her choice had perhaps itself been the rut, developing its own inertia because she had assumed that, to be 'fulfilled,' she had to reach out beyond her perceived boundaries of a traditional woman's role in the household. Perhaps, however, she longed to assume wholeheartedly the roles of family matriarch, mother and housewife, but had felt guilty, and been unable to acknowledge this feeling. She was beginning to recognize this possibility, seeing that her assumptions had precluded any attempt to throw off the shackles of her constructed confinement. The possibility of revolt became real. Now, armed with the realization that this was a choice, made with no force other than pressure she had felt, at some subliminal level, a surge of accompanying energy surprised both occupants of the quiet office.

"Damn, … excuse me, Dr. Barth, but dammit! It's so stupid … I feel so angry at myself, wasting all this time, I really don't have to. I can't blame it on Ted, I mean, he just went along, you know, he thought he was helping me to self-actualize or something, and I thought I wanted it…"

She paused for a second, assuming a focused, determined expression while looking away, staring out the window.

Barth knew enough to keep his mouth shut and let her go.

"All this time, maybe I can't do this design crap because I DON'T WANT TO. It's just drudgery, so damn boring, what I thought I wanted and…"

Here she stopped again, but Barth steadfastly refused to intercede, sensing, in quiet excitement, that his client was on the verge of a revelation which, expressed in her own words, would have an authenticity and credibility he could never impart with his detached interpretation, no matter how accurate.

Catching her breath, Karen Leffler continued.

"Now, maybe I'm wrong, I don't know, but you know, Doc, I feel excited about this, I really do."

The force of her words, more than their content, informed him, as obviously as it did her. She'd struck a vein, rich with questions arising naturally from openness to a new perspective.

"Yes, I can tell, you've never been this excited before. I don't have to tell you that your energy right now should tell you a lot."

Then, as if to punctuate the catharsis, Karen Leffler exhaled, slumping in her chair, letting her arms dangle loosely over the padded sides, her outstretched fingers inches above the carpet. A smile took shape on her face as she looked directly at Barth for the first time since completion of her self-revelatory monologue.

"I feel exhausted."

"You feel like you've just experienced some great relief, maybe even an insight," he responded. Barth felt a twinge of remorse at the sound of his own voice delivering this cliche, a completely unnecessary interruption.

Karen Leffler had relinquished her presumed attachment to her "problem" with a stunning suddenness, after avoiding questioning of her assumptions for so long. Barth hid his astonishment only with some difficulty. Astonishment at the sudden infusion of energy she now displayed, along with her evident acceptance of the decision to abandon a goal she had set for herself without desire. *Desire was the key.*

"Karen, this is the perfect time to end this session. I think you know what's happened here, we don't need to over-analyze this. Let's call it a day and pick it up when I get back from vacation."

"Yeah, this is something... Thanks, Doc, for sticking with me through this. So, where are you going?"

"No plans. Just stick around and take it easy, catch up on some reading, maybe a few days canoeing in the Ozarks."

"Doctor Barth, you know, I think you could use a change of scenery."

"I'll take that under advisement," Barth replied in a mock serious tone.

"Anyway, this has been a great afternoon." Karen Leffler smiled at Barth as she stood up, grabbed her purse and walked out, in a jaunty manner, in marked contrast to her entrance.

He sat at his desk, trying to assimilate the impact of the session, writing a few summary sentences in the chart to jog his memory before their next encounter. The unexpected turn that the course of therapy had taken had an effect, not only on Karen Leffler, leaving with an air of confidence and energy she had not heretofore exhibited, but also on Barth.

In the scope of a few hours he'd been exposed to successive encounters, with Dave, Mabel Cavanaugh, and now, Karen Leffler, shedding light on the sources of inertia, frustration, and lack of contentment in his own life. The irony that he had derived an awareness of his own personal demons in the course of these meetings did not escape him. Barth had been aware of the malaise he felt in his routine existence, but the day's experiences jolted him into a more conscious confrontation, not providing answers, but certainly bringing questions into sharper focus.

How is it that Dave, in the shadow of what has to be one of the darkest periods of his life, has an optimistic frame of mind, and he's not denying the rough times that still lie ahead?

Barth had fully expected he'd assume the obligatory supportive role for his friend, but was struck with the observation that Dave had moved, emotionally at least, well ahead of his expectations under the circumstances. During the period of his own separation and divorce, many years behind him, he was a virtual recluse, to the extent that his social life had been reduced to work-related contacts. He was hardly able to find the energy to get out of bed at the time, in contrast to what appeared to him as self-generated optimism and a refusal to surrender on the part of his friend.

Mabel Cavanaugh had, similarly, exhibited evidence of the resiliency of human beings in rough circumstances. Alone, but not really alone, she had constructed for herself a serviceable alternative world that didn't conform to expectations typical in her living situation. She, too, had given Barth something to think about, based on her refusal to acquiesce and accept the expectations others had for her.

And, finally, no less emphatically, Karen Leffler, the obstinate client with whom he'd been engaged in an interminable, frustrating wrestling match through countless sessions. Suddenly, without prior hint of insight, she had pulled and pushed herself to a point of recognition and acceptance he hadn't thought possible. He was, momentarily, elated that she'd experienced what he hoped was more than a passing lucid moment. It dawned on him, however, that he had been a witness, but not much more. Perhaps he was not even a catalyst for the transformation, merely an observer, a bystander who happened to be in the right place at the right time. Barth couldn't elude the nagging feeling that his efforts did not warrant plaudits in this case. Karen Leffler's "breakthrough" was something she likely could have, would have, achieved on her own, just as Dave had somehow achieved his present equilibrium, just as Mabel Cavanaugh, the frail octogenarian, had constructed her own private, stimulating world in the confines of an antiseptic nursing home.

It's possible I won't ever see her again.

He was being left behind, jilted, by his client, an inevitable occurrence, indeed, a goal of therapy, but under these circumstances, a bit of a shock, the feeling exacerbated by the underlying conclusion he drew from the day's experiences.

I'm the one in a rut, I'm walking dissatisfaction, I'm the one who needs to do something.

Even as he was saying this to himself, he had no plan, no method available to him. Experience, moreover, was on the side of the inertia that kept him on the daily route from his apartment to his office, and back. He was envious of Karen Leffler, and Mabel Cavanaugh, and Dave.

Something will come to me.

Rumblings

I reckon I got to light out for the territory. — HUCKLEBERRY FINN

Barth dropped the receipts for the practice in the bank deposit box, neatly wrapped in an accounting slip filled out in Eleanor's elegant hand. On leaving the office that afternoon she'd been the last to see him out. "Have a nice vacation, Dr. Barth. See you in two weeks. Make sure you send us a postcard."

Eleanor's low chuckle underscored the fact that she'd been with the practice long enough to know that, more likely than not, Barth would be "visiting" at some point during his "vacation" to check his mail. Typically, he'd leave town for a few days, for a hiking or canoe trip in the Ozarks, or a drive to Des Moines to stay a couple days with his mother, but extended out-of-town jaunts were the exception. Once every two years he attended a convention, but these junkets could hardly be described as bona fide vacations. His vacations were as routine as his workaday life.

Barth had phoned in a take-out pizza order, deciding to relax at home this evening and mull over the day's events. He canceled an invitation to see a movie with George and Sarah McKelling and was thankful this wasn't the night they'd chosen to set him up with a friend from Topeka. Barth wasn't against occasional forays into the world of blind dating, but this activity required a reserve of emotional energy utterly lacking this evening. He easily recalled the unrelenting awkwardness of these encounters, not to mention the worst of all experiences, being with someone new and knowing you'd rather be anywhere else, a feeling sometimes materializing within the first five minutes. Barth was sufficiently empathetic to assume that such feelings were likely mutual in these situations. He hated the bar scene at this point in his life, but at least quick escape was an option under those circumstances. Best of all, he had to deal with neither of these situations this evening.

He stopped to pick up his pizza and, following a quick mental accounting, concluded he had no need for more provisions, at least not tonight. He could decompress, muse over the day's events, and decide whether he would, after all, take a few days for a canoe outing in the Ozarks.

Once he'd finally settled in, on his living room sofa, beer and pizza set out on the coffee table, he reached for the remote, hesitated for a second, then dropped the idea. Instead, Barth found himself, with time to relax, preoccupied with the questions that had dogged him a couple of hours ago. The succession of thought-provoking encounters on this singular day placed a continuing demand for his attention that refused to be stifled.

What sense is there to all this?

The simple question he posed to himself suggested that, if he only thought about it long enough, there was a conclusion, a lesson, a message waiting to be discovered. This nagging assumption wouldn't let go, wouldn't give him the freedom to be distracted.

Damn this! Do something, get this over with!

He tried a more concrete tact in an attempt to make some progress—replay and reflect.

What is it about Mabel Cavanaugh that's bugging me?

She's hardly the first oddball patient, elderly or otherwise, I've met over the years, won't be the last, so what?

Her story was fascinating, unique, to be sure, but so were those of countless patients in countless settings he'd worked in over the years. Nothing there.

Then it hit him.

It's her, right now. She's not just sitting there, telling stories about her past. She doesn't have all the time in the world to show family pictures and regale me with tales of the old days. She's not obsessed with all that. She's complaining and impatient about her work RIGHT NOW. She won't play patient, won't let staff treat her like a patient, wouldn't give me the time of day if I'd treated her like a patient. This woman has better things to do. Why the hell should she be jabbering with me?

Will I be as vital when I'm in my eighties? Hell, no, I'm not as vital now.
No wonder I'm sitting here thinking about this lady. One down.
Lunch with Dave was easy.

He's the one going through hell, rebuilding his life, and I'm sitting on my butt in
my living room, on vacation, gorging myself on pizza and beer, and I'm envious of
him? He's gone off the deep end with this Duchess, and he'll be completely miser-
able by next month, back in his post-divorce funk.

Barth recalled his incredulity on seeing his friend, in the midst of his chaotic
universe, energized, optimistic, and refusing to be bogged down by the detritus
of his broken marriage. By comparison, Barth, without an obvious crisis in his
personal world, with important aspects of his life under control, or, at least, predictable, was downright somber.

Even the briefest of encounters, with Eleanor, was a reminder, a living
point of reference. Another index of the lack of satisfaction in his own life,
something that, until today, Barth might not have denied, but treated as an
ordinary expectation, too ordinary to warrant sustained attention, much less
significant changes.

It would take a sledgehammer blow to knock him out of his complacency,
push him over the edge.

This is where Karen Leffler made her entrance into Barth's anxious
ruminations.

This woman drains me for a year, refuses to stay with anything long enough to
make progress, convinces me she has no desire to look closely at her problem of the
week, taunts me with a hundred close brushes with insight, even seems to enjoy my
inability to work with her. What does she do? – She breaks out of her rut, leaving
me in her dust. Even Karen Leffler has something to teach me!

Barth laughed at this observation. The cumulative impact of these encounters amounted to one huge confrontation with himself. In each of these replayed
vignettes Barth discovered irrefutable evidence of his personal malaise and the
contrast with his present state, stretched out on his couch rehashing the events
of the last ten hours. The vitality and satisfaction he'd witnessed shattered any
assumptions he held regarding the inertia-driven course of his own life.

Here I am, two weeks vacation in front of me, vegging out on this couch with
no plans, no desires, frittering my life away. This is ridiculous! No, I am ridiculous!

He recognized the impatience he often felt when working with Karen Leffler, now directed at himself. The random alignment of this day's interactions was conspiring to illuminate the humdrum, uninspiring pattern of "activity" that was his life.

Barth continued sitting, slumped back in the couch, shoeless feet spread on the coffee table, his posture and gaze frozen while his thoughts raced. He felt a growing sense of alarm.

Is this my mid-life crisis? Who cares? It doesn't matter what the hell it is, what it's called, this is real. I can do something, … or I can just rot.

Everything he had experienced this day reinforced a growing conviction that he was compelled to do something, to act. Perhaps it didn't matter what, so long as, at a minimum, it wasn't what he'd been doing up to this point—going through the motions, tending to business as it came up, without any personal evaluation of fulfillment in his life. He could see, or assume, a degree of this nebulous fulfillment in the lives of today's cast of characters. Having witnessed it in others, Barth became determined to find it for himself, before it was too late, one way or another.

How? What can I do? What do I want to do? How in hell do I get started?

Barth grasped for answers, but none were forthcoming. In the meantime, anxiety was overtaking him. He could feel himself sweating in the comfort of the air-conditioned room. He tried recycling his thoughts, hoping that, by doing so, something would emerge as a solution to his dilemma. A direction, a sign, some suggestion of a course of action, providing, at a minimum, the illusion that he was productively grappling with this hovering crisis.

Nothing came to him, nothing concrete, just the repeated conclusion that he had to act. He had to do something, whatever it was—he could no longer accept the status quo in his life's routine. This was progress of a sort. He'd reached a decision, even if it hadn't yet assumed a tangible, concrete form. Sitting there, feet pulled up on the couch, he allowed himself the illusion that he had achieved something. He only needed to hammer away at the problem he had posed for himself. His anxiety began subsiding with the confident conclusion that he was motivated to act, that he wouldn't lapse into a state of inaction, even if he couldn't immediately come up with a plan.

His mounting frustration had reached a critical point, and Barth decided he had to make an exit, to anywhere, now.

Just get out, a change of scenery, inhale the night air, it doesn't matter.

He was restless to move, slipping on his shoes, grabbing a jacket and leaving everything in the apartment as it was. Housecleaning could wait. Obeying this urge, he eased his car out of the apartment complex lot and headed north on Holmes. He had no idea of a destination, but it didn't matter, it felt good to move, even aimlessly. He turned on the radio for company and was comforted by the sound of Jimmy Liggins and his Drops of Joy, singing "Lonely Nights Blues" on Chuck Haddix' "Friday Night Fish Fry." Spurred by this audio cue, Barth decided to drive downtown, to the old jazz district in the 18th and Vine area. Maybe he could calm down and dull his isolation, at least for an hour or two.

The jazz district, former stage to the likes of Basie, Parker and Big Joe Turner, was a hollow shell of its ancient glory, not quite jumping, even on a Friday night. It could be described as drifting somewhere between the dilapidation of decades of neglect and the resurrection of the city council's tourist trap dream. The Blue Room, however, Barth's destination, had an atmosphere adequate to his present needs. Even when crowded, the piano bar was a source of listenable music, soothing, dark, and with a guarantee of undisturbed anonymity. Barth occasionally came here alone, but always felt like an outsider, not sufficiently cool or sophisticated to appreciate the nuances of the piano meanderings he nonetheless enjoyed, not an inhabitant of this section of the city, and not one of the sightseers steered here by the visitors and convention bureau propaganda. He was able to feel a measure of relaxation, however, enhanced by the smoky haze. As it turned out, it was a lucky decision on his part. Tonight Ida McBeth, a Kansas City institution and a favorite singer of Barth's, was on the bill. Her brassy, spirited, bass-driven rendition of "A Lot of Livin' To Do" could kick him out of the depths of his doldrums.

Barth found an empty seat and decided to wait until her next set, scheduled to start within the hour. He sipped a beer at his corner table, watching couples, smiling and laughing, glad for the opportunity to get out and become lost in the warming embrace of familiar melodies. He pulled a crumpled pack from his jacket pocket and lit up a cigarette. He wasn't a regular smoker, not by a long shot, not like his college days, but this was one of his few remaining vices and, he figured, one over which he had some control. In the office, smoking was universally condemned by his colleagues, and none of his friends smoked, but he occasionally surrendered to the urge, especially at anxious moments like the present. Eventually, the combination of smoke, the background music of the three-piece band, beer and change of scenery had its desired effect. Barth was losing his edge, and figured that this storm, whatever its source, would pass.

This is just a day in the life, a different day, but nothing to get bent out of shape about.

"You waiting for someone?"

Barth hesitated, then realized that the woman, bending and displaying her bountiful cleavage, was talking to him.

"No, just relaxing."

"Want some help relaxing?"

"No, thanks… Thanks anyway."

"You change your mind, you let me know, honey." With a sway of her hips, she turned and sashayed in the direction of the bar.

I'm sure she'd relax me, I should have said yes… No, who am I fooling?

Barth took a long, last drag from his cigarette, then mashed it into the ashtray with his thumb.

He had no urge to stay late, although he had nowhere to go tomorrow and no appointments to keep. He figured he had reached a satisfactory emotional equilibrium, and he left. He would catch Ida later, under more normal circumstances. The drive back home was relaxed, and Barth began looking forward to the prospect of sleep. By the time he entered the apartment he'd convinced himself that the early evening stirrings were under control. He still couldn't identify a way to solve this "problem," but for the moment was quite willing to let it go, chalking it up to something akin to male menopause. *Maybe it just doesn't matter.*

An overwhelming fatigue began setting in, and he decided to succumb to its demands. He couldn't foresee anything else to be accomplished right now and had no desire to stay awake watching bad TV. He carried the remainder of his dinner to the kitchen before getting into bed. Despite the still early hour Barth knew he'd have no difficulty falling asleep, and, following his extended internal dialogue, he thought it a good idea to marshal his physical resources in order to attack the unresolved questions in the morning, if they were still with him. Or, perhaps he would awake with the insight to action he longed for and had resolved to obtain, by any means.

For once, this is going to be a vacation worth remembering. Maybe.

Barth awoke from a fitful, unsuccessful attempt at sleep and, looking at the clock on the nightstand, saw that it was only three a.m. Tired and restless, unable to abandon himself to sleep, hardly half alert, he nevertheless knew that he had to tend to this nagging, unfinished business now... or never. He was agitated, staring up in the darkness.

I can't let this go. No, this won't let go. I have to do something, this is it. Deal with this, get it over with, then sleep.

He began reviewing the events of the last day again in nauseating detail, thinking that, by doing so, somehow he could find the way out, a way out, of his dilemma. *Out, out, out!* ... Again he heard Eleanor's mocking tone as she made the remark about sending a postcard.

Is it so obvious to everyone but me that I'm tied to the same routine, day after day?

It's obvious, he realized, an insight any idiot could have divined.

I have to try something else, anything, even if I can't think of the right thing. Anything will be better... I can't wait around here for life to happen to me. I won't rot anymore... or will I? Hell, maybe it's already too late.

A sense of dread, even fear, was building with this last thought, not a new one for Barth, but now felt so strongly he was aware of breaking out in a sweat, his whole body filling with a growing tension. Occasionally, when dealing with similar bouts of anxiety and unease, he'd been able to rely on his powers of denial, convincing himself that this was idle ruminating, that his life was under control and rewarding, that it was even selfish of him to desire anything more than the life he had created. Years ago, after his divorce, Barth experienced a long period of emptiness, but survived by investing more energy and focus in his practice, ultimately the most reliable aspect of his universe. He hadn't ruled out the possibility of finding someone with whom he could share the intimate joys and sorrows of his life, someone he could, in short, love, but it just didn't happen, and his floundering attempts at dating over the years convinced him that the probability of finding someone was, to put it mildly, low. Still, he derived sufficient enjoyment and stimulation in his professional role and in his social network, such as it was, to continue without a strong sense of existential angst, except occasionally when he had too much to drink and alcohol dissolved his defenses. Now, even in the absence of excesses of this sort, a sense of growing dissatisfaction with the inertia of his routine had emerged, had erupted, stealing even the reliable refuge of sleep.

These thoughts were magnified by his awareness, unsurprising for his age, of his own mortality, and the conclusion that, if something was going to change, it would only be as a result of his own action, whatever that might turn out to be. Time was slowly, imperceptibly, but certainly, running out.

All right, I am going to do something, dammit, I am going to do something, and I'm just going to make a decision—NOW. Right, wrong, I just don't care, that's not important, that isn't getting me anywhere.

The impulsive quality of this train of thought was out of character for Barth, but as he lay there, repeating the conclusion to himself, his body began relaxing for the first time since waking, a physical signal reinforcing his confidence. Something drastic was called for, he didn't doubt that, but the next step would become clear—he only had to keep his energies focused.

As he lay there, trying to formulate a plan, trying to latch onto a fragment, something that could provide a glimmer of progress, a vague sensation, a few seconds' snippet from this now momentous yesterday, intruded into his consciousness. Just as it had occurred then, a low rumbling became gradually louder, until it eventually demanded, commanded his attention. An idea started taking hold. He began studying it, turning it over, playing with it, then, finally, seizing it for his own, starting the process of filling in enough details to make the idea believable, convincing. A visual image formed in which he was included, a participant in his projection of a plan.

I can do this.

He had, at long last, arrived at a starting point. Even with its impractical, unrealistic aspects, he'd finally, irrevocably, made a decision. Barth began entertaining the implications of his newly-formed intentions. Remarkably, he was feeling an infusion of enthusiasm in which time, and sleepiness, were completely forgotten.

Desire was the key.

This would be an opportunity to jettison the "junk of life," Barth's designation for the everyday annoyances that wasted precious time and energy, serving as permanent diversions from the most enjoyable aspects of living, as far as he could tell in his routine existence. This broad category included such tasks as waiting in lines, filling out bureaucratic forms, doing his taxes, and waiting for red lights when there was no one else in sight. Well, maybe he couldn't chuck all of life's junk, but certainly enough to provide an illusion of freedom lasting four weeks. Two wouldn't be enough. No e-mail, no appointments, no internet, and it was certainly a requirement that he ditch the cell phone, the electronic tether to the whole system in which he was thoroughly enmeshed. In the world he inhabited these conveniences had effectively reduced risk, even in the hinterlands, to an option, but his instincts, seemingly dormant in the reaches of his memory, now demanded these choices. The irony of this whole process was not lost on Barth; the obsessive planning and thinking through that was required in order to obtain even a temporary freedom from the routine in which he was, at the very least, a willing conscript, and, more accurately, an active participant.

Uncharacteristically, the next step was clear to Barth, now very much awake. He had to act, to start moving, before his inertia had a chance to reassert itself. Before letting himself sleep, he must complete some act, a concrete step in the service of his plans, something that would make their realization more or less inevitable. Or at least make turning back conspicuously embarrassing to him.

Without hesitating, he rolled over to his left side, reaching for the phone on the nightstand. He punched the number and held the receiver to his ear, anxious for a response.

"Hello, who is this?" The voice was certainly recognizable, and so was the fact that its source had been fast asleep.

"Dave, this is Greg. Listen, I know it's late, I have to talk with you, I need your help."

"Greg? What the hell are you doing? It's three-thirty. Somebody die?"

"No, but maybe somebody being born… again. Look, I know this is weird, but I think you'll understand. I've been trying to decide what to do and now I know, and I need your help to get started."

"You been drinking? What the hell's going on? You need a ride?"

"No, nothing like that. I'm fine, in fact, better than I've ever been, but I need your help. I know I can rely on you."

"Hey, Greg, look, you know I'll do my part, whatever it is that's burning your butt. Can't it wait till morning? I have to tell you, I'm not alone here."

"Oh, sorry…"

Barth was briefly disoriented by this last bit of information.

"Sorry, Dave, sorry, yeah, this can wait, not too long though. Can we meet tomorrow?"

What the hell was Barth up to? Dave sensed the urgency in his friend's voice and his own response was automatic.

"Yeah, of course, buddy. Just let me take care of things here. How about we meet at the Corner at nine. We can talk about this, whatever it is. Will that work?"

"Yeah, fine. Thanks, Dave. Get back to sleep." Barth hung up without waiting for a reply. He'd been caught off guard by the faux pas of interrupting his friend's personal life, realizing at the same time that it was okay.

They sat at their window table, sipping coffee while waiting for their orders. Dave looked out on the waking street, then turned to his companion, venturing an observation.

"From anyone else, not really such a crazy idea, but from you, Greg, this is discombobulating. Sounds like you've made your mind up, though, so now it's a matter of getting the details out of the way. Even something like this requires planning."

"Yeah, I know, sure, but I thought you'd help me get started before I change my mind. I can't afford to sit on my ass and think this over or you know as well as anybody I'll never get going."

His friend managed a confirmatory laugh.

"Okay, I guess you know what you have to do at the office. You can put me down as a backup. I must owe you at least a couple months over the last ten years. Since you want to get going on this, let's go to Engle's this morning and

take a look. You don't have time to go through ads and hope you can get something that'll do what you want without breaking down. If they have anything it'll
cost you more, but it'll be ready to go, and this is no time to worry about saving
a few dollars."

"Thanks, I knew I could count on you. Just tell me what to do. I'm ready."

Dave couldn't recall the last time he'd seen Greg so energized, and was glad to
be playing a part in his friend's transformation, no matter how fleeting it might
turn out in the end. Truth be known, he was enjoying a vicarious thrill from the
opportunity to play a role in what might well have been viewed as a shopworn,
but nonetheless romantic notion, hitting the road for literal and symbolic freedom, no matter how temporary. The road trip.

They were wandering around the showroom at Engle's an hour later, with
Dave providing a crash course in motorcycle typology and his judgment regarding the merits of the used bikes in stock. He scowled when Greg started com-
menting on the colors of the bikes.

This is going to be difficult.

Finally, with some arm-twisting on Dave's part, Barth settled on a touring
bike with low miles and a presumably low need for maintenance, a bike that
could be mastered by a novice in a short period of time. Atypical of Barth, he
struck his bargain with the salesman without haggling over the price, satisfied
with a deal that included bags and needed accessories—a helmet, jacket and
gloves. Barth was willing to pay cash on the condition that the bike, including
temporary plates, could be readied to leave that day. Dave would ride the bike to
Barth's place, while Barth figured out how to remedy the minor deficiencies that
precluded immediate takeoff, namely, the absence of a license and the ability to
ride. He'd ridden his uncle's trail bike on the cow pastures of his farm, but that
was decades ago. In his frenzied state, however, these were minor details.

During the next two days, Barth threw himself into preparation for what he
viewed as the great escape from his own reality. The frenetic pace he maintained
during this time would have amazed those who knew him, including Barth
himself. He pushed himself to complete preparations, convinced that pausing
for reflection might result in abandoning the project that was growing in importance with every passing hour. With Dave's help, he learned the rudiments of
the bike's operation in a local K-Mart parking lot, took the written test, passed

it, then took the riding test and, surprisingly, passed it on the first try, thanks to liberal scoring. He called Eleanor, informing her of his change in plans without divulging any details regarding the exact nature of his getaway. Instead of two weeks he decided four would be required for his purposes, whatever those were, and he instructed Eleanor to make the necessary notifications and schedule changes. He could imagine her reaction and wasn't ready to deal with it just yet. Suddenly the predictable Dr. Barth was becoming enveloped in an air of mystery for the office staff and colleagues.

He sketched out a tentative route, highlighting remnants of Route 66 heading west on a series of road maps, for no reason other than the romantic notion of traveling on parts of the old road. He wouldn't plan specific stops; it made no sense anyhow, considering his utter lack of riding experience. For once he'd embrace the notion of a lack of detailed day-to-day plans, resolving to just go. He made one concession to planning, calling his little sister, who lived in a small town in the mountains of western Nevada. He hadn't seen her in ten years, not since she'd headed west and married, and this was an opportunity to remedy the situation. Kate, surprised and amused upon hearing her brother's plans, was as puzzled as anyone in Kansas City, but ultimately encouraging, sensing the importance of his mission.

"Sure, Greg, we'll be glad to see you, whenever you get here, it doesn't matter, just call when you get close, this isn't the city, you know."

"Great, tell the kids their uncle from back east is on his way. I'll see you sometime in two or three weeks if everything goes okay."

"Take care of yourself, Greg, and don't hurry, be safe."

This would be his only planned stop during the trip west. Barth figured he could make it to Seattle, a city he'd never seen, then worry about getting back, but he refused to spend time thinking about that detail. Everything had to be devoted to going, leaving, to the idea of seeing and feeling his present self receding in his rear-view mirror. He was obsessed with the still uncertain prospect of his impending journey, afraid that, if he allowed himself an opportunity for analysis, his plans would collapse in a sea of practicality and commonsense. He couldn't afford to let that happen, he told himself, or he'd be forever trapped in this life, with no one to blame but himself. He'd be the nursing home resident he pitied, sitting outside on his rocker, lamenting the trip he never took. Anxiously, he told himself he was, for once, not going to let that happen. Barth kept replaying the image of the city skyline shrinking in his mirror and, by doing so, began feeling comforted. As the time of departure approached, he was enjoying a degree of confidence.

I am going to do this, after all.

By Tuesday morning the vision was beginning to materialize. Office details had been covered, Dave had assumed responsibility for checking on routine matters on behalf of his friend, and the packing was finished, thanks again to Dave's help. The cases were filled with the bare necessities for the trip and the camping gear strapped to the topcase in a web of bungee cords, creating the image of a two-wheeled packhorse. Barth christened the bike with the name Rocinante, a self-mocking admission of the quixotic nature of an expedition that was nevertheless as critical to him as anything he'd done in recent memory.

Viewing his handiwork, with Dave standing by, he managed a relaxed, confident smile, knowing the beginning was but minutes away.

"Thanks for your help, especially for not trying to talk me out of it. I don't expect you'll hear from me for awhile, but that's really a good thing."

"Don't hurry, my friend, see what you can, stop when something calls to you, and don't spend time worrying about stuff here. It'll all be waiting when you get back."

"I hear you. See y'all later."

Barth was ready.

First Turns
(The Pilgrim's Progress)

Barth had the irritating sensation of being held back. The start and stop of Kansas City traffic, an annoyance hardly noticed in his daily routine, was making him impatient, eager to hit the first stretch of unfettered highway asphalt. Surrounded by streams of vehicles heading to workplace parking lots, Barth was a trapped animal desperately seeking the nearest escape route. His imagined freedom wouldn't be official until the fixed photograph in his mind was replaced by the traffic and cityscape receding in his rear-view mirror. He was on the verge of enjoying this dream becoming reality, absorbed in the elation growing with each city block separating him from the Gregory Barth of yesterday.

The hot sweltering morning, typical Kansas City in July, had less effect than usual on the lone rider seeking nothing more, for now, than his first look at a new horizon.

A biker passing from the opposite direction signaled Barth with what he would come to know as the "biker wave," index and middle fingers of the left hand extended downward in a "V." Even two policemen riding their white and black Kawasakis greeted him in this manner. These salutations signified Barth's admission to an exclusive fraternity with its own code, although he wondered if the bikers, seeing his packed bags, had mistaken him for a veteran of the road.

No matter, I'll get there soon enough.

Once on 71 heading south he was quickly in fifth gear and could feel the air rushing through his jacket and helmet vents. This was a cleansing sensation, cool air blowing the ties to yesterday behind him, the signal breath of new life, or so Barth imagined. He snapped his visor shut with a quick push and sat back, riding with the traffic at speed toward the suburbs. The low buzzing of the engine between his calves was a new form of stimulant, perhaps addictive.

Now it's really happening, I'm doing this, this nerd has hit the road!

He reminded himself of the lessons Dave had drummed into him during the last three days. Stay focused on the road, the conditions, the whereabouts of vehicles. Avoid becoming a statistic in the course of this adventure. Barth was conscious of the need to maintain a hypervigilance required for detecting dips and turns, potholes and changes in the road surface that would have no impact on four-wheeled vehicles but could spell disaster if not accounted for by the biker. The slope of the road, the angle of the crown and shoulders, and, of course, weather changes, required a heightened sensitivity to his surroundings he hoped to acquire without penalty. In the meantime, on this flat stretch, he could enjoy the cooling breezes swirling around him.

Soon he reached the suburbs, passing exits for Grandview, Belton and Harrisonville, outer limits of his everyday universe. Not quite in the country yet, the traffic was nevertheless thinning out and he could safely steal glances at the changing scenery. Barth became convinced he was actually making his escape. The upcoming towns and villages on the signposts had no associations for him other than names on the maps he had studied the last two days. Everything from this point on would have a newness and promise of adventure matching the intentions that were the reasons for this trip.

This is it, this is not a dream!

Barth was indeed slipping the bounds of his own life. The trailer park off to his right, unwelcome in the city, was for him a harbinger of *terra incognita*, a sign that he'd already entered another world. The motor's steady ticking and the gentle winds that would become his companions through changing vistas were, at this moment, new sensations.

He sighted a sprawling farmhouse, a quarter mile from the highway, with rusting implements whose purpose was a mystery to Barth, resting untended in the fields. The squat, wide profile of an old Ford tractor was recognizable, from childhood memories, in what remained of its faded gray paint and traces of red script lettering. It sat deep in parallel ruts close to the highway, captured and partially hidden by overgrown weeds and an emergent oak tree twisting its way around the rear axle. It was, Barth guessed, an unlikely candidate for rejuvenation. Behind it a surrounding vista of tall green cornfields attested to an accelerated growing season, and unending stretches of soybean rows bore witness to the changing nature of farming in this region during the last couple decades. The western Missouri terrain was rolling, with mild undulations that didn't obscure the rider's ability to scan the road far ahead. Technically, this was the prairie, absent the wild grasses and flowers that were long ago supplanted by cash crops brought by cultivators on the tail end of westward expansion. The closest approximations to wild flora here were bunches of crown vetch in the median between the lanes. Their purple flowers had a sweet smell in the July sun Barth had never noticed before.

Curves in the route came slowly and predictably, offering the novice ample opportunity to plan his moves well in advance. He attempted holding a line in the middle of the lane, not because it was required under these conditions, but as an exercise, an opportunity to gain confidence in his ability to exert control over the machine. At some point he would be forced to stop quickly or make a sudden turn in an emergency, and there was no better time to prepare for that exigency than the present. When no traffic was visible Barth started swerving back and forth in play, testing the limits of his newly-acquired skills. The weather, road conditions and absence of traffic rendered this an ideal opportunity for honing his riding abilities while enjoying the scenery of the western Missouri hinterlands. He was maintaining an easy, sixty-five mile-an-hour pace, punctuated with occasional bursts of speed on flat stretches to break up the monotony and provide an assessment of the bike's capabilities. Barth was immersing himself in the fulfillment of his newly-adopted role as cross-country biker, enjoying every second of the experience. He was, in this moment, a child unburdened by the responsibilities that lay behind him at an ever-increasing distance. The succession of towns on this route clearly demarcated the steady, undeniable progress of the riding pilgrim in his new world.

After an hour on Highway 71 his attitude became easy and relaxed. Barth was confident he could handle the requirements of operating the bike while taking in changes in the landscape and allowing himself the anticipation of unknown adventures. Things were going easily; even a few isolated dark clouds appearing in the sky between Butler and Nevada couldn't dampen his spirits. Part of the whole experience, he reasoned.

To be expected, and dealt with, that's all.

A sharp, unexpected turn demanded Barth's attention and, as he emerged from it he was confronted by an admonition, in blood-red capital letters on a white signpost, to "PREPARE TO MEET THY GOD." Barth hoped this didn't signify the presence of an upcoming road hazard.

He entertained the idea of stopping in the metropolis of Nevada for gas, but quick calculations informed him that he had plenty of fuel and, anyway, he didn't want to linger in Missouri any longer than necessary. He could easily reach the Oklahoma border by late afternoon, even at his relaxed pace, and find a cheap motel or campground for his first evening on the road.

His outlook began changing, however, as the wind picked up, swirling and buffeting him in gusts, requiring strenuous effort to maintain his line on the road. He slowed down, lessening the wind's impact, only to note spreading rain-drops on his visor. A scattering of threatening white thunderheads was visible in the sky. It would have made perfect sense to stop and put on his rain gear, except for the fact that there was no place on this stretch of highway to pause; the gravel shoulder was too steep and narrow to provide a reasonable margin of safety. A surge of panic went through him as the rain increased, now streaking down his windshield and visor, but Barth kept thinking, if he could maintain a steady pace, he'd ride out the rain or make it to the next major stop, Carthage, or even Joplin. Cars and trucks were now passing him with regularity, heightening his anxiety, splashing him in their wake. He flicked on the switch for the extra driving light but didn't notice any increase in visibility, now restricted by a dark, threatening sky. All this took place in the span of a few minutes. This was Barth's first test of his beginner's riding skills.

Hell, I should have known this was going too well. Too late to turn back, just keep focusing on the road, keep moving. You'll get through this. I have to do this. Go!

He was cautiously, nervously optimistic about his prospects for overcoming this early impediment to fulfillment of his road fantasy. He was also acutely aware of the risk of early disaster.

The road surface was completely wet and likely slick, but Barth managed to keep a straight, slow line, and his initial panic subsided. The effort required to avoid a calamity was demanding every ounce of attention and strength he had to spare, and panic was a luxury he couldn't afford.

No quick moves, just stay straight, not too close to cars, keep a lookout for a promising stop, off road, underpass, it doesn't matter.

For a fleeting second he envied the safety and comfort of the passing drivers, gawking at the rain-drenched fool.

Twenty miles out of Nevada Barth spotted the sign for the Lamar exit and made his decision without hesitating. The rain was coming down in sheets, limiting visibility to the flickering taillights of vehicles. He edged toward the shoulder, hoping to increase the distance between him and the passing cars while searching desperately for the exit ramp. The odometer glass was fogged, providing no clue regarding the proximity of his immediate destination. He cursed the rain and kept up his lookout.

Surely there's no way I can miss the exit, even in this damn rain.

At long last, after what felt like an eternity in the torrential downpour, a large green and white sign pointed to the Lamar exit, and Barth readily complied with its directive. Thankful for an opportunity to slow down and, finally, come to a stop, he determined that the town was somewhere off to his left, though it wasn't in sight. He did, however, spot the small bank, with its drive-in window, and made a snap decision, heading in that direction, pulling around in the lot and positioning himself under the extended awning covering the drive-through lanes.

The relief Barth felt with the protection from the rain was palpable. He stopped quickly, alighted from the bike, and lifted it on its centerstand. He removed his soaked gloves, then his helmet, placing it on the seat while enjoying the sensation of standing still and letting his tense muscles relax. He looked over to see the woman, through the lighted window of the bank, peering out at this drenched specimen. She smiled, then looked away—perhaps she wanted to avoid giving the wet intruder the impression she was laughing at him, perhaps she felt the proper etiquette under the circumstances was to let him recover in peace. In any event, Barth was grateful for the respite from his ordeal. He was safe for the time being. He was also thoroughly soaked and cold, shivering after being too tense to experience this bodily reaction. He had no desire to resume riding in the rain at this moment, tempting fate again on the road, but was only slightly less miserable standing still, cold, wet and shaking. His patience was being tested only a few hours into his adventure, and his demeanor was as damp as his clothes.

Forty minutes later, the rain began to subside, to an extent that convinced Barth another try was called for. He mounted the bike, started the motor and eased out from under his temporary shelter. The rain was lighter, enough to be encouraging. He boldly turned into the on-ramp, accelerating while merging back on to 71. The rain still ran down his windshield and visor, but visibility seemed reasonable.

This is to be expected, he told himself.

I'm going to have to learn to adapt. Just keep straight and keep rolling.

He was tired, plain tired. The concentration required to stay on the road was draining his energy reserves, and the shivering cold was hardly restful. The wind at speed was whipping even this light rain through him. It didn't take long for Barth to make his decision.

If discretion is the better part of valor, then forget about Oklahoma today. Find a room in Joplin, dry out, get a good night's sleep. Nothing wrong with stopping now, I don't have appointments to keep.

Satisfied with his change of plan, he concentrated on the road ahead, knowing the cloud-darkened sky would be getting darker anyway, making his decision all the more inevitable.

It wasn't long, even at his reduced speed, before the first signs for Carthage and Joplin appeared. These provided reassurance for the wet rider, with their promise of a genuine rest. He could certainly make Joplin now, find a place to crash and be satisfied with the knowledge that he had at least two worthwhile accomplishments under his belt. He had actually started this thing today, against the inertia of his life's routine. Secondly, he'd survived, or was surviving, his first real challenge on the road. As he approached the outskirts of Joplin, it also occurred to Barth that he was at the intersection of old Route 66, an achievement of sorts. Getting on 66, even the short stretch accessible in Joplin, would mean a change of direction. He would actually be heading west. Tomorrow would be another day.

Once in the city limits, Barth started searching for the first cheap motel off the highway. While waiting out the rain in Lamar he'd thought about calling directory assistance to reserve a room, but then remembered the cavalier manner with which he decided to leave his cell phone behind. *So much for foolish bravado.* He soon spotted the Super Seven, a reliable, comfortable haven at the right price. Tuesday evenings were obviously not a busy part of the week; he noted only two cars in the lot when he wheeled around to the main office. By the time he parked the bike in front of his room the rain had become not much more than a misting memory, but Barth had lost his desire to continue, at least for the moment. He was glad for the break from riding after his first day on the road. He detached his bags and dropped them on the floor, then decided that, before getting out of his rain-soaked gear and settling in for good, he'd grab something to eat from the strip mall adjoining the motel. Barth walked into the Gas'n'Go and picked up a six-pack; then, rather than spending time looking through the other fast-food joints in the mall, added the only hot food available in the store, a couple of warmed-up pizza slices, to round out his dinner.

He stripped naked back in the room and relaxed in the warm shower, letting the accumulated grime, sweat and cold wash away while he stood still, enjoying the ultimate relaxation, the opportunity to just let go. After hanging his soaked riding clothes from the shower curtain rod, he put on a pair of clean shorts, then sat at the small table next to the window, flicked on the cable, and prepared to enjoy his dinner. It occurred to Barth that this was a re-creation of the Friday evening, just four nights ago, when pizza and beer fueled his rumblings of dissatisfaction and a nagging need to do something.

I guess some things never change.

Barth laughed at this observation, realizing a change had taken place, or rather, he had initiated this change, this out-of-the-ordinary detour he hoped, at the very least, would include experiences more enjoyable than what he'd been through today. This day's ruminations were certainly different than those with which he was preoccupied last Friday evening. Instead of comparing his own life with those of people encountered in his routines and finding reason for disappointment, he had been preoccupied, for the last few hours, with immediate survival on the road. Now he could enjoy the simple pleasures of a warm shower and a dry place to sleep, at the end of a longer day than he had anticipated.

This, he thought, *is progress of a sort.*

Barth awoke early the next morning with the first hint of sunlight peeking through the window curtains. Minor aches and pains made their presence known as he propped himself up and swung his legs over the side of the bed, but he was rested, and, more important, ready to begin today's chapter with renewed energy. After shaving, out of habit rather than necessity, and putting on a dry set of clothes, he walked over to the coffee shop in the mall and had a relaxed breakfast. Yesterday's ordeal now seemed minor, part of the extended learning process he had begun and now believed he could finish. The separation between last week's life as city-dwelling professional and his new role as vagabond biker seemed wider after his first day's ride. Sitting in the booth, soaking in the warm sun through the window, his conviction regarding the necessity of this adventure became even stronger, knowing he had successfully negotiated the first significant obstacle. Barth reasoned that the more distance he could put between himself and Kansas City, the more likely he could complete this mission, whatever its purpose. The warmth, the sun, the coffee, and his reflections on his progress thus far had a replenishing effect. He was as ready and eager to set out as he had been twenty-four hours earlier, but now he had a touch of experience under his belt.

I can do this.

"Does it look like rain today?"

Barth posed the question to the waitress behind the counter, partly in an attempt to establish contact after the last day's extended isolation.

"Maybe, could be, I don't really know."

Barth realized that the question, now assuming some importance to him, was merely air-filling chit-chat to her, and her response was to be expected.

Likely, she's got no stake in today's weather.

A walk around the motel parking lot before returning to his room had the effect of loosening him up for whatever lay ahead in today's ride. Stopping here and there, he kicked stones off the asphalt into the uncut brush surrounding the lot. He was close enough to the highway to hear and see the traffic heading for known destinations and was comforted by the thought that he had, for the moment at least, a respite from his own ritual. Even at this initial stage, Barth was able to make the observation that his morning plans weren't dictated by the clock. He was switching from one activity to the next only as it seemed to him the right thing to do. Even then he could change his mind.

I don't know if this is freedom, but it'll do for now.

He repacked his bags slowly and methodically, carefully folding his not-quite-dry clothes and placing them in a garbage bag to keep them separate. Twenty minutes later Barth was sitting on the bike, surveying the surroundings as he prepared to set off.

All right, Rocinante, let's get this show on the road.

With the renewed hum of the engine he eased the clutch and felt the bike jerk, hesitate, and lurch forward. He was still a novice rider after all. As he sped up the on-ramp to Route 44, he reminded himself that, after spending all day yesterday heading south on 71, he was now, for the first time, going west, straight west. This was a new beginning, the metaphor of the westward-heading pioneer repeated for even Barth. Every day now held the implicit promise of a new adventure. Route 44 out of Joplin followed and sometimes overlapped old Route 66 as it wound toward the Oklahoma border and the next major city, Tulsa. In the meantime, the sun and the light breeze were perfect this morning, conducive to a relaxed, constant pace once he left the city limits.

He couldn't recall the last time he had experienced the excited anticipation of a new day on two consecutive mornings.

This is really the craziest thing I've never done before.

Barth was on the lookout for changes in terrain that would serve as a sign that he'd entered new territory, but he could hardly object to the sight of the lush green pasture land and wooded sections filling his peripheral vision. He had unknowingly adopted the rhythm and pace of the westward traffic and, while alert to his surroundings, was in a receptive, meditative state. Crossing the Oklahoma border he felt a brief surge of adrenalin, but quickly resumed his relaxed enjoyment of the road and countryside, leaning back in his seat as far as the handlebars would permit. Kansas City seemed much farther in his past than twenty-four hours. The rookie rider started laughing to himself at the idea of experiencing a sense of accomplishment in the span of a single day. Time and miles would determine whether the feeling was justified.

He continued riding in this vein until he was forced to stop at a toll booth on the Oklahoma Turnpike. On starting again he experienced the same hesitation and jerking in first gear he'd noticed in Joplin, but again chalked it up to his inexperience with the bike. The hitch disappeared at speed, and he settled into the easy reverie of the day's ride.

Almost imperceptibly, the hill country of eastern Oklahoma asserted itself, a new form of natural beauty that placed a greater demand on the rider's attention. His focus was at one point diverted by the curled-up carcass of an armadillo, forcing a quick jerking maneuver to the outside lane. Not an uncommon road hazard in this country, but an exotic sight to this traveler. Further notice of the fact that he was in new country came in the form of license plates announcing the names of tribal groups from the Indian Nations territories scattered throughout central Oklahoma.

His memory jogged, Barth started singing the remembered remnants of a verse from a childhood song. "Way down yonder in the Indian nation, a cowboy's life was my occupation, in the Oklahoma hills where I was born." He laughed at the sound of his attempt at singing. At this moment, countless years later, he'd acquired firsthand a new visual backdrop for the Guthrie song. Signs along the road reminded the tourist that the hometown of Will Rogers wasn't far ahead, another distinctive character in a distinctive land. Perhaps three, if you counted the biking psychologist. That's it, Barth thought, a TV melodrama based on the adventures of an Oklahoma psychologist who makes house calls in the small towns along the road. He was at least sure that it had never been done. *Maybe there's a reason no one's tried it. Oh well, next subject.*

In the midst of this rolling reverie he began planning the next step in today's ride. He could stop in Oklahoma City, get something to eat, gas up, and stay the night, unless he felt like moving on while it was still daylight. In the meantime he was enjoying the ride westward in a way not possible in yesterday's rainstorm, when the goal had been reduced to survival. He was approaching Tulsa, the first real city since Joplin. Oil and Oral Roberts, the only associations that came to mind, and he could see no sign of either, not that he expected to. After paying the toll for this section of the Will Rogers Turnpike, he entered the traffic stream going directly through the city. In the bright, direct sunlight, the wind buffeting his jacket continued cooling him while he looked to his right to take in the symmetry of the ascending mountain of buildings in the city's commercial center, from a distance creating the impression of a glass-walled volcanic eruption. A pretty skyline, perhaps a friendly city as well, but Barth was content to coast through and maintain course to Oklahoma City. Now he was crossing the Arkansas River, a wide, flat stream forming the western border of the downtown area. It hardly looked capable of supporting watercraft more substantial than a pioneer's canoe. A sign noting the nearby Osage Indian reservation tempted him, but he was feeling too lazy to turn around. He was still exhilarated by the sensation of continuous movement.

The relaxed attitude he was able to assume on this bright summer's day was providing a prolonged opportunity for meditation or rumination, but Barth was content to concentrate on the road ahead, absorbing the scenery of the city and the hilly green countryside. It was more than a bit ironic that he had craved the chance for isolation to contemplate untold aspects of his present life status, yet having achieved a more or less ideal setting, he preferred to let his mind succumb to random thoughts and sensations in the order they occurred to him. Another instance of having his plans thrown aside, although, unlike during the rainstorm, Barth, and not nature, was responsible for the throwing. At this moment his attention was diverted to the names of towns and villages denoting the uniqueness of the area. Broken Arrow, Muskogee, Okmulgee, Okfuskee, Okemah. Another country, or, as declared on the state's license plates, "Native America."

Other than the motel clerk and the waitress in the diner, Barth hadn't communicated with another human being for more than a day now, an unanticipated aspect of his *en route* experience. He wasn't lonely, however, at least not now, but was intrigued by his reaction to such a prolonged period without interaction. He was enjoying the unfettered freedom to indulge himself in any direction of thought or feeling without fear of interruption. It was a new form of play. He realized that, as long as he tended to the demands of the road, minimal now, he could choose any topic as the subject of the moment's contemplation, or surrender his attention to some curious or compelling feature of the changing landscape. The choice was absolutely his, and any option of consciousness he chose to exercise was completely unencumbered by time considerations. No alarm clock, no cellphone interruptions, no appointments, no foreseeable commitments constraining or dictating the course of his mental meanderings. By itself, this insight demanded and held Barth's attention for unnumbered minutes while negotiating the gentle curves and straightaways that characterized

Route 44 between Tulsa and Oklahoma City. He was beginning to experience a sense of freedom and even joy he hadn't anticipated in his imaginings. The difference now was that he had a real sense of the answer to the why of his prior assumptions.

"Let it roll, take it in, let it wander, go wherever this takes you!"

Barth made the statement loud enough to hear it, partly in continued amusement at the sound of his voice in the absence of another listener, partly to punctuate, emphasize, the felt insight he wanted to hold onto, a new, valued landmark of this rolling adventure.

He was making good time on this stretch of highway, not out of a desire to hurry, but because this section of road was ideal for easy cruising. Occasionally checking his speedometer, Barth was surprised by his speed and made a conscious effort to let off the throttle. Perhaps everyone else on the road was in a hurry to get to their destinations.

That's fine, but I don't need it, slow down. I'll get there soon enough, wherever the hell I'm going.

He continued in this vein, maintaining a steady speed and alternating his attention between the immediate vistas of the Oklahoma countryside and the personal and professional Barth he'd left in Kansas City, if only temporarily. His musings in this direction weren't centered on specific questions, problems, tensions or existential crises, but appeared as beginning exercises in technique, concentrating for brief intervals on his newfound realization that he could engage in a sort of play with these subjects, if he wanted. Or, he could ignore them completely. Without question, the riding pilgrim was in the midst of the most enjoyable part of the excursion thus far.

A couple uneventful hours passed in this manner until he was alerted to signs of the city, this time, judging by the traffic volume and the number of lanes, a substantially larger urban area than Tulsa. Barth concentrated his energy on the task at hand, staying on 44, avoiding impulsive lane-changing drivers, and watching for road conditions, the latter consideration of increased importance with the sudden appearance of the dreaded bright orange barrels.

Just like Kansas City.

He leaned forward, enlarging his range of sight. The potholes and grooves in the road, real dangers to any biker, demanded attention.

Barth had no desire to stop in Oklahoma City, but decided to make his way to a truckstop once he left the busiest traffic behind him. He'd take a brief rest, gas up, and decide where to spend the night, maybe in a campground if one existed within the next fifty or so miles. Right now he was immersed in his first real test of city freeway riding. Tulsa had been undemanding, but this was different. His riding skills in these conditions were not yet well-honed. He could only hope that his heightened sense of fear would see him through. Large trailers on the highway were bad enough, but could usually be avoided. Now he was suddenly, unexpectedly finding himself hemmed in by the large trucks, forced to maintain a careful speed and position, hoping his existence on the road had entered the consciousness of the truck drivers. At least he didn't have to cope with a rainstorm. Occasionally, drivers followed him at a distance close enough to increase his anxiety, but there was nothing he could do, just keep moving, keep a good lookout, and hope. It occurred to him for a second, as in yesterday's rain, that he was operating on the stupid end of the judgment spectrum, but, once again, he confronted and quickly dismissed this conclusion.

Doesn't matter, just keep going, keep going, eyes on the road, eyes on the road! Not too close. Look for an opening. Check the mirror. Speed up! Watch the car in the next lane. Onward and upward.

His reserves of energy were being sapped by the immediate and unrelenting demands of high speed positioning, yet Barth somehow maintained his composure while coping with this new source of stress. After the first shaky minutes he arrived at the realization that he would survive this new test. The thought generated a glimmer of confidence, enough to get him through this challenge.

Eventually he reached the western edge of the city, at which point the volume and intensity of the traffic began to wane. Barth knew he was weathering another learning experience. Taking a deep breath, he allowed himself to feel a measure of the fatigue he had acquired in the last twenty minutes, a seeming eternity. Within fifteen minutes of leaving the city limits he sighted a beckoning invitation for a rest stop with available gas, and gladly accepted.

Oklahoma Detour

What is that feeling when you're driving away from people and they recede on the plain till you see their specks dispersing? It's the too-huge world vaulting us, and it's good-bye. — JACK KEROUAC

Barth again felt the hesitation and lurching while leaving the rest area and merging onto the highway. It was definitely worse than the slight hitch he'd noted in the shifter this morning. The bike seemed fine once he reached fifth gear and was up to speed, but even a mechanical moron like Barth knew this wasn't a problem he could ignore.

Second day out, I should know this is going too smoothly, but…I've got time.

Again, he reminded himself, this whole wild adventure wasn't based on any notion of a schedule. He could turn back toward Oklahoma City, and get there before nightfall, but he would not, this time, take the logical course of action. Stupidly, perhaps, stubbornly, he decided to make for the first town where he could find a place to crash and, hopefully, a mechanic to set things straight and get him back on his way. That decision out of the way, Barth relaxed, rolling on the throttle, leaning as he entered a long, swooping right-hand turn he found himself handling with ease.

Practicality be damned, at least for now.

Yes, still a rank beginner, to be sure, but he was enjoying his newfound sense of mastery, no matter how rudimentary his skills. Perhaps it was only the newness of these sensations, but he had, nonetheless, dipped his toes into the waters of a different world, one with exhilaration in his grips he would not easily relinquish.

The professional Barth is gone now, long live the King!

Barth laughed, first, to himself, then, with the realization that the man he'd left in Kansas City still exercised control, he forced a guffaw, loud enough for his own hearing, followed by another, this one a reaction to the silliness, to his ear, of the first. He'd never listened to himself laugh before, and now, for the first time in ages, was confronted with a mirror of his ludicrous self, boy rider as adventurer. He enjoyed the absurdity, the loose feeling and absence of a required focus for his attention other than the demands of the highway. He laughed again, louder this time.

"Hot, it sure must be hot now, but I don't care, I can't feel it, let's go, Rocinante!"

Barth laughed again, at the ludicrous notion of himself as Don Quixote on wheels. He was, he was sure, a ridiculous caricature of something.

The traffic had thinned out when he saw the sign listing two towns, Red Feather and Henley, at distances of ten and fifteen miles. He'd choose one as his stop for tonight, just choose it, in the next few minutes. It was too late in the afternoon to expect to find a place where he could leave the bike, assuming there was a place to leave it, so he'd concentrate his efforts on finding a place to eat, somewhere to sleep, and making inquiries of the locals regarding his mechanical needs. With luck, he'd get the bike repaired and back on the road again at a reasonable hour tomorrow.

By the time he reached the exit for Red Feather the sun had begun sinking into the horizon. *Time to leave the highway.* There was no immediate evidence of a town to be seen from the exit ramp, just a sign with an arrow pointing in the direction of his destination. He turned south and, emerging from the underpass, continued down a narrow road, in a southwesterly direction. There was no traffic and the only signs of civilization were rusted farm implements abandoned in a field and a couple of working "stripping wells," slowly, steadily pumping, as they had in the plains and rolling hills throughout eastern Oklahoma. Barth occasionally spotted a house or barn along the route, set back from the road with cottonwood trees and scattered pines near each dwelling. The road was heading straight west, parallel with the highway, he assumed. The hesitation after each upward shift was now irritating, but he didn't doubt he'd be able to reach the town he could not yet see.

Eventually Red Feather appeared on the horizon. Even as he was heading in, on its outskirts, Barth could see the whole town, straddling the road, and the plains enclosing the north and south boundaries, without turning his head. He wondered about the odds of finding a meal and lodging, not to mention someone with the expertise to work on his bike. As he rolled into town he observed a scattering of small, one-story ranch houses on the periphery and, nearer its center, two-story, Victorian-era homes, with their tall, narrow windows and wraparound porches adorned with ornately carved and painted wood railings. The road widened considerably as it became transformed into the town's main street. A few scattered cars were parked at an angle to the sidewalks. Most of the old storefront buildings, with tall doorways and large windows, were boarded up. He reached the town's main intersection, with no sign or light cautioning him to slow or stop, and kept going until he came to a well-lit convenience store still open for business.

"Could you help me out? I'm looking for a place to eat and a motel for the night."

The girl behind the counter recognized Barth as a stranger in town, simply because she didn't recognize him.

"No motels here, you need to get back on the highway and keep going till you get to Centralia. If you go out of town that way you can't miss the truck stop, it's open for another couple hours. That's the only place here where you can eat after six."

"Thanks, I appreciate it." Barth could think of nothing else to say and didn't need gas or anything from the store, so he headed out and started up his bike, scanning the town before taking off again. A couple cars passed on the street in front of him, but the town was otherwise empty to his eye. Not a solitary soul was walking on the wide sidewalks fronting the main drag. The world of human interaction in this isolated hamlet was invisible to him. No evidence of activity; only a few lit windows hinted at life in Red Feather.

Allowing for the now expected hesitation, he eased his bike into the empty street and continued heading west, the quiet town receding in his mirror. A few minutes later the diner came into view—a small, whitewashed shack set back from the road with a large gravel parking lot. It was the area's busiest outpost, with two eighteen-wheelers and at least five other vehicles parked out front, including an antique, rusted-out pickup that caught Barth's eye, simply for the fact he would rarely see such a vehicle in the city.

He parked the bike off to the side, far enough to ensure that it wouldn't be accidentally knocked over, and removed his helmet and gloves, glad to stop but somewhat concerned about the bike's uncertain status and the fact that he had no immediate prospect of a place to crash for the night. Nevertheless,...

The interior of the diner, unlike the experience he had of Red Feather, was bustling, full of the sounds of conversation, silverware, and clinking china. It was inundated with the smells of fried foods and cigarette smoke. The place seemed much larger from the inside, with booths in front and a counter with six stools, all occupied. A couple of women, wives or girlfriends, were sitting in the booths with men, but otherwise, the diners looked like workers who'd just punched out after a long, hot day on the road or in the fields he'd just passed. For the most part they were animated, enjoying their separate conversations. It was possible everyone knew each other here, except for the stranger who had just entered. No one took particular notice of Barth, however, except for the waitress behind the counter beckoning him to step forward.

"I don't have a seat for you right now, mister, but if you don't mind, John over there is just gettin' up to pay his check and I can sit you down with Sed, he don't bite or nuthin."

Barth laughed, feeling welcome at receiving an invitation to join the group, given without question or hesitation.

"Sure, I don't mind, I've been on the road all day and I could use the company."

"You and everybody else here, except Sed, and he spends his time keeping us on the road."

Barth followed the direction of her glance and observed the individual he assumed was the object of her reference, an older, thin man with jet-black skin and a long, scraggly, black-and-white beard covering the front of his bib overalls. His race itself was enough to set him apart in this place. He was sitting alone while his dining companion was settling his bill with the waitress. Surely, Barth thought, there's a story here, as he reflected on the events that had led him to this place, a hubbub of human activity he could never have guessed existed.

The waitress signaled Barth to follow her to the corner booth.

"Sed, here's the stranger who belongs to the bike. Now you can ask him about it." Barth's arrival had been noticed.

"Sure, sit down, make yourself comfortable, and take my advice, tell Annie you want the pork chops, they're only two days old." The man laughed out loud, the waitress glared at him in mock disgust, laughed herself, and Barth, catching the joke, joined in. He dutifully ordered the pork chops and iced tea.

"Name's Sedley, Sedley Crump, call me Sed, welcome to the metropolis of Red Feather."

He extended his hand and Barth noted the strength and enthusiasm of his grip.

"Gregory Barth, call me Barth, I guess everyone knows everyone here."

"Well, you got that right, even the truckers know everyone, this place has been here so long. You're here by yourself, this late, so I assume you're not visiting anyone, just passin' through."

"Yeah, I've had a little trouble since Oklahoma City and decided to stop and see if I could find a place to crash, something to eat and someone to check out the bike. I can see I was wrong. I'll have to head out and find something down the road. The food looks good, though, so I'm going to relax for now."

The old man nodded and smiled at Barth, then turned his head to the window.

"We don't see many bikes here, off the highway, especially foreign bikes like yours. I notice it has a drive shaft and looks like more than two cylinders."

"Three cylinders, yeah, you've got a good eye. I wouldn't know except that's what they told me when I bought it."

Barth was now interested, even intrigued with this stranger, an observant man more wrapped in mystery than he might have guessed a minute ago.

"It hesitates when I shift gears now, but it's all right out on the highway, so far, so I think I'll be okay until I can get it looked at."

"Hmm, where you coming from?"

Sed had been momentarily preoccupied, with what Barth couldn't guess. Barth proceeded to tell his story, such as it was, feeling surprisingly comfortable with this stranger, even talking about the mixed motivations that had served as the impetus for this extended road trip to who-knows-where. This man was listening, with increasing interest, although Barth himself hadn't thought he had much to say or that there was anything unusual insofar as his disaffection with his situation was concerned. He was, however, enjoying the novelty of having something to talk about outside of his personal history prior to leaving Kansas City.

The old man looked at him, smiling again, offering the observation that, "Yeah, everyone gets the notion, once in awhile, maybe once in a lifetime, to look somewhere else, for something else, even if you don't know what that something else is. Most people don't do anything about it though, just let it fade away and die. Mind if I smoke?"

"No, not at all, go ahead." Smoking while eating, strangely enough, bothered Barth, but he was in Red Feather, after all, and the company was well worth such a small price. His pork chops arrived and the smell was inviting, reviving him. Each man sat and enjoyed his respective sensual delights, halting the conversation briefly in the midst of the continuing din in this lively place. Sed pulled a cigar from a shirt pocket and began a series of practiced motions, unwrapping the object of his desire and cutting, lighting and slowly inhaling, savoring the ritual. How was it that this stranger had somehow identified with his own quixotic expedition?

"Mr. Barth, if you're not in any particular hurry to get goin', I could take a look at the bike. It doesn't sound like anything major to me, and I'll guarantee you won't find anybody in Henley or Centralia who knows a damn thing about bikes."

The significance of the waitress' earlier remark about Sed and his knowing interest in the motorcycle was now apparent to Barth, who realized his dining companion had thus far revealed little about himself.

"Thanks for the offer, I really appreciate it, but I've got to hit the road and find a place to crash, so I think I'll keep going till I find something."

Barth had wanted to accept Sed's offer, but knew it was getting to be too late to take him up on it.

"Well, I understand, Mr. Barth, but you're welcome to stay with me, I've got a couch you can sleep on, and we can take the bike to my shop tomorrow if you like. No need to keep goin' in the dark if you don't have to."

Barth was struck by this man's generosity. Even more intriguing was the possibility of getting to know more about this stranger. His normal caution was set aside with this thought and the reminder of his own motivation. This man had a story, Barth wanted to hear it, and there was no way he'd turn down this invitation for a new adventure, a major reason for this traveling search in the first place. Besides, he had no desire, with his inexperience, to ride the roads tonight if he could avoid it.

"Sed, I can't refuse an invitation like that, and I'll pay whatever you charge if you'll take a look at the bike."

"Oh yeah, I know you will."

They laughed together and got up. Barth insisted on paying the tab for both dinners and Sed did not object. It was dark now, but the diner was still busy, with a couple just entering being directed to the booth they had shared. No one seemed to notice the odd-looking pair as they walked outside. The air had cooled considerably and the moon shown brightly in the evening sky. There wasn't a sound to be heard except for their boots on the gravel lot. Sed walked to the old truck Barth had noticed earlier, a veteran Chevrolet pickup with faded paint the color of which he could not determine in the darkness. Sedley Crump and his truck were kin.

"Nice looking truck you got there."

"Yeah, it gets noticed and it's good advertising. People think, 'If that ol' black geezer can keep that junker runnin', surely he can work on my car.'"

"Can't argue with that." Sed's self-description wasn't exactly what Barth expected to hear.

"You get your bike started and follow me when I pull out."

"Gotcha."

Barth started the bike and sat waiting, listening to the smooth hum when Sed started the old truck and noting the absence of smoke coming from the tailpipe. As Sed turned the truck toward him he clearly saw the old chrome grill between headlights perched on high rounded fenders. Sed headed the truck toward town, with Barth riding close behind, until he caught a whiff of the exhaust, enough to cause him to slow the bike, increasing the distance between the vehicles. Shortly, the truck left the road, heading south on an unmarked dirt path Barth hadn't seen on his way out of town. Barth followed, keeping the bike in one of the parallel ruts, completely lacking artificial lighting. The single taillight on the old truck didn't provide much in the way of illumination and Barth didn't want to follow too closely; the dust thrown up behind was an unpleasant surprise in the darkness. He hunched up on his footpegs, minimizing the shocks from the bumpy path, trying to keep his eyes on the truck as it rolled along while avoiding unseen hazards. Slowly the two vehicles worked their way down the trail, now far enough from the main road to block out any noises except their own.

Barth looked up, beyond the truck, and detected a dark silhouette with a familiar but unexpected shape. He slowed the bike to a crawl, approaching what now appeared to be his destination, a plane sitting in the middle of the open terrain. It was the only object breaking the straightedge of the late night horizon, save for what appeared to be a single, tall tree close by. *What the hell is this?* Not any plane. He recognized, from its outline, a relic of aviation history. Even in this pitch-dark evening he could identify it as a C-47 military transport plane of 60-70 years ago, propped up in the rear, its stabilizer in the air, making it appear to be rolling down a runway.

As they approached he could see he'd been correct, but the profile view, in the darkness, hadn't revealed what could clearly be seen now, the missing wing, clipped just outside the empty engine nacelle. Sed pulled up, turning the truck so that it was parallel to the wingless plane, stopping within a few feet of its side. Under the remaining wing stub was a frame of welded steel beams in which the fuselage was cradled, elevated from the ground exactly as it would have been with the original wheels and struts. *This is where he lives*, thought Barth, laughing to himself at the confirmation, as if needed, of the quirky, offbeat nature of the character who had befriended him.

"We're not in Missouri, anymore, Toto," he thought out loud, enjoying the prospect of what lie ahead. Whatever it was, it would be something unavailable to his experience two days ago in a world now far away. He wheeled around, pulling up alongside the truck, while Sed, already out, grabbed a bundle from the truck's bed and started climbing a metal stairway up into the belly of the plane. In a second, light shone from the interior through the former passenger windows and Barth, who had parked the bike and gathered his cases, followed up the metal steps. He entered, stepping onto solid plank flooring, turning to his left to get the best view of the interior. Except for the continuous curvature of the walls, the room, which was basically the length of the fuselage, did not betray any conspicuous evidence of its original purpose. Comfortable-looking furniture, an oak bookcase, appliances. This was, without question, a lived-in home that didn't lack domestic amenities.

"This place is something else," he said, in obvious amazement, too absorbed in the experience to say anything original. "I want to know the story behind this."

"Sure," Sed replied, "Just set your cases on the table by the couch and make yourself comfortable, I'll be back in a second." Sed walked toward what, a half-century ago, must have been a fully functioning cockpit, and opened the door of a small refrigerator occupying what had once been the navigator's compartment, just as if it was the most ordinary thing in the world. He returned to an old stuffed chair opposite the couch where Barth was now beginning to relax and set a beer on the table. Barth couldn't believe his luck. Looking for a place to sleep, and nothing more, he'd been invited to a shelter he could never have anticipated in the far reaches of his imagination, from someone obviously living in a world well removed from his own. He was a ready student for lessons like this, in an exotic classroom that was the product of his host's creative genius, an encapsulated universe quite apart from the mesquite and tumbleweeds he imagined were adorning the flatland on which the plane sat.

This was definitely more stimulating than the Motel 6 and cable TV he had anticipated outside Oklahoma City.

Barth slumped on the couch, relaxing while taking in his surroundings.

"This is an incredible place. Where in hell did you get the idea to turn a plane into a home?"

"It was here, that's all. I needed a place to live and it was sitting here so I moved in."

This was hardly an adequate explanation to Barth's ears.

"How did a plane like this get to be out in the middle of nowhere?"

"Well, the way I heard it, it was a transport plane for the Army Air Corps, used to shuttle troops between Fort Hood, Texas and Oklahoma City. It was forced down during a run with engine trouble. They sent a couple of mechanics to work on it but they couldn't fix it, so they carted off the engines and left the rest of the plane where it sits. The war ended and they just forgot it, left it here to rot."

"What about the wings?"

"I took 'em off myself when I fixed it up. They just got in the way so I put 'em out back. Didn't want to take the chance that a Texas tornado would come along and make this thing airborne again."

It took a second for Barth to recognize Sed's deadpan expression as a disguised attempt at humor, but he managed a laugh. Scanning the room, he was struck by the books—in stacks on the floor, lying on just about every flat surface, and crammed into a line of bookcases he couldn't help noticing when he entered the plane. Large format art books, novels, poetry, politics, history—the scope of his host's personal library was amazing to behold.

Lacking any hint of separation, the functional divisions of this abode were blended, with a central aisle, a reminder of the structure's original mission, tying all the disparate parts together in a single, extended living space.

"How'd you come to live out here in the middle of nowhere?"

"I was a kid livin' in Memphis and lost my job when the bar I worked in on Beale Street closed. I had nothin' to lose and figured, what the hell, this is a sign, time to go someplace else, so I walked across to the other side of the river an' headed out."

Perhaps it was the residue of his professional persona kicking in, but this was definitely less information than Barth was looking for.

"Well, how did you end up here?"

Sed, a man not used to being the focus of anyone's particular interest, except from a visual perspective, began warming to his audience, and continued.

"In those days, a young black kid, they called us negroes back then, if you were lucky, didn't stand much chance hitchin' rides on any account, and you sure didn't take chances on back roads. It took me a couple days to get across Arkansas, just as hot as it is now. By the time I reached this place I was beat, starvin' hungry and thinkin' to myself, 'Sed, you dumb-ass, you coulda stayed at your auntie's house for awhile, made a little money on the docks, and you'd be sleepin' now, takin' it easy.' I was in a place where I was thinkin' I probably needed to turn around, but then I thought, it would take me a few days to get back and maybe, just maybe, I could find somethin' if I just kept goin' west.

Other people done it, surely there must be a place for me. I knew my chances for findin' somethin' were bad where I came from, so I figured I'd put up with the hot sun awhile longer. I thought I could make it to California, like the Dust Bowl people. So I kept goin'. Like the ol' sayin' goes, when ya ain't got nuthin', ya got nuthin' ta lose. Being a foolish thirteen-year-old kid didn't hurt either."

"I can't even imagine that," was all Barth could respond with, but it was the truth. He'd never been as alone and desperate as the boy in this story. "How'd you wind up here?"

"Well, I was waitin' for a ride and I'd have taken one anywhere I guess, just to keep movin', you know, when this woman stops her car and asks me, 'You lookin' for work?' This was a white woman, you see, and she didn't say 'boy,' or 'Hey, nigger,' or nuthin' like that, and those days, that was indeed a strange thing. A very strange thing."

This was a story and a history lesson, a first-person account more stimulating than the biographies Barth could hope to hear in most client sessions.

"Anyway, I was scared, honest truth, maybe this was a trick, you know, Emmett Till, but this wasn't Memphis, that was what I was thinkin', and this lady was by herself, so I thought it might be all right. Anyway, I had no prospects, nuthin' you know, and I could sit and be in the shade for a few minutes. So I says, 'Yeah, maybe I could use some work, what you got Missy?' She says she needs a dishwasher in her diner, I says I could do that, we go back and forth and the matter gets worked out. She says, 'Mrs. Colter, not Missy,' I say 'Okay,' and get in her car and she drives us out of town and I think, 'Where we goin'?', but I don't say anything, just keep my eyes open, tryin' not to fall asleep."

Barth was silent, riveted to this account of a world foreign to him, not wanting to interrupt. Sed, on the other hand, sensed that his guest's interest was genuine and, after a brief pause, continued.

"Mrs. Colter takes me to this place, just a stuckout nuthin' place on the road, in those days way outside town, and it's the place where the trucks stop, goin' both ways. Only there's no trucks there, nuthin' I could see 'cept another car and a house out back, a little house. She takes me in and sure, it looks like a diner, but there weren't no customers, just a few tables and a counter and everything you need for a diner, but no customers. She explains that the busy time is at night or real early in the mornin', not in the afternoon. This starts makin' sense to me, you know, so I'm feelin' not so nervous, and she shows me around, where the sink and everything is out back and what I need to know. Then she asks me my name and says 'I ain't heard of a name like Sedley before,' and I explain it's the family name, from the Sedley plantation outside Robinsonville in Mississippi where my family comes from. Whites in those days would say something or laugh, but she didn't laugh, she just says, 'Okay, Sedley, let's get you something to eat,' just like that, and you know, I reckoned I was in a different place right then, like a new country, just the thinkin' I had when I crossed the Mississippi."

Sed paused again, short of breath after what was, for him, an extended monologue, as a perceived courtesy to his guest, but Barth was determined not to let this pass if he could help it.

"How'd you get from there to here?" he asked, waving a hand while scanning his immediate surroundings to make clear the meaning of his question.

"Well, let's see, she put up a cot in the back room for me to sleep in. I had no place to stay, of course. The man who worked there before me lived in town, and I had no money. Her husband, John, he wasn't so sure about me, but I guess they had a need strong as mine right then, so we both took a chance and somehow things worked out."

"For a kid going by himself so far away from home, you had a lot of guts."

"Well, I thought I might stay a little, then keep goin', make enough to get me on a bus you know, but things worked out fine. I was just a dumb kid and they gave me a place to stay. I wasn't ever hungry after that time, and they paid me some too. Not a lot, but it was regular and they never cheated me, and let me say I never would've cheated them either. I missed some things, of course, I didn't know nobody out here. This isn't exactly Memphis, as you've noticed, or California, but I didn't care so much right then, I figured to go on later, and, like I said, things worked out."

Sed stopped here, as if to signify the end of his story, but, for Barth, this was only the skeleton—intriguing, to be sure, but obviously lacking important details. The man who sat across from him was many years removed from the anxious adolescent hitchhiker in a strange land he'd just described. His voice and demeanor belied the confidence of someone quite familiar, and satisfied, with himself and his surroundings.

The interior of this unique living space attested to an imagination represented by wide-ranging interests and a level of education different than what Barth would have guessed, based on Sedley Crump's story. The library alone struck Barth as one in which he could himself become absorbed, surely finding something to his liking, and the computer setup in the tail section was used… *for what?*, he wondered. Barth also took notice of a scattering of LPs and CDs in a cabinet, suggesting a range of tastes he didn't associate with his stereotyped notions of the Oklahoma hills. Van Cliburn, Yehudi Menuhin, Coltrane, Woody Guthrie, Maria Callas, even an album of Allen Ginsburg reading poetry. This evidence did not fit the history he had absorbed thus far, and he wanted, he needed to know, something of the untold biography, at least enough to make the connection between the boy in the story and the storyteller plausible.

"I hope you don't think I'm rude or anything, Sed, but that just sounds like the beginning. How'd you get from the diner to here?"

"You're right. I'm just not used to tellin' the story," Sed replied, conscious that his tale was more complex in the telling, and weighing the realization that, yes, he'd been through a lot in this life, and it took a stranger's curiosity to bring this conclusion to his awareness. After a few seconds pause to consider these thoughts, he resumed.

"Well, things worked out okay. Like I said, I had a place to stay, food to eat, a little money, and the Colters treated me fine. Mrs. Colter looked after me, like I was a foolish kid, which I was, and made me do things I didn't like, at least at first. She took me into town one day and set up a bank account for me. I couldn't even imagine that, and she made me put a little money in it every week, and she kept the bankbook, which I didn't like, so I couldn't do somethin' stupid with the money, which I would've, you can believe that. At first I was suspicious, you know, I mean, I was young, but not stupid, and it wouldn't be the first time a cracker ripped off a nigger who worked for them. That kinda thinkin' all disappeared after awhile with the Colters, and I got to know this was a smart thing they did for me. It got so that I'd look at that book, every week, and think 'This is somethin' I've got some money,' and it seemed like a lot, and then, I began to know that she was lookin' out for me, and I liked it, and didn't think too serious about goin' farther again. She started to read things with me, newspapers mainly, and she didn't laugh at my readin' at all, just kept showing me words

I didn't know, and kept at me like that, every day, until I could find the words myself and look them up, sometimes even show her words she didn't know. You know, when I ditched Memphis, I figured I was going to see a different world, but I didn't think of finding it here in the middle of nowhere."

Sed was looking wistfully, at nothing in particular, summoning up energy to continue with his story. Barth sat still, not wanting to say anything that might break the spell.

"Anyway, the Colters were real good to me, and when we went into town, nobody messed with me, mainly 'cause I was with them, or they knew I was. John had me help him in the back lot, he worked on cars when people stopped and needed help, and later he bought the garage in town. I started spendin' time with him there, and he showed me practically everything I needed to know to work on anything with wheels and a motor. There was more money in it than washin' dishes and workin' around the diner, so later I just started going in with him all the time and Mrs. Colter hires a kid from town to take my place. That's when I decided to look for a place to stay on my own. By then I was used to livin' outside town, goin' in when I wanted to have some fun or see somebody, spendin' every day at the garage anyway, so I liked the idea of the peace and quiet out here. Back then there was nothin' out here besides the diner and the road, no houses, and I sure could not afford to build one. I knew about this plane, heck, everyone knew about it, but no one bothered it, it was too far out of the way, even for the kids, and for years we all thought the army would come back and claim it. I got the idea I could stay in it awhile, just sleep here, clean up at the garage, and look around until I found a place of my own."

Barth laughed, the idea seemed strange to him in the telling. At the same time, nothing seemed more natural to him at this moment than relaxing in his surroundings, as if he were in the parlor of any house, anywhere, listening to a friend. He might be sitting in the belly of a plane, he mused, but he was actually a guest in someone's home.

"It seems a little weird, the idea of living in a plane, but I'm sitting here and I'm thinking, 'What the hell, it's comfortable', and it works."

Barth offered his brief observation, hoping not to change the momentum.

"Yeah, it was strange at first, but you know, you can get used to anything after awhile, and the price was right. I took it as a challenge, trying to figure out how to make this into a real living place, tearing out seats, putting in a real floor and walls. After a while one of the guys who brought his trucks to the garage came out here and drilled a well for me and that's how the plumbing got put in. For the first couple years I got by with kerosene for light and heat and ate dinner in the diner, like tonight. When they run lines out on the road past the diner, they put one all the way back here, that's how this finally got finished. I'm so used to the place now, and the quiet, that's the best part, I don't think I could live anywhere else."

All in all, an amazing story, thought Barth, although he still wondered about details, like the land the plane was sitting on and any claim the army might still have on the plane that obviously was not missed. One question, however, wouldn't remain unasked, perhaps as a product of his professional role, even if he was prying.

"Doesn't it get lonely out here, don't you ever feel like spending time with someone besides yourself?"

Sed had no sense that his guest was intruding. This was a perfectly logical question under the circumstances. He responded without hesitation.

"Well, yeah, it does get lonely. When I first came out here I'd go to Oklahoma City or even Tulsa once in awhile. You could meet people there, meet women and have some fun. I even thought about leavin' a few times back then, but it always come down to feeling comfortable here, having friends and no real trouble. When Mrs. Colter died, that was twenty years ago, John needed help to keep things goin', and I couldn't leave then, you know, after all he did for me. He stayed out here and kept the diner goin' for awhile. He didn't really need the money, but he felt like he owed it to his wife to keep the place she started, and he basically let me run the garage. That was a great thing, believe me, to be runnin' the place and everybody bringing in their cars and trucks. I got respect and I was a long way from the stupid kid that crossed the river when I came out here. I thought I would meet someone, get married maybe, but it just didn't happen. Sometimes I would hook up with a lady, but she wouldn't have anything to do with a crazy man living in a place like this. I knew after awhile I couldn't leave, so that's the way it is you see."

"What did Mr. Colter think about you staying out here?"

"Oh, he never said anything, he didn't talk about personal stuff much, that was for Mrs. Colter. He just figured, live and let live, you know. He and I were sort of alike, kept to ourselves a lot, and liked it just that way. Like I said, the quiet is the best part of this place, I can hear my thoughts clear, if you get my drift."

For a guy who enjoys peace and quiet, thought Barth, *he's been doing a lot of talking,* but he could see the man's point. Here you could choose the time and circumstances of your intrusions, and maybe he was just looking for the right audience for his story.

"I couldn't help notice, you really have quite a library here."

"Well, being out here gives me a chance to do my reading, I've been doing it since Mrs. Colter started me out. It got to be my habit, something I could depend on to see other parts of the world or follow someone else's thoughts when no one else was around. I was using the library in town way back then, but when I got to the point where I could, I just started buying books I wanted to read, so I can take my time and look at them whenever I want to."

"Didn't you ever want to get out yourself and see some of the world in these books? I mean, nobody's keeping you here. You could just take off anytime, see some of these places and stay as long as you want."

Sed grinned. He'd heard this question many times before.

"Oh yeah, of course, I could have blown this place a million times, any time I wanted, maybe finish the trip I started when I left Memphis. I coulda done that, but, you know, after awhile, after the first years here, it just seemed like the right thing for me to stay. When I was a kid, I thought, I want to keep going, make it to California, this was just the place I stopped because I had to, I couldn't get no farther then. When the Colters took me in it seemed to me this must be the way it's supposed to be, people lookin' out for me who need me here too, it was just right that it worked out. After awhile, it just seemed to me this is my place in the world. I have people I know, people know me, nobody bothers me, and I was, I am, somebody here. People depend on me and I know I can depend on them, and nobody gives a damn that I'm the crazy ol' black dude livin' out in the plane. Gives everybody something to talk about, you know, and that's okay by me. Besides, now I'm part of this place, even more with the garage."

"What do you mean? You could probably get a job as a mechanic anywhere you wanted to go, if you wanted to."

"Yeah, you might be right, but you don't understand. When John passed, a few years ago, he left the garage to me, completely. It was a surprise, and then again, it wasn't. Anyway, I got my own business here, people know me, I call the shots, and it gives me freedom to spend time out here. I could go too, if I want, but this is what I was lookin' for all along. I just didn't know it until it happened."

There was an extended pause, for the old mechanic a chance to relax from what was, even with breaks, an extended monologue, and, for Barth, time for the realization to sink in that he and his host were, at least in one respect, very different people. Barth had set out on this impulsive excursion to who-knows-where in an attempt to find who-knows-what, but never envisioned someone attaining this level of personal satisfaction in what would otherwise appear to be the epitome of an isolated, solitary existence. Barth could see, however, a kindred spirit of sorts in the man sitting across from the "aisle" from him. Just as a young kid had crossed the river at Memphis to look for something, Barth had left Kansas City in his concrete wake for something, he really didn't know what at this point. On the other hand, doing so at this time in his settled middle-aged existence hardly seemed the least bit rational in comparison to Sed's trek westward which, out of necessity, was exactly the "right thing to do," as he put it. The irony of the lost man with the formal education sitting across from the found man with the self-education of experience wasn't lost on Barth. While sitting in the belly of this immobilized relic he had experienced a good deal of travel during the evening, a flight he could not have anticipated.

He now felt the fatigue of the road setting in, suspended for a few hours while he was absorbed in the journey of another man's life.

Sed made a few inquiries regarding Barth's own situation, but these prompted no detailed responses from Barth, whose life experience at this juncture hardly seemed, as he sat there, the stuff of which a compelling story could be fashioned. Either out of politeness or a sense of his guest's need for rest, Sed didn't press the issue, hospitality taking precedence over curiosity. He sensed, however, that his guest wasn't typical of the bikers he saw traveling through this country, many of whom had stopped in his garage over the years. Here was someone whose route was obviously not determined by its proximity to specific sites and towns.

Instead, Sed concluded, this was a rider with a different mission. What it was he couldn't guess, but his route was an opportunity, perhaps the setting, for its success, however that could be defined, divined. His guest's reluctance to discuss his own past or present intentions was interpreted as a sign of an unsettledness he likely wished to avoid for the moment, and Sed would of course respect this choice. Things would sort themselves out for this guy, too, Sed thought, as long as he was willing to keep looking. He had also detected the presence of a kindred spirit.

"Well, Mr. Barth, it's getting late, I've got a garage to run. I'm going to put some music on, if you don't mind, and lie down. You help yourself, the frig is full, the toilet and shower are down that end," he said, pointing at the tailsection. "Tomorrow we'll go in, I'll look your bike over. I don't think it's anything major, you'll be on the road again before noon."

"Thanks, I really do appreciate this Sed. I couldn't have wished for anything better than meeting you tonight. I hope I can return the favor sometime."

Barth, realizing how tired he was, looked forward to sacking out in this quiet outpost on the plains.

"Well, goodnight." They were out of words now, shifting into their separate worlds. Sed walked toward the cockpit section, extracting a pair of rimless glasses from his overalls, then stopped for a few seconds and put on some music. Barth, after removing his boots, was lying on the couch, looking up at the ceiling while the first strains of soft, soothing violins reached his ears. He thought he recognized it, Debussy's *La Mer*, he was almost certain, but wasn't going to break the silence to ask. He was beginning to appreciate the peace in the sanctuary Sed had created for himself. Speaking now, only to satisfy his curiosity, would have been disrespectful.

Losing himself in his thoughts, Barth mused over the notion that this experience, meeting this solitary, sharing and seemingly well-satisfied man, more than validated his impulsive decision. This glimpse of another universe, not viewed through the pages of a novel or on the screen of the art movie house he frequented, was real, tangible, not created for his enjoyment, but no less stimulating and provocative.

He was, for the moment, a participant in Sed's story, a bit character, but this was real, he knew. Even as he began dozing, he realized how far he'd come in a few short days from his life routine, how he'd unexpectedly been invited to share a glimpse of a life experience he would never encounter even in the most direct, naked, confession-laden sessions with clients in his suburban office.

"Time to get up, Mr. Barth, I've got a garage to run and you'll never find your way out of here by yourself."

Barth rolled over on the couch, rubbing his eyes. He glanced at his watch. It was 6:00 a.m.

"You can clean up at the sink up front. When you're ready just follow me into town and leave the bike at the shop. I'll look it over while you get some breakfast."

"Thanks, I'll be ready in a few minutes."

The enthusiasm and energy in Sed's voice was palpable. Barth couldn't recall when he'd been so eager to get started on a workday. He stood up, absorbing the early sunlight through the cabin windows, and grabbed one of his cases. Sed walked out the entryway while Barth headed toward the front of the plane, located the sink, as if it was the most natural thing to expect in this unusual habitat, and splashed cold water on his face. Looking out the window above the sink, he studied the southern exposure in the bright morning light. The view consisted of gently rolling hills covered with the buffalo grass of the plains, unbroken by any evidence of civilization outside the immediate vicinity of the plane. A thin, scraggly tree, obviously planted, provided a sliver of shade hardly worth the effort. He noted two structures arising from the earth that he couldn't immediately identify. Studying them for a few seconds, he determined that these were the plane's wings, planted upright in the ground and painted white, providing a windbreak of sorts, perhaps that was their function. To the east of this wall was a garden, neatly planted rows of corn and fruits and vegetables he couldn't identify.

Barth emerged from the plane with his bags, descending the steps like a passenger from another era. It was hot, even this early in the morning, and the sun even brighter than he had sensed a few minutes ago. The view north was, if anything, as sparse as its southern counterpart, broken only by traces of the dirt road, quickly disappearing in the distance, and the power line, the only visible connections to the outside world. He spotted no landmarks on the horizon signifying the presence of a town, and the absence of any of civilization's sounds reinforced a sense of eerie isolation. The feeling was disconcerting to Barth as he stood surveying the landscape, until it dawned on him that this setting was perceived by his host as peaceful, relaxing, and conducive to a contemplative and meditative existence.

He turned to find Sed, busy packing items in the truck bed, and now could see its faded green paint and the black fenders, likely original. The plane also sported a faded green, of a lighter shade, and a faint white outline on the fuselage he guessed was its military insignia. The tail of the plane was propped up by an elaborate welded structure of interlocking steel beams, testimony to the creativity of the man who had many years ago appropriated and transformed it completely.

Barth walked to his bike and reattached the bags. Sed was sitting in the cab of the truck, the door open, engaged in no particular activity. When Barth was helmeted, Sed closed the door and started the truck, without uttering a word. Barth waited until the dust thrown up by its rear wheels had subsided, then headed down the road in its wake. The house with the clipped wings faded into the distance and the scenery, for a couple minutes, did not differ in any direction. The path he was following and the position of the sun provided the only sources of directional information.

Finally, the odd-looking caravan reached the main road and headed east toward town, now within sight. Two ancient red brick four-story buildings hugged the main street, sticking up into the bright, clear, morning sky. Sed turned south at the main intersection after passing the convenience store where Barth had sought directions last evening and headed east on the first side street, pulling over in front of an old brick building Barth guessed was his shop. Barth parked behind the truck and dismounted while Sed opened a large wooden garage door, revealing a long, cavernous interior harboring a half dozen vehicles, a lift, and walls and benches covered with tools. The stamped tin ceiling with peeling ivory paint hinted at another purpose for the building, in another time. Tires were hanging from massive wood crossbeams, and there was an enclosed room, probably an office, off to the side in the front of the building. Barth couldn't imagine that there were six vehicles in a town this size requiring maintenance at any one time, but Sed assured him he was never wanting for business. Cars, trucks and tractors, at times even farm implements, were brought in, sometimes towed, from all corners of the county. He had hired an assistant, who would be here in another hour, to meet the demands of the business.

"You just leave the bike where it is and get yourself some breakfast, walk up to the corner and you'll see the diner, right across the street. Take your time. With luck, I can take care of the bike by the time you get back."

"I'm in no hurry, I'll buy you breakfast if you're interested."

"Thanks, I like to get started early and I have the coffeepot in the office, that's all I need."

"Well, thanks, I really appreciate your help and hospitality, I hope you know that, Sed."

By now Barth had gotten used to, if not completely comfortable with, the familiarity of the first-name basis he had with this man, as well as the economical quality of much of his conversation. He understood there was no need to say more.

"See ya in a while."

"Yeah."

Barth walked off toward the town center, soaking in the warmth of what promised to be a hot Oklahoma summer's day, hopefully to be enjoyed from the seat of his repaired steed. He crossed the main street at a lazy pace—nothing more was required here. The only moving vehicles in sight were at a safe distance in both directions. Sounds of conversation could be heard coming from the modest café on the corner, through the screen door with the whitewashed wooden frame and milled dowels marking it as an original component of this old red brick edifice. As he entered a few of the seated patrons looked up, then resumed their conversations. He wasn't sure, but it seemed that these were the same faces he'd seen at the diner. Barth sat in an empty booth and a middle-aged woman with short bleached blond hair emerged from behind the mechanical cash register to take his order.

"Morning. You're the guy with the bike at Sed's place."

Had it not been for last evening's experience, Barth might have felt paranoid at the observation, but he understood it was meant as a combination of greeting and recognition. In this town any "outsider" was quickly registered as an item of local news, and the acknowledgment shouldn't be interpreted in a sinister manner.

"Yup, that's me. He's working on it right now. Could I have some coffee and a couple eggs, scrambled, with toast?'

"Sure thing, Honey. Take my word for it, your bike will be in the best shape of its life when he's done. You can take that to the bank."

"Thanks. I get the idea that a lot of people here feel that way."

"You got that right. The man's a wonder."

She turned and disappeared in the back. Barth was struck with what he now concluded, on the basis of his own experience, Sed's accounting of his story, and the corroboration of another stranger, was the universal admiration with which this man was regarded. No wonder that Sedley Crump, who might seem the ultimate misfit in this setting, regarded himself as one who had found and made his home, as satisfied an individual as any Barth had ever known.

No surprise he never made it to California.

Barth enjoyed a quiet, leisurely breakfast while other customers, with more definite destinations than his, left to fulfill their obligations. He glanced at his watch, thanked the waitress, and leisurely retraced his steps to the garage, observing more traffic and activity in the waking village.

When he arrived at the garage there were three men in the building discussing business with Sed. They nodded in greeting and Sed paused for introductions. Again it was apparent that these strangers not only knew Barth's identity, but accorded him a modicum of respect as a direct product, he now assumed, of his association with the proprietor. Barth listened in silence while two of the men discussed their automotive problems with Sed, making arrangements to have them attended to, and determined that the third, a young kid who looked to be about high school age, was Sed's hired hand.

When the men drove away, Sed introduced his employee simply as Tom and the younger man excused himself to work on a project in the rear of the garage.

"Well, did you have a chance to look at the bike?"

"Yeah, I did."

Barth interpreted the look on Sed's face as consternation, causing him to pose the followup query with hesitation, if not trepidation.

"What's the verdict?"

"Well, the problem isn't all that hard to fix, but the thing is, the part you need has to be ordered, probably from the U.S. distributor, I imagine somewhere back East."

Barth was crestfallen. He hadn't imagined this scenario at all and, despite the fantastic diversion his mechanical difficulties had made possible, was eager to set off on the road. He was, nonetheless, able to make the transition to acceptance of his fate with no visible sign of distress.

"Well, I guess it's gotta be fixed sometime, it might as well be now. I'll just have to figure something out, what I'm going to do."

Sed noted Barth's reaction and sensed the depth of his disappointment despite the equanimity of his expression. He looked down at the floor of the garage for a few seconds, without saying a word, then, directing his gaze so their eyes met, displayed a broad smile and began laughing, confusing Barth for a few seconds, after which he realized something was up.

"I'm sorry, I couldn't help myself. I hope you're okay, but that look of yours was worth it. Truth is, all you had was a loose clutch cable. Took me two minutes to tighten it at the handgrip."

He continued laughing, not as energetically now, and Barth, who otherwise would have felt himself the victim of the joke, couldn't help but laugh out loud. It wasn't only the relief he felt in receiving the diagnosis, but what he regarded as the most important aspect of this brief interaction with the master mechanic. A man with the judgment and circumspection of Sedley Crump wouldn't have bothered to initiate such a ruse with anyone for whom he had no regard or interest, and this level of confidence rendered Barth a partner in the joke between two friends. It was amazing the respect that he accorded this unique character, based on less than a day's contact.

"You got me, you really got me, Sed. I was ready to start making other plans, I don't know what, but I can tell you this, wherever I end up, I won't forget this, not as long as I live. You can bet on that."

"Well, I've enjoyed it too. Now you need to get moving, while you have a whole day of good weather in front of you."

"What do I owe you for the bike?"

"Nothing. Just enjoy your ride, that's enough for me."

The two men stood facing each other for a brief second, then shook hands. Barth understood that nothing else need be said. He walked over to the bike while Sed stood and watched him put on his gear, mounted, then switched the key on. The engine sputtered, then came to life, in its reliable manner. As he started to let out the clutch, now with no slack, he turned toward Sed, still standing in the same spot.

"Thanks again. If I ever come back this way I'll stop by."

He slowly inched the bike forward and nodded one last time. Sed returned the gesture.

"Just keep looking, that's enough."

Cross on the Road

Everybody has choices, only some don't see 'em, an' others, they jus' don't choose ta choose, that's all. — REV. AMOS TUTWILER

L eaving Red Feather and returning to the highway, Barth couldn't help knowing he had, briefly, left his mainstream existence. Back on the main road, perhaps he wouldn't have another encounter as singular as that experienced through his glimpse of the life of Sedley Crump. No matter, it was now official, he'd met someone he couldn't know in the comfort of his apartment, and the decision to become the temporary wheeled wanderer was validated.

If nothing else happens on the road except for the change of scenery, this was definitely the right decision, no doubt about it.

Not exactly a conquistador on the trail of El Dorado, but Rocinante had already been good for the discovery of a vein of humanity he hadn't found in Kansas City. The air, he was sure, was fresher here, the sunshine warmer, and the road was his welcome mat. Barth wasn't cocky, he was too smart for that, but he had confidence in his ability to make this journey, now founded on more than the desperate determination with which he'd set out. He had, in addition to the road miles under his belt, a confirmation of his legitimate status as biker-explorer, bestowed on him by those he'd encountered thus far, if only by the absence of any challenge of his credentials.

Today's riding was a relaxed, uneventful opportunity to survey the gently rippled terrain of the Oklahoma landscape while heading west toward the Texas panhandle. Lush green grass and scattered clumps of wildflowers waved gently in the light wind, cooling Barth without demanding any compensation in his riding. It was a good day to dawdle, and if he did see an excuse for leaving the highway, there was nothing to stop him.

There's gold in them there byways.

Having taken the exit to Red Feather out of necessity, he would be sure to take some exits by choice, hell, on a whim. This wasn't a race—after all, he had four weeks for road-roaming, and damn if he wasn't going to take every last minute of it!

Barth passed another group of pumpjacks sucking the last pockets of crude from the earth beneath the green Oklahoma hills. With large steel heads at the sky end of each rocking arm, their silhouettes gave the impression of slow-motion woodpeckers, the bobbleheads of the plains. For all their rhythmic machined movement, however, they weren't going anywhere.

He continued cruising, oblivious to passing cars and trucks except as safety demanded. Assuming there was a better than even chance he wouldn't duplicate this trip in his lifetime, he wanted to scan the countryside as much as possible while maintaining his line and a safe speed. Unattached to a schedule or itinerary, Barth imagined this was what was meant by the phrase "freedom of the road." Occasional gusting winds from the south, however, served as stern reminders that this freedom didn't come without the responsibility for attention to changing conditions. It wasn't the wind *per se* that was giving him a problem. He had learned to compensate for its direction by leaning the bike into the wind to maintain his line. The hard parts were the abrupt changes in its force or direction that would sneak up on him, requiring quick shifting of his weight and pressing his grips to keep the bike upright.

Maybe I'll get this right by the time I reach Seattle.

Thirty miles out of Red Feather he was passed by a pack of bikers riding in staggered formation, their bikes emitting a steady, loud, irritating roar. Each rider was sporting a black leather jacket or vest that couldn't have been comfortable in the hot sun. Barth could make out the common emblem displayed on their backs, a spoked bike rim and tire with a broken thunderbolt passing through the hub and, in large white letters sewn on the black background, the words "Okie Outcasts."

Barth nudged Rocinante to the edge of the road to accommodate the riders, passing him one by one in a steady progression. He nodded to them, about twenty in all, each in his turn nodding back or, in the universal language, extending two fingers of the left hand in the rider's salute. The greeting was notable coming from these bikers, easily distinguished from the intruder except for the choice of two wheels. They were riding large, heavily-chromed cruisers and the closest thing to headgear was a bandanna tied in the back. Barth, riding his chrome-less touring bike and wearing a full-face helmet, was an alien in these parts, but if it mattered to anyone in the group it wasn't evident. He watched as they proceeded, steadily disappearing even in this straight, flat stretch of interstate. A twinge of envy at their camaraderie was supplanted by the knowledge that, lifestyle choices aside, he was constitutionally incapable of being a joiner for any extended period of time. Even Dave, as good a candidate for best friend as anyone Barth knew, was someone he rarely saw more than twice in a month's time. He was more like the recluse Sedley Crump—friendly enough, but jealously guarding his solitude.

Now he was hungry, despite the breakfast in Red Feather, and decided his appetite was an excuse to take another detour off the beaten path. Elk City, just ahead, would be his last Oklahoma stop before the Texas border. *Maybe just another stop, maybe not.* Barth signaled, though no one was in sight, and leaned Rocinante into the exit curve, easing the throttle and slowing until he could see that stopping was unnecessary. All he had to do was follow the line of the old cracked macadam road toward the outcropping of ancient brick buildings that established beyond doubt the town's existence.

Red town drowsing in the hot Oklahoma sun, empty cars parked at an angle on each side of the wide-open main drag. Occasional stares from casually dressed passersby *en route* to errands and business appointments. He wheeled the bike slowly westward, acutely aware of his outsider status, but immune to any inference of abnormality. This was a working assumption by this time.

Just for the heck of it and his curiosity, Barth pulled the bike in at the midpoint of the main street and dismounted, leaving his helmet perched on the seat. He assumed that here he didn't have to spend energy worrying about such things. It felt good to stand up, stretch his legs and walk, even after such a short morning ride. Heading east on the sidewalk, for no particular reason, he took in the storefronts. A barber shop, hardware store, insurance agency, antique store, law office with a stenciled window sign advertising a solo practice, and a pharmacy, all with tall, curtained windows open to the late morning sunlight. On this weekday the other strollers, exhibiting more purposeful pacing, nodded to the obvious stranger in what appeared to be a genuine attempt at welcome. The sporadic "Hiya" was reflexively returned, and Barth was beginning to warm to the villagers and the weather.

He was seized with an unexpected feeling akin to nostalgia, a familiarity evoked by memories of another time, another place. Except for the names on the storefronts and the change of fashions, this was the main street of Marceline, the small Missouri town where he'd spent his childhood. Just large enough to require stop signs, the center of an agricultural county, where familiarity was a given. Throughout his adolescence Barth had been eager to escape his hometown. College had been the key to freedom from his small-town prison, but now, he realized, there was much that he missed. Barth recalled that time, when he'd been on a first-name basis with everyone his own age and knew all adults as "Mister, Missis, Ma'am or Sir." A simpler time, so far away, yet vivid in the moment. The morning sun warmed him much as it had during lazy childhood summers.

"Hey, biker, ya lookin' for the Dog?" An old man in faded bib overalls and a wide-brimmed straw hat, sitting on a public bench against an old brick building, spoke to Barth.

"The dog? I'm sorry, what's that?"

"Oh, I saw ya parkin' yer bike an ah jus 'sumed ya were lookin' fer the Dog. That's where the bikers hang out."

"Well, I wasn't, but which way is it?"

"Jus' turn and head back past yer bike two blocks. Ya won't be able to miss it, that's fer shure."

"Thanks, appreciate it. I think I'll head over there. Thanks a lot, mister."

"No problem. Used to ride myself, in my younger days. An Indian, four-cylinder, big bike for those days ya know. Anyway, welcome and good ridin' ta ya."

"Indian, classy bike. Thanks again." Barth didn't know what he was talking about, but somehow recalled the Indian name in the pantheon of revered motorcycles. He'd already turned and begun strolling past the storefronts, continuing until he reached Rocinante, readying himself for the short ride to this bike hang-out. Heading west he soon came in sight of his destination, fronted by a group of chromed cruisers pointing out to the street, leaning on their sidestands. A true biker bar, no doubt about it, even if he didn't see himself as a true biker. *Maybe this isn't such good idea*, he thought, but quickly changed his mind, reminding himself that opportunities for small adventures were all part of this, exposing himself to worlds foreign to his own when he had the chance. Barth pulled up alongside the bank of gleaming cruisers and parked, not too closely, lest he offend these bikers by unknowingly breaking an obscure rule of riding etiquette.

Above the entrance of the sagging wood-framed structure was a painted oval sign in a rusting wrought iron frame. It depicted a sleeping dog with its legs outstretched over an old wooden porch. The name of the establishment was painted in dark green letters against a white background—El Perro Perezoso. The sign and the name definitely fit this hot, lazy afternoon. It also fit the building, a large, unpainted wood shack, not much more, looking incapable of resisting a barrage of gusting Oklahoma breezes. Barth stepped on the shaded plank porch and entered, immediately finding himself in a different world from Main Street of Elk City. The interior was dimly lit, with a long antique bar facing from the back wall and several tables randomly scattered over the unfinished wood floor. Rustic was the word that came to mind. An assortment of beer ads was flanked by gaudy colored posters announcing past appearances by blues, country and folk singers, including some Barth recognized. A juke box, with pulsing lights, loudly broadcasted the voice of Howlin' Wolf belting out his classic "Evil."

I'm not in Kansas City anymore, at least any part I know.

In a corner near the entrance, tables were pulled together and a group of bikers was sitting, engaged in animated conversation. As far as Barth could tell, they gave him no notice. As he stepped to the bar he could see that these were the Okie Outcasts who had passed him an hour ago.

Barth seated himself and began studying the menu, written in chalk on a blackboard hanging from the wall. When the waitress approached he ordered a pork sandwich and a Lone Star. He imagined this to be the typical biker's lunch, and, right now, it looked good to him. Dave would have given him hell for the beer this time of day, but one couldn't hurt. He could assume the role for the time being, at no cost to him or anyone else, he was convinced.

The raised volume of the bikers' voices diverted his attention to the corner table, where he witnessed a commotion among them, some now standing. What he heard wasn't a cacophony of clinking glasses punctuated by loud laughter, but an argument regarding a subject he couldn't guess from his seat. He was curious about the reasons for the disturbance, but smart enough to disguise his interest. Barth couldn't follow the conversation, but picked up an angry outburst from a huge figure facing away from him.

"Look, I know it sucks, you moron, you think I like this, you goddamn idiot? We can't walk away from this, no fucking way. You don't like it, just stay out of it, but we ain't gonna forget it. You think about that when *your* turn comes!"

With that, the speaker stood and stomped toward the bar. His presence was as conspicuous as his voice. He was a few inches on the plus side of six feet and a few pounds on the plus side of two hundred fifty. His large, round head was cleanshaven, with a surplus of facial skin folding over in his cheeks, and one small, unadorned gold hoop hanging from his right ear. Large biceps had escaped from the sleeves of his black T-shirt, complemented by black leather chaps and boots. A faded, indecipherable tattoo adorned the upper half of his left arm and it wasn't an understatement to describe him as an intimidating presence. He stepped a few feet to Barth's left and stood there, silently, fidgeting, until the woman walked over to him.

"Yeah, Bones, what can I get ya?"

"Some iced tea, Joanie, thanks." He was obviously upset and the waitress just as obviously knew him well enough to leave it at that. *Let him simmer down, whatever it is, he'll be okay in a few minutes.*

Barth, taking his cue from her, relaxed and rededicated himself to his lunch. When Bones stepped up beside him he didn't react, except for a nod of recognition.

"We see your bike when you rode up. From Missouri, huh?"

"Kansas City."

"Lot of ridin.' Headed any place special?"

"Seattle, I think. At least that's the plan. Sort of a vacation, getting away for a change, see some of the country."

"Good for you. None of us does much of that, just ride around here, get together for lunch, foolin' around. Whaddaya do in KC?"

Barth was always hesitant to talk about his work with a stranger, but he couldn't weasel himself out of answering the man's question.

"A shrink, really, that's bizarre, I can't believe it."

"Well, it's true." Barth couldn't guess where the stranger's remark came from and didn't know whether he should be insulted, but continued to let discretion rule.

"No, no, that's not what I meant. It's just weird that I step over here at this moment and run into you. Amazing, that's what it is."

Barth was mystified, but guessed this guy Bones would reveal all in due time.

"Look Doc, we got a situation here, pretty bad right now. I gotta ask you a professional question. Okay with you?"

Barth was smart enough not to risk refusing him.

"Well, all right, just keep in mind, you get exactly what you pay for, and I'm not getting involved in whatever was going on over there, okay?"

"No problem. Listen to me, I've got a question for you. Do you think anyone who wants to off themselves is crazy, I mean certifiable, nuts, whatever?"

"What the hell are you talking about?" This guy had Barth's undivided attention.

"Really, do you think a person is automatically mentally ill or whatever you guys call it if he wants to just end it all?"

"Well, I guess I'd have to say no, not automatically, I suppose there are circumstances where someone who wants to commit suicide might actually be perfectly sane, even if it seems illogical to everyone else. I can't give you any kind of rule or anything. Just depends. So don't quote me on that."

Barth was baffled by this question out of left field, but decided to let well enough alone. This wasn't a therapy session, no need to press.

"Yeah, I know. Just wanted to get your opinion, see what a professional has to say. I appreciate your time and hope you see nothing but good ridin' all the way, pardner. Thanks."

With that, Bones patted Barth's shoulder with a surprisingly light touch and walked over to the space he'd previously occupied to pick up his tea. He stuck a bill on the counter and smiled at the waitress.

"This rider's lunch is on me, Joanie."

Barth's gaze followed him as he returned to join his colleagues. He still couldn't figure out the role he'd just played in this minor drama, but guessed that the question and his response were connected to the goings on in the corner.

A few seconds later Bones waved to him, the gesture meant as an invitation, an offer from the Outcasts he knew he couldn't refuse. Despite his reservations, curiosity got the better of him. Barth picked up his beer and wandered over to a chair that had been pulled out for him. As he sat down Bones made the introductions, nicknames or surnames Barth would never remember, and Barth followed suit, volunteering his basics. He was immediately the center of attention, a diversion for the group that, as Barth found out, was comprised of local, workaday people for whom this was an extended lunch break, not the hardcore biker gang he had imagined. There were five women here, none of them looking the part of the prototypical biker babe. The fact that Barth was a novice rider seemed not to matter; his road thus far was, for the most part, out of their radar, and they were interested in even his limited riding experience. It was amazing to Barth that none of the listeners was aware of the existence of Sedley Crump, although Red Feather was less than a couple hours' ride from here. They were fascinated by the tale of the mechanic who made his home in an abandoned army transport plane and envious of Barth's chance encounter.

Shots of tequila were shoved in Barth's direction. He was at first hesitant to accept, reasoning that he shouldn't compromise his still tenuous grasp of riding skills. He was, however, reluctant to reject any aspect of this invitation to sit with the Outcasts and complied.

"So, you're the shrink. What do you think we should do about Harris?" The question, coming from Lila, a red-haired woman on the opposite side of the table, caught Barth off guard.

"That's what I asked you about before. Harris is one of us. He was hit by a drunk on the road two months ago and he's a quad now, stuck in a damn bed for the rest of his life. He can't do nothin' for himself, only talk, and all he talks about is getting it over. He can't even do it himself, he wants us to do it for him. The guy's been our best friend since we were kids, all of us, and hell, we don't know what to do. That's why I asked you about being crazy."

Bones leaned back in his chair. His out-of-the-blue question now made sense. Another voice chimed in.

"Yeah, I don't think we can do this but, you know, if it was me, man, shit, I wouldn't want to be layin' in bed rottin' all day with no control over nothing. Hell, the man can't even piss without help. How can he have any dignity left, I ask you?"

The question, obviously rhetorical, and just as obviously right on target, went unanswered. Other voices chimed in, all in agreement that their comrade was, indeed, living a life none of them considered worth much, deprived of all the things he loved most. Every one of the Outcasts felt an obligation to Harris to respect his wishes, but all were powerless to do anything. If Barth had told Bones earlier that the then anonymous person was indeed "crazy" they could have at least taken refuge in the delusion that Harris's demands weren't real, weren't valid, but Barth's response had done nothing to alleviate the communal anxiety. And, after all, when it came right down to it, their conflicted intuitions were dead-on. There was no satisfactory way out of this dilemma.

None of the riders wanted to abandon Harris to his nonstop misery, and none of them could take responsibility for doing what, under like circumstances, might even be their own preference. Harris was a loyal, reliable friend. He would give a buddy his last dollar, and the fact that they sometimes referred to him in the past tense wasn't lost in the discussion. Everyone present, including Barth, was a bit uneasy. They were experiencing their own helplessness, mirroring that of the rider now depending on 24-hour care to maintain a poor shadow of what they considered living.

"Maybe he'll adapt, adjust to his new reality, you never know, six months from now he might see things differently."

Barth's words weren't convincing, not even to himself, but he had nothing else to offer. A few members of the group nodded in assent, grasping at any straw. Collectively they seemed, for now, resigned to the absence of any prospect of resolution. It dawned on Barth that, despite the free flow of tequila, which he had continued to consume, these weren't hardcore drinkers, not by any stretch of the imagination. The alcohol in this instance was meant as a palliative, a feeble attempt to dull the edge of this undeniable shared crisis.

As the energy at the table subsided, some of the riders made it known they had to leave and return to their jobs, but no one left immediately, and nobody seemed to care much about such details. Barth was feeling drowsy, abnormally fatigued when he considered how little he'd done today. He had a vague sense that his plans might have to be changed, that he'd be riding out of Elk City later than planned. He recalled hearing Bones, who he now recognized as the group's unofficial leader, say something about tomorrow night, but that was all. Things were becoming hazy. He sensed he was relinquishing control, not voluntarily, but because his present state left him no choice.

The bright sunlight filtering through the curtains warmed his face. Barth instinctively turned away, waking as he did so.

What the hell is this? Where am I?

Bewildered, disoriented, he sat up, opening his eyes to what he could see was a small, single bed in a small, sparsely furnished room. Scanning his surroundings he noted, first of all, he was fully dressed, except for his boots, and, secondly, his gear was neatly stacked on a dresser next to the window. A table lamp had been left on, its light barely noticeable in the rays of daylight invading every corner of the room. A print hung on the wall next to the window in a cheap plastic frame. The image was a hulking leather-clad blacksmith swinging a hammer down on an anvil outside a red barn with large oak trees and forested mountains in the background. It dawned on him that he was somewhere in Oklahoma, in a motel—at least that was his initial determination.

How in hell did I end up here?

Lacking any recollection of the evening, Barth nevertheless concluded that he was physically intact and there was no immediate cause for alarm. He swung his legs over the side of the bed and sat up, rubbing his eyes. Instinctively slapping his back pocket, he determined that his wallet was in its place, then stood up, surveying the scene. A little woozy, but he could maintain his balance. By now he'd regained a degree of consciousness sufficient to aid him in his quest to obtain an explanation for his circumstances.

It must have been the tequila, that's it, oh yeah, my head's still in a spin, but what's this?

Barth walked to the window and was immediately reassured at the sight of Rocinante, parked in the lot just outside the door of his room. Somehow, he concluded, he had managed to get here without getting himself killed, but details eluded him. Everything since lunch with the Outcasts was beyond his powers of retrieval.

Okay, that's gone, time to put yourself together.

It had been years since he'd actually been drunk, but the hazy feeling wasn't unfamiliar. He was rejoining the world and set about taking the steps required to restore himself. The shower was exactly what he needed, and after digging out a fresh set of underwear and getting dressed he was ready, even eager, to re-enter the outside world and start riding. He packed his gear, grabbed the room key lying on the dresser, and opened the door to feel a warm, gentle breeze welcoming him back. Barth spotted the office and entered, greeted by a smiling woman behind the counter who didn't seem the least bit surprised by his appearance. The strong smell of brewing coffee was energizing.

"I guess you're feelin' better this mornin'."

"Yeah, that's putting it mildly. I hope I didn't bother anyone last night."

"Mister, you weren't in any condition to bother a soul, not as far as I could see. You weren't much more than a sack of potatoes when your friends carried you in here."

One mystery, at least, was solved.

"How much do I owe you for the room?"

"Don't worry. That was taken care of yesterday. You're good here. Help yourself to the coffee. It's fresh."

"Thanks. Don't mind if I do. I'm heading out in a few minutes. If you see those guys again, would you thank them for me? I doubt I'll be back this way anytime soon."

"Sure. You be careful, you hear? Shiny side up."

"Will do. Thanks a lot." Barth poured himself some coffee and turned toward the door.

"Oh yeah, I almost forgot. You'll be needing this." She extended her arm, dropping his bike key into his hand. "I was under strict orders not to give you this if you were the least bit wobbly." She laughed, and Barth couldn't help joining in.

"Thanks again, ma'am."

Outcasts indeed, he thought to himself as he revved up Rocinante and headed her in the direction of Main Street to grab a late breakfast.

Seated in the bar at the Lazy Dog again, Barth was now fully awake and functioning, not the state he had reportedly been in when he left the place yesterday. He was alone in here today, late Friday morning, by his reckoning. He smiled at the realization that the last fact didn't come immediately to his awareness, but required a few seconds' thought. Two nights in Oklahoma, with as much adventure as he could have bargained for, and he hadn't even reached the Texas border. Today he planned to cruise through the Texas panhandle, maybe stop for a late lunch or early dinner in Amarillo, he had to at least stop there, then spend the night somewhere in New Mexico. He could gas up here in Elk City and continue westward at his now customary leisurely pace. He wouldn't have to think about stopping for a while and could wait until Amarillo to consult the map and plan his next move.

I could get used to this ad hoc travel itinerary.

The road Barth was laughing at the domesticated version—he'd be sitting in his Kansas City office right about now, his day's activities governed by his appointments calendar. *I'll return to that life soon enough.*

An hour later he was on the interstate and Elk City was another memory to dredge up someday in the distant future. He kept his visor partly open to let in more of the cooling breeze, just in case his state of wakefulness was less than optimal after the alcohol-induced lost evening. His middle-aged body was reminding him to exercise a little moderation, even in the midst of this less-than-rational road venture. He couldn't guess whether he would be worn down and road-weary when this trip eventually came to its end, or whether he'd be hardened and conditioned to demands he hadn't subjected himself to in even the far reaches of his memory. At this moment, however, he was enjoying the sensation of the moving vistas surrounding him and the comforting, barely audible hum of Rocinante's powerplant, doing its work beneath his seat. This feeling was becoming an addiction.

The presence of the occasional large truck, invariably passing him, was a reminder that he wasn't off the beaten path, but the traffic was nevertheless sparse. Elk City was apparently the largest metropolis in this section of Oklahoma. The towns he passed now, as far as he could tell from his moving perch, were more in the way of villages or hamlets. Barth wondered about the reasons for the existence of these places, the whys and wherefores of the people who stopped in a particular place to begin the process, knowingly or otherwise, of settling a site that would eventually give rise to an intersection, a few businesses, and, finally, a town which would somehow survive the vagaries of natural and economic hurdles that could thwart any such enterprise. The bend in a river, vast expanses of arable land, thick forests, veins of coal or gold in the earth, or merely the place in the plains where a migrating party stopped for water or rest, these were some of the reasons for a town's coming into being. He knew the midsection of the country had also been populated by immigrants from Europe who'd been swindled by land speculators' convincing advertisements for cheap, fertile land requiring barely a nudge to transform it into a lush, self-sustaining Shangri-La. Barth wondered if the fields of coreopsis, the purple verbena, and patches of green, hardy buffalo grass visible from his padded perch were any different than the flora greeting those ancient immigrants.

It occurred to Barth that Oklahoma's history had unique chapters explaining some of these outposts of civilization. The Trail of Tears that led from regions east of the Mississippi and ended in this state, then a territory, with its survivors, the Cherokee and the other nations alluded to in the "Native America" slogan stamped on the license plates. Then the Cherokee Commission of the 1890s that purchased fifteen million acres from the tribes to open the territory to the land-hungry settlers hovering on its borders. On the other hand, he supposed there were settlements, by whatever name they were called, that had disappeared in the forced migrations of the Dust Bowl days of the '30s memorialized by Steinbeck and Woody Guthrie. After that, the migrants by choice and tourists passing through on America's Highway, the 66 Barth had been shadowing on his own westward journey. No one, he concluded, could be viewed as a permanent resident, except by the measuring stick of a few years, more or less. Traveling, east or west, north or south, was a permanent aspect of the human condition, the towns and cities giving rise to an illusion of anchored stability.

Enough philosophy for today. Lean back, look around, feel the wind, relax.

Even at his deliberately leisurely pace, Barth was putting miles between himself and Elk City. The scenery, mildly undulating hills and low, stubborn vegetation, was exotic to his eyes. When he crossed the border into Texas he tried to detect evidence of a distinct change in topography, as if it was a perfectly reasonable expectation, but none was apparent. That didn't stop him from imagining a transition to a Texas frame of mind in which he could hear the strains of Willie Nelson songs and the plaintive wailing of Joe Ely, Jimmie Dale Gilmore, or The Sons of the Pioneers. Having no prior direct experience of Texas, this aural image would have to do for now. For Barth, the music evoked a singular picture of the Texas high country, full of romance befitting his status as a two-wheeled cowboy.

Here I am, riding Rocinante into the Texas sunset.

There was simply no other way, through his limited powers of imagination, or via a substance-assisted boost, that he could have created the knowledge of his senses, the incontrovertible experience of being here, in this moment. At times however, the direct sensory knowledge wasn't an advantage. When a cattle hauler pulled up alongside him, with large pink and white fleshy noses poking out from the trailer's grating, Barth attempted to shorten his encounter with the intense barnyard smells by slowing down. Sometimes the opportunity to be one with nature wasn't quite what it was cracked up to be.

Be here now. Yeah, I'm sure that's a Texas meditation.

At that moment he tensed up, reflexively easing off the throttle, milliseconds before seeing that the traffic, nonexistent a minute ago, was bunching up. As he approached he could see it was moving at a crawling pace. Barth's first instinct, based on the frustrations of his daily commutes in Kansas City, was to curse loudly at the forces conspiring to thwart his progress, but he refrained, partly because he was in the open, where he could be heard, possibly in violation of some Texas statute. He also reminded himself that he was in no hurry and he suspected, out on this stretch of open highway, the slowdown was out of the ordinary, although he could only guess the cause. Probably a construction bottleneck, but he had no clue from where he sat.

In a matter of seconds, he came to a complete stop. He was surrounded by vehicles in both lanes–drivers running their engines in apparent futility, or, like him, shutting off the ignition and waiting, with varying degrees of patience, for the obstacle ahead to be revealed and removed. Cars and trucks in the eastbound lanes were moving sporadically, gathering speed from the site of the problem, but there was no communication, at least that Barth could receive, to inform him regarding the length or cause of the holdup. Barth tried to relax, closing his eyes briefly, then looking at what he expected to be a moving line of vehicles that had yet to materialize. After countless additional minutes he realized this wasn't any ordinary delay; surely there would have been adequate planning on the interstate to prevent this degree of gridlock.

Having the advantage of an absence of destination or deadline, he was able to convince himself to be resigned to the unknown. This was not, despite the resemblance, the deadening, frustrating experience of being stuck in rush hour traffic on I-435 in Kansas City during his drives to and from the office.

Eventually, after another half hour by his reckoning, traffic started moving, in a jerky, start-and-stop rhythm. The height and girth of the trucks ahead of him blocked the view of what he now sensed must be a serious event, and once he reached the crest of the next rise he could clearly see at least a half dozen distinguishable flashing red and white lights off in the distant median. And then, suddenly, the cycling whine of a siren was in his ears. A white police cruiser sped past the line of traffic on the right side, nearly off the shoulder, whipping up a trail of dust. The car came to a screeching stop several car lengths ahead, its four doors flung open simultaneously like extending wings. Four officers in gray uniforms emerged; two stood by the edge of the road while two crossed the traffic to the median. A very serious accident, no doubt about it. Still, Barth was stuck in this rolling queue, unable to do anything but sit and guess. His impatience and curiosity were supplanted by chills and an acute anxiety, intensified by the fact of being trapped in this traffic, a new, unwelcome feeling in his open-air adventure. There was no opportunity for escape from what he now believed must be a gruesome reality.

Steadily, inexorably, he was herded to the point at which the tragedy became visible. He could see the remnants of a sedan, crushed, accordion-style, from the rear, in the median. Closer to the westward lanes, an overturned trailer was lying on its side, its grill smashed, but otherwise looking intact. In the lane farthest from him he could see two men with rakes spreading that substance used to soak up gas and oil and other accident-related fluids. There were at least three state troopers' cruisers parked in the median with lights flashing. Officers were standing in both lanes, energetically waving orange signal sticks to control the traffic while tow trucks and an ambulance could be seen parked off the shoulder of the eastbound lanes.

Barth's level of trepidation and horror spiked sharply when he realized that the lights on the ambulance weren't flashing. As his bike reached the vicinity of the impact the most ominous view of the scene couldn't be ignored or suppressed. White-garbed med-evac personnel were standing in a group with a couple of the officers and, next to them, in plain sight, were two partially-covered bodies. Another man, who Barth guessed to be the operator of the overturned rig, was standing separately, accompanied by one of the emergency medical staff, but in no obvious physical distress.

Unfortunately, for Barth, he was moving at such a slow speed that he was afforded time enough to linger over the scene while passing. He could clearly see the shattered rear window of the crushed car, with dark blood spatters visible on the shards of glass still attached to the car's roof. The sight sickened him. For a fleeting moment he thought he'd have to lean over and vomit, but he managed to return his focus to the western horizon and the still slow movement of the traffic. He was cold now, shaking, the sight and realization of inexplicable, accidental death dominating his thoughts to the point of distraction. Somehow, he was able to keep moving. He didn't have any idea how, but eventually he was rolling at a steady snail's pace, fast enough to stay in second gear. With the press of moving traffic slowly thinning out, it was now late afternoon. Much time had passed since he'd been forced to slow down, and the sun was within touching distance of the horizon.

Barth's mood had shifted dramatically. He was anxiously obsessing about the fragility of life. Even though such casualties were an everyday occurrence, boring news when glanced over in newsprint or blaring out from TV screens, the reality here was inescapable. The sight was devoid of abstract qualities that might render it tolerable, even forgettable. The fact that he knew nothing about the victims wasn't important. It was enough to know that two lives, with histories, routines and desires, had been snuffed out. Barth knew that, after an indeterminate length of time, he would return to "normal," but the realization had no impact on the turmoil he was experiencing, even as he somehow continued executing all the subtle adjustments keeping the bike moving forward in a straight line.

"Vrr…oo..m.." The roar, felt and heard at the same time, erupted from behind, then alongside, between him and the car in the left lane.

"Hey Doc, what the hell you doin' here? Let's get the fuck out! Follow me."

The order was barked out by Bones, even larger in profile seated on his booming Harley. Without time to think, without thinking, Barth turned his bike to center, twisting the throttle, pulling behind the big cruiser. He didn't know it, but he'd become a lane-splitter. Instantly, he was a rolling renegade, weaving between lanes, alert to the jutting rearview mirrors threatening his progress. His pulse racing, his hands tightened on his grips. He was riding.

The bikers progressed in tandem through the slow traffic, gradually putting the worst of it behind them. There was still a glimmer of daylight left when Barth saw what he first imagined was some form of vision. It was a cross, a huge, towering, shining metal cross, clearly outlined against the expansive Texas skyline. It was in the median area, with parking. Without thinking the matter over, Barth pulled over, following Bones.

Barth guessed Bones' action wasn't triggered by a religious impulse, but the reason didn't matter. Barth wanted the opportunity to get off the bike, maybe get his head straight. When they had parked and dismounted, Barth started walking, slowly, in circles, to obtain a degree of equilibrium and calm. Normally as grounded as the mammoth metal marker in the background, Bones also appeared unrooted, pacing aimlessly by his bike, staring at the pavement. For Barth, now was as good a time as any for a cigarette, and after what he had seen he figured he needed one.

There were a few cars in the lot and stragglers reading the signs containing information regarding the history of the monument, which he learned was the largest free-standing cross in the northern hemisphere. This was the middle of nowhere, so to speak, so the location made its presence even more intriguing, but Barth, in his present state, had no desire to know more about this curiosity. He was alone in his thoughts, for the moment.

"Hey, Doc, you know smokin' ain't healthy, don't you?"

Barth nodded.

"You holdin' up okay? You don't look so good right now."

"That accident back there, it just really hit me. I can't believe how hard, I'm still shaky." Barth let out a long, slow drag.

"Tell me about it. The whole thing just sucks. One of the paramedics stopped here. He says it was a mom and daughter. Car stalled on the road, that's what they think. She was reaching over the back seat to grab her kid when the rig plowed into them. Man, I can tell ya, I ain't quite right myself." Bones's left foot tapped nervously on the pavement.

Barth felt a twinge of reassurance in this shared distress. At the same time a sudden chill shot through him at the reappearance of the image of the crushed car and shattered glass.

"I was thinkin' Harris would have traded places with them any day. That's how he would have wanted to get out. Nobody lucky here, not by a long shot."

Barth thought this was a strange perspective, then realized Bones had been wrestling with ideas of death and dying since Harris' accident, while he himself had a safe distance from these issues until now.

"Yeah, I can see that. You really can never tell when the big foot is coming down and where it's going to land."

This was Barth's half-serious, flippant shorthand for the uncertainty and fragility of life, but it was the only response he could come up with, and it seemed to fit.

"You got that right. No gettin' around it, that's it."

Barth said nothing in response. Both riders stood quietly, surveying the now normal flow of traffic as if there was some reason to in what was now the beginning of nightfall. The only illumination, aside from headlights on the highway, was provided by the well-lit specter of the huge metal cross. If there was something to be learned from the symbolism, Barth was unable to make the connection.

"Well, it's time we get our butts moving. No good hangin' out here, waitin' for an insight that ain't never gonna come. Why don't you come with me, Doc, you could use the rest and I guarantee you'll unwind with us a lot easier than you will in some fleabag motel."

"Where you heading?"

"Just a place out in the sticks where a bunch of us hide out Fridays. You'll be able to let yourself go any way you want and be in a better place when you get rollin' tomorrow. We both need to chill out. Just follow me."

Barth was heartened, and flattered, by the invitation, nodding acceptance and turning to his bike. This guy was right, he had a strong need to be in the presence of other people this evening, and his intuition had led him to conclude that, despite the brief nature of their contact, Bones wasn't exactly a stranger.

He crushed the cigarette with his heel and mounted Rocinante. He was ready to ride.

Why he was following Bones down this lonely, bumpy road, he couldn't say exactly, except that he was beat, tired and without any reasonable expectation of reaching an outpost of civilization, a bed and a roof, in the immediate future. In his shaken state, the silent confidence of Bones had a calming effect, and Barth was susceptible to the implicit promise of safety and comfort. The invitation was especially welcome and Barth, sticking with his determination to let slip the usual rules of suburbanite survival, had impulsively turned his bike to follow in the wake of his fellow traveler. *Why the hell not?* Bones needed to crash as much as he did right now and he obviously knew his way down this unmarked, unlit road, actually more of a trail. If there was a moon in the sky tonight it wasn't yet in evidence. There was no hint of a horizon visible, only patches of old road illuminated by their headlights.

I'd better lock into the taillight of Bones's bike and stay close, there's no way I can find my way back now, might as well keep going...

His riding partner slowed and Barth did likewise. They were approaching a rise, likely the closest thing to a hill in the area. As Barth reached the crest, he noted flickering lights coming from a stationary position somewhere in the distance; he couldn't judge how far in the darkness.

His momentary change of focus was abruptly interrupted as he was jolted and bounced from his seat. He reflexively tightened his hold on the grips, at-tempting to keep the bike upright. The front wheel came down, plunging into the packed earth of the rutted road, and he managed to keep the bike up while the rear wheel touched, propelling him forward with a burst of speed. Okay, he recovered instantly, while moving ahead. He had hit a rock, something, while he was temporarily distracted, but had somehow kept his cool, and couldn't take time to reflect on what had just happened. His companion was now farther ahead, the red light from his rear fender fading, and the only choice was to pull on the throttle or be stuck here in the Texas plains.

Barth was guessing now, gambling, outrunning his lights, struggling to catch up. *What the hell is there to lose, this entire episode is a gamble,* he thought to himself, emboldened, feeling no trace of fear, speeding up and zeroing in on his target. He was reveling in the irrational confidence he was experiencing in the moment, fully aware that another such surprise might not be followed by the same lucky recovery. *Whatever*, Barth thought, *just keep going.* The exhaust of the forward bike was becoming louder and he was closing in, close enough to ease off and resume riding at a more reasonable speed. He had reached a level of relative safety, sufficient for the quick luxury of the thought, *What doesn't kill me makes me stronger*, followed by his own laughter at his ridiculous indulgence of machismo and the visual image of a bearded Nietzsche fearlessly rolling on the throttle. In the coolness and darkness of the night, accompanied only by his thoughts and the muffled exhaust of the bikes, he had the sensation of a transformation, perhaps minor, perhaps temporary. Nonetheless, Barth knew, in this moment, he wasn't the same person who had inhabited his Kansas City office a few short days ago.

Bones slowed down, and now the lights he'd seen before became distinct, a grouping of separate points indicating a camp. Barth detected the dark outlines of tents and the silhouette of a parked van against the evening sky. As they approached he could make out two groups, each illuminated by campfires and scattered lanterns. A wailing lone harmonica, mixed with scattered bits of muffled conversations, reached his ears. He didn't dare take his hand off the clutch grip to check his watch, but his newly-acquired reflex, reminding himself he had no use for this information, kicked in as they pulled to the side of the camp where bikes were parked. His leader-guide swung around, stopping at the end of the row, parallel to the other bikes. Barth followed suit, glad to know he was done riding today.

"Hey, Bones, what is this?"

"Just people getting away for a night to chill out. Mostly locals, some of the riders you saw back at the Dog. Don't worry, they're cool. Take it in, be a player if you want. Enjoy the Sky Club and I guarantee ya, you'll be in spirit drive tomorrow once you get rollin'."

Barth thought about asking Bones what he meant by "spirit drive," but figured he should already know, in which case he didn't want to display his ignorance more than absolutely necessary.

I'll know soon enough, just follow his lead Hell, it's another experience—Isn't this what I'm looking for?

The encounter with Sedley Crump had taught him the value of being open to new adventures, and the previous day's experience assured him that trust wasn't an issue insofar as Bones was concerned. Barth unhooked the cords holding his sleeping bag and slung it under his arm.

The pair walked silently together toward the largest of the gatherings, twelve people seated around a low, struggling fire providing a flickering light, but little heat, left to burn itself out. The bikes in the background and the relaxed atmosphere reminded Barth of a scene from a Frederic Remington painting. He thought he recognized a couple of riders from the Lazy Dog. Some sported black leather vests with the broken thunderbolt Okie Outcasts insignia, but there was more variety in looks and dress than Barth expected to encounter in a bikers' outing. As they neared the group a couple of its members looked up and one nodded, in recognition of Bones and the stranger with him.

"Hey Bones, where ya been, guy? Having so much fun selling insurance you forgot about us derelicts?"

"Well, much as I'd like to, it's a bad addiction, like maggots drawn to a carcass with y'all."

Coarse laughter and familiar greetings followed the exchange. Bones found a space in the circle and sat on the grass, pointing to a spot opposite him where Barth quietly settled. He was tired, no doubt about that, but knew the present company would have a more relaxing effect on him than the opportunity to flop down, alone, in a bed at the nearest Motel 7. Being around people simply felt great after the recent reminder of life's fragility.

He lazily turned his head, surveying the two groups. There were men and women who, by their dress, he could readily identify as bikers, and others whose roles he couldn't guess. Behind the bikes were a couple of parked vans and three pitched tents, leading to the conclusion that this wilderness setting could not by any means be adequately described as a biker hangout. The campers exhibited common features of either a relaxed contentment or an engaged enjoyment of their company. To his right a man and woman were talking quietly to each other, apart from the rest of the circle, attracting no notice. On his left was a tall, slender woman, stretched out on the ground with her feet pointed toward the fire. She was facing away from Barth, her dark hair falling over the back of her neck and finally resting on the ground.

Barth decided to be a relaxed recipient of the night's energies and entertainments.

A soft but firm voice from a man seated next to Bones demanded, and received, the attention of the surrounding parties. "Okay, y'all, it's my turn, the moment you've all been waiting for, so listen up, children."

The interruption of the separate conversations had the desired effect. It was obvious that the invitation was neither surprising nor unwelcome. In the brief silence, with an occasional cigarette lighting the perimeter of the circle and open wine bottles making the rounds, a young man with a short scruffy beard was soliciting attention for his contribution to the festivities. Without introduction, he began reciting words from the pages of a thin paperback held in his left hand. Barth was sure he recognized the black and white cover, even from this distance, as one of the poetry books published by Ferlinghetti's City Lights bookstore in San Francisco. The easy rhythm and crisp, clear voice of the reader underscored a long and loving relationship with the lines, including a plea for "Gratitude to Mother Earth, sailing through night and day..." The audience savored both the reading and the reader's love for the poem. Allusions to the relation between the writer and his natural surroundings, the primary theme, led Barth to believe he was listening to something by the Beat poet Gary Snyder. It hardly mattered; the lines conveyed a message of intended harmony between men, women and the natural phenomena framing their existence, one not lost on the stragglers in the cool night air and endless, unobstructed sky. Although these people were strangers to Barth, in this shared moment he knew why they were here, and didn't feel out of place.

The end of the reading was followed by a brief, respectful silence and an approving sentiment from the woman lying next to him.

"John, it's too bad you're stuck in that cubicle where no one can hear you. I'll bet no one there guesses you have a voice."

Concurring laughter followed, then a brief reversion to their separate preoccupations, broken by Bones's commanding voice, its girth matching his physical presence.

"Mr. Barth here is riding through from Kansas City. I dragged his butt here from that big wreck. Anyway, don't be shy, no strangers here, you're safe in this part of the wilderness. Feel free to take a turn at bat if you like, anything's okay except for something that offends our delicate sensibilities."

The group laughed and Barth, hoping to maintain his blissful anonymity, said his thanks and sat back. The woman lying next to him sat up and turned to him.

"You play anything, guitar, sing, anything?'

"No, not really, many years ago I could, just a little, but no singing, not me."

Any belief that this response would be sufficient was quickly scuttled when she yelled to a guy sitting in the other group. He walked over and, at the woman's request, took the guitar slung over his shoulder, handing it to the newcomer. Barth hesitated, wishing to decline the invitation but feeling, at the same time, a refusal was selfish under the circumstances. Besides, he thought, no one here would be critical if he made the attempt. There was nothing to lose. He took the instrument, placing the body in his lap, curling his fingers around the neck and pressing down on the steel strings, lightly picking a few notes with his fingers.

Barth began playing, hesitantly at first, knowing his desire to be inconspicuous in this group would be irretrievably thwarted once he'd plucked the first few notes. He wanted, however, to make a contribution to the evening, a thanks for the understated welcome he had received from this assembly of self-designated outsiders in the Texas wilderness. He was playing one of the few pieces from his childhood over which he could still demonstrate a competent command, an instrumental succession of eighth notes with a distinctly Spanish motif. As he played he became oblivious to his surroundings, imagining himself to be the musician in a painting he loved, *El Jaleo*. The flickering campfire reinforced his vision, and he was vaguely aware of the attention of his audience. Finishing with a flourish, he looked up, attempting to divine any evidence of a consensus.

Nods and smiles, all around.

"What do you call that?" The question, from the dark-haired woman next to him, now sitting, at least indicated some interest.

"I think it's called 'Country Dance,' something like that, by a guy named Carulli."

"That was pretty, perfesser, really nice."

Barth hardly expected the piece to enhance his chances of blending in, but her smile belied the mocking tone in her voice, and he understood that his contribution had been accepted and enjoyed as he had meant it to be. After a few more appreciative remarks, he was able to sit in silence and enjoy the continuing mishmash of readings and songs. He was feeling tired, still mildly disturbed when afterimages of the accident scene intruded into his consciousness. Bones's intercession, however, and the hospitality of these strangers, had gone far toward settling him down, and the prospect of sleep in this company itself had a sedating effect. Exercising his usual tendency to caution and restraint, he refrained from the opportunity to sample any of the assorted stimulants proffered by parties in this gathering, except for swigs of wine when a bottle made its way to him. Finally able to relax, he laid back, resting his elbows in the cool grass, surveying the group as one of the men read aloud from a book of poems by the California writer, Charles Bukowski.

The woman who had complimented Barth's playing introduced herself as Ina and asked about him-where he was from, how he'd connected with Bones, where he was headed. She seemed interested in his story and intrigued by the notion of his escape, however temporary, from his life in the city. It was apparent, however, that her interest did not amount to envy. Ina, for her part, had lived in the area most of her life and was the single mother of two sons. She taught school in a nearby town and had left her children with a neighbor for a night off with her friends, her version of temporary, satisfying escape. In a few minutes' time, this woman revealed as much of her personal life to this stranger at the fireside as some of Barth's clients might have in the first hour of counseling sessions. Ina was only recently divorced, from her high school sweetheart, after ten years of marriage, and had been adopted by the members of this gathering through the urging of a woman who also taught at the school and was now lying on the grass on the other side of Bones, with whom she was having an animated discussion. Instead of being distraught following her recent split, this woman was enjoying a newfound liberation. The Friday night outings had become an outlet for personal explorations denied her before now. Ina had become a part of this community, a group of individuals whose bonds had nothing to do with jobs, status or the roles they assumed in their respective lives in the nearby towns. All outsiders in their own manner, they had coalesced in the night in the Texas high country around the struggling fires for the warmth and rest the setting offered, with no role expectations.

Ina had a direct smile, honest and connecting, inviting a return smile from the stranger. Barth gladly obliged, sensing comforting warmth in this woman. And, for the first time in the course of this interaction, he allowed his thoughts to wander with his eyes, indulging himself in the enjoyment of the striking sensuality that began with her eyes and smile and continued along the contours of her body in his slow, absorbing gaze. He knew nothing about this woman except for the brief outline of her present circumstances and, for the moment, didn't care. It was enough that Ina stirred feelings he hadn't experienced with a woman or expected to for a long time, longer than he could immediately recall.

Does she share any of these feelings? How should I interpret her attention? Barth had no answers to his questions. He couldn't even venture a guess. *Perhaps wishful thinking is clouding my judgment.* He wouldn't press the issue now, there was no reason to other than his previously submerged desire, and that alone wasn't enough to risk the relaxation he was enjoying.

"Do you mind if I smoke?"

The question surprised Barth. Even if he had minded, he couldn't refuse this woman any request at the moment and, in this open air setting, it hardly made sense.

Why did she even bother asking?

"Of course not, go right ahead."

She lit up and sat back, so that her shoulders were on a line with Barth's, and they silently enjoyed snippets of ongoing discussions they could catch and the singing of Bones, who had assumed the role of group entertainer for the time being with his loud baritone, not seeming to care whether anyone was listening. The visible fires, audible entertainments and interactions from those in the other group contributed to the sense of community, and Barth understood that his own history was of no particular concern to any of these temporarily transported villagers. Hell, it was of no particular concern to him at the moment. All that mattered, all that had mattered since the words exchanged with Bones on the highway, was the capacity to accept the individuals and suspend any predilection to judgments based on any usual personal criteria. Except, of course, singing ability.

The hypnotic effect of the glowing embers and the warmth from the fire, combined with the effects of the wine and the soothing impact of Ina's presence, drained the last remnants of anxiety Barth had been feeling since the trauma of the afternoon. He guessed Ina might be feeling the same and eagerly accepted her silent smiles when she glanced in his direction. He imagined she was as lonely as he was and had a need to be comforted and reassured as strong as his, at least, perhaps, for the evening. He was carried along in this belief and lost himself in the seconds, minutes, while the entertainments and discussions continued, a restorative time, a respite for the participants from the wearying days and nights of the past week of their lives. Barth was, once again, experiencing the feeling of escape from the clutches of his confining, restraining and unfelt existence. An illusion, perhaps, but it would do for now.

"Where are you going from here, Greg?"

Barth caught himself, not having a ready answer and not having an idea of the reason for her question.

"I'm not sure, just west I guess, I'll keep going for awhile and see what I can."

"So you're headed back to KC once you've finished riding?"

The question had a sharp point Barth could not miss. After all, he may have traveled farther, but he was, ultimately, in the same boat as these Saturday-night escapees.

"Yeah, I guess so, probably, but I really don't want to think about that right now."

"I think I understand, didn't mean anything by asking, just curious, that's all."

Ina laid her hand on his knee, a gesture meant to soothe the restless soul. Barth, for his part, didn't know how to respond to her touch and decided to do nothing. This was unfamiliar territory for him, at least in recent memory. Barth was hardly immune to the siren call of desire, even considering the long drought of personal experience in this regard.

This sympathetic woman had a naturally relaxing quality in her physical appearance that mirrored the casual aspect of her conversation in its impact on the stranger. Her dark brown hair was mussed, ending somewhere well below the collar of an old denim shirt, open to reveal a gray sweatshirt which, like the rest of her wardrobe, emphasized comfort. She stretched her legs out in an attempt to absorb the maximum amount of heat from the struggling fire.

"I probably feel the same way about going back to Kansas City as you do going back to work Monday after being out here."

"No, I don't think so. I like being with the kids, it keeps me feeling alive, I just need a change, like everyone else out here, so I can relax with people my own age and recharge my batteries. The Sky Club is sort of my church, if you know what I mean."

"Yeah, I think I do."

Barth certainly understood what it meant to need a change, but, unlike Ina, he could not imagine, not at this point, experiencing an eagerness to return. *Maybe in another week or so.* He decided against letting his thoughts linger here, however, preferring instead to revert to his romantic meanderings. Bones, meanwhile, had begun another song, a ballad perfectly suited to the Texas high country surroundings, and a few of the night revelers, uninhibited and familiar with the lyrics, joined in or hummed in attempted harmony. Ina lay on her side, facing Barth, and closed her eyes. Barth studied her outstretched form, imagining the possibility of a perfect ending to what had been a disturbing day on the road. He would enjoy the remainder of this evening in the serenity of this lost communal outpost, letting nature take its course. In this moment he was willing to allow himself the revelry of these warm imaginings, stirring deeply entrenched memories so ancient they seemed to be chapters from someone else's history. Layers of encrusted thought patterns were being dislodged as easily as the dry dust on his boots. He could believe, for these few minutes, that he was a part of the surrounding landscape, that he was absorbing a measure of the tranquility of these isolated hills that had drawn Bones, Ina and the other night campers. Bones's voice, weaving through the night air, would not be mistaken for Joe Ely or Jimmie Dale Gilmore; still, it had a melodious, plaintive quality that was exactly in place in this setting. The nods and smiles, even the lack of attention from most of the night owls, were comforting to Barth, now feeling acceptance and welcome without question or reservation. He was experiencing a genuine, replenishing connectedness. This was the same social impulse, he thought, that had bound the earliest generations of *Homo Erectus* around their night fires, created for the necessities of warmth and cooking game.

Ina had dozed off, when a woman from the neighboring group walked over and knelt over her, putting a hand on her shoulder, gently nudging her into a groggy wakefulness.

"Ina, honey, time for bed."

Ina looked up at the woman, who took her by the arm, and struggled to her feet. She shook her head, pulled on the ends of her sleeves, and nodded, smiling at Barth.

"Well, it was nice to meet you, Greg. I hope you get some sleep tonight and have a safe trip if I don't see you again."

"Thanks, Ina, this is really something. Nice meeting you. Goodnight."

Barth watched as they started walking, hand in hand, toward the makeshift shelters beyond the far group. His gaze followed the two women as they disappeared into one of the tents, closing the entry flap behind them. The flicker of desire he had allowed himself was abruptly extinguished, or at least doused, without hint or warning. Perhaps Barth should have been disappointed, but he couldn't help laughing, to himself, at himself, it didn't matter. The spark of something he hadn't felt in ages had been snuffed out, but this wasn't a cruel joke. An unexpected turn in an unanticipated sequence of events, to be sure, and certainly not his druthers for this cool evening in the relaxed romance of the Texas plains, but Barth wasn't consumed with frustration or longing.

Instead, turning his head upward toward the clear sky, he stared intently at the panoply of starlights whose names or sources he couldn't divine. Lone travelers through the sky looking down on the lone traveler staring back from his vantage point in that patch of planet Earth known as the Texas Panhandle. During these minutes he believed he'd shed some of the alienation and boredom that had impelled him to undertake this odyssey to nowhere in particular. Without specific goals or achievements in mind, he was reveling in the experience of being adrift, and accepting the companionship of this new set of friends, all with their own odysseys.

"You were barkin' up the wrong tree that time, mister."

Barth looked to his right and nodded to the long-haired guy sitting on a colorful Navajo wool blanket. His grin conveyed no trace of levity.

"Yeah, I guess. You just never know, it was relaxing just talking to her anyway."

"What Ina went through, put up with in her marriage, it can't hardly be a surprise that someone at some point might figure you can't lose nothin' by takin' another road, if ya know what I mean."

"Yeah. I think so."

Barth was at first surprised by the personal reference, as well as the note of empathy coming from this stranger in the Texas Panhandle. Another reminder of his own prejudices.

"Name's Turner. You a friend of Bones?"

"Well, he brought me here tonight. I'm Greg."

"Oh yeah, you were at the accident."

"Yeah. Well, I was there after it happened."

"Rough stuff. Even for a bad stretch of road like that. The whole county's talkin' about it. Guess you don't need to be dwellin' on that more than you have already. Good choice to come out to the Sky Club meetin'."

"Bones kind of insisted, actually, and I'm glad he did. This place is great."

"Bones is sort of in the business of taking care of people around here. He just never stops doin' it at work or play."

Barth didn't know what Turner meant by the remark, but figured he'd find out soon enough. He couldn't see how such details could be important to him at this moment.

The two of them started a conversation based mainly on contrasting their backgrounds, although, as the time passed, it gradually dawned on the two nighthawks that they shared more than either of them would have guessed. Turner had been born and raised in the little crossroads town of Groom, known to the rest of the world as the home village of the giant steel cross Barth had seen yesterday. According to Turner, the image of the cross was so ingrained that, in all the surrounding towns and countryside, where people should have known better, the belief that Groom residents were "Holy Rollers" was resistant to contradiction. Turner noted that the very ground they were sitting on was the site of camp meetings where, years ago, itinerant preachers and snake-oil salesmen, often working in tandem, whipped local crowds into a frenzy on Saturday nights, the best available combination of salvation and entertainment available in the sparsely populated plains of that distant era. It was only later, he wryly mused, when more established churches sprang up in the small towns, that the "competition" was spurned as outside the pale of respectable Christendom.

It seemed that, as if they were deliberately challenging the characterization, Turner, and his friends, conspired to spend the bulk of their childhoods somewhere in the margins between civil respectability and outright flouting of the law. By his accounting, they'd been spectacularly successful in this regard until shortly after high school, when they were prevailed upon, or "urged," as Turner put it, to voluntarily enlist, or just plain leave. With no meaningful options, and no plans, Turner found himself in the Army's 3rd Armored Division at Fort Hood and, shortly afterward, in the desert sands of southern Iraq.

The experience had been brief for Turner, without significant exposure to combat, but it had served as his taste of a world outside Groom and the first direct experience of his countrymen from regions with weirdly-accented speech. He had decided, however, that he disliked the restrictions of army life as much as he had the social limits of his rebellious youth. He returned to Groom, intending to stay only as long as it took to decide his next move. He'd taken an assistant manager's position in the Buffalo Market grocery outlet in nearby Lakoshna, where his military experience had given him an aura of credibility sufficient to override lingering memories of his local past. Turner intended to stay long enough to finance his escape from the territory, wherever that lay, but found the routine surprisingly tolerable and, a few years ago, had been promoted to his present position as manager. Like Barth in his Kansas City base, Turner had long ago established a predictable routine for himself, including regular attendance at the Friday evening Sky Club meetings, to which he rode on his decked-out sea-green ElectraGlide with the other Okie Outcasts.

Barth marveled at the interest Turner displayed regarding mundane aspects of his own existence. Barth was the "big city" guy, a description he would hardly have fashioned for himself. Turner's first question in this part of the conversation revealed contrasting aspects of their lives forming the basis of their interest.

"You know what I want to do if I ever get out of here? Go to a real baseball game, in a real stadium. What's it like to see a major league game?"

"It's okay, loved it when I was a kid, but you know, it's work too, you have to plan your time, figure which way to drive to avoid the traffic, and be prepared to spend your money every few minutes, on parking, tickets, programs, bad hot dogs, and three hours of non-stop noise."

"You don't sound like much of a baseball fan."

"I know, but I am. I love the game itself, but you know, what you have to go through makes it an ordeal. I mean, on a Friday night like this, fantastic weather, open sky, great people here hangin' out, why would you want to trade this?"

"Maybe you're right. Never thought of it that way. Still like to see one someday. Just once."

"Hey, everyone should see at least one."

Both men, from different worlds, had focused on some strongly-shared feelings that evening. About the same age, having taken advantage of singular opportunities available in their distinctive subcultures, they were long-settled into routines of their own choosing, affording each certain cherished comforts and a respectable measure of security to boot. Here, in the restive setting of the quiet plains, however, it was evident that what they shared most in the moment was the urge to move, no matter how briefly, and see something else, soak up a little experience of other worlds, other perspectives, before it was too late. It was ironic that Barth, likely the most sedentary of the two, had assumed the role of pioneer in this regard, and perhaps the additional role as catalyst for Turner's inner rumblings, not much different from those rousting Barth from his fitful sleep a few nights ago.

Finally, sleep could no longer be denied. Turner stood up, inviting Barth to share his tent, but Barth declined, comparing the chance to sleep in the open country with Turner's baseball game fantasy. Turner understood instantly, saluting his kindred spirit, then turned, walking into the night.

Guessing there was no established protocol, Barth decided to stay put and placed his sleeping bag under his head, stretching out and settling in for the duration.

For the next hour he could hear laughs, singing and other entertainments punctuating the otherwise still atmosphere of the evening. To Barth's hearing, the sounds were a soothing background, evidence of camaraderie and mutual celebrations of life lacking any hint of conflict. Gradually lapsing into a needed rest, he reflected on the confrontations with life and death he had experienced in the last few days. Uncovered and exposed in the night air of this foreign setting, he had the sense that he was starting to shed some of the skin in which he had been trapped for untold years, but he didn't dwell on this subject. The need for sleep demanded, and captured, his body's attention.

The break of morning was accompanied by sounds of tent flaps opening and closing, the sporadic clanging of cooking utensils, and the strong, erotic smell of brewing coffee, but there were few traces of conversation. Barth was wakened by the sensation of warm, direct sunlight tickling his eyelids. As he sat up in the same space he had occupied around the campfire he shaded his eyes with his open hand. He could see he wasn't the only one who slept where they sat. Motionless bodies were arrayed feet first around the still-smoking embers of the fire. Looking around the site, he spotted other waking campers, emerging from tents and open vans within a hundred feet of the spot where he was sitting.

Barth stood up, surveying the scene and the remnants of the Sky Club. The topography looked the same in every direction, with no trace of a road or trail visible even in the morning sunlight. He was still disoriented by these wide open vistas.

He walked over to a group sitting around a tall enamel-coated coffee pot and eagerly accepted a cup and an invitation to sit. There wasn't much in the way of conversation this morning, no discussion of Saturday night plans, just occasional references to chores on the return to Elk City and reminders of the accident scene they were bound to witness. There was an absence of background noise, with no audio hints of civilization other than the sounds of the waking riders. Then, sometime around eight, the place started coming to life with determination, as if the signal had been given to break camp.

The air was punctuated with the periodic starts of air-cooled V-Twins, sputtering, then roaring to life, defiantly announcing their intentions to carry riders to their destinations. There was no mass migration of the camp revelers, who left the grounds either singly or in pairs, eventually emptying the site until it began resuming its prior status as an unmarked stretch of Texas countryside. Barth, with nothing to pack, sat in silence, watching the exodus of riders to their homes, weekend jobs, and families, some to spend the remainder of the weekend in routines that would not differentiate it from any other, except for this brief respite. As he began his own trek to his bike, sleeping bag tucked under his arm, he spied the unmistakable round figure of Bones, crouched next to his bike, absorbed in the task of fastening his gear to the seat with bungee cords. Barth stood next to his own bike, watching this man, a figure he hardly knew except for his unrestrained welcome. He had to say something to the enigmatic character who had shepherded him through the drunken stupor in Elk City and the trauma of yesterday's vicarious death experience. He stepped over, waiting silently, until Bones acknowledged his presence with his upward gaze.

"Hey, listen, I know we're heading in different directions and we'll never see each other again. I just want to make sure you know you and the rest of the Outcasts have made my time here something I won't forget."

"Well, Doc, I never figured you for such a sentimental guy. After the shock we got yesterday it was a good thing to get out here and sleep under the sky, commune with something bigger than both of us. That's the reason us working fools come out here in the first place. Just a different choice of drug. Remember, live 'til you die."

With this he stuck out his hand. Barth didn't hesitate to take it firmly in his grasp.

"Happy trails."

Barth's feeble attempt at an apt, hip phrase was nevertheless accepted for its earnestness. Any more words would have been superfluous. Bones nodded, straddling his bike, and the V-twin roared to life. Barth stood still for a few seconds, letting his gaze follow the dusty wake of the cruiser as it retraced the trail they could hardly see last evening.

He was riding out himself a few minutes later, horrified when he saw the rocks and deep ruts in the trail, entirely outside his awareness the night before. In this case ignorance was bliss; he was more anxious now that he had a clear view of the obstacles in his path. He was nevertheless able to navigate his way back, following the settling dust of the other riders. Once he reached the highway he took a quick look back and, seeing no traffic, pulled out, yanking the throttle hard, punctuating the end of this episode.

Barth was conscious of being alone again once he was at speed, hoping for nothing more than a lazy, uneventful day's ride, arriving in New Mexico this afternoon and spending a night in a roadside motel in a comfortable bed. Even a touch of boredom could sometimes be welcome, so long as it was temporary.

The air was drier now, the vegetation sparse, and the horizons more distant. He wasn't in desert country, but he could sense the transition from the green Oklahoma hills in Red Feather. He now had the feeling he was actually in Texas, in the West of his imagination. Barth half expected to be dodging tumbleweeds blown in his path and sighting longhorns being herded along by Rowdy Yates, but these images didn't materialize. Instead, he was greeted by roadside invitations to the pleasures and attractions of Amarillo, the first city of any size since he'd passed through Oklahoma City.

As he was toying with the idea of stopping in Amarillo, something in his peripheral vision jolted him, stirring up emotional residue of the last two days. In the ditch off to his right, between a couple of billboards, were three crude wooden crosses, about two feet high, each painted white and draped with colorful, fresh flowers. *El descanso*, the resting place, a phrase that would become part of his vocabulary in the not too distant future. The sight generated a spasm of anxiety that gave way to additional reflection on the temporary, fleeting and unpredictable nature of life, including his own. Barth was saddened at the reminder of another human tragedy and resolved that, although he didn't have a clue how, he would try making the most of his own brief stay on the planet. With that, he was able to recover a semblance of calm.

When he reached the outskirts of Amarillo he decided, in keeping with his dawdling pace, to stop, for no other reason than to say he'd seen it, whatever there was to be seen in an hour's time. He exited at the intersection of 40 and Interstate 27, smack in the middle of the downtown area, heading north in busy traffic that gave him doubts about his decision, but managing to leave the freeway in short order onto Amarillo Boulevard. Heading east, he passed the Amarillo Livestock Auction, a large, obviously viable business, a reminder that he was in the real west, instead of Kansas City, whose stockyards hadn't seen a live steer, other than in the American Royal rodeos, in at least fifty years. Barth slowed to a reasonable gawking speed now, circling north on Whitaker and doubling back on Amarillo. People were walking the streets and driving alongside wearing boots, jeans, western cut shirts with contrasting piping, hats and turquoise belt buckles that undercut any notion that western wear was only a caricature.

Right now he wished he had radio access to test his theories regarding local stations, but was nonetheless impressed that, despite the media-driven homogenization of culture, things were a bit different here, at least on the surface. No further analysis was necessary; Barth was content to sample the visual offerings. Turning and heading south, he got an eyeful when he ran into The Big Texan, a huge, sprawling restaurant with an extended covered porch, painted in a bright yellow with blue trim, the same color scheme as the Sunoco signs of his youth.

Naturally, an enormous steer stood overlooking the parking lot, assuring visitors that they were, indeed, in Texas. Barth was compelled to stop, knowing he was entering a tourist trap. He couldn't resist the gaudy chic of the place and its advertised promise of a free 72-ounce steak to anyone who could devour it in 60 minutes. He wasn't about to take up that challenge, but he figured a smaller bite of Texas beef was worth trying.

When a waitress approached, she greeted Barth with a hearty, but disconcerting, "How y'all doin?" Barth was convinced of her sincerity but jolted by her delivery, in a pronounced New York accent. He made the adjustment, however, as he had done so many times in the last few days, and eagerly accepted the information provided by this transplant. Before taking his order, she regaled him with grand descriptions of Palo Duro Canyon, just a few miles south, "The Grand Canyon of Texas," full of colorful rock formations, hoodoos, and a romantic history of thousands of years of habitation, undisturbed until Coronado and the conquistadors passed through in 1541. Barth was enthralled with her description, and grateful for her hospitality. When she left with his order, he mulled over the possibilities and, knowing he might regret his decision, determined to keep heading west, stopping at Arizona's Grand Canyon instead. He couldn't see everything and, reluctantly, had to make choices. An hour later, he was back on the road, satisfied with his taste of Texas.

Five miles west of Amarillo he made a brief stop, at the Cadillac Ranch, to see firsthand the ten Cadillacs buried nose down in a line at the same precise angle, fifties era relics with rusting rear fins pointing skyward. Every exposed inch of the cars was covered with sprayed-on graffiti. Whether this was art or not, he had no idea, but it certainly was ingenious and eye-catching. He was no less interested in these buried artifacts of his own youth than the group of European tourists gawking and photographing themselves posing with the Caddys.

A middle-aged white-bearded man left the group and walked over to Barth. He introduced himself as Stanley Marsh, the "ranch" owner. After an exchange of introductory pleasantries, Stanley, who somehow determined that this visitor was interested in these things, explained that the idea was based on the notion of the ancient American dream, the modern incarnation of ten covered wagons heading west. Barth, whose present travels were a slight reprise of the vision, warmed to this interpretation. Stanley informed Barth that he was free, if he chose, to spray-paint his own message on one of the rusting carcasses.

"Thanks, I think I will."

Barth walked toward the procession of finned sculptures, pausing to pick up a spray can from a large cardboard box. Ordinarily, his impulse was to avoid what he might otherwise have concluded were obvious tourist gimmicks, but, for some inexplicable reason, all he could think was, *why not*?

He approached one of the resting hulks, pausing for a second before its exposed roof, then, aiming the can, sprayed the words-

I WAS HERE, THEREFORE I WAS

The deed completed, Barth smiled at the realization of the transient nature of his message, soon to be masked by another. It occurred to him that this sheet metal graveyard was a monument to the temporary, fleeting nature of just about everything. Formerly immaculate symbols of wealth and prestige, now rusting hulks, forgotten like the popes his Catholic playmates had attempted to memorize, or the names of presidents who would be completely erased from memory centuries from now, except in the footnotes of unread Ph.D. dissertations. Decay, death, shrinking traces of memory, these were the rule. It occurred to Barth that here was another reminder of death, the auto burial ground.

Then, grudgingly, he laughed, not defensively, but because it dawned on him that he was viewing the world a tad on the morbid side. Just as suddenly as this fit of philosophic meandering had appeared, it was broken, come down to earth like the buried bows of the land barges on either side of him. Barth laughed again, to himself, finding a bit of needed equilibrium and perspective.

Get a grip.

He was able to regain some sense of normalcy, not denying the lessons of the past two days, just placing them in a larger perspective.

Too serious, way too serious, time to ride.

He felt like a tourist after his Amarillo experience, but then, he was, this was indisputable.

For the next two hours he maintained an even cruising speed, in the vicinity of a comfortable sixty, heading straight for the western border of the Panhandle.

Fields of beautiful wildflowers, the same bright yellow as Kansas sunflowers, could be seen in the distance in the foothills of the changing topography, with pointed rock formations appearing more frequently. The blue sky enveloping this bright sun seemed to go on forever. Surely it was much larger here than he'd ever seen it in Kansas City. Endless, sparsely populated vistas on both sides of the road now resembled backgrounds for the great Technicolor westerns made half a century ago. Spectacular was the word that came frequently to this gringo. He could almost imagine himself turning Rocinante northward through the pass to join the posse.

At Glenrio, straddling the border, he officially entered New Mexico, the "Land of Enchantment," according to the state's plates. Barth left the highway for a brief look at this honest-to-goodness ghost town, a small town made even smaller when the highway bypassed this section of Route 66. He got his first look at real tumbleweeds, rolling over cracks in the crumbling concrete, passing by stragglers like himself who stopped to gawk at the emptiness. He imagined what it might have been like when the windows of the Little Juarez Diner were unbroken and this road was the main east-west artery in this part of America. At one time Okies, Arkies and Texans passed over this spot on the map in their attempts to escape their dust bowl desperation.

"So long, it's been good to know ya…"

Roads, even highways, can migrate.

Barth twisted the throttle, heading back to the highway. He stopped for a few minutes at a rest stop to use the facilities, stretch his legs, and drink a *horchata*, the refreshing concoction of milk, sugar, cinnamon and vanilla common in this region, cooler than the water he carried in his topcase, and especially welcome in the heat. He was now fifty miles from Tucumcari and decided to stop there for the day.

Interstate 40 now followed closely the remnants of Route 66, the mother road that once carried travelers from Chicago to California. Progress had obliterated much of the old road, though Barth had noted intact sections as far back as Oklahoma City. Progress had also taken its toll on other structures of archaeological significance. Barth sighted a pueblo in the distance to the south with crumbling walls and a missing roof that might have disintegrated a century ago for all he knew. The clash of cultures represented by these two artifacts was further underscored by the presence of a roadside stand that attracted Barth's attention, causing him to stop and take a closer look.

At one end a group of Navajo blankets and rugs was draped from aluminum frames, their distinctive geometric designs and contrasting colors beckoning to decorators and tourists alike. At the other end, hanging from interlocking poles, red chile *ristras* were drying in the sun. Painted clay pots were being sold complete with yucca plants and, of course, there was a selection of turquoise and silver jewelry. A large glass-covered pan contained fresh loaves of the frybread that, he would learn, was a staple commodity in the diet of the native American cultures of the southwest. Barth successfully resisted these temptations, not because of any immunity in this regard, but because his means of conveyance didn't allow for any such indulgence. Space was a precious commodity on the bike and had to be reserved for essentials.

As he returned to the highway he observed the sky suddenly turning gray, then dark. Moments later, he was subjected to what had to be a relatively rare occurrence here, a cloudburst and a light rain. He was forced to pull off onto the shoulder and unpack the drybag mounted on his seat to gain access to the raingear packed beneath his sleeping bag. This was certainly an unexpected development. He hadn't anticipated any need for these items until California or Oregon. The pants and jacket were a bright yellow and added bulk and weight, but the protection, in terms of both visibility and keeping him dry, were well worth it. At least he was able to get them on before the rain drenched him. The misery he had experienced on the road to Joplin less than a week ago was still a vivid memory.

He resumed his journey, confident the rain would have little impact and that he'd reach Tucumcari within the next hour. In the next few minutes the rain, which couldn't have been described as heavy by any measure, subsided, and Barth was now riding on dry pavement, although the sky remained gray. If the sun re-emerged he would stop again to remove his gear, otherwise overheating would be a possibility, even at speed. The road was perfectly straight now, with no hints of surprise, inviting a relaxed hold on the grips while he leaned back, cruising in fifth gear. It was like riding on a rail; all he had to do was maintain a steady speed and the bike would do the rest.

The sighting of a mesa in the distance, with gold and red coloring and vertical shadows in continuous lines from the peaks to the foothills, was further confirmation that the rider was in a three-dimensional visual paradise, if not the land of enchantment. Barth could only wonder about the ability to survive in this country in the time of the Anasazi, or even in more recent eras of the region's history. He couldn't help but become infected with the sense of romance and mystery that the landscape fostered.

About ten miles east of Tucumcari he spotted a car off the road, its driver kneeling beside the left rear fender, dangerously close to the highway's edge. Acting on an impulse, Barth slowed and pulled over on the shoulder, stopping directly behind the stranded vehicle. As he did so, the driver stood up, turning in his direction. She was Hispanic, insofar as Barth could determine, with a thick long black braid hanging down her back, dressed in faded jeans and a black denim shirt. She stared at the stranger while he dismounted, not saying a word. It occurred to Barth that he might inspire a measure of caution, if not fear, appearing as an apparition hidden beneath his helmet and baggy yellow raingear.

"Need some help, ma'am?"

He removed his helmet. At least she could see his eyes.

"Maybe. The wheel nuts are stuck tight. Mechanics use too much airgun on them."

By this time Barth could see that she had jacked the car up and removed the spare. This woman knew what she was doing and would certainly have managed the situation herself but for a lack of brute strength. It was also apparent that he was going to be embarrassed if he lacked the muscle to dislodge the pesky offenders. Picking up the jack handle, he strained mightily to budge the first nut, and, to his amazement, it gave way to his muscular persuasion. In like fashion he was able to remove the other five and replace the flat, assuring the maintenance of his faux macho status. The woman, who had been standing by silently, watching him, expressed her gratitude.

"Thanks mister. You saved me from calling the tow truck."

Barth picked up the flat tire and laid it in the trunk.

"Don't mention it. I've had a few people do me favors on the road this week. Time I helped somebody out. Now I've done my work for the day, all I have to do is ride and rest."

"Where you riding to?"

"Well, just to Tucumcari for now. I'll find someplace to eat and a place to sleep for the night and keep riding west. That's the plan."

"If you stay in Tucumcari, here's a place you should stop. You can eat good and find a room, not too expensive."

She extracted a yellow matchbook with red print from a pocket and handed it to the stranger, displaying a slight smile as she did so.

"You don't need to wear that in the weather here."

"Yeah, it was raining a few miles back."

"Well, I got to go. I got to go to work. Thanks again, mister."

"No problem. And thanks." He waved the matchbook in her direction and stood watching while she started the car and pulled away. She wasn't much for conversation, but he didn't doubt the genuineness of her gratitude. Still, he wished he'd been able to prolong this first encounter in the land of enchantment.

Estrella's Story

This land is your land, this land is my land... — WOODY GUTHRIE

My name is Estrella Corbalon. My family is from the Zapotec Indian people who lived in Mexico even before the days of the New Spain. Today I still remember the smiling days when I was a child in the mountains before the years when we lived in the desert and the city. I remember the corn, looking up at the corn that is so high, and I am so small, and men with big knives cutting the corn, burning the corn on the hills to make it grow again. I remember the smell of the smoke, that smell I liked, not like the smell of the smoke of the maquiladoras. Not like the smell every day and every night in Ciudad Juarez. It was the smoke of the late year, the smoke of celebration. It was the smoke we make ourselves, not the smoke of the city that makes us prisoners, smoke that makes everything dirty and has the smell we never escape, even inside the apartment. We were so poor, all of us were poor in those times, so we did not know it. Only now can I know these things. I remember I was very happy then, so many years ago.

The time in Ixtlan in the Oaxaca when police came and made the troubles for the people in our village, bringing the guns with them, I remember this. I know Mama was scared. I was not old enough, I did not understand. We lived in the mountains where no one says we must leave for a long time. We had the small fields of corn, the *milpas*, and we fed the cornstalks to the cows. After the time of the troubles the families started to leave the Oaxaca. My Uncle Javier left first and goes to the north, to the Sonora, and we heard nothing for a long time. Then he came back and talks to my father and then they left, Uncle Javier and Father. They worked by the Yaqui River picking chili peppers for seven dollars a day, wearing gloves and scarves to protect them from the itchy plants. Then they went to Magdelena, near Nogales, and cut down the mesquite trees to burn for charcoal for *El Norte*. When they got jobs in the Ford factory in Hermosillo Uncle Javier came back to Ixtlan and we left with him the long way after many days.

This was the way then in Oaxaca. When there was no water for the *milpas* and there was no work on the ranchos, or when there was trouble for us in the mountains, the men leave for the north, to Sonora, or Chihuahua. They come back to their families when the work was done, sometimes not before many months. I remember the roads, the truck bouncing on the roads, taking all of us to the end of the mountains. It was so many days moving to the flat areas, to the Sonora where Uncle Javier, he is Mama's brother, is already living. We were the *desplazados*, like many others, but I did not think this then, I only knew the moving was part of the living and did not know that it was not the same for everyone when I was a child.

We lived in a worker's house near the Ford factory. I could go to school, even learn English in the school and watching Oprah on the television after school with Mama and Manuel or listening to the radio playing the Tejano music or the rock'n'roll for the people in *El Norte*. Uncle Javier is always wearing his old black hat and comes with Father from the factory every night in the summer and they sit on the porch, listening to baseball games and drinking beer. Father talks of the players and I remember many times he talks about when he is a boy and he meets the greatest, Martin Dihigo, *El Maestro*, the Dominican who plays in Cuba and plays in Mexico and the States and is the only player in the Hall of Fame in the United States and Cuba and Mexico and the Dominican Republic. Uncle Javier talks about the old movies and his favorites, Delores Del Rio and Ramon Navarro and the one he loves, the beautiful Marguerita Cancino, the lady who is later Rita Hayworth. They are not old men then, but they talk like old men, of things they remember when they were children and the baseball and movies of many years ago. What happens today in their lives is not so interesting to them.

We had no land then, no place to grow corn and no animals. We are not so hungry in those days, but I missed Ixtlan and the mountains. I did not like the heat of the Sonora desert and the smell of the Hermosillo smoke. There was troubles with the boys, the drugs, the *narcotraficantes,* and always there was the killings. Mama is always afraid about Manuel then, maybe he will be killed or maybe when he is older he leaves with the men crossing the border at Nogales to work in Arizona or California. He makes trouble with his friends sometimes and then he would not go to school at all, he says why should he go to school?

When the jobs are gone in the Ford factory we left Hermosillo and came to Ciudad Juarez, a place with more smoke and bad smells and maquiladoras where Uncle and Father can work. Father works in the factory to make washing machines and Mama washes and sews clothes in the apartment where we live, four of us, and Uncle Javier when we first came there. Uncle Javier could not get a job then, but he bought a car, an old Toyota Corolla. He fixed it and then he would drive it during the days as a taxi. At night he and Father take turns driving the car and the one who wasn't driving sleeps on the couch in the front room under the window. I take Manuel with me during the day to the corners on the busy streets where we sell gum and cigarettes to the drivers and the Americans who cross the border for a few hours. I can buy leather shoes for women from one of the shops and hang them from their heels on the sides of a cardboard box. I always get the red or black or white shoes so they are easier to see. Sometimes we can also make money selling the Cuban *cohibas* to the American *touristas* who drive in our streets, but mostly they want the *Montecristos* that are so expensive and they can buy in the shops. Manuel would go to the school in the church only sometimes and I would stay home and help Mama with the laundry and watch Oprah on the television to learn English. In those days everyone who works in the maquiladoras and in the cities on the border like Ciudad Juarez believes they are living there only a short time, only until the days they will be watching Oprah on the other side of the river. It was the religion, we believe that since we are all suffering and we are all working very hard, somehow we will be able to cross the river and stay in *El Norte*, the real heaven for us who breath the air of the maquiladoras every day.

So many times I remember, when my father and my uncle drive the car at night, sometimes they come to the apartment when they are finished, always very late, and they are very drunk. I think it is their way to forget the days, living every day in the ugly place with the smoke and the dirt and remembering the days in the mountains in the south, before Ciudad Juarez, before Hermosillo, before the time of the soldiers in the Ixtlan. Mama was always angry and scared in these times. She shuts the door to the room I shared with Manuel, and she yells at them until Uncle would leave, then I hear her shut the door to the other room, and my father would be in the kitchen. It was worse when my father comes home alone, then my mother screams sometimes and I can hear her so clearly, I am scared and so is Manuel but we do not leave the room. When Father leaves the kitchen to go to the factory in the morning we can hear him and we stay in the rooms until we hear the door close. I always ask Mama if she is hurt, she always says no, she is all right, she is only worried about Manuel and me. Manuel was very upset about Father shouting at Mama, he tells Mama he will protect her but Mama says it is all right, he must say nothing. I talked about these things with Manuel and we always agree, we are going to make Mama happy and safe one day. We do not know how we will do this.

When Manuel left he was so young, he was fourteen years, but it is no surprise, not to me, not to Mama. My father never talked about Manuel leaving. Manuel does not tell us anything, but we know he crosses the border. Maybe he reached the other side of the Rio Grande with his friends, maybe he goes to El Paso by himself in one of the cars and trucks that cross every day. We do not know, all Mama and I can do is wait and hope and pray. Every day we think we will get a message from him and we will know where he is and he is safe. One day, it is two months later, there is a post card. There is no name, but there is enough so we know. It says "Mama, I am in San Diego, I am working now, I am good. Adios." We are glad, then we thought Manuel is safe, safer than in Ciudad Juarez or Reynosa or Matamoros or Nuevo Laredo or Tampico, where there is little work and drug wars with the Zetas and Sinaloa that cause many to die. The ones who die are the young men like Manuel, or the ones that try to stop the killing, like Alejandro Dominguez, who is killed by the drug gangs a few hours when he is the police chief in Nuevo Laredo. This is the time that is *La Inseguridad*, even now, when *la nota roja*, on the back page of the papers, shows the bodies in the streets, with no heads and no arms.

After that, the cards from Manuel come every month, cards with pictures of San Diego and beautiful skies and the California ocean and promises from Manuel that he is saving money for Mama and me. Mama does not show the cards to Father and we never talk about them when he or Uncle is around. Then, after awhile, the cards stop, and there is no messages at all from Manuel. Mama does not say anything, but we know, somehow, we know, and then Mama becomes sad and cries when she is alone.

One day I came home and Mama and Uncle Javier are sitting at the table in the apartment and I know something terrible is happening. They are both quiet when I come in. Then Mama tells me to sit down at the table. She says that two men from the factory came to the apartment in the afternoon, they told her that Father was killed in the morning in the sheet metal stamping machine. I see that she has been crying a long time, but I cannot say anything, and we are all quiet. Accidents in the factory are not so surprising in those days, but it is another shock for us. We survived so much since we left the mountains in Ixtlan, and it is only worse. Manuel is gone, now father is gone. We cannot even bury him in the mountains, there is not enough money, and we have to bury him in the ugly city, in this place of strangers. I miss the mountains. We know it is much harder for all of us.

Then I know it is my turn, there is no one else. Someday I will go to *El Norte*, maybe I can take Mama with me. I do not say anything to Mama, she will worry and say no, it is too dangerous, it is better to stay. I leave the apartment early in the morning and go farther, closer to the border traffic. I can make more money and practice English with the taxi drivers and the Americans who buy the shoes and hats and belts and cigars. I am listening for the information how to cross the border and who to talk to, who to trust. This is a big problem, this is a dangerous place, gringos from *El Norte* are many times kidnapped for money and the police are not trusted, they are told to choose, *la plata o plomo*? It is not difficult to learn the ways to go to *El Norte*, that is no problem, but the easiest ways are too dangerous and Mama could not go those ways. She cannot walk so far. The safe ways cost money, money for the *polleros* to take us, so I learn to sell more and stay away from home longer. I also find out the ones to be trusted, who are the ones to talk to about these things. All the time, I think Mama knows what I am thinking, but she is quiet.

One night, I come back to the apartment and Mama is not there, she has gone to the mass. Uncle Javier is not driving the Toyota, he is sitting by himself, on the couch, drinking, I think he is drinking all day. I go to my room and close the door and decide to stay there and read until Mama is back, but Uncle Javier starts yelling "What are you doing in there?" and opens the door and stands next to my bed. I am scared of this voice, he is drunk but not sleeping like most of the time when he drinks.

"What are you doing, woman, you go into your room and you do not even say anything to your Uncle Javier? Are you ashamed of me?"

"No, Uncle Javier. I am very tired from working on the street today, that is all. I only want to sleep now."

"Tired? You sit on your ass and sell cheap shoes and you are tired? How hard is it to sit and take money from the *touristas* on the street?"

I was very angry then, too angry to be quiet, and Mama was not there to stop him.

"Yes, I am tired, I am standing in the hot sun, not sitting on the couch and drinking beer all day in the cool room."

I knew at the moment this is a mistake.

"So you want to sleep now, senorita. I will show you a different way to sleep."

Uncle Javier grabbed my wrists hard and pushed me down on the bed and then he fell on me. I try to scream then but his hand is on my mouth, pushing my head into the pillow, then his knees are on my arms. I am trying to kick my legs up, but this does nothing. I cannot move, he is too heavy, he pushes my head and takes his other hand and pushes it down into my blouse, grabbing my breast with his large, cold hand. I see his eyes, he looks down at my face, and he is angry, and very strong. His breath is close to my face and stinks with alcohol, a smell I hate.

"Yes, you shut your mouth and I will teach you how to sleep," then he says "You won't be hurt unless you fight."

I hear his words, but I will not listen. I try to move, but I cannot move, just my feet, it is useless, he is too strong, too heavy. Now, what makes me very afraid, I know by his eyes he is more drunk and more crazy than I have ever seen him. Now I think I might die, he might kill me, I do not know what will happen and I close my eyes and try to turn my head. His hand is still on my mouth and it is difficult to breath, his big hand is against my nose. His body is pushing into me, he is breathing very hard, I can hear his breathing, his hand is pulling and ripping, pushing my stomach and on my legs. I am so scared, no one can hear me. I am trapped.

Where is Mama, where is she? I scream inside, but there is no one to hear me, even if I could speak. The walls are my prison now.

Later, I do not know how much time has gone, I am lying alone on the bed. I hear the footsteps and then I hear the door slam. I feel weak, very weak, but I know, I must move, I must move before he comes back. In a few minutes I am standing, then I dress myself, and I run down the stairs to the street. I am almost falling, I am still weak, but I go to the street. Most of the time the streets are too dangerous at night, but tonight I am scared to be alone and the noise of the street now makes me to feel safe.

It is cooler outside, after walking some time I am better, I am still afraid, but I can think now. No one I see knows what happened to me but I wonder if someone who looks at me can tell. Then I am so mad I think, "I don't care." I get angry that this happens to me and I know I can do nothing here, I must go, that is all. I must go. Before I would think about going someday, but now it is different, I must go now. I am afraid of going, but now I am afraid to stay. And I am afraid to leave Mama, so I must find the way to take her with me. That means I must go back to the apartment, so I wait until I am sure she will be back, then I go back up the stairs and see she is sitting in her chair, waiting for me. She is surprised I am not there. Uncle Javier's black hat is not on the table. I say nothing to Maman, just goodnight, and close the door to my room.

That night, I am so scared, I don't know what my uncle does if he thinks I will tell someone. I am alone, I am ashamed, and I am also angry, very angry. So angry about what has happened to me, when there is no reason, so angry about what my father has done all the years to Mama, so angry at myself. I should have left before, like Manuel. Now I am trapped here in the dirty town, there is no one to talk to, I cannot even tell Mama what has happened, and I know it will happen again. So many times I think I will take Mama away even if she does not complain, somewhere she can be safe, now I have to go for myself to be safe, I have to leave here, and I will. Then I think I will take the money I have hidden for Mama and use it for both of us. Give the money to a *coyote* who takes us out of here to a place where we will start life again, where we can be safe. I will take her away from here, out of here, somewhere in *El Norte* where we can breathe a better air. I only know we cannot stay here. I know who to talk to, this is not difficult. I don't know the places, then I don't care, it is for me to take Mama and leave, that's all. I know I will tell her when everything is ready and I know she will come with me, she will not stay here alone.

The western ways, into Arizona and California, are the dangerous ones. I remember the stories about the *coyotes*, who take people on these trails through the rocks and the heat and the cold nights when it is so dark. Sometimes they are left in the desert, on the Devil's Highway, where many died and more die today, drying up in the wild land and the hot sun without water, always afraid of the border police who take them back, where they have nothing, less than when they left. Then they try again. Some of these are caught again by the police, and some will die before they are taken back, how does this happen? But this is the easiest way to go, this is also the cheapest. If we have money and good jobs, would we leave our homes to go to El Norte to be illegals? No, we would not. The east ways, through Matamoros or Reynoso or Nueva Laredo are also not so safe, these places are for the smuggling of the drugs by the *contrabandistas*, much easier than people, and *Los Setos* are always killing each other there, or taking people and demanding ransoms, and the police will not help. They are busy helping the *narcotraficantes*. Ciudad Juarez is the best way, if you can pay to ride the trucks. The truck riders are the lucky ones, there are not so many of them, the bribes take care of the border police, but this needs much more money, even more now because there are more police and it is not so easy to hide people on the trucks and buses. I know, everybody knows, this is the better way. When someone rides in the trucks, after awhile we will find out about them, we will get a letter, sometimes a phone call, and then we will know the person is safe in *El Norte*. The western ways, these are not so good, families are waiting to hear something from the sons, the husbands, and the daughters who go by *los caminos* west. Many times we hear nothing, or maybe we will hear from somebody else and then know that a person does not live, does not survive the trip, or sometimes, like Manuel, is killed after he makes the trip. The Ciudad Juarez way in the trucks is better I think, and that is why I decide to go this way with Mama. It is not possible to go west with Mama, she is not so strong, so the Ciudad Juarez way is the only way. I am lucky, I have hidden the money since the time we left Sonora. The *coyotes* want four thousand pesos, there is no choice. This is the price to go to El Paso.

I know from Uncle Javier's friends, the drivers that he drinks with, and the drivers that I sell cigarettes to every day, how to find the truck shipping people. I go myself to find them, I do not want anybody to know, not Mama, she will be too scared if I tell her. When I find the *coyotes* they tell me the safe trucks are the ones carrying the big air conditioners for buildings, they will not look at all of these on a truck and we will have to sit in an empty box.

It is only two days after when I tell Mama we are going and I have made the plans for us and she must go with me, and I am going, I am not staying here in this dirty town anymore. I am surprised by her. She knows I am going, she knows I am leaving and I am not coming back, and she does not ask me why. She does not tell me no, I must stay, she does not tell me she is staying. She is quiet for a little, then she says

"Yes, we will go when it is time. I am ready, my Estrelita."

Mama goes to her trunk, with her nice clothes, she says nothing, then she takes a beautiful wool *rebozo* and then puts it around my shoulders.

"You will need this, we will need this."

Mama pulls the silver chain with the Virgin around her neck out from her blouse and there is a white cotton bag. She opens it and shows me money, a lot of money.

"I have saved this for many years. I know you will to leave here someday, just like Manuel. Now we will go together."

I am surprised for a few seconds, then Mama holds me close. We do not talk about this anymore. It is decided. That night we are ready, we are going when there is a truck for us. We can take only money, and clothes, and photographs with us, but we cannot stay, that is the way it is. I cannot tell anyone, not my friends, not any of the workers in the factory, it is too dangerous. We do not say anything to Uncle Javier. When it is time I call the number and now we must hurry, we must go to the factory place now, before the truck is loaded, there is no time. Mama is ready and no one we know is around that night, no one to hide from and no one to say goodbye to, no one, but we are not sad, not now. There is no time, it is just for us to go.

The streets are full and busy that night. I am holding Mama's arm and walking with her as fast as she can walk down the small streets. These are the streets where we do not walk when it is the night, but tonight is different. When we are on the main streets in a few minutes and we are lucky that night, we find a taxi to take us to the place of the maquiladoras and pay the driver to take us to the factory gate where the *coyote* is waiting, sitting on a chair next to the guard, laughing with him but quiet when we get out of the taxi. He waves his hand to me and I take Mama's arm and pull her with me. We do not say anything but look to see we do not fall in the dark with the moon on the big trucks in the lot. When he comes to the truck he stops and looks around, then puts a ladder to the back and waves to Mama to climb in the truck. Then I climb up the ladder and see a white sign inside the truck, *Materiales Peligrosos No Permitidos*. The coyote, a big man, climbs into the truck and asks for the money and counts it, then walks to a large wood box in front and opens one side.

"In here, both of you, now."

Then I thought, he might kill us.

We are both afraid, but it is too late now. Mama gets in the box, it is tall enough to stand up if we want. I get in and we sit on the floor, close, and the coyote looks in the box and says, "Be quiet, no noise, try to sleep."

We say nothing but are more afraid now, it is all dark when he closes the door, then, a surprise, we hear pounding, he is pounding the door with a hammer. Now I think they will not kill us. I hold Mama and we say nothing. We are still, we hear more men, they are loading boxes on the truck, close to us, then farther away.

How can we do this?

But I know we cannot stay, there is no choice anymore. We sit together in the dark, we are afraid to talk.

An hour later, we are awake, we hear, we feel, the motor running, then we feel the truck move. The next life is beginning and I am afraid, but I am also excited, maybe Mama is feeling the same now, but we do not speak. In a few minutes we know we are on the road, we are going.

I held Mama close in the box so she would not be afraid, but I was. It was hot and wet and the wood feels hard on our bodies, we were sitting and there was no room to lie down. The noise was always the same, the engine noise does not stop, and we could not sleep with the noise and the shaking we feel every second. The darkness was frightening to me, but I could not show this to Mama, she needs me then. We did not talk. We did not know the time, the day, or night, only the noise, the shaking, and sometimes the truck would stop, we could not know why or how long and then we would try to sleep, we were so tired. But we could not sleep, the noise and the shaking was too much all the time. I do not remember if we were hungry, but we had no water. We were so thirsty and tired in the dark. Mama prayed sometimes. I could not pray then, I remember I thought we will die in this box, and I was angry, so angry. Why were we dying in this hot, shaking box, we had done nothing! The God of my childhood lets this happen to me, lets Manuel die in California, lets Father be killed in the maquiladora, lets me and Mama die in this dark box. There is no God in this truck with us, no God would let Uncle near me and caused this!

I was too tired to cry even though Mama could not see me, I cannot say anything to her. She says nothing, there was nothing to say. We can only hold each other in the darkness, we have to hold each other and that was the only thing I knew then, I am not alone and she is not alone. Maybe Mama will die in that box and I will be alone, maybe I will die in the box and Mama will be alone. I was afraid, but I could not say that, only keep feeling her in my arms. It was all horrible and does not stop. I thought I was protecting Mama, but maybe I was killing her, maybe we should have stayed in Ciudad Juarez.

I thought the drivers had forgotten us, then I thought they are letting us die in there, maybe they want us to die, they must know how afraid we are. Maybe they know we have money and they will just take it after we are dead and drop our bodies in the desert like the others. Once the truck stopped and I thought they would let us out now, we must be far in the United States, out of El Paso even, but nothing happened, and we could do nothing.

Then I heard the dogs barking. I knew we are not across the border yet. We could hear men outside the truck, sometimes they were speaking, but we could not understand what they were saying. I was afraid they are going to open the truck. Now they will find us. Then the talking stops and the barking of the dogs stops. The money that we paid for this, maybe it is worth it. We are so tired, so hot, we finally can go to sleep. We went to sleep, then sometime the truck started again. I remember, I held Mama so she would not be so afraid, but she said to me,

"Estrelita, don't worry now, it will be okay for us, don't be afraid."

I was surprised, I could not say anything then, the truck was moving, but I knew then, Mama is the strong one. She was the strong one when Father was killed, and I knew then why it is easy for her to leave with me, because she needed to take care of me, not what I thought, I needed to bring her so I could take care of her.

I still do not know the hours we were in the box. Mama does not know I think, we do not talk about this now, not about this, not about my father, not about my uncle, not about my brother. I know it was a long time, hours, then the truck stopped. We were tired but we were awake and we could hear the noises of the truck doors and then, the unloading and we know it is near the end.

Then, two men talking to each other, then talking very loud, saying

"You in there, make a noise."

Mama hit her hand on the side of the box, many times, and the men started hitting the top with their tools, then, finally, the light, the bright light in our eyes, the cool air from outside. Our eyes hurt for a second, but we knew this was over now.

"We are sorry, we could not stop before, they were looking at the trucks, we would have been caught. You must hurry now."

The men knew we suffered much and gave us water and poured water on our heads. We were in a place with a lot of trucks and men unloading the trucks. We could not be seen and the two drivers lifted us out, we were too weak. Then they carried us over to a small truck and we had to lie down in the back of the truck, on a rug on the floor, but it felt good, we could lie down, not sit like we did in the box. The men covered us with blankets so we would not be cold and told us to make no noise, but we are too tired to talk and Mama was so happy to see the sunlight. One of the men drove the small truck and we did not see anything then except the sky. The sky was so nice then, the sky in the United States; it was so beautiful and blue. We looked up to the clear sky with no smoke. For me and Mama, it was so different. We are safe here.

It is strange that I feel so different here sometimes, in this place that belongs to our people so long ago. This is still the land of my people, I believe this. If we are illegals, this does not matter, the border is only a line, a line that is hard to cross sometimes, but it is a line that will always be crossed. Mama's father crosses the border many times in the years of the *braceros,* when many thousands go through El Paso every year to dig sugar beets and pick the tomatoes, the cucumbers and the cotton in Texas. He comes from Chihuahua to work in the Texas places. Mama still has his card he always carries with him. His name, Alexios Campoya, is on the card, and the permiso writing that says he can cross this line, and how long he stays, and his picture. He is a very young and very good-looking man. This is the only picture Mama has of him.

Before the time of the *braceros,* there are the years of the *repatriados,* when the families, the people who look like me and have Mexican names, are taken by the planes and trucks across the border to Mexico, even when they are born in California and Texas. My great-grandfather, Mama tells me, in the time of the revolution, crossed this line many times with the campesinos who are fighting with Villa. The American general Pershing crossed the line too, but he is not so smart, he does not find Villa when he hides in the Sierra Madre. The border could not stop Villa, it does not stop Manuel, also it does not stop Mama or me. Even the fence will never stop the ones who want the better living, even in shadows. The mountains and the desert here are not so different from the mountains and the desert on the other side of the border. But it is different, I know, it is safer here, safer for me, safer for Mama, safer for Matias, who does not know, who will not know, unless he also crosses the line someday.

Matias was born here, the year Mama and me came to Tucumcari. No one asks me, only how I was feeling, even Mama did not ask me. I could not tell her. Maybe she knows, but she never says anything, and I could not tell her, not then, not now. I think she must know, but it doesn't matter, she could not do anything, and now that is all over. When Matias was born, Mama was with me and she spends all her time, when she is not working, taking care of Matias. He has grown up here with us, with his friends, and he is a good student. Matias is a good boy to me and Mama and the drivers and the workers like him also. He sometimes helps to wash the trucks or works inside the diner with me. He will not be a *cholo.* His home is here.

This is how we come to Tucumcari. It was a much different time then, not a good time, but not a bad time, we are too busy, we work cleaning the rooms at the truckstop and cooking in the kitchen and cleaning and washing the floors. There was work all the time except when we could sleep, but we have the room in the back of the diner for us, then later the motel rooms for the three of us, and now Mama will have her own house. Mama also helps with the food in the kitchen, she changes some of the food with no taste and uses the ancho, chipotle peppers, chile peppers and Grajillo peppers, and the drivers like this very much, and today Mama is the boss of the kitchen. We are safe here and after a while we do not worry so much. Mama works hard and she never complains, not at all, and talks to the other workers who speak Spanish. I did not talk so much to people at first, my English is good enough, I just did not want to talk with others for a long time.

My life here has been good these years, I am able to work inside because my English is good and Mr. Corrigan, who is the owner, he lets us live in one of the motel rooms. Mr. Corrigan trusts me and helps me to learn all the work in the diner and the truckstop. Later, when he goes somewhere, I am running the diner, and he is very happy how it is here when he is gone. He has other business and can make money while Mama watches the kitchen and I do the rest. After a few years I have started to be the manager of the diner and the truckstop. I am the boss here and the one who is here every day, every night. Mama does not have to work now, but she is boss of the kitchen, she watches over me and Matias and she knows people from the church in the town. I do not go to the church, but my friends and my life is here, that is enough. Tucumcari is my home, the only home I want, Mama and I will stay here and Matias I hope also, but that will be his decision when he becomes a man someday. I know he will not become a *cholo*, he will not disappear in the world like Manuel before. I never have a desire to go back to Mexico, never. There is nothing for me there. Mama, I know she thinks about Mexico, and sometimes, she asks me to write a letter for her, a letter to Uncle in Matamoros, but I always refuse. This is something I cannot do. She becomes angry with me, so I think she does not know and cannot understand. She forgets and then it is okay, and she is happy in her home here with me and Matias, and she knows I will care for her as my father did not do. She watches *Telemundo* to remind her of her home, but I know she is happy with us. We are building a house for Mama now, a place where she can be in the quiet and Matias can go see her.

I know my life is hard sometimes, but it is not so hard like others I know, there is no room for crying. Before we are in Tucumcari life is *una lucha*, a battle, for Mama and me, but today it is different. Mama is comfortable now. Matias is growing in this good place and does not know the terrible things. Here we are no more the *desplazados*, and Matias, he will never have to know what this means. There is no smoke from the maquiladoras in our eyes and we are in our home now for many years. I do not know why these things happened to me, the good things and bad things. I know the mornings and the nights and the days that come and make the life and that is so much, there are the friends here and the drivers, the family that makes me happy. This is so much, I know this. I never think to go back, to cross the border again, there is no reason, everything is here. *Asi es la vida.*

Dancing in the Desert

It's hotter than Mojave in my heart. — IRIS DEMENT

B y the time Barth veered off the highway and headed into town, the sky was clearing and he was able to get a long view of the isolated mesas to the south. The road into town, Tucumcari's main street, was a surviving remnant of Route 66, two lanes running in an east-west line bisecting a core of small shops, a laundromat, car lots, restaurants and houses. There were no big city malls or high rise buildings blocking the view of the nearby mountain from which the town derived its name. The sand hills lying between didn't diminish its dramatic impact but highlighted the fact that the rider had entered another world. The mountain was its gateway marker. It was an ideal lookout across the great expanse of territory for the Comanche Indians during the 1880s, when the nearby settlement was known as Liberty. The word Tukamukaru, in their dialect, translates roughly as "to lie in wait for someone or something to approach." The Apaches, however, maintain that the mountain derives its name from the story of two star-crossed lovers, Tocom and Kari, destined to their desert demises, a southwestern Romeo and Juliet. *Could there be something in this mountain*, Barth wondered, *lying in wait for me?*

He considered the possibility of staying for the night as he passed the Blue Swallow Motel, a biker hangout recommended by Turner. In the bright sunlight it had a tired, washed-out look, but there were hints of character missing from the Motel Sevens along the road. First, however, he was going to tend to the pressing matter of his appetite, preferably with some southwestern cuisine. Barth passed small and inviting Mexican restaurants, including one named La

Cita, with a seafoam green and pink concrete sombrero entryway, but decided to look for the Tucumcari Truckstop, its address printed on the matchbook which was his bounty for the good deed he had accomplished an hour ago.

The lady had seemed straightforward enough. He had no reason to question her recommendation, his only connection to this town. She'd instructed him to stay on the main drag until he reached its western edge, at which point he couldn't miss the place. Sure enough, after five minutes' ride, he turned into the front lot, filled with parked cars and trucks, and others that were fueling up.

The truckstop was a hive of activity, drivers entering and leaving the diner and the motel rooms in the narrow one-story strips behind and to the west of the main complex. Outside a group of Native Americans, older men, were gathered around a table, smoking and exchanging stories. An older woman, with long black and gray-streaked hair and a long white skirt, divided at regular horizontal intervals by zigzagging dark red embroidery, tended the bougainvillaea covering the front wall. At the diner's entrance Barth surveyed the busy scene inside for a few seconds before spotting an open booth far in the back. He navigated a course through the crowded front section, adjusting his hearing to the din of conversations surrounding him. The sweet, melancholic voice of Patsy Cline, singing *Crazy*, was beckoning to him from a jukebox he couldn't see on the far side of the U-shaped front counter. Appealing to another sense was a blend of exotic scents indicating that no ordinary truckstop fare was served here. His untrained sense of smell detected an enticing mélange of spices, including chile peppers.

"What can I get you, mister?"

The question came from a Hispanic kid with short black hair, red T-shirt, jeans, and an old pair of white sneakers.

"Let me see a menu, thanks."

Surely, this kid is too young to be working in a place like this.

"Oh yeah, how can I find out about a room for the night?"

"Wait a minute mister."

The kid turned away and headed through the crowd. When he returned, he was accompanied by none other than the woman Barth had assisted on the road. In this light she was even more attractive than she appeared during their initial meeting, with an abundance of coarse jet black hair hanging down her back in a single thick braid and high cheekbones, speaking to Mayan heritage. A smile enhanced her even, dark complexion, a smile he hadn't seen during their earlier encounter.

"I see you managed to make it here after the expert repair."

She laughed lightly. "Now I see you, also. Matias says you want a room. How many nights you staying?"

"Just tonight. Rest up and head to Flagstaff tomorrow."

"I'll take care of it and Matias will take your order when you're ready. Ask for me when you pay up front and the room will be ready."

"I'm sorry, ma'am, I don't know your name."

The fact that this information hadn't been exchanged earlier was evidence, thought Barth, of a mutually-shared reticence with strangers. His request, on the other hand, was not a pro forma bow to required etiquette. He wouldn't have made the inquiry except that his interest in this woman had been inexplicably aroused.

"Estrella, and Matias is my son. Matias, this man fixed my car, you treat him good."

The boy nodded, looking directly at Barth.

"What's your name, mister?" No shyness here.

"Barth, Greg's my first name, you can call me Barth."

"Matias, you bring Mr. Barth his food and then I want you to find a place to sit where I can see you finish your homework."

"Matias can sit here if he likes."

"Okay, as long as he studies and doesn't bother you."

The boy's mother turned and disappeared while he waited for Barth to place his order. Matias dutifully carried out his responsibility, leaving the stranger to his own amusements. Instead of pondering his next moves, however, deciding whether to explore the local flora and fauna, and choosing his next stop, Barth's attention was diverted elsewhere.

"Estrella." He repeated this exotic name, sounding every melodic syllable over and over to himself. At the same time, he attempted to maintain his focus on the woman as she hustled between customers and employees. He was out of earshot of the interactions he witnessed, but it was obvious, from her energetic, businesslike manner, that she was in command in this arena. This was her home turf. The reactions he observed supported the conclusion that those who had the opportunity to be around this woman on a regular basis viewed her in exactly the same way Barth had sized her up in his brief acquaintance. Her unheard words were met with looks and nods signifying respectful attention. Estrella waded through the front section toward a destination behind the counter, apparently oblivious to her status as one of the few females in the establishment other than the counter and kitchen employees.

As he sat, absorbing this woman's presence, he was developing an interest in Estrella independent of her unmistakable physical attraction. By any standard of beauty she would have been noticed, but her attractiveness, at least to Barth, was based on the unseen. There was a story behind this woman. It was also apparent that their brief exchanges hardly signified a lack of things to say on the part of this woman; certainly not a shortage of thoughts worth attention, but, more likely, a deliberate choice to be only as revealing as required under the circumstances. Barth was energized, resolving that, unlike his usual approach to situations involving the opposite sex, he was going to take an active role. This was different from the encounter with Ina in the campground—the arousal of dormant primal drives was not the driving force behind his curiosity. He wanted to know something of this woman, another chance encounter in his westward travels.

Just as he resolved to somehow initiate contact with Estrella, the boy returned to his booth, setting a plate of fish tacos in front of him. Tucked under the boy's arm was a dog-eared spiral notebook which he opened after sliding down the bench opposite the stranger. Without hesitating, Barth turned resolution into action.

"What grade are you in?"

"Fourth grade next year."

The boy's interest was hardly aroused by Barth's awkward attempt to start something, but this was all he could come up with on short notice.

"You get good grades?"

"Sometimes."

No doubt about it, the boy wants to escape this conversation as soon as possible.

"What do you like in school?"

"I don't know, everything, except arithmetic." Barth had located a foothold, and fully intended to exploit it.

"Hmm, yeah, arithmetic is hard, but it's important, you know."

"I know, Mama says that, she makes me see Mrs. Tanana now so I can learn it better. It's hard."

Progress. The kid was talking to him.

"You're doing arithmetic this summer?" Barth tried to sound sympathetic.

"Yeah, I need to do my homework. Mama won't like it if I don't get it done."

"You know, I'm pretty good at arithmetic. You need some help, let me know."

This bald-faced attempt to ingratiate himself with the boy had better-than-expected results.

"Really, Mister, can you help me now?" The kid knew better than to decline the offer.

"Sure, I've got nothing else to do. You show it to me and we'll try it. And you can call me Barth, okay?"

"Deal, Mr. Barth. Here it is." Matias turned the pages, not waiting for additional confirmation, thinking he'd better take advantage of the offer before this man changed his mind.

This was blatant, unabashed exploitation. Barth wasn't deluding himself about any altruistic motivations for his actions, but felt absolutely no guilt. *After all*, he rationalized, *I could make a small contribution to the boy's education, and who knows…?* Under these circumstances he didn't have the luxury of waiting for an opportunity, he had to create it. His initiative was uncharacteristic, and right now he was glad for the inconsistency.

He figured Matias was about ten years old. The absence of a noticeable accent in his speech, unlike that of his mother, supported the conclusion that he'd been raised in this country. As for Estrella, the critical question for Barth, as he saw it, was her attachment status. Boyfriend, or husband, he'd seen or heard nothing which could provide a clue one way or the other, but he was confident that this small mystery, at least, would soon be solved. On the other hand, he knew this was foolish under the circumstances. The realization, however, had no impact.

Time to get cracking.

The subject was multiplication tables, and Matias was struggling with them, although he was able to obtain the required answers with ease using his calculator. At least this wasn't beyond Barth's intellectual reach, just a matter of rote learning. Barth assumed the teacher's role and, once he had determined a good starting point, neither too difficult nor too easy, he began a back-and-forth question-and-answer exercise with Matias, making sure he wasn't the least bit judgmental. This approach seemed to work—the boy gradually warmed to the stranger and the attention he was getting from an adult. At the same time, he seemed to be making progress in the task at hand. They established a rhythm in their work, oblivious to their surroundings, when Matias' mother walked up to the booth, sizing up the situation.

"So, you fix tires and teach arithmetic...I'm impressed." She smiled directly at Barth.

"Well, the lesson is worth every cent he's paying for it."

She laughed while Matias, sensing the lesson was over, slid off the bench seat, grabbing his book.

"Mama, I'm going to Mama Graciela's now."

"Okay, you take her supper back for her and don't watch television all night."

"Yes, Mama. Thanks Mr. Barth." Matias turned to leave.

"You're welcome. If you're around later we can try some more."

"All right." He ran toward the front and disappeared around the main counter.

"I hope you don't mind, ma'am, I thought I'd try to make it a little fun for him."

"No problem, Mr. Barth, anybody who helps Matias with his school is a good person to me. He's very smart, you know, he just needs help to get going sometimes."

"Oh, I can see he learns quickly if he's having fun. If he's here later maybe I can give him another lesson. I'm just relaxing and getting cleaned up before I decide where I'm heading tomorrow. Can you tell me what a stranger should see around here? I have no idea."

"The mesas out of town are supposed to be beautiful, people come here sometimes just to see them."

"Are they difficult to find from here?"

"Not hardly. You can see them from the parking lot. When you're driving straight west you stay on the county road that starts a mile from here and keep going. You can't miss it."

The woman smiled at the stranger as she snatched up the plates from the end of the booth. Barth would not have guessed it, but her thoughts were of him as she walked away. She had stolen occasional glances of him and Matias during the last half hour, trying to figure out what they were up to and then, satisfied things were okay, wondering why a perfect stranger would invest the time with Matias. Her long-held predispositions toward men aside, she believed that Matias needed more contact with an adult male than she could make possible. On the other hand, the men who passed through here rarely showed other than a few seconds' interest in Matias and, besides, she wasn't always confident regarding the life lessons some of them would have for him. As for advice, she hoped the recommendation regarding the mesas was good. Estrella could only guess herself since, despite her years in Tucumcari, she had never ventured outside the town to take a close look.

Barth sat for a few seconds, indulging himself in thoughts of this newcomer in his road trip adventure. She had a story worth the time, if she'd tell it, but would he have a chance to listen? Rather than take a wait-and-see attitude, he decided to see if he could increase the odds of getting to know this woman.

He stepped to the front to pay his tab and, without hesitating, leaned forward to the woman behind the counter.

"Excuse me, the woman who waited on me, her name is Estrella."

"Yes, she is the manager."

Barth was not surprised.

"She married?"

"No," the woman smiled, "She's way too busy for any man except her son."

"Thanks. I'm staying here tonight and she told me to ask about the room now."

"Yes. Number 24 out back. Here's the key. Checkout is noon."

Barth stretched out on the narrow bed, still dressed except for his boots. Since leaving Kansas City he hadn't slept on a bed as comfortable as his own. Still, the motel beds, Sedley Crump's couch, and even the hard earth of the Texas Panhandle felt great after a day's ride. He was finding that he had a capacity to sleep just about anywhere when it came right down to it, waking each morning as refreshed as he could desire. He wasn't ready to doze off, however, finding himself engaged in a more pleasurable preoccupation.

Who is this woman, Estrella, what's her story, why am I so attracted to her?

Barth had no ready answers, just a fascination with the exotic, mysterious nature of this woman. There was no denying a proud, independent nobility in her bearing that added to the attraction of her physical beauty. He allowed himself the fantasy of believing she could have an interest in him, a man who was just another in the succession of strangers passing through this stretch of 66. Anything was possible, of course, but after a few minutes lingering in this reverie he concluded that realization of this newfound desire was improbable. This was nothing more than a fleeting, pleasant diversion. Besides, he was traveling west, this was a pit stop, what was he thinking?

Time to get back to reality.

He got up, gathered his clothes, wrapped them in a pair of jeans, and walked out, picking a path through the eighteen-wheelers and pickups in the side lot. Passing the truckstop entrance, he headed east, walking on the shoulder of the road toward town. Even from a distance, he could see the bright red, white and blue neon invitation of the Blue Swallow Motel, rendering the site alluring in a way that had escaped him during the day. Halfway between the truckstop and the Blue Swallow he located Anastacio's Laundry-Mat, another landmark he'd passed on his ride into Tucumcari.

Once inside, Barth saw that he was alone and stripped down to his boxer shorts, shoving everything into an available washer. This was a degree of informality he would never have allowed himself in Kansas City, where there was always the possibility of being recognized. No one here this Saturday night. Barth was sitting on a bench with no background noise save the vibration of the washer in front of him. His fifth night out of Kansas City, none too exciting at the moment, but after the experiences of the last few evenings, that was okay. In one sense, however, this day brought with it another in the succession of surprises. Sitting and staring at the bare white enamel of the washer, Barth wasn't enjoying the restful interlude he'd anticipated. This time, however, it wasn't a vague stirring of unease attributed to his road adventure.

The image he had of her now was not that of the stranded driver out on the highway, but the proud woman in charge of her personal domain, competent and confidant. Barth was intrigued, and undeniably attracted. He knew her story was one he'd like to hear, if he had the chance. She was obviously from a world much different than his. She was also beautiful in a way he could only describe to himself as some form of impelling feminine force. *Here I am, another day out, and another person I'd like to know.* Barth tried to avoid dwelling on this line of thought any longer. He was more of a realist than that.

The front door swung open and a young woman entered, her arms wrapped around a large plastic laundry basket, two small children trailing in her wake. She looked at Barth and veered sharply away toward the front corner, shuttling her children in the same direction.

I must be a scary sight, some pervert here to prey on her or her kids, that's what she's thinking.

Barth realized that, from her perspective, caution was reasonable. He sat still and quiet, hoping a lack of response would ease her anxiety. After all, he was the stranger in this strange land.

By the time he returned to his room it was already dark, a clear night with another bright moon. He packed his clothes in the top drawer of the dresser, after tugging hard on the pulls to urge it open, stuck as it was through the layers of beige paint accumulated over a period of forty, maybe fifty years. The simple décor and furnishings, he guessed, were fairly ordinary when the place was built, half a century ago, but now had acquired a homey charm not accessible in the motels adjoining the busier highway exits. Lying on his bed, staring up at the dingy off-white ceiling, he started playing with a continuation of the train of thought he had begun earlier in the same room. Barth couldn't distinguish between curiosity and desire as he replayed these musings, and he was not one to initiate anything under the circumstances. His history with women, even in familiar surroundings, was against him and, besides, he was passing through, riding west, and had no business going beyond these tentative, if attractive, imaginings. Land of enchantment or not, perhaps this *terra* should remain *incognita*. Finally, there was the small matter of this woman's own situation. Barth had not an inkling of her perspective of anything whatsoever.

After a few more rounds of these ruminations, Barth was able to reach a conclusion. Not exactly a course of action, that was still a foreign commodity to him, but, in this case, not an absolute necessity. It was possible, he reasoned, to just hang out awhile, maybe another day, take in the scenery, imagine away at his leisure, see what, if anything, might happen. After all, as he kept reminding himself, he wasn't on a schedule, and didn't have to go anywhere in particular tomorrow. His only certain destination in this meandering, his sister's place, was for an uncertain date, at best, as a result of his own unpredictable, unreliable skills as a novice rider. His inexperience had its advantages.

He awoke early Sunday morning, well-rested, with no plan in mind other than a leisurely pace. By the time he entered the diner for breakfast, it was crowded with drivers. This was another day for them, not a rest day in any sense. He was well aware of the obligation gap existing between him and most of the other diners—mainly, he had none demanding his attention this morning. Barth was an interested observer, traveling voyeur, lazily taking the opportunity to survey the entire cast of early-morning customers while keeping an eye out for the woman who had piqued his curiosity.

A group of women were gathering outside the diner, on the west side. It was obvious they were headed for church, at least by their dress—skirts, blouses and light jackets, in bright blues, yellows and reds. Some were wearing low heels. They were engaged in friendly conversation and were waiting, probably for a bus. Barth spotted Matias, dressed in a white shirt and black slacks, accompanied by a similarly dressed boy, joining the group. Right behind Matias, Estrella stopped and said something, briefly attracting her son's attention. She was dressed in tight black slacks, a white cotton blouse and running shoes-obviously she was not going with the group. One of the older women approached her and, although Barth couldn't hear the words between them, their facial expressions and, in Estrella's case, hand movements, indicated mutual familiarity and the less-than-cordial nature of their conversation. When a light blue bus pulled into the diner's front lot the older woman took Matias's hand and turned to board with the rest of the group. Estrella looked on, silently, for a second, then, without looking back, headed straight to the diner's side entrance, disappearing in the direction of the kitchen. Barth was puzzled by the confrontation, guessing the older woman was Estrella's mother.

He had diverted his attention to his coffee and breakfast when Estrella reappeared, pausing to say something to the cashier before surveying the customer landscape. She spotted Barth and, in a surprise move, headed straight to his booth.

"Same seat. You are comfortable here?" She laughed.

"Yeah. I guess I feel safe here." Barth laughed at himself. She had him pegged.

"Everybody off to church? I saw Matias all dressed up."

"Yes. Mama takes Matias."

"What about you?"

As soon as the words left his lips, Barth realized this was much too personal a question.

"I don't go. Nothing for me. Just here. This is enough."

"I see."

He didn't, of course, but figured he had pried enough. Still, her quick, no-nonsense response told him she was as forthright as she was businesslike.

A tough woman, here.

"Why don't you sit and relax a few minutes? It doesn't look too busy right now." Barth had nothing to lose.

Surprisingly, she accepted his invitation, gesturing to one of the waitresses with two fingers extended as she assumed her seat. Fortified with fresh, hot coffee, they sat together. Barth was hopeful.

She told him her story, from the beginning. It had been awhile since she had talked about herself, about her life, even in outline. She found the telling surprisingly easy, however, because Barth was such a good listener. True, it could be assumed he had acquired some talents in this regard as part of his professional training, but Estrella knew nothing of this. What she could tell, as she spoke, was that this man, a stranger two days ago, was interested. He wasn't a passive audience, unreactive to what she had to say. On the contrary, Barth was an involved listener. He would frequently interrupt, not in a probing manner, but in order to clarify the meaning of parts of Estrella's story, to make sure he understood, as much as it was possible, the story as she meant it to be understood. He wanted to know what the words meant, of course, but he also wanted to know what was important to her, and why things were important to her. It quickly became clear to Estrella that Barth wanted to know her, that his attention was not to be distracted from this goal. This was an entirely new experience for her, to be the focus of sustained and interested attention, and this had an effect on her narrative. She could feel herself, in the act of telling, becoming more open about her life travels than she had ever been. After awhile she did not hesitate, not at all, in divulging some of the personal facts of her history. She recounted details of her poverty-stricken existence in Mexico, of her wandering, subsistence life, with its childhood joys and adult hardships. She did not tell Barth what her uncle had done to her; this secret would touch no ears. She had never said a word of this to Mama. Even with an audience like Barth there were limits.

Estrella was glad, finally, when she was able to get to the parts of her story that followed settlement in Tucumcari, the last chapter in her life as a *desplazado*. She smiled with the realization that her story might have sounded a fairytale quality in its ending.

When she finished, she paused, looking silently at Barth, who returned her gaze across the table while making an observation.

"Estrella, you're an incredible woman, incredible. I listen to you and you know what I think, I think 'How does this woman go through all of these things and survive?' No, more than that, more than surviving. You've made a life here, a good life, and you've done it yourself. You are remarkable. That's all I can say."

She smiled at these remarks. Estrella had never thought of herself, or her life, as "remarkable," in any way, but she knew this was his honest reaction; it was obvious by the way he was listening. The tone of respect with which his words were spoken was unmistakable. On reflection, she accepted the observation that, yes, perhaps her life was in some aspects remarkable.

"You are a very good listener, I should say the word 'audience,' Mr. Barth. I never tell anyone before this much of my life. Never."

"I'm glad you told me, Estrella. I've heard lots of stories about people's lives, but never one like yours. It makes me feel ordinary, you know, listening to you."

"Ordinary, Mr. Barth. I'm sure, you are not ordinary. I'm sure that is not true. Why do you say that?"

"Well, only because I know my life, and now I know some of yours, and I can see big differences, that's all. And please, Estrella, call me Gregory."

"Tell me about the difference, Gregory, what is your story?"

"I'm not sure it's all that interesting, to tell the truth."

"Say it to me. I want to know this."

She looked him straight in the eye. It wasn't possible for him to avert his own gaze without seeming impolite.

Barth began, slowly, tentatively, divulging the basic facts of his own past, a fairly routine middle-class life trajectory, one in which major life decisions had, in most cases, been his, perhaps expected by others, but not forced by external dictates, threats or deprivations. He had ups and downs, to be sure, in his personal and family life, but even then, during what he considered low points in his own existence, questions of real, basic, elemental survival were absent. His crises were of another sort and, at their most distressing points, did not entail the desperation his listener had known first-hand. Barth didn't spend much time recounting his story, not because of any lack of desire to respond to her query, but because, for him, it was just not that compelling and could not be, no matter how it was embellished. He was even a bit ashamed, from his perspective, at having so little to say.

Estrella, for her part, didn't sense Barth's lack of interest in his own story. The brevity of Barth's account yielded much to her ears. Above all, she could tell that this stranger, from a world completely foreign to her, except perhaps through her Oprah-filtered exposure, had followed expectations, sometimes his, sometimes not, and that he had, despite obvious advantages, been unable to achieve a degree of satisfaction in his life equal to her own. Indeed, it was clear to Estrella, especially through Barth's description of the last few days, that the biker was, in a very real sense, among the *desplazados* himself. Estrella felt a degree of empathy for Barth beyond what she had experienced based on the sum total of his behavior toward her and Matias.

"So you travel now, not in a box on a truck, but you ride your bike, maybe looking for something?"

Barth was startled. *It's undeniable*, he thought, but he was caught off guard by Estrella's summing up of their differences in the space of a single question.

"Yeah, I guess you're right, but, unlike you, I don't think I have any idea what I'm looking for. *Nada.*"

They laughed together.

"Maybe when you keep riding you will find whatever it is."

"Maybe."

Barth had no desire to embark on a philosophic tangent he knew would solve nothing. If it was possible to find "whatever it is," the accomplishment would have been attained by this time in his life.

"Well, Gregory, I need to get back to the kitchen before Mama and Matias get back." She stood and hesitated, smiling at him, before walking away.

Right then and there, Barth made a decision. Without any semblance of a plan or crystallized intention, he was going to stay, stick around for a day or two, rest and explore some of the surrounding territory, including the mesas. He was in no particular hurry, he reminded himself, and had nothing to lose by lingering for a while before heading west again. He harbored no illusions about this woman, whose story he found extraordinary. She knew he was passing through, just like all the truckers served here everyday and, besides, this woman did not require even the temporary diversion of another man in her life. That was apparent. Still, when he thought about it, with all the other reasons for hanging around, the mere presence of this fascinating woman, if nothing else, tipped the scales in favor of staying.

When he left the diner he spotted a group of Hispanic men gathered in the parking lot, near the first of the stretched-out buildings housing the motel rooms. One man was explaining something, in Spanish, and the others were listening, without interruption. Barth slowed his pace, though he knew there was no possibility of finding out what was going on. Meeting his glance, the speaker paused and gesticulated, summoning Barth with a gruff "Come here." Surprised, offput, but curious, Barth stepped to the edge of the gathering, conscious of his gringo status, but intrigued.

"Biker man, we see you stay here. Want to make some bucks to pay your gas?"

"What are you talking about?" Barth was puzzled but sufficiently interested to linger.

What the hell is this is all about?

"We make a house the next three days out here." He pointed to an area well behind the motel rooms where Barth could see square mountains of cinder blocks and a large dugout area, roped and staked, marking four sides.

"You need dollars, work with us two days, cash dollars, that's it. You interested, we need more men." He paused, then barked, "Be here tomorrow, seven hours."

The others turned their focus on Barth while he was being addressed and just as quickly turned back to the speaker when he finished and resumed speaking in Spanish. Barth was just as quickly ignored. He nodded, a nod of recognition, of thanks for the offer, not one of assent, and resumed the trek to his room, where he stretched out on the bed to unwind and consider everything he had absorbed in the last couple hours. This was a new twist in his adventure, and he considered it for a few seconds. He didn't need the money, certainly not the minimum wage, likely less, to be made from working with them, and this didn't fit into his idea of a vacation, or whatever it was he was doing. The "offer" was disorienting, likely based on his rough appearance. On the other hand, this might provide a sliver of a glimpse into another culture, and maybe some physical labor would be good for him, if his body could take it.

No, on second thought, this isn't for me.

Barth was restless, ready to do something, and decided to walk into Tucumcari and get a better look, then maybe give his bike a much-needed wash later in the afternoon. He headed out again into the day, wearing sunglasses to screen out the bright sun, now directly overhead. Near the front entrance he witnessed the same group he had seen that morning, now stepping out of the bus. The head honcho of the workmen he had encountered earlier was engaged in conversation with one of the women and Matias, still in his Sunday clothes, walked over to Barth.

"Can I sit on your bike, Mr. Barth?"

"Sure, go ahead, better not do it now, though, not in those clothes, the bike's pretty dirty and I'm sure your mom won't like it."

"Okay, thanks." He ran back to the women standing by the bus and grabbed the hand of the older woman Barth had seen talking with Estrella this morning. She was the one who'd been talking with the workman. At Matias's urging she started walking with him in Barth's general direction and paused, smiling at him.

"I am Graciela, grandmother to Matias. Jorge says you make my house tomorrow. Gracias, Senor."

She reached out for Matias's hand, aimed a nodding smile in Barth's direction and, without waiting for a response, headed off toward the back lot, child in tow. The connection hit Barth, causing him to reassess his decision. If he was sticking around for a day or two on the off chance of getting to know something about Estrella, he didn't see how he could get out of the house-raising. If Graciela expected it, he couldn't very well disappoint her and risk disappointing Estrella. Here he was, miles from home, deliberately removing himself from everyday entanglements, and he could feel himself falling, even slightly, into a web, but this was different. Despite the man's brusque manner, he was going with this. Tomorrow morning, seven o'clock. In the span of a week, the office chair filler had been transformed to vagabond voyager, and now, volunteer roustabout.

Barth walked into town, passing the laundry and heading toward the Blue Swallow, the forties-era adobe-walled motel near the town's center, now serving as an orienting landmark for him. The town was alive, not bustling, but alive, locals heading toward destinations with the preoccupied look Barth knew others had seen in him not so long ago. There were no skyscrapers here, Tucumcari was not yet that prosperous, but this was not a ghost town either, even though the empty railroad depot and its status as a stop on "America's Highway," old Route 66, suggested better times in decades past. Cars, bikes, and trucks stopped here from the highway, not like the old days, but this was still a stop, the largest between Amarillo and Albuquerque. Smaller, fewer trees here, despite the town's age, less shade to filter the straight, inundating rays of the hot sun. Now the heat was in his skin, not modulated by the wind pushing him back in his seat, whipping through his helmet vents.

He turned, heading north off the main street, into a residential neighborhood, far enough to find himself walking on the street's edge, past the section where sidewalks ended. He could see the country beyond the town, a sort of dreamscape if he raised his gaze high enough to eliminate the tops of the telephone poles and galvanized metal roofs from his vision. Briefly, he created for himself the illusion of entering a nature-bound sanctuary, a sensation he played with, enjoying its novelty. The solitude in his sight mirrored the solitude of his soul in this moment.

Barth was well aware of the alternating experience, during the last few days, of exposure to and contact with individual lives inhabiting his route, on the one hand, and the singleness of the thought conversations indulged while en route to the next stop. Immersing himself, for a time, in other lives, foreign to him, then reviewing each episode, looking for its connection, if any, with his own existence. To this point, he had a sense of disappointment in pursuing the idea of a connection, making comparisons and, invariably, finding his own life direction, if you could call it that, wanting. He'd begun his journey without a readily identifiable aim, nothing he could verbalize, but there was a strong need which had impelled him to hit the road. Now, a few days hence, he found that, instead of satisfying that vague, nebulous desire, whatever its source, he was hungry, his appetite whetted, even more than when he left Kansas City.

The thought was mildly disturbing to Barth, but there was a difference. A week ago he might have felt its presence, and let it be suppressed before reaching the surface of his conscious ruminations. Now, he was letting this disturbance linger and run its course, examining it openly, in short bursts, knowing he would do it again somewhere along the route. This expectation, by itself, represented a small, but significant change in this traveler's outlook, and the realization, he concluded, was a form of personal progress.

Estrella's story, and her person, made a strong impression on Barth, now attempting to figure out why he'd become preoccupied with this new actor in his road theater.

What am I hanging around for? I should be moving, now, not staying. What is it about her?

To be sure, there was the exotic, physical attraction of this woman stimulating his desire—that much was undeniable. It wasn't enough, however, to warrant the energy he was expending, certainly not enough to consider lingering in Tucumcari. Perhaps it was something of the character of this strong survivor that he admired, making her own way without the usual supports. The situation didn't entirely make sense to him.

I should just leave and be on my way.

He walked far enough in the direction of the north end of town to exclude all signs of civilization from his peripheral vision. In front of him lie the sands and scrub brush of the wilderness, mesas and isolated rock formations in reds, oranges and yellows in the far distance. Now his gaze caught the outline of an abandoned car, a rusting relic accentuating the romantic nature of the vista he was surveying. The landscape was met by the vivid bright blues and fluffy white cloud formations of an uncluttered southwest sky, undisturbed by any hint of motion. The abstract nature of the vision contrasted with the very concrete questions and feelings Barth was attempting to sort out. He stood there, on the edge of town, absorbing a summer horizon unlike any he'd ever known.

By the time he made it back to the truckstop it was late afternoon. He had eaten nothing since the morning and decided to grab something in the restaurant and tend to the cleaning of his bike later. After the long walk he was enjoying the sounds and the bustle of the crowd and the trucks pulling in and out of the lot. The first wave of the dinner shift was being seated. His own booth, he could see, was still unoccupied, waiting to be claimed by the midwestern biker.

Matias ran up to him, out of breath, just as Barth began scanning the menu.

"I sat on your motorcycle Mr. Barth, it's real cool."

"You didn't take off anywhere, did you?"

"No, you know I can't do that." Matias laughed.

"Get your homework done?"

"There's no homework on Sunday, that's silly. Mr. Barth, Grandma Graciela says you and the others are building her new house tomorrow."

"Yeah, that's right."

Barth was reminded of his commitment, one he couldn't recall having made. Matias was also a reminder of his incentive. Hell, he had nothing to lose, except for a late night, and, from what he could see, there wouldn't be that much going on here anyway. He'd eat, take it easy and get to bed early.

"Can you help me with my homework tomorrow, Mr. Barth?"

"I don't see why not."

"Thanks. I gotta go." Matias turned and started skipping up the aisle toward the front. He went to the counter and stopped next to his mother, who was standing by one of the tables, taking an order. She was wearing a long, black cotton dress, its hem almost touching simple, unadorned black leather sandals. The image Barth had was of the elegant mistress of an old Mexican hacienda, missing only the matching lace veil. Estrella bent slightly to listen to her son, then, in a deliberate motion, turned toward Barth, who caught her glance.

The men were polite, that wasn't a problem, but the language and cultural gulf separating them from the stranger could not have been overcome in years. An older man with a graying moustache, a black, ancient fedora, and a rawhide bolo tie held together by a large silver and turquoise clasp, was the unofficial foreman. He was slowly pacing the perimeter of the site, occasionally pausing, delivering short commands, in barely-audible Spanish. The other men were wearing white, wide-brimmed, tightly-woven straw ranch hats to block out the bright sun, while their new colleague sported a dilapidated, faded brown cotton baseball cap he'd stuffed in his saddlebags. Barth stuck out in this group, of course, but accepted his misfit status. He quietly followed the lead of the other men, assuming his place while unloading truckloads of lumber, concrete blocks and shingles. For their part, the men kept up a steady banter of jokes and loud exclamations without letup, talking around the stranger. Occasionally one would offer a cigarette to Barth, which he politely and gratefully declined, or, during breaks, swigs of iced tea, which he did not. A pit for the basement had already been dug out and a concrete floor poured, leveled, and set to cure. Now the foreman directed the others in the task of systematically hauling over the blocks as needed and the cement buckets that were filled by men operating a portable mixer. Barth, assuming a place in the group carrying the concrete blocks, quietly and happily threw himself into a rhythm of lifting and walking which mimicked the other men, optimizing the speed with which the work proceeded. The communal aspect of the enterprise, the voluntary coming together of this group, based solely on the need to be met, impressed the stranger from a world where workmen were bound together only temporarily, and then only by a guaranteed wage.

Just before noon the work stopped when three women arrived at the site with baskets of wrapped fresh tamales, spiced with Guajillo peppers, and a wagon with ceramic crocks of hot coffee and ice water. Barth recognized Graciela, the matriarch who would soon be living in the rising structure, and Matias, who ran over to him, grabbing his arm.

"Mr. Barth, can I sit on your bike again? Mama says I have to ask you."

"Sure, Matias, but I want you to do something for me. If I pay you five dollars, will you wash the bike? It really needs it, and I'll be too tired when we're finished here."

"You bet, right away, Mr. Barth."

Matias did a half-jump, half-skipping step, turned and ran, without looking back. Graciela smiled at Barth and walked toward the other women, heading to a spot about twenty feet to the north of the foundation. Barth's gaze followed the three women as they talked beyond his hearing and he continued watching as one of them, brandishing some sort of garden tool, began digging at a spot in the field. He could see one woman unwrapping her apron and grasping a handful of plants that she placed in the dugout hole, after which she hand-packed loose dirt around the roots. Curious, he tapped the arm of the man working next to him and pointed, making it clear he was asking a question.

"Snakeweed," he responded, adding "for arthritis," pointing to his knee. Later, Estrella would inform Barth that this was a traditional remedy used in the Sonora and that Graciela refused to be treated with anything in pill form. In her logic, pills were drugs, and drugs were the obvious cause of her son's death. She trusted only the local *curandero,* a folk healer, and his recommended combination of herbs, chiropractic, and spiritual arts, for her medical care.

The work proceeded smoothly the rest of the day, so quickly Barth could actually see the house taking shape. The cinder block walls weren't attractive, but the emphasis was on simplicity, cost and function, and the emerging structure met these requirements. As the walls began rising, pipes were laid in trenches dug for water lines, to be connected to the main outlet from the truckstop. Metal conduits were run from the rear of the structure for wiring to be installed by one of the men now busy nailing fresh-cut two-by-fours to hold the roof. Not a union electrician, Barth guessed. The house would be quite comfortable for Graciela, a place to call her own. She would have her own kitchen and bedroom for the first time since the flight across the border.

Barth kept his commitment to help with the heavy lifting and felt only minor back and shoulder pain at the end of the day, but this was enough to force a decision to get some rest and cancel the ride he had planned for the late afternoon on his newly-washed bike. He had another session with Matias at his booth, this time with reading homework, but only caught a few glimpses of Estrella that evening as she darted in and out of the kitchen area, exercising her generalship of the place. He continued to savor the moment of close contact he had enjoyed with her yesterday, knowing anything more was precluded by his leaving, probably in the next two days.

Barth was surprised when, by late afternoon the following day, the rough work was done, enough so that Graciela began moving in while the finishing work, including the painting of the exterior and wiring, was being completed. He was amused while watching men brush on the pink color Graciela had chosen for the house. Not just pink, but a bright, darkness-defying pink, one of many such colors which were not unusual here or in the Tejano regions from which most of the workers had come. He enjoyed the open sensuality of the vibrant, shimmering pink as he watched it applied, knowing that an attempt to do the same thing in his part of Kansas City would undoubtedly result in a citation for violating a municipal ordinance.

There was nothing more for Barth to do, so he sat idly by with a couple of the other men and relaxed until the foreman announced that enough had been accomplished for today. He would join the rest of the house-raising crew for a dinner by invitation in the restaurant, prepared by Graciela herself as thanks to her adopted family. For a brief moment, Barth felt accepted by part of this subculture.

As he stood up to leave, the foreman approached one of the men sitting next to him, spoke a few words and then, looking at Barth, motioned him to follow. The three walked back toward the truckstop until they reached one of the motel rooms. On entering it was apparent this had been Graciela's residence and their mission was to carry the remaining packed boxes to the house. Seeing how little was left in the place Graciela had called home until a few short days ago, Barth could only marvel at the speed of the communal house-raising and home relocation.

Barth picked up an antique portable record player by its handle and nestled a large cardboard box of records in his right hand. He knew, from Estrella's story, that neither of them had carried anything substantial during the harrowing trip across the border that night years ago, so the records he was transporting would have been acquired since then. He couldn't help being curious, but followed the two men with their loads back to the new house. Graciela was standing at the newly-connected sink, sorting cooking utensils into drawers and watching Telemundo on a small television resting on a shelf at eye level. She smiled as they entered, greeting the older foreman and nodding silently to Barth. The foreman, in turn, doffed his fedora, bending to kiss her on the cheek.

When Graciela saw what Barth was carrying she stopped her sorting and motioned with her hand, directing him to a small table against the front, still unpainted, drywall. Barth understood that he was to set up the player and eagerly complied. He placed it on the stand, opened its lid, and plugged it into an outlet that had been connected and screwed into the wall in the last hour. Following her implied instruction, and his own curiosity, Barth opened the box and began removing its contents, one item at a time. The records were old LPs and even older 78s, relics of musical entertainment Barth hadn't seen since childhood. He recalled unnumbered instances when he had visited his grandmother and played her records, perhaps of the same vintage. He'd been entranced by the magic of sound produced by the careful placing of a steel needle on thin black vinyl discs. Then the records had artist's names like Tommy Dorsey, Glenn Miller, Artie Shaw and Deanna Durbin. The records he was now sorting through listed performers completely foreign to him, names like Flaco Jimenez, Los Hermanos Cardenas, Jose Morante and Narciso Martinez, also designated on the label as "*El Huracan del Valle.*"

Barth lifted a 78 for a closer look, one with a cobalt blue label with gilt lettering, a Bluebird record, probably from the '30s or '40s. The song was "Panchita" and the artist was listed as "Lydia Mendoza y Familia." He noticed other 78s and LPs by the same singer, obviously one of Graciela's favorites. In the photos gracing the album covers the woman stared out at him with dark, inviting eyes, cradling an elaborately decorated acoustic guitar and wearing long, billowing, colorful dresses giving her the appearance of a blooming flower.

"La Alondra de la Frontera."

Graciela had noticed Barth's interest and dropped her chores to say her thanks and good-byes to the other two men as they left. She pointed at the album cover Barth had been studying and, when she realized her failure to be understood, bent down, picking out the record he had looked over a few seconds earlier, "Panchita." Graciela pointed to the outline of the flying bird on the label and, in a rare display of recognition, Barth understood.

"The Songbird of the Border."

"Si. La Alondra de la Frontera."

Graciela smiled at the success of her new student, but she intended to provide him a more important lesson. With Barth kneeling attentively on the unfinished wood floor, she searched through the box, retrieving another record, a recording titled "Mal Hombre," also by Lydia Mendoza. Her slender fingers lovingly cradled its edges, a tribute to its status as a cherished object, although its once shining surfaces had long since turned a dull black through decades of playing. Her look was reverence, as if she was holding the plastic crucifix hanging from a nail on the unpainted drywall behind them. In that case, however, the attitude did not represent so much a choice as it did the tacit recognition of a common thread in the fabric of her life, like the air she breathed. It was obvious that Graciela had listened to this record hundreds of times in her lifetime. It was just as obvious that she was thrilled to share her old joy with the gringo stranger who seemed interested.

Through the pops, hisses and other ingrooved imperfections, the power and authority of the voice of Lydia Mendoza exerted a hypnotic hold on Barth. Although he couldn't understand the lyrics, he guessed the singer was telling the tale of betrayal by her lover. This was a strong, determined voice—Lydia Mendoza was singing of her own certain survival while delivering a dolorous condemnation. Barth was hooked, nodding in vigorous approval. With the addition of a pedal steel guitar and a Southern accent, this singer could match any expression of anguish and strength in, say, the recordings of Kitty Wells or Tammy Wynette.

"Gracias, Senora. Muchas Gracias."

Barth stood up, making an exaggerated bow to Graciela in an attempt to express the thanks he felt but could not otherwise communicate. Graciela smiled, grasping his hand with both her hands. She knew she'd made a convert, and, more importantly, knew something of consequence about this stranger.

"I'll see you at the dinner tonight. I need to change my clothes."

Barth grabbed his dirty shirt for emphasis and stepped toward the open front door while Graciela nodded, her silent smile following him.

Inside the restaurant, Barth surveyed the tables, looking for a place to sit. As he was searching, Graciela vigorously motioned for him to sit by her at the counter. She was speaking to Estrella in Spanish. Barth listened intently to a conversation he couldn't understand. Graciela was animated and emphatic in her voice and gestures, directed to her daughter for a purpose he could not guess. He occasionally picked up isolated words and phrases, "la musica" was one such example, but, more importantly, he understood that he was a more than tangential subject of their exchange. At several points Estrella's mother paused, turning her head and looking directly at him, smiling as she did so.

What in hell is going on here? I hope these two are not arranging a marriage.

He sensed a difference of opinion between them regarding a topic he could not divine, but it appeared that, after a couple minute's discussion, Estrella had reluctantly agreed with her mother's insistence on her position. As Estrella rose from the counter, Graciela looked at Barth, smiling again, nodding her assent to him while pulling her brightly colored rebozo over her shoulder and holding a lit cigarette out away from the stool. Barth, for his part, returned a polite smile that didn't betray his puzzlement regarding the conclusion whose subject he could not fathom.

"Mama says I should take you to the dancing tonight for the workers." Estrella informed him of the party planned in conjunction with the house-raising. Graciela had made arrangements for the celebration to take place in a warehouse on the north edge of town that doubled as a dancehall, and, according to Estrella's account, her mother believed he would feel more at ease under the circumstances if his invitation was accompanied by the offer of an escort. Estrella seemed a less-than-eager conscript for this mission, but was unwilling to engage in prolonged resistance to her mother, especially in this public setting. Barth understood her dilemma, but chose not to demonstrate any empathy.

"Great, I'm sure I'll enjoy this. Thanks for the invitation, this is very generous of you. This is an experience I don't want to miss."

Barth smiled, turning his head in unspoken thanks toward Graciela, who was observing the exchange from her counter seat. Estrella explained the logistics of the evening to Barth. She would be picking him up in her truck around eight and driving them, Barth, Matias and Graciela, to the dance. The stage was set for the next unanticipated venture in this vagabond's travels. Barth was anxious for this next episode to begin.

The mariachi band paused, regaining its collective breath after the last number, then a large, middle-aged man with slicked-down, jet-black hair stepped onto the stage, showered by loud bursts of applause and shouts. Without introduction, he launched into a slow, ballad-style love song, his body swaying widely and gracefully, his eyes fixing on the adoring women in the audience, his audience. Estrella was no less enamored of his voice and confident presence than the other women. He reminded her of the singer Juan Gabriel, the Divo de Juarez, who could be heard on any of the local Hispanic-oriented pop radio stations. As a young girl she'd listened to the song "No Tengo Dinero" so many times it had seemed like the background music of her life. Juan Gabriel had come from a poor family background like hers, singing his way to stardom in churches, parties and weddings, much like the performer in her hearing, and she was feeling a connection between her past and present. At this moment she was replaying pleasant memories of her childhood, a seldom-experienced aspect of her Tucumcari life, except via the megawatt border radio stations whose signals penetrated the New Mexico night.

Barth, sitting next to her, had no inkling of Estrella's reveries, but he was, nonetheless, enjoying her open smile as she sat quietly intent during the performance. He couldn't understand the words to the song, but the tenor of its message was obvious, and he imagined it was the song itself eliciting her enjoyment. Barth was also caught up in the singer's energy, unmistakably directed at each of the dancers and seated admirers. This wasn't the polished Latino pop he was used to, not the restrained sound of Chan Romero's *Besame Mucho* or Richie Valens' *La Bamba*, not even the dance rhythms of Tito Puente, the only Hispanic recordings ingrained from his own distant past. This guy was giving his audience everything he had—there would be no second takes. Barth himself fell under the spell cast by the singer, even as he wondered how the man with the boot-blacked hair and middle-age spread was inviting a reaction best described as enchantment. *Is this ability a common trait in this culture, or is it only coincidence that I was introduced to the charms of Lydia Mendoza a few hours ago?*

As the singer left the stage the band resumed its fast-paced energetic style, punctuated with sharp brass flourishes. Couples in the audience began dancing with a wild, fierce energy, determined to leave it on the floor. Now one of the band stepped forward, an accordion strapped around his shoulder and, as if on cue, a young boy, possibly his son, stepped out beside him, dressed in traditional Mexican costume and holding a *bandoneon*, a smaller relation to the man's instrument. This was truly a family affair, through the ties of blood, culture and, more than likely, histories of their journeys. Now the Tejano music of the border took center stage, with polka-like rhythms rousing the whirling couples to even more feverish exertions.

Out of nowhere, an urge to join the crowd seized Barth, and, before he could suppress it, he stood up, extending his hand to a surprised Estrella, content up to this point to watch and listen. Perhaps entranced by the emotional aura of the crooner's performance and its associations for her, she didn't hesitate, taking Barth's hand and jumping to her feet in a manner as out of character for her as it was pleasing to him. Without a word, they moved to the edge of the dancing throng and began imitating, as best they could, the ritualized back-and-forth movements of couples within their sight. They adopted the beat of the loud bass as their own rhythm, and the focus of their looks became each other's eyes. Their mutual shyness was temporarily set aside. Even during those dances in which the only physical contact occurred while they swung each other with their hands clasped, Barth thought he sensed warmth beyond mere politeness.

He had a reserve of energy he hadn't suspected after the last two days and was intent, as was his partner, on using as much of it as possible on the dance floor. Onlookers, including Graciela, were amazed and entertained by Estrella's joyous abandonment, a striking contrast to the controlled taskmaster whose discipline made the truckstop the success it had become under her management.

During breaks they sat together, gathering strength for the next round and engaging in light conversation. Their smiles, now mutually obvious, filled in the gaps. When the evening finally came to an end, around eleven, tomorrow being another workday, Barth felt drained and exultant, walking quietly beside Estrella. Graciela had taken Matias to her new house an hour ago.

The shyness and reserve both had exhibited a few hours ago now returned, although neither seemed uncomfortable. Estrella, who'd been the reluctant escort, smiled to herself as they walked to the truck and took their seats, without any words spoken. Within minutes they were parked in front of Barth's room. Ordinarily, he would have leaned over to kiss her goodnight, but he was anxious and didn't want to risk, despite his rising desire, the possible violation of cultural rules. He reminded himself that, for all his fascination and attraction to this woman, he was still a drifter passing through her life and it was presumptuous to act otherwise.

"Well," he finally stammered, "I had a fantastic time, Estrella, you're a great dancer and this is something I won't ever forget."

"I'm very glad, Mr. Barth, I had fun too."

"You know, you really can call me Gregory, or Greg."

He wondered just what she had meant by "fun."

"Yes, Gregory."

"Anyway, I think I'm finally going to take a ride out to the mesas tomorrow. I need to at least get a look at them while I'm here."

He slid in his seat toward the door and grasped the handle.

"I have not been there and I want to see it also. Is it possible I can go with you?"

Barth could hardly believe his ears. This wasn't only a wish fulfilled; he knew this woman well enough to realize there was nothing typical in her request. It took him all of a millisecond to respond.

"Of course, that would be great. How 'bout breakfast and take off around nine?" Only with great effort could Barth manage to contain his excitement.

"That's good." She saw no reason to elaborate further.

"Great, then. Goodnight."

Barth swung the door open and stepped out, confident she had not detected his suppressed jubilation.

"Goodnight."

She smiled and, once the door was shut, started the truck, driving off into the night.

Until this moment Barth had wondered whether it was a wise decision to stay in Tucumcari, but staying had made possible this fantastic stroke of luck. Another night, another world, but he had shared this one, for a few hours, with a truly beautiful woman who'd consented to spend her evening with him. He wasn't a part of this subsection of the world, but that, of course, was exactly the point.

Barth was incredulous at the idea that he could persuade anyone to ride with him under any circumstances, but the fact that Estrella had asked for this ride was something on the order of astounding. He couldn't, of course, let on the fact of his amazement, nor must he do anything to convey the anxiety he felt at the prospect of safely and competently transporting this exotic passenger. He was, however, consoled by the thought that he wouldn't have to struggle to make conversation.

"Sure, it's easy, all you need to do is sit back, hold on and relax. I'll do the work, you enjoy the scenery. If you're afraid, just tap my shoulder and we'll turn back, that's all."

Barth hoped his face wouldn't betray the lie of his complete lack of experience with a passenger. Should he overcome this hurdle, he determined to manage the task he had set himself with a sufficient show of confidence to allay any fears she might have. Estrella, on hearing the word "afraid," decided she had no choice but to reaffirm her acceptance of the invitation. Besides, she was intrigued by Gregory Barth, this newcomer in her life, and convinced, through her observations of his interactions with Matias, that he could be trusted. It also occurred to her that, in her years in Tucumcari, she'd seen very little of the local scenery beyond the town's edge. Finally, the ride afforded the opportunity to escape her responsibilities for a short time, all she could afford, but the closest thing to a break in her routine she could remember.

"Well, let's go now, Gregory, as long as you are not too fast and we are back here before five." She swung her right leg over the seat and positioned her feet on the pegs while Barth held the bars. He got on, started the bike, and slowly let out the clutch, attempting to detect the differences in handling the bike would require with a passenger. When he reached the friction zone and the bike began edging forward, he pulled lightly on the throttle and started heading out of the parking lot. Once he turned onto the road and shifted, he began feeling confident he could manage the handling demands and perhaps even enjoy the opportunity to see the beautiful New Mexico scenery with this beautiful New Mexico woman.

Damn, life is good, what more could I ask for than to be here, now?

He laughed to himself at the reference, but it was true, this was an exhilarating experience, underscoring the incredible nature, the vital necessity, of his middle-aged foray into this unknown world. The sight of clumps of pinon, common throughout this area but foreign to his eye, served to reinforce a sense of enchantment and the knowledge that he was, indeed, a very lucky man.

Estrella, in the meantime, took a deep breath, settling her arms around Barth's torso, as if it was the most natural act in the world, venturing a look over his right shoulder to see what lie ahead. She loved the sensation of the wind in her face and the idea of being free, no matter how briefly, from the rest of her world. She was amused at the observation that it had taken the catalyst of the gringo biker passing through to provide a larger window on the land she called home all these years. The little she had learned about Barth in the last couple days also made it obvious she and her rider had traveled very different roads to get to this ride.

She tapped Barth's shoulder, pointing to the entrance of the road leading in the direction of the mountains. Although they hadn't discussed a specific route beforehand, Barth slowed, leaning into the turn without hesitating. It really didn't matter, he reasoned, any direction they headed would provide vistas he'd never seen, and he was convinced by now that they were all spectacular. He trusted her judgment implicitly, and feeling her firm hold led Barth to believe that the trust was mutual. The act of riding two-up on the bike reinforced this feeling since, unlike four-wheeled travel, it required constant give-and-take adjustments on the part of both rider and passenger. Occasionally, while accelerating and decelerating, he felt her body shifting against his. The sensation wasn't an unexpected aspect of riding two-up, but for Barth, with no prior experience, this was entirely new. At first he tried making shifts and speed changes as smooth as possible, minimizing any distress Estrella might be experiencing from sudden jolts. Gradually, imperceptibly, sensing no hint of discomfort from his clinging passenger, Barth began investigating these sensations in a subtle, deliberate manner. He could feel the changing tension of her arms around his waist and was aware of his enjoyment of the sensation, especially when she tightened her grip during acceleration or while leaning into turns. Early on in the ride he developed, apparently without her knowledge, the ability to tease the throttle slightly, inducing a tightening of the hold of his rider's arms.

What might have been considered a distraction from enjoyment of the boundless natural beauty of the desert surrounding them had become a preoccupation he wanted to explore further. As long as his movements were executed in conjunction with oncoming curves or other road conditions requiring changes in speed or lean, chances of discovery were low. These sensations were provoking erotic feelings, and Barth began to question himself.

Is this pure lust I'm feeling, is it something more? What is this?

The forced lack of spoken communication and face-to-face contact under the circumstances heightened the intensity of these sensations. The situation was perfect, in this respect. He could allow himself the exploration, these feelings without acknowledging them in any overt manner. He could wonder, even fantasize, about his growing affection for Estrella, while simultaneously enjoying the reality of her closeness.

The opportunity to commune with another human being in this setting was reason enough for the ride, especially after the solitary miles he'd traveled in the course of his westward odyssey, but the present experience was eliciting a reaction the unromantic Barth couldn't have anticipated. Anything, including this, was within the realm of possibility, but the potential, much less the realization, hadn't been a significant element of his conscious thought for years. Barth reflected briefly on his disastrous marriage, many years distant, his subsequent uninspiring dating history, and what he realized was his implicit assumption of a continuing existence absent any sustained heterosexual relationship. Until now. The rhythmic physical prompts from his unsuspecting passenger aroused in Barth a flood of sensations and thoughts both unsettling and exciting, another in the series of unexpected twists and turns in his continuing adventure.

The first road sign in miles, announcing an approaching crossroads, diverted his attention. The demand of this external aspect of his reality also had an immediate impact on Barth's musing regarding his feelings for this woman he had known for but a few short days.

What sense does this make? I'm going my way, she's staying here in the life she's made for herself. Exploring these feelings is ridiculous. I know it, I'm sure this isn't anything more than a pleasant interlude for her. I'm riding on and she's taking care of business, including her mother and Matias. Don't be stupid, just enjoy this for what it is, a great day, a great ride in the desert with an intriguing woman, that's all this is and all it should be. Chill out and ride.

Barth followed the dictates of these conclusions, relaxing while slowing the bike during the approach to the barren, hardly noticeable intersection, and again as he resumed, without stopping, the trip toward two towering red rock formations in the distance. The dark shadows on this side of the rocks provided an excuse to stop and obtain relief from the midday heat, and the possibility of cooling down from the stirrings of emotion, attraction, and lust he had been coping with during the last hour on the desert road. The shadows were not a mirage, a conclusion confirmed by the sensation of a distinct coolness as the first fingers of shade reached out, touching the path of the rolling intruders. As the road entered the gap between the two natural monuments, the sense of unending openness of the desert surroundings was quickly supplanted by a feeling of being closed in by the solidity of the permanent walls. The guest-riders couldn't know as they approached the twin stone towers that the sense of awe they were experiencing was mutual; their wonder at the existence of the massive sky-blocking monuments was shared. Barth slacked off the throttle, downshifted, slowed to a crawl, then pulled over to what he thought was a perfect spot for a more leisurely-paced viewing. Estrella expressed no surprise at the stop, carefully alighting at her chauffeur's signal.

"This is incredible, you can't imagine how different this is from where I live. There are no mountains, only buildings are this tall."

"I think I can see these rocks from the roof of the diner, but being here is very different. I wish Matias will be able to see this."

"He really should. Maybe we can bring him out here."

Barth knew the probability this would happen was next to zero, as did Estrella, but felt it was okay to say it anyway. She smiled, but said nothing.

As they walked toward the narrowest part of the gap between the formations, with only the width of the road separating the walls, the sun's light was blocked, and they had the strange sensation of sudden darkness in the middle of a very bright summer day. The only sound was their footsteps on the old road. Barth had no desire to break the silence with a casual, gratuitous utterance, but the lack of conversation magnified the tension he was experiencing. Estrella, for her part, was acutely aware of the implications of this situation, but was also absorbed in the fact of this striking interlude, in terms of activity, scenery, and company. Venturing forth like this with Gregory, a man she'd known for only four days, elicited thoughts of the last major trip she had taken from home, ten years ago, in the more complete darkness of the packing crate. Then she had an excitement based on fear, fear of the ride itself and fear of an unknown destination, all experienced in the context of necessity, lacking real options. Now, she was venturing into unknown territory by choice, and was feeling no fear. Instead, she was somehow able to bring herself to trust this experience and the man she had freely chosen as her guide. The dancing last evening had convinced her she could feel safe with him and relax, enjoying the sensation of holding this man in her arms as much as he enjoyed his role in creating it.

They stopped, looking out at the segment of landscape framed between the dark walls of the natural cavern where they stood.

"I can't get over the beauty of this place. It's amazing we can be here all by ourselves, like being alone in an art museum."

Barth had felt the need to say something to maintain contact, lacking the excuse for silence provided by the bike. She sensed his anxiety, but could only smile, nodding her assent. Nonstop conversations with regulars and strangers never presented a problem for this woman in her natural habitat, the daily hustle and bustle of the truckstop, but this was different. The feelings stirred by the power of the surrounding vistas were matched by the wonders they were experiencing within, barely contained tensions exerting control of their attention, beyond the reach of their senses. Estrella had been held back by another force that Barth couldn't know, her history, but its grip on her was wilting in the hot sun.

It was then that Barth extended his hand, gently grasping hers, given in turn without protest or surprise. The unspoken connection assumed a physical aspect, different than the contact of custom while dancing last evening. The desert explorers continued walking together, silently pacing in a direction that led nowhere in particular, if it mattered. Estrella looked up at her partner, returning Barth's undisguised smile with one of her own, then quickly turned her head away.

What is happening now, what is this?

Barth had no readily available answer to the question he posed to himself as they continued, approaching the end of the closed-in area where the road re-entered the unshaded desert. Re-emerging into the afternoon sun, the blinding light striking their eyes required a momentary pause. Barth and Estrella stopped, surveying the wild open space, as eloquent in its silence as the hand-holding couple that stood there, absorbing its beauty. A minute later they turned, retracing their steps, still hand-in-hand, each savoring the silent presence of the other. Their footsteps, the only sound to be heard during the return to the bike, fell together, synchronized, an unspoken cue for Barth's next act.

Impulsively, he stopped, placing his free hand around her waist, pulling her towards him and shifting his weight in one unmistakable motion. She understood the move without need for translation and complied readily, willingly, as she had last evening. Together, swaying and turning, they smiled at each other, duplicating their steps on the dance floor. There was a gentle, lilting quality in their movement matching the thin, light desert atmosphere surrounding them.

"You are a good dancer," she offered.

"It must be the desert air."

A minute after they had begun waltzing in the sand they stopped, openly laughing at their sashaying shenanigans. Barth leaned forward, kissing Estrella's forehead, as much as he dared with his newfound dancing partner. She said nothing but continued smiling and holding his hand while they resumed their walk to the bike.

"It's nice to be crazy once in awhile, don't you think?"

Barth made the simple, honest observation without expecting a response.

"Yes, you are the *vaquero loco*, riding into town, and now I am the *vaquera loco*, this is the truth." She laughed at her own observation. At the same time, she realized she hadn't laughed like this for as long as she could recall, except for the required responses to her customers' bad jokes and lewd remarks. Her words and actions were unforced, immediate, unfiltered reactions to the openness of the natural setting and the undeniable attraction cultivated in the beautifully barren landscape. Anticipating the inevitable end of this brief interlude, this interruption in her life, Estrella resolved that she would not question it further. Simply, uncharacteristically, she would enjoy the respite from her routine while it lasted.

Barth, meanwhile, was at a loss to explain the course events had taken in the last couple days of his life, much less to predict where they were leading, but there was one, single fact beyond dispute. His interest in this intriguing, independent, beautiful woman was becoming a strong, dominating attraction. He knew his lingering presence in Tucumcari, staying for the dance and the house-raising, was for the sole purpose of making some form of continued contact with her possible. He also realized, mirroring Estrella's thoughts, this prolonged stop on his westward journey would end at some point in the immediate future. He accepted this conclusion, but couldn't escape the anxiety he was experiencing as he confronted and acknowledged the inevitable ending of this chapter of the unfolding adventure. A mixture of the delight at discovery of these newfound feelings and the melancholy that came with the realization of the temporary nature of their relationship absorbed him as they reached the bike. Barth noted the reflected glint of the sun off the chrome fenders and remembered to compliment Matias's work to Estrella. They seated themselves in silence and, without hesitating, Barth started the bike and followed the slow turn in the road to begin the return trip. Both riders understood the turn their relationship had taken in the last couple hours, a change evident in the tight hold she had around his waist and, on his part, the certainty with which he could now interpret her grasp. The mutual affection of the riding vaqueros was unspoken, but undeniable.

Hours later, the riders occupied a booth, lazily taking in the blazing sunset through the west window and ruminating, in silence, over the events of the day. Supper, with Matias, had included the spicy *Albondigas Locas*, a rich soup that was a diner specialty. Graciela, occupied with the supervision of the final tasks associated with the move into the nearly finished house, stopped by to pick up an order of the soup. She thanked Barth for his help in raising the structure and easily persuaded Matias to leave with her and watch television.

Sipping coffee, Barth and Estrella exchanged awkward smiles, enjoying each other's company, wondering what would happen next. Estrella asked Barth, as she had before, for particulars of his everyday life back in Kansas City. He patiently answered her questions, wondering why she'd be interested. After all, he thought, *If my life there is so damn interesting, what am I doing out here?*

Barth asked her again about growing up in Mexico and her coming to Tucumcari, but elicited only a reluctance, in marked contrast to the detailed disclosure of her past a few days ago. Perhaps, he thought, her reluctance had the same source as his own, a predisposition to view the past as lacking any intrinsic attraction. In fact, Estrella's reticence was a product of their increasing familiarity. It had somehow been easier to divulge details of her personal history to a sympathetic stranger passing through than to this man with whom she had become close enough to share a motorcycle seat.

"Are you thinking about the ride? Did you enjoy yourself out there today?"

"Of course I did, Vaquero Barth, what do you think, I dance and ride with all the bikers that stop here, I have dinner with each one and they meet my mother and Matias?"

She didn't attempt to hide her laugh, realizing that, even after the last few days, Barth needed reassurance. She reached a hand across the table, covering his, a gesture signifying the desire she was feeling as well as her response to his question.

They exchanged small talk, occasionally interrupted by patrons paying their respects to the manager or employees with concerns demanding her attention. Barth was patient through all this-he had, after all, been the beneficiary of her undivided attention for as long a period of time as anyone in this place. Gradually, the dinner crowd was reduced to a few incoming stragglers. Estrella gave parting instructions to the counter manager and nodded to Barth, signaling him to follow her outside.

They walked together in the cool evening air, past Barth's ride and room, heading straight toward the rear of the complex and the uncluttered night horizon. He made a few remarks about the clear sky, about being able to see so many stars and the brightness of the moon, stating the obvious because he could think of nothing else to say. The silence between them was making him anxious. She nodded, agreeing with a simple "Yes, Yes, that's true, you're right," for the same reasons and to let him know, without elaboration, that she was still with him.

Barth thought, *this is nice*, a memory he'd savor in a few days, but this was the awkward time, things had gone as far as they were going to go, as far as they should go.

He knew this, as much as he had fantasized otherwise, and was struggling to accept the fact that, things being what they were, it was time to face facts, to start making the transition to being elsewhere. Out of nowhere, without explanation, the words and music of a childhood memory intruded, Marty Robbins' song, *El Paso*. None of this was evident to anyone but him, not Estrella, keeping pace as they approached the last of the detached motel units, the one she called home.

She knew, of course, that, despite the events of the past days, the ending was near, and expected it. She had, however, also become frantic, without letting it be known, especially to Gregory. There had arisen in her, especially today, an acute awareness that she was letting herself close to something that had never been part of her life, an experience she knew, at some level, was a vital component of living. That is, for most people, but one which she, out of necessity, then out of a need to survive and, finally, out of habit, had denied herself. The satisfaction of the life she'd made for Graciela and Matias, and herself, was suddenly, unexpectedly undermined by the realization she could feel, walking with Gregory. Estrella sensed deprivation and resentment she would never have allowed herself to consider before this moment, which was different, in one important respect. Now, now in this instant, she was not lacking in one single, critical element.

They reached the room at the end of the row, her home. She took Barth's hand, directing him to the concrete step that served as a porch. They lingered, silently, under the light of the single naked bulb hanging over their heads, while she searched for her keys. She opened the door, leaving the key in the lock, and turned to Gregory with a fierce, wild-eyed look. Barth, who'd been dreading the moment, desiring to get this over without unnecessary dawdling, was thrown off guard, completely befuddled. He leaned into her, extending an arm, and offered himself for the obligatory goodnight kiss.

The two arms enveloping his body were filled with a strength of purpose and passion which startled Barth, catching him completely by surprise. She pulled herself into him as he stood there, for the split second it took to interpret her touch. Her eyes were open to his as he bent to kiss her, kiss her in a way leaving no doubt regarding the intensity of his own suppressed feelings. In the passing of a second the reservations, the rational restraints governing their behavior, all fell away, so completely there wasn't time to exhibit surprise. They kissed, held each other and, without a word, continued in the natural course of their conversations of the last few days, when they might easily have done otherwise. Estrella firmly grasped his arm as they entered her room, crossing the threshold to their desired unknown.

Perhaps it was a sense of the press of shared time, a commodity they wouldn't waste, that jettisoned preliminaries. Barth uttered a lone, pleading "Estrella" as they fell together, still holding each other, in slow motion, on the single bed against the south wall. She only smiled, returning his look, her eyes clearly visible even in the dim light leaking through slivered openings in the front window curtains. They fumbled, fiddled and accommodated while continuing to kiss—touching, exploring and pushing against each other in a fevered rush of unleashed desire and unabated groping, their bodies awake and responsive. In the midst of the most universal of human experiences, they were immersed in the miracle of the perfect fit and fluid shared rhythms. They were excitedly, deliberately submerged in the smells, tastes and touches of the other they had barely sampled, though imagined, in the last hours.

Neither Estrella nor Barth felt obligated to utter anything other than random, emphatic, simple affirmations of understanding requiring no translation. For Barth, Estrella's open physical warmth was savored as no experience he'd ever had with a woman. He could hardly believe his fortune, that she would share herself with him so completely, but he did not question—the feeling of his hand sliding down the soft skin of her back and legs, her long hair falling on his cheek and forehead, these were immediately accepted fortunes.

Estrella, despite her overlearned caution with men, was convinced her impulsive act was justified. The hands that held her and the lips kissing hers were communicating tenderness and desire she'd found herself imagining with Barth. Now that she had come this far, there was no thought of turning back, just as there had been no such thought when she'd gone through hell that night, years ago, during the arduous journey to Tucumcari. Letting herself follow her instinctive yearning, she smiled in the awareness of her actions, in the fulfillment of desire. By this time, scant minutes after shutting the door to the outside world behind them, they had plunged, body and soul, into their private, shared version of paradise.

The "ordinary" charge of this most intense encounter was magnified, for each of them, by struggles that normally were dormant, nearly extinguished, elements of everyday existence. For Barth, the detached acknowledgment that he of course craved the saving pleasure of intense human contact had long been supplanted by the assumption that this basic need wasn't a realistic expectation in his life. He had resigned himself to this conclusion for such a long time that he rarely bothered to examine it, convincing himself, through years of practice, that he preferred the comfort of his existence. It had dawned on him, however, during the last week, that one component of his alarm at the news of Dave's girlfriend was his own unease. Not only the usual reaction of losing some contact, no matter how sporadic, with a long-time confidant, to his new relationship, but also the disturbing question of his own fortune in this regard. Was he actually satisfied with the life he had made for *himself*, or had he just built a reasonable rationalization upon which he placed an automatic, unquestioned reliance? The discomfort experienced during that long-ago lunch with Dave was now magnified to an intensity and immediacy that shocked him. It did not, however, inhibit him from giving himself to the woman whose arms were clutching his body with a strength and desire matching his own.

Estrella had experienced her own struggle in the last few days, one requiring her to surmount the facts and obstacles of her own history. Her reluctance to become involved, to any degree, with the opposite sex, was the product of long training and astute, intelligent observation. In her life, men had generally been threatening, abusive, or unreliable. She would never forget the treatment her mother had endured at the hands of her father, and, of course, the treachery of her uncle was branded on her soul. Her own little brother, who she dearly loved, had secretly left and abandoned his own family, leaving her and her mother to fend for themselves in an unprotected excuse for a home. She could at least forgive this. Manuel had only done what was reasonable and typical under the circumstances. His death, however, had reminded her of the other ways men had abandoned her. Even Matias would one day leave her, in a more natural way, she hoped. This entrenched personal history reminded her that she was deliberately making herself vulnerable to this new man in her life, one she knew, from the beginning, would be leaving.

Why did I let this happen, make this happen?

As soon as she asked herself the question, it was answered, emphatically, by luscious kisses and the tender warm hold of Gregory, her Gregory. However temporary their liaison, Estrella would not deny herself this chance of living, right now, of releasing anger and resentment, unjustly grafted on the person of all the men she encountered, and trapping her, all at the same time. She harbored no illusions. She knew this was as evanescent as the night, but, just as she had at other times in her life, she summoned the courage and determination to enter this *terra incognita*, something she had long suspected, even while avoiding it.

Neither of the lovers, in the midst of shared ecstasy, had any but the most fleeting thoughts of the morning after. Barth kissed Estrella with an intensity belying any semblance of the quiet, passive observer familiar to his friends and she, in return, received his kisses, giving him her own, with a deliberate throwing off of the control that enabled her to accomplish so much in the parts of her life visible to others. For the landlocked lovers, it was as if they had taken the heavy ropes mooring them to their lives and cast them off, their eyes wide open to the prospect of drifting who-knows-where. Right now it didn't matter.

Throughout the night the couple fell into the cycles of embrace, collapse, and exploration. They were letting themselves become playful and passionate, repeatedly crossing barriers they had made for themselves in sexually-charged situations over the course of years. As their reserves of energy became depleted, both souls were nevertheless experiencing fulfillment of desire for tactile contact with living that had too long been denied.

Eventually, the demands of their bodies asserted themselves in the form of the need for sleep, even in this once-in-a-lifetime night. The rhythm of their breathing became more regular, even and synchronized as they curled up in their nocturnal nest, still entangled, giving in to the inevitable. The heat of the day was long behind them, but this was of no importance as far as the two limp bodies were concerned.

When Barth awoke it was already seven and he knew he could easily lapse into another couple hours of sleep, but he was absorbed in the undeniable fact of the night he'd just spent in this bed. Estrella was missing, but his alarm passed as he realized she was likely attending to her professional obligations, not to mention Matias. He was somewhat dazed as he propped himself up on his outstretched arms, but had no difficulty recalling the evening and Estrella, indulging himself for the next few seconds with a cascading replay of the events and sensations of the night. Despite his lingering fatigue he had a distinct sense of being very much alive and a desire to rise and rejoin the rest of the human race.

When he entered the restaurant he was unnoticed by the noisy breakfast crowd and glad for the anonymity. He sat in the back and ordered the requisite coffee for starters, scanning the front as he did so but not asking for Estrella's whereabouts. She did eventually make her appearance, joining him in the booth.

They were sitting together, immersed in a mutual silence, mulling their vain attempts to explain to themselves what had happened. For Barth, what he had experienced was a reawakening, a confirmation of a part of him which, if contemplated at all, was in the abstract, something so distant in his past he couldn't actually recall it, not in any real sense. Now he couldn't easily control the stirrings of personal desire which had lay dormant, but, without any firm sense of direction to override his inertia, he was afraid of the effect he might be having on the beautiful, exotic spirit sitting across from him. This woman had shared something with him that hardly existed in his awareness a day ago. Unless he knew his own desire now, he had no right to disrupt her world any more than he had already.

For Estrella the last hours revealed to her a need—*was that what it was?* Unlike Barth, she had not even a distant memory with which she could, if she wished, draw a comparison. Her experiences with her father, her uncle, and her brother had formed the basis for her attitude toward the men in her life. It had never occurred to her that relationships with men could end otherwise, and this assumption wasn't shaken by her night with the *vaquero* Gregory. The surprise, the thing she could hardly believe, was her response to this man, letting him come this close. She was deeply puzzled by the strength of her passion, especially since it hadn't seemed like a struggle for her. She had acted as if the evening together was the most natural thing in the world, and perhaps it was, but she couldn't answer the nagging whys in her consciousness. Why had she made the choice that made the evening possible? Why now, why this man, why had this reached this point in a few short days, and why couldn't she make any sense of this situation as she sat here?

The silence between them was not a silence of denial; their periodic glances at each other confirmed this conclusion. Barth and Estrella felt a shared confusion, but neither would deny the seismic shift in the nature of their relationship, whatever it was now. And neither had any expectation that they could articulate to themselves, much less verbalize. Barth was absorbed in a mix of conflicting desires consuming him since the turnaround point of the afternoon bike ride. The mutuality of the attraction between himself and Estrella was unmistakable, not the wish-fulfilling fantasy he had indulged in his meeting with Ina at the campfire gathering. This time, however, he had a valid reason for hesitation. While the strangers of the night in the Texas hills could have had no expectations beyond the confines of that evening, no such assumptions applied to the couple facing each other in this Tucumcari truckstop. The relationship held at least a potential for more. Barth knew this, but he was also conscious of the problem on the immediate horizon.

Where is this going, where does she want to go with this, what expectations, if any, does this woman have?

"Estrella, if you don't know this already, I've become very fond of you, and Matias, and Graciela these past few days. Dancing with you and riding with you, I can't tell you how you've made me feel, you're an incredible woman, I never expected to meet someone like you, Never…."

Barth stopped in mid-thought, elaboration wasn't necessary. It was only required that he make his feelings plain, although he had reservations. His assertion of affection was belied by the stress evident in his facial expression.

"Yes, Gregory, I know, I also am surprised, I also don't expect things like this to happen to me, so I don't think about these things, not now, not for a long time. My life here is the same for many years, Matias and my mother. I accept this, our life is good here, but you come, and I don't know."

This admission, from the woman Barth had sized up as determined and self-assured, shook him, as he realized the impact he was having on her and the burden of responsibility he had willingly, if unwittingly, assumed.

"I'm sorry, I've just enjoyed myself with you so much, I let myself stay here so I could see more of you, and here we are. I don't know what to do. All I know is, I don't want to do anything to hurt you. I hope you believe me, Estrella."

"I know, Gregory, I know. I know you are a good man, I know you don't want to hurt me or anybody. I know this."

Barth couldn't hope to guess the basis of this woman's standard for judging the goodness in men.

"I'd like to stay, I enjoy every minute I spend with you, and I think maybe, if I did stay, you might feel the same way. I also think if I stay, then I leave, that won't be good for you, and we know it won't be good for Matias. Right now I'm just a guy with a motorcycle to him. If I hang around here much longer it won't be good when I leave."

Already, a palpable presence between them was the renewed awareness of the assumption that Barth was leaving, probably soon. While they were openly acknowledging a budding affection toward each other, they had quietly come to the realization that this embryonic relationship was coming to an end. They were realists, and they knew this conversation had to take place.

"I know Gregory, I know you are right. I have been thinking about these things also. Even when we are out riding I know these things, I know you will leave here. I also know how much I enjoy being with you. These days are good for you and me, but we must go on. I know that, Gregory, I know that."

She squeezed his hand, affirming the bond they had strengthened during the last few minutes, and again stealing an opportunity for the sensual pleasure of his touch.

"Estrella, you really can't imagine how you've made me feel the last few days. I don't know whether you understand this, but I didn't think it was possible for me to feel like I do now."

"Yes, maybe I don't understand."

She wasn't being dismissive of his feelings, but, at this point, she felt the wisest thing they could do was avoid further exploration. She was beginning to sense that she should protect herself and, at the same time, she really couldn't understand how he could be leaving now if he was experiencing the emotional turmoil she was attempting to block out. Business matters still demanded her attention. At this point the comings and goings of the manager and the stranger were drawing little attention, except from regulars who hadn't been in during the last week.

The relationship had taken a definite turn, crossing a barrier, but with its future still firmly planted in the unknown. They were sipping coffee together, smiling at each other, occasionally breaking the nervous silence with comments about the ride or the work ahead, but no allusions, except for their smiles, to the evening just passed. They nevertheless shared the realization that the night was an unexpected affirmation of their connection with humanity, through the mutual fulfillment of physical and emotional yearnings. Barth hadn't expected contact of this sort to materialize. Hell, nothing remotely resembling this experience had occurred in the decade since his divorce.

Estrella, for her part, empathized with the man sitting across from her, at least insofar as the matter of expectations was concerned. Much to her surprise, she had never closed herself off completely to the possibility of a close encounter of this kind, despite her history, but she never sought it out. Her best relationships with the opposite sex over the years in Tucumcari had been confined to either employer-employee banter or the casual flirtations of regular customers, both which were, however natural to her, also the price of business success. It was this success in the business, and her willingness to devote herself to it, that had built the home for herself and Matias, and was, even at this moment, the foundation of the new house for Graciela.

Estrella had allowed herself this interlude of involvement, whatever it was, with Barth, but held no assumptions regarding the future of the relationship. As far as she was concerned, she could only depend on what she had made for herself here. The bustling customer activity in front of her eyes was the present in which she was vested. Still, even she shared the insight that Barth had acquired in his lightning-strike vision in the Midwest a week ago, the suspicion that life might have something more of value to offer than the security of their self-made ruts. Unlike her booth mate, however, she also had the responsibility of her mother's care and the continuing devotion to her son and his future, sources of very real satisfaction. Allowing for the possibility of more, she could still live well with what she had, and be grateful.

In the next two days, Barth attempted lending a hand to the routine tasks of the business, those allowing an opportunity to be with Estrella or Matias, with whom he resumed his mentoring relationship. Matias enjoyed Barth's attention and they could be seen working in tandem, unloading delivery trucks, carrying supplies to the storerooms and attending to outside maintenance tasks. When it wasn't possible for Estrella to share lunch with them, Barth and Matias could be seen sitting opposite each other in one of the back booths, Barth reading a story from the sports section aloud and stopping to ask the boy to read a particular word he had singled out. They walked together to Graciela's house after lunch, taking her a meal put together in accord with Estrella's instructions. Since her efforts in contriving to get them to the dance together, Graciela had developed a strong liking for Barth. Under her direction, Barth dug out patches of earth behind the new house for her personal garden. He packed the dry dirt into rectangular berms, commonly used in this area to retain the little available moisture. Graciela raised some of her own spices, but it was more important that she have access to a personal supply of snakeweed which, when steeped in boiling water, made the tea she drank to treat her arthritis.

Neither Barth nor Estrella had any desire to prolong this moment. The events of their intertwined lives during the last few days had precluded much thought regarding the presumed ending to this chapter. The accident of their intersecting lives had left an indelible mark on both, but, despite this fact, they understood this time was coming. The words had already been said; there was nothing to add as they walked in silence toward the bike. Barth knew anything he might say now would be inane and clumsy, but, stopping for a second, he reached for her arm and pulled her to him, wrapping his arms around her in one last embrace. She held him, just as tightly, but they were unable to look at each other until the second they let go and Barth turned to walk away.

Barth mounted the bike and looked back at her, half-smiling, the closest thing to a smile he could muster under the circumstances, forgetting for the moment that his helmet now completely obscured any hint of facial expression. This was it, he told himself. He had never intended to become so involved. Even in the greatest depth of his immersion in this woman he knew this was a stop in his travels, that he'd be leaving and matters would revert to normal for both Estrella and the lone rider. He understood this, she understood this, and their parting was nothing less than inevitable. Besides, he kept telling himself, she was well established in her world, the world she'd created for herself and Matias, and further delay in his departure would undoubtedly make things more difficult. Yes, it was time, the awkwardness of this moment notwithstanding.

Estrella was experiencing an unease and discomfort mirroring that of the lover who'd ridden into her life and was now heading for territory as unknown to her as that from which he had come. The lover, she knew, the only one she'd ever regarded as such. She had understood that Barth, in the midst of a mission she couldn't quite understand, would be leaving. There was never any real doubt about that assumption. With their discussions of the matter, she also knew his leaving was the best thing. He was, after all, despite their intense interlude, still mostly a stranger who couldn't be expected to be a part of the life she had made in Tucumcari, far away from the world she couldn't imagine back in his Kansas City home. These days had been unsettling for her, shaking ingrained assumptions regarding her life here as the truck ride had for her and Mama, years ago. But, just as then, she would survive. It was time for her to rededicate her energies to the business and Matias. She hadn't told Matias about Barth's leaving, sure that she was saving him from a possible trauma, convincing herself that he'd soon forget the brief entry of the gringo biker in their lives.

She stood for a few seconds after their good-bye, staring while he checked his bags, and returned what she interpreted as his expressionless glance. At this moment it was no great comfort for her to know, as she had never known before, that she wasn't closed off from this part of living. Unquestioned assumptions regarding her ability to experience this kind of love, at least, were convincingly banished. She didn't linger, turning as soon as she heard the now familiar hum of the motor and walking, deliberately, without hesitation, toward the front entrance of the diner. She did not look back. There was work to be done, and this was life as she knew it.

Interlude

The man hunched over his motorcycle can focus only on the present instant of his flight... he is wrenched from the continuity of time... — MILAN KUNDERA

Barth was missing much of the scenery during the first stretch of Interstate 40 between Tucumcari and Flagstaff. In a fog, he was riding out of acquired reflex and habit, not much more. It wasn't fatigue depleting his reserves or blunting his ability to engage his surroundings. Since leaving the truckstop, his preoccupation with the last few days was diverting attention that otherwise would be directed outward, absorbing nuances of the changing terrain and imagined sights and towns beyond his visible horizon. For now, Estrella and Tucumcari were the extent of his horizon, miles behind him and here with him as the motor hummed its tune and the bike rolled steadily westward. He could still smell the perfume of her sex and feel the press of her enveloping arms on his body.

Leaving was the right thing, the best thing, for everyone involved; this wasn't in doubt. Staying longer would have made matters worse. Barth was an interloper in the world of Estrella and Matias and had no right disrupting their lives when he had no intention of sticking around. Besides, even considering the passion they'd shared, the touching of souls during the last days, he knew she had no expectation of anything more, and likely wanted nothing more. Estrella had built a life for herself far away from his and there was no energy for another change of course in her life. She was, at last, not nomadic in spirit, not at this point. Despite his present mobility, the same conclusion applied to him. He was realistic; he'd spent a lot of time during the last forty-eight hours convincing himself there was no alternative. Repeated ruminations of this sort led to the same dead end, until finally, a few hours out, Barth shifted gears, for the sake of his sanity, directing his thoughts in the same direction as his wheels.

I'm not running from anything. This is the best thing for all of us, getting out before I do real damage to their lives.

He was reassured by the thought. He was doing the right thing and it was time to re-orient his vision.

Go West, old man.

At the next opportunity, a town named Puerto de Luna, he exited the highway to gas up. At the pump he completed the ritual cleaning of his visor with the windshield squeegee, removing the fresh crop of bug guts clouding his vision. Afterward he parked the bike and wandered over to the attached fast food joint, grabbing a coke and cheeseburger. He needed sustenance for the day's ride, but refrained from engaging in anything other than quick exchanges of hellos with the truckers. For the time being it was enough to remain alone with his stubborn ruminations. When he remounted the bike he retrieved a map from the topcase to recheck his bearings. There was nothing in particular to note, Flagstaff was a long ride ahead, but it was all highway, straight through Albuquerque and on, unless he wanted to take an attractive detour. On further reflection, he decided to avoid what he expected were many such opportunities until he had left New Mexico behind. He was looking forward to an uneventful ride and, hopefully, an equally uneventful rest once he made it to Arizona. Boredom was the preferred antidote for the emotional turmoil of the last few days. He might reject this conclusion tomorrow, but now he was looking forward to a low-key stretch of road.

Barth was growing used to this open feeling, not so much the idea of the road, yes, that was true, but the openness he could feel by looking straight ahead, then to his right and left. Except for the few cities he had passed through, and none of these were great metropolises, none the size of Kansas City, he wasn't riding through caverns of high rises or even winding roads cutting through mountains, though he knew he'd be running into mountain country before long. Rolling hills, at the most, but the terrain rarely obstructed long views of the land. These vistas contributed to Barth's sense that he wasn't hemmed in. Whenever this ride ended, he knew he'd have the satisfaction of a real vacation from his hemmed-in life, as he saw it, for the first time in memory. This wasn't strictly true, of course, but there was a newness derived from the belief that, unlike past vacations, this was open-ended, in time and mission.

The remainder of the day, like the road, was straight and easy. Traffic was heavy, especially as he approached Albuquerque, and for a few minutes he had the same cramped sensation when surrounded on all sides that had filled him with anxiety back in Oklahoma City. This time, however, Barth was able to cope with the pressure by maintaining a steady focus on the car directly in front of him and keeping a constant distance. By the time he reached the Rio Grande he felt he had chalked up another minor victory. His riding skills, and his confidence, had improved considerably since Kansas City, and this wasn't the challenge it might have been a week ago. He was still aware of the need for vigilance, maintaining the assumption that some idiot driver wouldn't see him if he attempted to pull out, but he wasn't frozen into inaction and knew his judgment regarding safe moves was becoming reliable, almost automatic. He wasn't cocky, just confident of his growing skills. Moreover, his wasn't the confidence of a child, born of blissful ignorance of the risks, nor that of old men who are well aware of the dangers, but beyond caring, not giving a damn about consequences. Barth's air of assurance was founded on the gradually acquired knowledge of his skills and limits. *Dave*, he thought, *would be amazed.*

As he reached the west bank of the Rio Grande it occurred to Barth that the river, on its southward journey, would be flowing past El Paso, and then Juarez. He recalled Estrella's harrowing account of the night she and Graciela spent in the suffocating heat of the locked, moving trailer during their escape from a world of abuse and maquiladoras. By comparison, Barth's present escape was a lark, nothing at all. He toyed with the idea of heading south on 25 to Las Cruces, only an hour from the Mexican border. Hell, he might as well, he'd never be this close again and the thought of Mexico was a strong draw for him. Well, at least for a second. He thought again of Estrella's story, of her description of the dark streets, shady sharp-knifed characters, and the necessity, even for long-time inhabitants, of well-honed survival instincts. Instantly, he realized, an inexperienced gringo like himself, traveling alone, didn't have a Chinaman's chance. The basis for the phrase, a relic from his childhood, was unknown to him, but he knew its meaning. He kept the bike on course, straight ahead.

Between Albuquerque and Gallup, near Grants, the road took a northwest bend between the San Mateo and Zuni Mountains, near the Acoma, Zuni, Laguna and Ramah Navajo reservations. Barth's interest in exploring a Native American subculture, something he'd considered since Oklahoma, was now flagging as a result of his growing fatigue. It might be the altitude, he thought, noting that nearby Lookout Mountain was higher than 9,000 feet, an unimaginable elevation in Missouri. The Cibola Forest was thick with mountain pinon, giving it a pale green coloration not seen in eastern New Mexico. Topography and vegetation had changed dramatically since leaving the lowlands of Tucumcari, a world away. Still, as he was leaving the Land of Enchantment, Barth knew the spell cast upon him hadn't been broken, not by a long shot. That would occur, of course, with the tolling of the miles and days ahead.

Invigorated from the night's sleep, Barth decided to leave Flagstaff early that morning and head straight for the Grand Canyon, although his departure, at a time when the sun hadn't yet made its appearance, wasn't dictated by necessity. Rather, he felt energized and, despite the time and distance now separating him from Tucumcari, he was unable to stop thinking about Estrella. Perhaps, while alone on the road, he might arrive at some semblance of a conclusion regarding the meaning of their brief, but unforgettable and intense encounter, for lack of a better term, since affair couldn't begin to describe what he was feeling while recollecting the last few days.

He stopped at the front desk long enough to drop off his key and pick up one of the Grand Canyon tourist maps. The local paper lying on the counter announced a controversy involving the decision to allow snowmaking equipment at a resort in the nearby Cococino National forest. The action was offensive to members of the Hopi tribe and Navajo Nation who claimed the plan to use treated wastewater to make snow would taint a mountain they considered sacred. Barth still held on to the hope of making some sort of contact with an Indian culture in the Southwest, but this would have to wait; perhaps this wasn't an auspicious time for any such adventure.

It was too early to stop at one of the local coffee bars. He could have used a dose of caffeine for the road, but decided to move on, minimizing the chances of getting caught in what he imagined would be a bottleneck of summer visitors to the canyon in a few hours. The cool air at this altitude had a rousing effect, pressing against his exposed neck while he coasted through empty streets. Nothing in the local scenery attracted his gaze for more than a few seconds in the sleeping town, and he guessed that, weeks from now, he'd have little to tell regarding his brief stay here. He could see that this town had a different feel from Tucumcari, passing yuppie coffee bars and wilderness supply stores like Babbitt's, catering to the park region visitors.

On the other hand, he realized that the lack of an experience of lasting memory in Flagstaff was an indication of his present detachment, not a reflection on the town. After all, nothing in his consciousness could compete with the lingering impact of the woman from Tucumcari, her image stubbornly interfering with attempts to direct his attention elsewhere. All the more reason for heading directly to the Grand Canyon, a vista he was sure contained enough natural drama to distract him, at least for a few hours. Barth twisted the throttle, focusing his attention while turning onto the main road out of town. Route 180 would take him through the Kaibab National Forest and to the south side of the canyon. He could continue through the Painted Desert, getting a glimpse of the nearby Navajo Indian Reservation before stopping in the park, taking some time to contemplate, and deciding his next move.

The morning air was bracing, blowing up the waist of his jacket, waking him in the absence of morning caffeine. The road was thickly bordered with short pines on both sides, a definite change from the sparse, scrubby vegetation of eastern New Mexico. No signs of desert flowers or cactus, at least none he could see from his rolling perch. Barth was feeling triumphant as he headed northward, surveying changes in topography and vegetation he otherwise would have enjoyed only while flipping through the glossy pages of *National Geographic* in his dentist's waiting room. He relished the thought of regaling his office colleagues and Dave with firsthand accounts and exaggerated tales of his wild westward wanderings.

They probably think I'm crazy for doing this. I don't care, better than boring.

This destination, along with the stop in Nevada to see his sister, was the only planned part of this western odyssey. The choice had been made simply because it was on the route and he figured that, at his advanced age, it was about time he'd seen this natural wonder in person. Only when getting close to the park, however, did Barth start feeling something akin to excitement. He would have experienced this feeling before, he thought, but his preoccupation with Estrella had demanded all his contemplative energies. Finally, however, after the first road signs listing the distances to the Grand Canyon, he was able to shift gears, if only because it was evident he wasn't going to arrive at any resolution, if one was to be had, regarding this woman. Some internal mechanism kicked in, providing him a respite, for the time being, from this eruption of thoughts and emotion.

Having made it down the trail this far, Barth decided to relax and sat on a large, flat outcropping, his legs dangling freely. It was still early in the morning and there were only a few hikers to be seen this far from the rim. The morning sun illuminated the upper edge of the west rim, but the air hadn't yet warmed to a degree that would be described as insufferable heat in the afternoon. It was, in fact, cool where Barth sat, and he kept his jacket on while surveying immense, irregular landscapes he'd only seen in photographs. Red and orange were the predominant colors of the rocky formations closest to him, turning to a purplish hue in the distance and a dark blue, with a vague hint of stratification in the sections of the canyon walls farthest away on the horizon. From his seat near the North Rim he could easily spot and identify key landmarks within the canyon itself. To his left, the peak known as the Vishnu Temple, with its sharply stratified summit nearly as high as the clearly visible rim in the background, then Coronado Butte, dead ahead from where he was sitting. As his gaze wandered to his right, the Horseshoe Mesa came into view, with its planed-off surface clearly visible in the valley of the canyon and, farther to his right, Wotans Throne, at least as elevated as his own vantage point and topped with green shrubs and scruffy trees adapted to this altitude. Looking above the walls of the canyon in a southeasterly direction he could detect, thanks to the clear sky this morning, the outline of a distant mountain. This landmark was one of the San Francisco Peaks, nearly a hundred miles distant from where he sat.

Barth was struck with the raw beauty of the craggy asymmetry, a stark contrast with notions of attractiveness that pervaded the civilized world, with its emphasis on smooth surfaces, rounded curves, straight lines and its worship of regularity. Here, in this natural, open to the heavens cathedral, unpredictability ruled, not as an absolute, to be sure. Gravity was still king here as elsewhere, but the landscape presented a panoramic challenge to his scanning eyes, with firs and brush dotting the cliff walls and fissures of unknown depths begging to be explored. The pleasure in this vista was derived, not only from its vastness, too large to be enjoyed in a single sitting, perhaps in a single lifetime, but in its perpetually changing nature. In his scanning meditation Barth noticed slight changes in the shadows of the canyon opposite his perch, changes taking place in the span of a few minutes. With the nonstop course of these natural changes, no two visitors would ever have the same experience of its wonders; even the same visitor would never have identical horizons to absorb. Dreamlike malleability was the rule here.

The sighting of a group of hikers far below him temporarily broke the spell of these musings. He couldn't see them distinctly—the members of the group, moving at the same pace, gave the impression of a slow-moving caterpillar crawling and twisting along the trail. In the darkness prevailing at the canyon's bottom Barth imagined that the hikers must have a much more confining sense of their immediate universes than he enjoyed from his elevated perch. He recalled the fleeting image, on that last afternoon of what he was beginning to think of as his prior life, of the biker leaving the parking lot from his office window.

His thoughts drifted to the malaise that had reached its height a few short weeks ago, the driving force for his wanderings. Perhaps it was the sameness and predictability in his particular corner of the world that impelled him to take to the road so impulsively. Perhaps there was some innate desire to experience, more directly, the serendipity, the chance occurrences, which were ultimately the source of the incredible scenes before his eyes. Barth was convinced that his journey, with its unforeseen encounters, was the product of some inner stirring, perhaps a yearning for surprise now being fulfilled well beyond his imagining. Before this instant, he had somehow known this venture was necessary, even vital, to his wellbeing. Now, for the first time, as a spectator studying the peaceful, unfathomable canyon, he began acquiring a sense of a reason for this trip, a yearning to expose himself, in some small measure, to the unknown, gaining knowledge of his reactions to the unexpected demands placed upon him. Barth reflected on these notions without reaching conclusions, although the train of thought, provoked by the splendor of his immediate surroundings, was the source of a feeling he hadn't experienced for as long as he could remember. For want of a better term, Barth thought he could describe his present emotional condition as a form of contentment, no matter how fleeting.

I'll take it, he mused, knowing that he could become absorbed, without notice, in the uncertainties of the road, not to mention his life generally. His life routine seemed as distant as the Kansas City he'd left behind. Although he would return to his prior life, he was sure it wouldn't be lived the same way. Not after this.

He recalled the story of a man, Wilbert Rideau was his name, somewhere in Louisiana, who'd served forty-four years in prison for murder, finally freed after the sentence was appealed and reduced to manslaughter. On his release, into a world vastly changed during his confinement, he was asked by a reporter to list his wishes for his remaining years. The self-educated ex-con replied that he wanted to become a writer, honing the craft he had learned in the pen, that he wanted to experience the thrill of riding a roller coaster and, not lastly, he wanted to see the Grand Canyon, to experience its "vastness," to "let it soak in." Barth couldn't speak to the first two choices, but at this moment he certainly understood the last of the freed man's desires. After years of enforced claustrophobia, the idea of unlimited natural space, without convincing hint of boundaries, must have the strong erotic force of any deprived need accruing over prolonged intervals. Barth was enjoying the freedom of open space as he sat with his legs swinging over the edge of the outcropping, though he wasn't entirely free of the emotional tension remaining from the time in Tucumcari. His personal vistas had, during these days, expanded to an extent exceeded only by the natural horizon he was enjoying.

In a matter of minutes the eastern walls of the canyon had quickly and dramatically darkened, in contrast to the now bright sunlight flooding the horizon defined by their upper edges. Looking down to the canyon's center, the illuminated formations now appeared in darker and lighter shades of red, with scattered patches of green detectable from the center of the east-west line of his gaze to the ledge on which he sat, soaking in the warming rays of the morning sun. The unease that had pushed him out of the regularity of his day-to-day life in Kansas City had largely dissipated. Other than the preoccupation with the woman he'd left behind, he was completely unencumbered.

The stillness in which Barth had been enjoying this succession of thoughts and observations was abruptly interrupted with a loud "whoosh," a sudden rushing sound coming from his left up the canyon wall. Startled, he instinctively leaned back, catching sight of a large dark shadow sweeping over him. At a distance of two hundred feet from where he sat, a dark, winged specter swooped downward in the sky to an outcropping of rock below him. A giant black bird, its wingspan in excess of six feet, by Barth's estimation, folded its wings as it dug its clawed feet into the rock. Barth could see the object of the bird's flight, a companion flier already settled on the same jutting perch. If the two feathered conspirators, now hunched together, had taken notice of their observer, there was no sign. The dark bony foreheads and beaks of the large predators were rotating in tandem, surveying the valley below. They appeared as ancient sentinels overlooking their kingdom rather than scavengers whose sole motivation was the prey constituting their next meal. Feeding primarily on carrion, there was no need for silence in their flight. These were California condors, the largest flying birds in North America.

Barth sat there, carefully still, while it occurred to him these were the first examples of exotic wildlife he had encountered since leaving Kansas City, not counting the Outcasts. His direct experience of the world had expanded considerably in the last few days. He was also aware of the power of this majestic natural scenery to upend his midwestern notions of sensory stimulation. Here he was, surveying, savoring, the succession of visual vistas, all made possible, to his thinking, as a result of a gash, a gaping wound in an otherwise smooth, even landscape, nothing less than spectacular in its beauty and grandeur. In his corner of the world puny rises not much higher in elevation than speed bumps were legitimately considered hills. Barth laughed to himself to think that the overweight, drab, colorless condors, which could be generously described as ugly, repulsive-looking creatures, attracted much human effort and dedication in service of their survival and protection, having narrowly escaped extinction a few decades ago. Even entrenched notions of perceived beauty and value could be overturned in this setting. If Einstein was correct in asserting that the greatest of all experiences was the mysterious, his own silent mystification, as he sat, taking in all the canyon had to offer, would be savored long after he had left the road.

He began thinking about his next move. Since leaving Joplin he'd been heading straight west, with only short detours from the highway. The trip north from Flagstaff was the farthest he had been from the interstate since Kansas City. It made no sense to head back south to 40 and Barth had no desire to go north and catch 70. Eventually he would be riding into Nevada to see his sister, but he could afford to take the smaller roads for the next few days, slowing down a bit, taking the only chance he might ever have to absorb more of the territory that had, at best, been a two-dimensional vision for him. Maybe ride to Escalante, not far from here, maybe Bryce Canyon, maybe Zion. It didn't matter, it was all the same to him. All the same, since it was all new and, he knew, all bound to be uniquely spectacular.

I'll make my choice soon enough, I can leave that for now. Don't rush, don't be in such a damn hurry. It really doesn't matter, you'll get there.

Satisfied he had convinced himself, he leaned back on his elbows, staring up into the bright sky, his eyes following the vague contours of a lazy, lone cloud formation, a long wisp, more of a whitish streak, misplaced in this indisputable summer day. Barth thought it possible that he had begun to acquire a little patience. He was able to let his eyes linger on details of his surroundings he would have overlooked before, but then again, he thought, he had a more inviting choice of details to study out here. In this wide-open natural setting, he pondered the reasons for the sense of well-being that was so easily induced. There was the obvious, of course, the absence of the routine pressures, demands, annoyances and constraints of his everyday existence. There were no reminders of any of these out here, and that fact, combined with his powers of denial, tended to loosen the civilization-induced grip of anxiety. Symbolically, it seemed to him, the greater the amount of open space, the more diluted his anxiety would become. Back in the city, spending most of his time within the confines of walled rooms or closed cars, his anxieties would remain concentrated and potent, capable of perpetuating the "normal" experience of everyday life. Thus, psychological and physical decompression were directly related, in the same way the interaction of volume and pressure in gases were predicted in Boyle's Law in his freshman chemistry class. This was a cockamamie theory, Barth concluded, but it had entertainment value, and didn't cost him anything.

When he left the Grand Canyon, Barth was riding north toward the Utah canyonlands, with their promise of new choices of spectacular landscapes. He entertained the idea of heading in a northeasterly direction toward Monument Valley, just on the Arizona side of the border, but was gripped with a strange hesitation. On the one hand, there was the potential thrill of being in the midst of the high-rise stone formations and endless open spaces he'd seen in the Technicolor westerns of his youth, the John Ford-John Wayne showcases that had seemed so unreal, so dreamlike to him. This was also Navajo country, another inducement. He was hesitant, however, worried that these vistas might be despoiled by civilization's encroachment, that maybe it was better to leave the old magical images undisturbed.

On further reflection, Barth realized there was another, stranger reason to head toward one of the other sites. It was the notion, at once recognized as irrational, of heading in an easterly direction, even for a short interval. The whole idea of making this escape from his routine was to head out, to leave his safe anchorage behind him. Heading east, even for a few miles, somehow felt like retreat. He realized this was a brand of superstitious reasoning. It was laughable that such an idea could get a foothold in his rational mind. Still, he concluded, *Why take the risk?* The servant of his silliness, he kept Rocinante in her northward line.

Lake Powell and the Grand Staircase-Escalante areas were a short ride from the Grand Canyon, easy choices for Barth. He knew nothing about either until he studied National Park brochures he'd picked up after talking to a couple who'd been hiking in the area. He was again reminded of the extent of his own ignorance, never having heard of the largest national monument area outside Alaska. Once he got there, he was able to take in only a small fraction of what the area had to offer, but it was enough, more than enough, to shock him into an appreciation of the power of nature, just as the Grand Canyon had done. Barth had never imagined as much red rock as he saw in Escalante—wide striated ribbons winding along the river, large jagged rock formations emerging abruptly from the desert areas, wind-swept dunes transformed to stone hundreds of centuries ago. The fifty miles between Escalante Rim and Lake Powell were connected by the so-called Straight Cliffs, fifteen hundred feet high and running the entire distance, with only a few gaps.

The name reminded him of a feature of these vistas that he had at first found to be somewhat disorienting. Whenever he attained a vantage point completely excluding evidence of civilization he observed a lack of the straight lines through which his movements were shunted in the city. Here, straight lines appeared only at a distance, in the abstract, the lone tree pointing skyward, the horizontal plane of the horizon. The taming of the wilderness could be seen as a struggle between the stubborn existence of nature's curves and irregularities and the desire to assert, to impose on the landscape, lines with their certain destinations. Practicality, predictability, these, Barth knew, were the necessary virtues of the lines from which his world was constructed. He recalled his reaction, years ago, when the rolling expanse of open lawn in front of the Nelson Gallery, where he and Dave held their monthly lunches, was stocked with new trees. He remembered his revulsion on seeing them planted in regular, measured ranks and columns, like stormtroopers goose-stepping their way through the countryside. The mute, naturalistic, bronze Henry Moore sculptures peacefully inhabiting the gentle rises must have suffered some degree of disgust at the appearance of the uniform intruders.

An image of other curves from nature followed close on the heels of these thoughts. The outlines of a human form. Her lithe, undulating, sensuous body. Was it a coincidence that the present environment felt so comfortable, so inviting? An unexpected, even illogical connection, perhaps, but an insight nonetheless worth savoring. After a few seconds indulgence, he forced himself to switch the focus of his attention and start walking again.

Barth had to be careful while indulging in short hikes in this area. Unlike his experience in the Grand Canyon, it was possible, with little effort, to find yourself in a spot from which absolutely no trace of civilization was visible in any direction. This possibility did not, however, induce a noticeable quantum of anxiety. On the contrary, Barth became ecstatic at the realization that, despite the depredations of his species, here was an area on the planet not much changed since its re-discovery by small groups of intrepid explorers in the 1870s. This had also been Indian country, the home of Anasazi cultures that disappeared centuries ago, but again, Barth observed no direct evidence of this aspect of the area's past. He had a notion to view the "staircase," maybe even climb it, until he was informed by one of the Bureau of Land Management employees that the staircase consisted of a series of cliffs covering a 40-mile stretch from the Kaibab Plateau to the Paunsaugunt Plateau, encompassing an altitude change of nearly a mile. Barth was a tourist, clear and simple, and not about to make a conscious mistake that could be easily avoided. He resolved to absorb as much of the area's inherent beauty as he could through short walking excursions. Otherwise, he might suffer a fate akin to that of wandering cattle here, attracted by the beauty of the woolly locoweed that caused them to go berserk, even die, after eating its toxic leaves. His natural reserve, the thing that kept him from venturing out from his protected environment all these years, would stand him in good stead here.

Barth's decision to spend the night at one of the nearby park cabins turned out to be as right as his decision to take this particular detour in the first place. It was, by any estimation, the definition of simplicity—four walls, a roof, a single bed and a sink. Absent were any of the usual distractions. There was no television, no radio, not even a Gideon's Bible. It was a minor victory of sorts that he missed none of these. The walking and riding occupying his hours since leaving Flagstaff had been more than sufficient stimulation. He was filled with images of unending cliffs, the hidden Escalante River, a kaleidoscope of blues, reds and sand, the endless stretches of terrain without telephone poles, and cacti, yucca, shrubs and flowers he could only have seen otherwise in the confines of a climate-controlled botanical garden. The day's exercise was more than enough for his body's demand for sleep. Still, he couldn't help but lie awake in his bare, rustic room, rewinding and replaying his memory of the day, reminding himself he would have missed all this but for the cumulative impact of a single day in his life. He recalled one brief moment in that day, watching the well-dressed biker from his office building strap a briefcase to his motorcycle and leave the parking lot. At the time Barth had viewed the guy with a touch of disdain, the faux freedom rider heading off in the sunset. Now Barth was more sympathetic. He gave the guy credit for at least having a dream, if he did, and making an effort, if that's what it was, to make an escape.

I hope he succeeds.

The next morning Barth left early, without breakfast or coffee, eager to get to nearby Bryce Canyon. It was so close it made no sense to miss it and then, he concluded, to continue heading westward to Zion. This was, he knew, the most superficial of explorations of these incredible sites, but then, an adequate look would require every bit of the four weeks he had allotted for this trip. His freedom was not, after all, limitless, and this was certainly better than nothing.

Bryce was another in the succession of surprises to Barth, compounded by the fact that he'd never heard of it until coming out here. Unlike Escalante, with its cliffs, mountains, and canyons emerging from and diving into the earth, Bryce Canyon was a complete dropping off, a sudden, gaping chasm with clearly visible edges, including the one on which he was standing. Unlike the Grand Canyon, with its vast, open spaces filled with large, impressive formations, this canyon was populated, or so it seemed, by thousands of irregular, standing sandstone towers, huddled close together as if petrified in position countless eons ago. The striated spires could be seen for miles, but the opposite rim was close enough so that thick forests of bristlecone pines, Douglas firs, Ponderosa pines and juniper, mixed with spruce and aspen, were visible. Barth decided to hike down into the canyon on one of the paths to get a closer look.

The irregularly stacked sandstone pillars, called hoodoos, stood in silent witness to the millennia of eroding forces required for their creation. Barth followed the clearly marked Navajo Loop Trail into the canyon, acutely aware of the danger of wandering off in a direction that would decrease his odds of an easy return. The bright morning sun became partially blocked while he was descending, and there was no sound other than his own footfalls. At times the stone columns surrounded him so closely he suddenly found himself isolated, able to see the sky only by craning his neck and looking straight upward.

Since leaving Tucumcari Barth had spent his time in a succession of natural wonders sufficiently spectacular, most of the time, to divert his attention from other matters, including the recently concluded experience with Estrella. She nevertheless intruded on his thoughts, especially at night. The power and uniqueness of these natural settings, moreover, reminded him of the hold she had established in his consciousness, an undeniable fact of his existence since that moment, only two days behind him, when he'd said good-bye to her. He realized that, while he was spending more time alone since Tucumcari than during any prior leg of his travels, she stubbornly lingered in his consciousness. Lacking contact with others, presumably able to focus his thoughts in any direction he chose, he was overwhelmed by the beauty of his immediate surroundings and drawn inward to images of the beauty he had known firsthand in her form. The natural beauties of inner and outer worlds momentarily lost any distinctions for the lone wanderer.

Centuries ago, the Paiutes told stories of the Legend People—birds, lizards and other animals that looked like people, but had committed unspecified wrongs and were turned into rocks by the all-powerful Coyote. If you looked hard and long enough in any direction in the canyon, you could see them now, standing and sitting together, some actually holding onto each other. A nation of mute red sand forms, with hearty, stubborn trees, some with exposed root systems, staking their claims in the open spaces. The effect was truly magical. Barth realized the futility of attempting to convey the sense of this place in words. He walked slowly down the trail, his pace reflecting the reverence with which he regarded his surroundings. Another place he could easily have explored for a stimulating week, but he accepted, with resignation, the fact that he had to go on, ride to Zion, take a look, then map out a route to Kate's place.

When he re-emerged from the trail there was a tour bus parked near Rocinante. A group of Italians was gathering by the rim, preparing to get their own look at the American version of the Colosseum.

Time to move on.

The few houses in the small towns along the road to Zion, arranged in clusters around a restaurant, gas pumps and mechanic's garage, did not diminish views of the romantic terrain. He was coasting now, up and down long, sloping hills through the highlands and valleys, only occasionally encountering cars or RVs heading eastward. It was another world out here, one which some would think of as desolate. Barth, however, was enthralled with the stark beauty of this country, filled with wonder thinking about the experience he could not know, of course, of living here everyday. The thought was another reminder that he had, at least since Tucumcari, been alone for the longest time in his memory, his only conversations those required to obtain directions and place meal orders. Accompanied by only the expansive scenery, the near-silent whirring of Rocinante's stalwart engine, and steady cooling breezes, it occurred to Barth that, despite the rarity of this aspect of the present experience, he'd made the transition with a surprising lack of difficulty. He was literally alone with his thoughts now, and, at the moment, without any alternative. What's more, he was enjoying the solitude, even as he had while dangling his legs over the edge of the Grand Canyon, where he was always within sight or hearing of other visitors.

Off to his left, away from the road, the sight of a solitary saguaro, with arms on each side pointing straight into the sky, captured Barth's gaze. He was momentarily entranced by the image of the lone sentinel, a Solon-like figure with its extended arms either waving a warm welcome to the visitor or shooing him away, warning him off the sand premises over which it presided, the Buddha in its unroofed temple.

Then, just as Barth re-directed his attention to the road, a wind-driven tumbleweed whipped across his path, continuing in a rolling, bouncing, skipping prance in the direction of the rooted cactus. The unanchored desert inhabitant rushed by, as if hurrying to its next appointment, without so much as a nod to the rider. He couldn't know, but even this specimen was an intruder, an immigrant to the desert. Originally the Russian Thistle, it flourished in the western plains after being brought over by the German-Russian pioneers who fled a Czar's oppression over a century ago.

It was no surprise to find that Zion, so close to Escalante and Bryce, was its own unique experience. Riding into the park's center, in Zion Canyon, Barth passed shops, restaurants, parking lots and campground areas full with cars and RVs. Bicyclists, buses and foot traffic were as thick as he'd seen since leaving the Grand Canyon, but the activity didn't detract from the magnificent cliff-and-canyon landscape and the heavily-forested mountains surrounding him. Once he located a safe parking spot for Rocinante, Barth stopped at the visitor's center to splash cold water on his face and pick one of the sites to experience this afternoon. He settled on Angel's Landing, a nearby peak that could be reached by hiking and climbing, requiring no special equipment.

He caught one of the shuttles stopping at the major attractions, from the Temple of Sinawava at the northern end of the canyon to Eagles Nest in the south. The bus was filled with sightseers along for the ride, young kids seeing the country and families on summer vacation. Barth felt like the odd man out in this company, as if he should explain his lone middle-aged presence to the other passengers, but he managed to shrug off the momentary discomfort. He got off and walked to the base of the mountain, where the trail began in a series of switchbacks cut in the stone walls with the sensible name of Walters Wiggles. Constructed years ago, Barth guessed this must have been a WPA project, each piece carefully cut and fitted by men grateful for any opportunity to work during the Great Depression. Whatever the origin, the work had been done well. The zigzagging walkway was aesthetically pleasing, functional, and didn't clash with the sides of the mountain into which it had been carved and erected. It afforded casual climbers the opportunity to reach respectable heights in perfect safety, but, eventually, the easiest portion of the climb ended, with a firm commitment to risk required to go farther.

Determined to reach the summit, Barth began the next leg upward, scaling the surface with careful foot placements and tight grasping of the iron bars protruding from the rock face, hammered in years ago, he assumed, by the same WPA workers. Unlike his hikes in Escalante and Bryce Canyon, he was never out of sight of other climbers, although their frequency tended to drop off with every increment of elevation. Eventually, breathing with effort in the altitude, he reached the top of Scout Lookout. Finally, a chance to stop, catch his breath, and absorb another awe-inspiring panorama. Ragged outlines of red and sand mountains touching the clouds, some at eye level from where Barth sat. Tough green pines and shrubs hugging the mountainsides and below, far below, the weaving line of the road through the canyon. Out in front of him was Angel's Landing, his destination, separated by a connecting section of the mountain strewn with boulders, smooth rock and hard edges to be negotiated with great care.

Barth got up and pressed on, sometimes walking, sometimes climbing, at times on all fours, on a knife-edge ridge with sheer twelve hundred foot drop-offs on both sides. He was mildly anxious while proceeding outward, but he knew, if he hadn't known before now, that he had no phobia of heights—if so, he wouldn't have made it beyond the Wiggles. Once, while creeping alongside a boulder leaning outward at an awkward angle, two young kids, they couldn't have been older than ten or twelve, raced by him like they were running down a sidewalk. Barth was too drained to be embarrassed.

Finally, he reached the far ledge of Angel's Landing. He found a smooth flat surface on which he set his tired butt, dangling his legs over the edge with satisfaction. From his perch he could survey as much of the earth below as he'd ever seen at one time, plane flights excepted. Barth wasn't alone on the ledge, but this didn't stop him from appreciating his accomplishment, one of the milestones in his adventures he wouldn't have dreamed himself capable of a few weeks ago.

At this moment, a rushing, cool wind whipped through him, causing him to zip his jacket and turn to his left, in the leeward direction, minimizing the chill. Out here, in the elements, as on the road, Barth was forced to adapt to conditions that hardly rose to a level of awareness back in Kansas City. He had become accustomed to the controllability of these aspects of living, through life in his apartment, car and office, environments not generally subject to the vicissitudes of weather, by virtue of the option of deliberate regulation. Out here, without the conveniences of home, he was forced to make adjustments constantly, but this requirement wasn't as onerous as might be expected. At this point, almost two weeks out, he was beginning to make the required accommodations to changing conditions automatically, even anticipating them. Barth had the satisfaction of a budding confidence, derived from the knowledge that he would somehow, some way, land on his feet in the ever-changing experience of the road ahead. It hadn't escaped his notice, moreover, that the safety and comfort, and predictability, of the place from which he had come, were vastly overrated.

Staring across the canyon to the shrinking shadows on the opposite peaks, he was aware of the immediate sensation of sitting on solid rock, how different it was, and yet, not in the least uncomfortable. Sitting on the bike seat sometimes made him saddlesore by the end of a long day on the road, but not once had he complained about this common riding malady. This was the price of a more direct sensation of the road than he could ever have acquired in his "cage." He smiled at the recollection of another direct sensation, the feeling of Estrella holding onto him, nestled close behind him during the ride to the mesas. The mixture of anxiety and sexuality was real, no fantasy, and not so very distant, as he allowed the memories an opportunity to grab his attention. Finally, however, he had to reassert himself, reassure himself that staying any longer in Tucumcari would have made the situation worse. Leaving had been the logical move—he and Estrella knew and expected it. Neither one of them, he was certain, had doubts.

Barth was knowingly rationalizing the situation, chalking up the time in Tucumcari as a brief but fantastic interlude that made him feel alive, one that would also be the source of dividends on the road ahead, even after his return. Of course, he knew, she knew, their lives, backgrounds, and personalities were just too different. There was simply no getting around that obvious, indisputable fact.

The climb and the train of thought had taken their toll on his energies, but he was glad he had ventured out, exposing himself to another variety of challenge. At least the climb down should be easier. It was still early. He could take his time, head out, hunt down lodging, and ride into Nevada tomorrow.

Barth was a reluctant traveler, for the first time since leaving Tucumcari. He knew he should move on, even if there was no particular hurry. Still, the spell of the wonders he'd witnessed and walked through the last two days exerted a strong hold on him.

Will I ever walk through these canyons and see these colors again? Will I find myself sitting in front of the TV, feet propped on the table, looking through travel magazines and thinking, yes, I remember climbing Angel's Landing and hiking one small part of the Grand Staircase, years ago?

The thought of this as a distant memory, possibly with no comparable memories to follow, was discomfiting to Barth, since, if he ever reached that point in time, it would certainly mean that he had surrendered to the path of least resistance, reverting to his professional, life-in-the-city existence.

Stop ruminating, jerk. Get moving.

Barth fired up Rocinante and rolled slowly out of Zion, heading north on 15. Instead of dwelling on fruitless thoughts about future reminiscing, he directed his attention to the task at hand. It wasn't necessary to hurry, but he should start thinking about the visit with his sister in Nevada. He was ready now. He had initially felt some trepidation about seeing her. After all, they had only sporadic contact, by phone or e-mail, for years, and couldn't be said to know each other, except in the most general sense. He had seen the visit as an obligation, long overdue, but now, after the last couple days alone, he longed for company and was glad for the possibility of contact with her and her family.

He'd take a break at one of the service spots he was bound to run into on his way out of the park and figure out the route he would most likely enjoy for his last stretch in Utah. Find a cheap motel for the night and start the next Wild West chapter in the morning.

The roadside stop was made up of one-story clapboard shacks, all in the same flaking, faded ivory paint, connected by open covered walkways and separated from the road by fifty feet of rough gravel. The sagging roof lines of the restaurant and adjoining garage confirmed the impression of at least a half-century of neglect. No effort was wasted on landscaping, just a few yucca plants scattered in the rocky soil and a couple of rusting tow trucks in the back. It wasn't necessary to dress up the place—there was no competition in this area for the tourists' empty gas tanks and stomachs.

This was as good a place as any for deciding which route to take into Nevada to Kate's place. At the far end of the lot Barth sighted a sidecar rig and headed that way, out of curiosity and the opportunity to commune with bikers after spending the last forty-eight hours alone with his thoughts. After parking Rocinante he inspected what his untrained eye guessed was a vintage setup, a black BMW with white pin-striping that was matched on the open sidecar. A spare tire was mounted on the rear and two bulging canvas duffel bags were lashed to the rack. The California tags indicated these were not riders on an afternoon jaunt. On the sidecar seat Barth spotted a couple of black half helmets and goggles that looked like props from an old movie.

As soon as he entered he saw the couple sitting in a booth. They had matching white hair, and black leathers covering each from shoulders to toes. They looked old enough, Barth guessed, to have been riding at least as long as their bike.

"Beautiful Beemer you got. What year?"

"'72. Where you riding from?"

The woman slid over in her seat, motioning Barth to sit.

"Don't mind if I do. I've just been walking around in the parks the last couple days, gathering dust and drying up. I'm Greg Barth."

After the last two days out of Tucumcari, the sound of his own voice, pronouncing his own name, had a distinctly foreign quality.

"Herschel, and this is my better half, Maryann. We've been riding three days from San Diego, out to see our daughter and her family in St. Louis. Maryann's officially retired and we finally have time to ride east. Where you heading to?"

"Right now, to see my sister in Nevada, then up to San Francisco and Seattle. I've never been there and I thought it was about time."

"Know what you mean. We always fly east, but this time we decided to do it right. Travel on some of 66, just for the hell of it, see some of the places along the way, Amarillo, Albuquerque, whatever looks good."

"Hersh wants to see Kansas City too. We've just never gotten around to it all the times we've been in St. Louis."

"Really?"

Barth's laugh elicited puzzled looks, until he explained. It wasn't just the obvious coincidence, but the idea of Kansas City as a vacation destination. Except for sporting events and the occasional convention, he'd never viewed his home as one of the tourist destinations in his part of the country. St. Louis, Lake of the Ozarks, Branson, but not Kansas City, regarded by even its inhabitants as flyover territory.

The couple began peppering him with questions. To Barth's surprise, he named a number of places of interest in his hometown. The jazz district, Union Station, the Nelson Gallery where he and Dave ate lunch, the Truman museum, and the Plaza area, although Hersh and Maryann didn't give the impression they harbored a desire for upscale shopping. Of course, the trite and true, the barbecue joints that comprised, in Barth's thinking, different sects in the local religion. Bryant's, the Holy Grail and his personal favorite, Gates, Rosedale, LC's. By the time he was finished, Barth was himself convinced Kansas City was worth a visit, especially if you were heading in that direction anyway. The irony of the fact that they were heading in opposite directions to fulfill their curiosities didn't escape them. Hersh and Maryann were veteran bike travelers, as it turned out, and proficient riders, systematically switching roles and positions on their rig for rest purposes and to provide changes in perspective along the way. They had traversed the entire west coast from Tijuana to Vancouver, but had never ventured east of Utah. Like Barth, they had their share of unanticipated adventures, including travel alongside an isolated canyon the previous day due to a map-reading error.

"My GPS takes awhile to get working," Herschel asserted, pointing to his head and laughing.

"Good thing, too, or we would have missed that beautiful canyon and the giant mesas. Not even a telephone pole, no empty beer cans, nothing you could see giving a hint of civilization except the road. One of the most incredible detours we've ever taken, and never heard of it, never read about it, absolutely nothing."

Barth was envious of the mutually supportive nature of their interaction. It was obvious this partnership of many years was the most important aspect of their individual lives, a togetherness underscored by the dried dirt distributed over their matching leathers. He was equally intrigued by their description of the road they'd taken yesterday and asked for particulars. Hell, he was this close, it was somewhere west of here, he might as well take it in. Even if it added a few hours on his way to Kate's place, that was nothing under the circumstances. *Carpe diem*, that was his motto, wasn't it?

The three bikers sat together, filling their stomachs, stretching their legs, swapping road stories and sharing insights gathered from the perspective of open-road warriors, no matter that Barth's own admission to the fraternity was relatively recent. For his part, although he enjoyed the enforced solitude of the road and the last days spent wandering in the park areas, he was thoroughly immersed in the opportunity to make contact again, a recharging interaction that reinforced the certainty in his decision to head west. He could see Hersh and Maryann felt the same way. He was providing them the chance to share an aspect of their lives he was uniquely equipped to understand and appreciate.

An hour later the travelers, bowing to the call of their roadweary bodies for sleep, got up and left the restaurant for their waiting bikes, where they exchanged knowing observations about the technical aspects of their rides and Barth confirmed the directions for the road they had stumbled on yesterday. Finally, renewed and reinvigorated by the roadside encounter, they said their goodbyes and Barth watched as Maryann, on the bike, and Hersh, almost hidden in the sidecar, headed out toward Flagstaff to hunt down a night's lodging. Likewise, Barth urged Rocinante forward on the same road from which they had just come, heading in the opposite direction, but seeking the same goal, at least for this night.

Stranded

Americans have no real identity. We're all... uprooted people who come from elsewhere. — LESLIE FIEDLER

B arth figured he was good for somewhere in the range of a hundred miles on a half tank, but chose not to tempt fate more than necessary in this country, deciding to make the prudent move and stop. He could at least eliminate one source of potential problems once he was off this road.

It was another novel experience, turning into this unpaved lot, with its two vintage dull red pumps shaded by the wood frame roof jutting out from the main structure. The ramshackle shed, structure was too elegant a word to describe the decaying assemblage of rotting whitewashed wood siding and ancient metal roofing, was surrounded by stacks of unusable tires and piles of auto salvage. Rusting tin advertising signs confirmed Barth's impression that this place had seen its heyday at least forty years ago, before the road's function as the main east-west artery in this region was ended by the construction of the highway. The lonely disintegrating outpost appeared to be losing its struggle to avoid being annexed by the surrounding desert, patient and confident of its inevitable victory. It was a wonder there was enough business here to sustain a human being. Barth surmised that anyone who chose to run this enterprise, such as it was, must necessarily crave solitude.

Rustling noises from inside the shed heralded the emergence of the presumed proprietor, an old man wearing baggy denim overalls, with scraggly white hair hanging out from the sides of a blue-and-white striped engineers cap. Without as much as a nod of introduction, he stepped outside, staring straight at Barth.

"What're you lookin' for?"

"Just gas and directions."

"You must know where the gas goes in that thing, so go ahead. Where you supposed to be going?"

His demeanor underscored Barth's observation that this man was not Sedley Crump. It was also obvious that the appearance of customers at this outpost wasn't exactly a welcome event.

"I'm looking for the turnoff to the old canyon road that goes north to Ridle's Gulch, looks like it should be close by."

The old man stood in the open doorway, staring at Barth with a combination of disdain and amusement. Barth guessed that the accumulated layers of dust and the two days' growth on his cheeks couldn't camouflage his status as the latest highway gringo. The man watched while Barth figured out the workings of the vintage pump.

"The turnoff is ten miles down the road," he stated, pointing west. "If you're foolish enough to ride that trail, you can't miss it. There's no other place to get off this road once you head out."

"I think I can handle it. Thanks for the directions."

"You're lucky kid. I was planning to take the day off."

"What do you do when you take a day off?"

Barth was actually interested in what anyone would do for leisure in this place.

"None of your damn business, sonny."

Pleasantries were obviously not part of this man's conversational repertoire.

Oh well, thought Barth, *it's a fair exchange—I got my directions and gave him a good laugh and a story for his drinking buddies. And, after all, I am a highway gringo.*

"Well, got to get moving, thanks for your help."

Barth shoved some bills into the outstretched hand.

"You got water in those bags? You're gonna need it where you're headed."

"Yeah, thanks, I keep enough on me so I don't have to worry about it."

The man's concern seems genuine enough, even though he probably thinks I'm a good candidate for buzzard carrion, Barth mused as he swung his leg over the seat and started the bike.

He's an old coot, but I suppose he's just another human being making contact in the only way he knows.

They hadn't exchanged names in the course of their interaction, but it was evident that wasn't a matter of concern to the old man. Barth urged Rocinante back on the road and gave the proprietor a perfunctory wave with his left hand. As far as he could tell, the salutation wasn't returned. A backward glance caught him standing, staring at the visitor, both hands in his pockets.

The road was demanding all his attention as a result of its decayed state. Cracks, potholes and loose chunks of broken asphalt dictated a slower pace than Barth would have preferred in the hot desert sun, forcing him to unzip his jacket to obtain relief. He was getting used to the constant need to adapt himself to the requirements of the changing terrain and conditions, taking pride in the observation that he'd been able, so far, to overcome the unpredictable obstacles he encountered. He wasn't, however, deluding himself into thinking he had become a proficient motorcyclist. He'd met enough bikers along the way to provide convincing confirmation of his novice status. Still, it was undeniable—he'd come a long way since Kansas City. He was sure Dave would be impressed with the riding skills he had acquired.

In the distance he sighted an undetermined vehicle heading in his direction. He couldn't actually see it, but dust clouds in its wake announced its appearance and direction. The flat terrain and desert heat suggested the possibility of a mirage, but Barth knew he hadn't been on the road that long, and besides, he could see a dark moving object at the head of the floating dirt. He kept his attention focused on the crappy road surface and the slow, steady convergence of the vehicles in the eerie stillness of the landscape.

The dreamlike, slow-motion vision, magnified by the absence of accompanying sound, quickly faded, supplanted by the gritty present, as more details of the still distant vehicle came into view. An old truck -sometimes it seemed this was the land of old trucks—was heading toward him, at a faster rate of speed than his own, shaking and jolting over the same road surface that was forcing Barth's caution. As the meeting of the vehicles became imminent, the truck slowed, in presumed deference to the lone biker. Barth could clearly see the faded green paint of the cab and the wobbling sides of its wooden stake bed. The driver's head, halfway out the window, was focused on what must have been a strange apparition under the circumstances. As the truck approached, the clanging of the bouncing cab grew louder, drowning out the subdued hum of his bike.

At the instant in which the two vehicles came alongside each other, Barth was looking directly into the craggy, sunburned face of the driver, a man who could have been a member of the same clan as the gas station owner. In that fraction of a second Barth waved in greeting and the driver nodded in return, exhibiting a puzzled look. As quickly as the encounter occurred, Barth was reminded of his isolation in this dreamlike vista of sun-baked mesas and distant sandscapes, now generating wavelike forms in the midday heat.

Five minutes later he spotted the road north, unmarked, but unmistakable as the only other man-made break in the landscape. While turning he noted the surface of the trail, nothing but packed earth ruts in a sea of short scrubgrass. It was nonetheless smoother and more predictable than the road he'd just left, allowing him to pick up speed and shift into fourth gear. Barth looked in vain for tracks of the sidecar rig, but traces of tire tracks not yet obliterated by the sand and wind assured him that this was indeed the road to Ridle's Gulch. He resolved to absorb his surroundings, territory as beautifully barren as any he'd seen. He could no longer see the main road in his rearview mirror, despite the absence of natural obstructions, only the faint trailing of dust signaling his immediate past. He was clearly in a world of his own, a stimulating and daunting realization underscored by the complete absence of sounds other than the smooth low whine of Rocinante's cylinders. Only the occasional variation in the distant horizon kept Barth from entering a seductive hypnotic trance.

The deceptive sameness of the terrain ended, without warning, when a crack in the earth following the contour of the trail opened, revealing a sudden drop in elevation within a few feet of the trail's edge. In the middle of the next curve, Barth could see a widening canyon below him, hidden completely to his view a few short seconds ago. The canyon's walls were at least a half-mile apart, and on its floor he could see plant life that could not have survived the constant heat of his own altitude. Yucca plants, Painted Indian and prickly pear were scattered about the sloping walls and floor of the canyon, as far as the eye could see, in sharp contrast to the desert landscape above the canyon's rim. The trail hugged the canyon's sharp edge, affording the rider a dramatic, spectacular view from a vantage point he couldn't have imagined minutes earlier. Hersh and Maryann knew what they were talking about.

Exhilaration was the sole sensation Barth experienced for the next half hour, wholly immersed in the sensory smorgasbord within his sight, hardly believing his good fortune. He reminded himself that he could easily have stayed in Kansas City, stuck in the inertia of the rut he'd created, with no inkling or awareness of this corner of the universe. He wasn't lost now, but was traveling with the euphoria of knowing he was in his own *terra incognita*. Still, even here, practical considerations were lurking, not far from his consciousness. It occurred to him, here, in the "middle of fucking nowhere," that, if he went down, he had no way to signal for help and, in this byway of a trail, the likelihood of another rider, or anyone, for that matter, coming across him, was probably minimal. "Forgetting" his cell phone, that arrogant gesture of independence, in this moment became his folly. He had no healthcare information with him and, hell, he wasn't even sure of his own blood type—*Is it A-negative?*

These practical concerns gave the lie to any romantic image of the lone pioneer Barth may have been enjoying. The beauty of the canyon, its stark display of unvarnished natural realism, with no hint of civilized intrusion, had its flip side, a darker aspect. He certainly knew this, at some level, but here, in the confrontation with this unimagined paradise, other thoughts hinted at ambivalence. Barth was absorbing the knowledge that "no man is an island" while proceeding further up the canyon route, scanning the road for obstacles as it narrowed, now not much more than two parallel ruts. At this moment he was seized with an unforeseen anxiety, realizing how foolish he was, viewing his personal predicament in such black-and-white terms. He was, after all, neither fully integrated into the fabric of his suburban existence, nor was he, or could he be, in any but a laughable, caricature sense, a self-surviving renegade striking out on his own. Hell, someone had made the trail he was following. Who knew, *Maybe I'm the 561st rider on this road.* In quick succession came a series of concrete examples confirming his wilderness-inspired epiphany. He had to worry about gas, of course. His travels were tethered, eventually, to the gas pumps, inescapably, inexorably, of course, tied to the corporate America he might otherwise claim to despise.

An ersatz rebel.

He was too acculturated to be a real trailblazer, an outsider for real, no matter how independent (lonely?) he viewed himself in his everyday existence. Glancing at his boots resting on the bike pegs it came to him that, of course, all his gear had been made in sweatshops feeding the consumer society from which he imagined himself alienated. Short of donning a loincloth and seeking his sustenance brandishing a makeshift club, it was impossible for Barth, except in a very narrow sense, to "light out for the territory." The long-cultivated delusion had, however, served a purpose for Barth, one with which he was well aware, scanning the terrain, interrupted only by the comforting ticking sound coming from the engine propelling him farther away from his last reference point. He had survived, even thrived, on the care and feeding of this delusion, the idea of freedom, for years, with a touch of arrogance, a source of comfort even in the midst of what he perceived as daily drudgery.

Diverting his attention from this train of thought to the immediate demands of the convoluted path the bumpy trail was taking, Barth found himself led to a new "insight," that it had taken this unplanned excursion into the solitary wilderness to make him aware of his connectedness, so to speak, his interdependence, with everything he'd sought to escape. This irony didn't elude him, not at all—instead, the full force of this canyon-inspired nugget of wisdom had its impact in the form of an outburst of laughter. At first, within, subdued, then, with the freeing impetus of the open setting, Barth let the laughter grow and, finally, he was laughing audibly. He embraced the humor of his insight, without reservation. He didn't care, didn't give a damn who might hear this self-imposed outcast—it didn't matter. He knew, of course, that his laughs, a source of sheer pleasure, joy even, were shared only by the pale orange walls of the canyon and a few scattered saguaros standing dutifully in place. A surreal scene, to be sure, but the freeing sensation filling Barth, as he accepted this absurdity, generated open laughter, unlike any witnessed by his friends and colleagues.

This was, all in all, a great, lightning moment, and Barth recognized it, jumping into it, laughing and mocking himself, or maybe his prior self, abandoned and without restraint. His determined, sacred search for whatever he may have imagined he was looking for was being transformed into a single, intense belly laugh displacing, elbowing out of consciousness, the serious preoccupations of the last few minutes.

At this instant, celebrating what he knew was a once-in-a-lifetime insight, the terrain, without warning, reasserted itself in the ever-changing balance between his mental meandering and the need to maintain vigilance. A sudden jolt shot through his seat, up his back and neck, followed by the sensation of his rear wheel sliding out from under him. Barth instinctively twisted the throttle, attempting to regain traction. Instead, the bike began an uncontrolled descent, the spinning tire churning up choking clouds of dust, enveloping the bike, now sliding tail end first over the ridge with Barth, braking and holding on, desperately attempting to stop the bumpy downward ride. His struggle to keep the bike upright failed and both bike and rider were falling backward, the bike on its left side, over the brush and rocks, until Barth let go and the bike slid, finally coming to a stop, about fifty feet below the trail.

"Shit!" was all he could muster, gasping for air. Lying on his side, halfway between the bike and the trail above, Barth was stunned and dazed. He lay on the dry ground, breathing heavily, trying to replay the seconds during which the ride had changed. He felt no pain as he lie still, slowly coming to the realization that he wasn't hurt, not seriously, just roughed up. His boots, gloves and helmet had served their purpose; he knew he could get up when he chose to. He turned his head, looking over his shoulder, searching for his bike. The handlebars and seat were showing from behind some brush, but from his position he couldn't see enough to guess at the damage. A thin cloud of dust from the newly-made break in the trail drifted over him. All was now silent as the nature of his predicament started sinking in. Looking up, it was apparent that getting back to the trail with the bike would be impossible, assuming the bike was in working order. This section of the canyon wall was too steep, not to mention rocky. The dirt below the trail would undoubtedly offer less traction than that which had just given way under him on the road.

Barth sat up, surveying his situation from a better vantage point, but with no better conclusion.

Well, no use sitting here. Let's get to it, find out what I need to do to get out of this mess.

He stood up, slowly, checking as he did for telltale pains, finding he was more dirty and dusty than injured. He paused, raising his visor, taking another look at the spot where the bike had ended its fall. It was on its left side and was surely banged up, but from where Barth stood it looked like it was otherwise intact. Perhaps he could find a way down the slope to the plain below and look for a break that would allow him a chance to regain access to the trail. He was a bit stiff, but bent down, slowly shuffling down the hill, around rocks and sagebrush, until he was standing over the bike.

It had slid on its left side, the up side was clean, as far as he could tell. The left mirror was bent, and the lid of the left case was lying separately a few feet away, its contents scattered in the sand. He smelled no gas and the tires looked good. Barth stood next to Rocinante for a minute, trying to figure out how to right the beast, while experiencing a pang of guilt for letting his faithful companion down in this manner.

"Well, let's see, push it up from the back, set it on its stand, now, … next step."

He sat on the ground, his back to the seat, forcing his feet into the earth, imagining the leverage he would need to raise the 550-pound behemoth. At least the bike was aimed upward, not parallel to the trail. He dug his heels in the rocks and sand, testing whether it would give way, then gave a tentative push with his back. The bike moved, enough to set both tires in contact with the earth. Barth braced his shoulders against the seat and tank, one hand on the ground, the other around the left grip, and threw his weight backward in a quick, forceful shove. The bike was now at a forty-five degree angle and he was able to turn his body, pushing, until finally, with a last surge of strength, he succeeded in righting the bike, enough to kick out the stand and let it rest, perpendicular to the trail.

After a quick inspection he determined that, while the tank and front fender had acquired a series of parallel scratches and the left signal light lens was missing, nothing was bent or punctured and no disconnected wires were visible. *The bike should run okay.* The problem was figuring how to get it back up the trail. Pushing or riding it up the steep incline was out of the question. Barth concluded that the most promising strategy would be to get the bike down to the canyon bottom, where he could find a way to ride it back to the trail at a point further north. He grabbed the grips, bracing himself on the bike's left side, kicked the stand up and released the clutch in short bursts, allowing the bike to slowly back its way down. After twenty minutes of repeating the procedure he achieved his goal, and the bike was resting on its stand on level ground. Barth retraced his route to retrieve the left case cover and the case contents, thankfully in a single scattered pile among the rocks. He re-attached the lid and repacked the case, except for a water bottle.

Stepping back from the bike, he walked past the point from which it had left the trail. He began scanning the canyonwall, searching for the hoped-for gentle slope, a gradient he could manage with the bike. Nothing was immediately visible, so he decided to ride the bike further up and survey the trail for possible entry points.

"Dammit," he yelled, his composure leaving him as soon as he tried starting the bike. Nothing happened, no sound at all, when he pressed the ignition switch. The key was in the on position. Barth had remembered to switch it off when he righted the bike, so the battery wasn't the problem. He searched again for evidence of loose wiring, but found none. The lights didn't come on when he pressed the button, neither did the horn. This was a complete mystery to Barth. He turned the key off while attempting to collect himself and tackle the immediate problem. No possible solutions came to mind. Gradually, a realization set in—he had no workable options to pursue.

All right, I'm stuck here now, who the hell knows what the problem is. I've just got to figure out how to deal with this.

Standing by the bike, pondering his dilemma in the late afternoon sun, it dawned on him that he was physically and mentally incapable of grasping an immediate answer. His left side ached and he was succumbing to a mounting fatigue since the fall. Hiking back down the trail was out of the question, at least for now. He wasn't lacking for anything critical, at the moment, so he made his decision.

I might as well set up camp and get some sleep, maybe something will come to me in the morning, maybe someone will come down the trail. At least I'll get some rest if I have to hike back and, besides, this is what I wanted, right? The chance to experience the great outdoors.

Barth didn't laugh at the last observation. He knew he couldn't take this situation lightly, but resigned himself to his resolution without extended rumination.

He began the process of setting up camp. Instead of putting up the tent, he set a tarp out on the ground next to Rocinante and laid his sleeping bag in a north-south line to provide a clear view of the changing sky. It was likely to get much cooler, but tolerable, he reasoned, so it was time to take advantage of his natural surroundings. He would commune with nature, as he had during his meditation in the Grand Canyon, the difference being, he was now an involuntary observer.

Settled and lying on the sleeping bag, he shifted his focus to the surroundings comprising his temporary home. In the waning light he could see shadows and silhouettes of the scrub plant life, yucca and varieties of cactus scattered throughout the desert basin. He could hear a gusting, distant wind, something he missed while he was still a tourist passing through on the trail. Sounds generated by this habitat's life forms were absent to his ear, although he imagined the desert coming to life during the cool evening hours. Barth wasn't anxious about the prospect, figuring he should just try to absorb the lessons of the night desert, accept his status as a shipwrecked wanderer, and be confident he would extricate himself from this predicament. If there was one lesson he had acquired, it was the knowledge that, when tested and challenged by unexpected twists and turns, he could, on his own or with the help of newfound friends and acquaintances, find a solution to temporary difficulties. This was knowledge he could never obtain in the course of his routine back in Kansas City, and this fact alone, Barth mused, made the trip worthwhile.

With his head propped up on one of his cases, the lone rider lay on his bed for the night, convinced things would work out. Putting his predicament behind him, he looked out on the desert landscape and the strikingly beautiful colors of the sky at sundown. Now he was glad for the opportunity, savoring a vantage point that would have been missed but for the break in the trail. The bright, flaming red sky was anything but a small part of a living universe. The heightened sense in this moment was that of being an observer of the natural processes around him and, simultaneously, feeling that he was being observed, or at least detected, in a manner he couldn't explain, by the worlds surrounding him. The detachment that characterized Barth's perspective in the life from which he had ridden vanished, for the moment, in the desert wilderness and the emerging starlight of the evening sky.

In this contemplative frame of mind it occurred to Barth that he had recently experienced a form of connection with another dimension of the natural world. Not so long ago in the course of his journey he had felt the passion, love and life of another, the physical and emotional binding to Estrella that reminded both of the common needs and desires of all human travelers. The attentions and interest of the boy, Matias, had also left their mark. In the absence of civilization's distractions, and certain that no one inhabiting this sphere had knowledge of his whereabouts, he didn't feel alone. The encounter with Estrella reminded Barth that he wasn't, after all, an alien on the planet that was his bed. This experience, he knew, made the whole venture worthwhile, awakening him to the necessity, the reality, of connection, even as he lay on the desert floor. It occurred to Barth that this idea of connection went even further. Sedley Crump, Bones, Graciela, even Herschel and Maryann—all of these celebrities in his personal road show had their own sets of connections, through which he had made contact via different entry points within the neuronal network of the universe.

He recalled the certainty he felt regarding the necessity of doing something, anything, to relieve the mind-numbing monotony that was his life as he lay on the soft mattress in his bed a couple weeks ago. Then he had been sure that something had to be done, that he had to do something, not knowing what, but it had worked out. Even in the precarious circumstances of his present predicament, Barth had no serious doubts in this regard.

The experience with Estrella was having a similar impact. He had to change this part of his life, devoid of any semblance of a close, loving relationship, before it was too late. This he knew, with the same degree of certainty he had regarding the value of this whole venture. Having reached this conclusion, however, he was doubtful regarding his prospects for another chance encounter with someone who could stir his passion and elicit admiration, for her stability, for her sense of assuredness in the world she had built for herself and Matias, and for her capacity to impart a serenity to others, himself included. On the other hand, his actions, he reasoned, had made it possible for all these things to happen in his life. All he had to do was avoid falling back into the rut that had been his life back in Kansas City, not to mention the one that had sent him reeling to this parcel of the sand and rock universe. The thought was oddly reassuring.

Serendipity, in the form of the accident that sent him rolling to his sandy bed in the cool desert night, was the source of a feeling of peace and satisfaction not unlike what he had experienced with his legs dangling over the edge of the Grand Canyon. On further reflection, Barth recognized a kinship with the temporary respite he'd shared with the Outcasts around the campfire in the Texas Panhandle. The tranquility of the evening in this wilderness, finally, conjured up the image of another lone, though not lonely, figure who had stuck in Barth's imagination as the result of an earlier lucky encounter. He could imagine Sed, in the cockpit of the ancient C-47, listening to a favorite piece of music, relaxing with the satisfaction that he'd done his job that day and that he was exactly in the place where he was supposed to be.

Will I ever arrive at such a destination?

Flickering specks of light, from beyond the mountains on the eastern horizon, danced on his eyelids, waking Barth at an hour he instantly recognized as earlier than he was used to, even during his time on the road. His body was comfortably warm in the bag; only his face was exposed to the still cool morning air. He'd slept soundly, oblivious to any potential dangers in his open desert bedroom. Well rested, he lay awake, having no reason to rise immediately, confident he'd resolve the dilemma that had landed him here.

He surveyed his immediate surroundings and was struck with an odd sensation, noting that he and Rocinante were the only visible signs of an alien civilization. In contrast with the Grand Canyon, with its beauty only tenuously protected from the ravages of a surrounding society, here, at least for the time being, Barth was an intruder whose survival was dependent on the beneficence of an unknown and indifferent terrain. Still, the lost wanderer stubbornly refused to ruminate about his uncertain personal fate, choosing instead to revel in an enjoyment that seemed out of place, given his predicament. His forced isolation had the side benefit of a wonderment Barth knew could be experienced in no other way. He was a lucky man, he reckoned.

He sat up, exposing his body to the morning's chill, reluctant to concede the necessity of getting up and confronting the demands of his situation. Finally, however, Barth acknowledged the obvious. He had to start moving, size up his situation and conceive a plan to get out of here. It dawned on him that he shouldn't be lying around, comfortable as he was, wasting the daylight hours, more precious now than a day ago, when he was traveling with the knowledge that he'd end up somewhere in a warm bed after a hot meal. Yesterday's certainties had vanished like a mirage in the desert air, and he'd better get used to that fact.

Time to decide and act.

As he stood up, surveying the horizon in every direction, he caught the only trace of civilization's intrusion into the landscape, the freshly-made gash in the trail where his unplanned descent had begun. Barth's frame of reference had changed drastically since that moment. The wilderness he had regarded, while a pilgrim on two wheels, as welcoming and peaceful, was now a potential threat, and he was no closer to a solution now than he'd been ten hours earlier. Worse yet, it was obvious that no one in the universe had any idea of his whereabouts, or was missing him, for that matter. As he saw it, he had two choices—remain where he stood and take the chance of becoming carrion for desert predators, or attempt to walk back the fifty or so miles to the nearest outpost of civilization, hoping someone would cross his path. It hadn't escaped his notice that not a solitary soul had come down the trail since he left it yesterday, not exactly a good omen for his imminent rescue.

Looking eastward, he detected no sign of any break in the view indicating the presence of a human being—no trails, no man-made objects, not even loose trash. As far as he could see, this was God's country, it wasn't man's, not yet. It certainly wasn't this man's, even if he did enjoy the view, and the perspective of the traveling tourist had now changed considerably. Barth knew that in a few hours' time he'd better be within striking distance of civilization or a shady place, and he needed to get moving.

Just as Barth was resigning himself to the prospect of a trek of indeterminate length, he was startled by a shaking, rumbling sound behind him, growing louder. He turned in time to catch the sight of a speeding truck bouncing and clattering on the trail above him. Barth jumped, running toward the rim, waving his arms, shrieking "Stop!" as loudly as his lungs would permit, over and over again. By the time he had begun running, however, he knew his attempt to gain the driver's attention was in vain. The truck was well down the road and it was unlikely that he was visible through the clouds of dirt thrown up in its wake or that he could be heard through the racket of the bouncing truck bed.

"Dammit," he yelled, his vain exclamation heard by no one as he finally made the road, watching the truck, at least a half mile away, speed on. No chance the driver was bothering to study his rearview mirror. No reason to in this place. Barth stood still for a few seconds, his gaze fixed on the receding image of the only sign of human life within reach of his senses.

No use standing here crying. Get moving. Now.

Barth pounded his fist into the air, then turned sharply, climbing down the side of the canyon wall, following the path cut by his sliding bike yesterday. Once he reached it he sorted through his gear, retrieving the essentials for his hike, including both water bottles. There was no reason to linger now. Barth re-traced his steps to the trail and started heading south in full stride, confident he would cross the path of another moving vehicle before dark. He realized he had no idea of the distance he'd traveled since his last contact with civilization. As usual, he'd been preoccupied with the natural surroundings or his own pensive wanderings, paying no attention to details like mileage. He had, however, set the trip meter on his bike when he filled the tank, so he could get the distance by trekking back down the canyon wall. He could, but Barth didn't have time or energy to waste at the moment and, besides, the knowledge would make no real difference to him. After this near miss he quickly realized a sense of mission unnecessary in his travels thus far.

I'd better make tracks.

Trudging south in the dusty trail ruts, Barth was conscious of the slowing of time. No doubt the sensation was due to the change in his mode of travel in the last twenty-four hours. No longer the *tourista* zipping through the countryside, his labored pace now tied him much closer to his desert surroundings. Instead of enjoying the opportunity to absorb the sights and sounds of the morning, however, his ruminations were of a more anxious sort. This wasn't a survival trek: he was convinced he was not in such dire straits. Still, he couldn't avoid the nagging feeling that his situation warranted a degree of seriousness and con-centration that didn't allow for casual reflection. He couldn't afford the luxury of wandering aimlessly or letting time slip away. For the first time since leaving

Kansas City, he was on a definite mission, and couldn't rest until he had achieved his objective.

Time now mattered.

Barth's relation to the desert had been flipped in the instant his bike left the trail. Nature had been his host, his entertainer, while riding through and choosing the vistas to which he directed his attention. Now, however, he was forced to assume a closer relationship with the rocks and scrub plant life. He had to maintain a single-minded focus, had to avoid wandering. The desert was now an obstacle, even a threatening presence, one that must be conquered.

The warming air held a more foreboding promise. This was the threat of unrelenting heat he knew was heading straight from the rising sun with every step. He was comfortable, even without the cooling breeze flowing over and under his handlebars, but this wouldn't last. Looking off into the distance, he detected undulations in the air causing distortions in the horizon. The heat waves generating this optical illusion were already present, and the phenomenon, even at a distance, was a taunting reminder to Barth, through the dancing images, that his turn in the desert heat was only a matter of time, and not much at that. Nothing in the landscape provided a credible hint of respite from the growing sun. The outline of a sandstone ridge off to the east, harboring only a vague promise of shade, could hardly be trusted where the combination of a lack of convenient landmarks and the distortions of desire rendered distance calculations nearly impossible. Besides, if he left the road and headed in that direction, sooner or later he'd have to return to make his way out of here. His logic had not yet been affected.

Barth had a vivid image of the searing heat of an average August day in Kansas City, with waving hot air no less hallucinating in its impact than the atmosphere surrounding him. He could easily recall the withering, enervating, three-digit temperatures forcing him to remain in the house, in the car, and in the office, except for short, quick transitions from one of these sanctuaries to the next. The difference between then and now was, of course, in the details. This was a Kansas City scorcher *sans* leafy elm trees, brown grass, asphalt boulevards, row houses, stone mansions and, most important, the opportunity to duck into shelter, bathe his body in air conditioning and his parched throat in the ice cold liquid of his choosing. Choosing, of course, but he had chosen to leave Kansas

City and, therefore, had chosen the unknown consequences to follow, including his present predicament. This logic, however, did little to alleviate his growing unease.

Barth maintained an even, unvarying pace, keeping his footfalls in a straight line in the center of the rut he was following. The more uniform and efficient his walk, he reasoned, the more precious energy he was conserving, and the sooner his mission would be accomplished. If his thoughts started wandering, okay, but his feet must not. The more automatic and trance-like his movements became, the less he agonized on his predicament, the better.

During the first couple hours he was able to maintain a steady gait without difficulty, but he had no sense of making progress. He was far from the place where he had started, he knew that, but was beginning to feel disoriented. While surveying the landscape, it was apparent there was nothing to which he could direct his gaze to inform him of a change in his position. Barth searched vainly for a landmark he could use to gauge his distance, but the desert in this stretch was not sufficiently differentiated to his untrained eye. There were no large trees or clusters of plant life close by, and the mountains were so far distant they were useless for this purpose. He reasoned that, as long as he kept moving on the trail, he'd be okay, but the thought was now less reassuring. He'd been sure he would have encountered a vehicle by now, that he'd be sitting, shaded by its roof, while heading for an outpost of civilization.

His watch informed him that noon was approaching, but the reminder was unnecessary. Barth was conscious of the sun burning directly overhead, and, most of all, of a heat like the breath of a furnace surrounding him. He was also aware of the approaching closeness of warping light waves that had appeared much more distant a few short hours ago. Doubts about his capacity to overcome his obstacles were beginning to materialize. He stopped, took a swig from his water bottle, and trudged on, knowing he had no choice. He was surprised this degree of uncertainty had overtaken him in what he considered a short span of time.

Surely, I can keep going until dark if I have to.

Periodically, surges of determination revived him and he was able to convince himself that there was somehow, inexplicable for now, a value in his present ordeal that he would appreciate retrospectively from the comfort of a motel room. As the afternoon wore on, however, these flashes of optimism alternated with increasing suspicions of his peril and a steadily mounting frustration accompanying the continuing absence of any signs of approaching civilization. The hot sun was depleting his reserves of optimism, and he had, despite his caution, already drank half the water he'd brought with him.

This is getting serious.

The realization haunted every step now.

His black leather biking boots, vital for protection on the road, were a distinct liability on the desert trail. He would have taken them off, the ground heat had long ago reached his feet, and constant rubbing was creating blisters, but he didn't dare. The bare road would have taken a greater toll for such foolishness and even this straggler knew this. He stopped momentarily, bending over slowly to untie the laces and loosen their stranglehold. He hoped this compromise would provide some relief.

When he stood up he felt lightheaded and had to take a second to get re-oriented.

Fatigue was beginning to take its toll, but Barth managed to continue down the road, placing his feet in front of him in a more or less automatic pattern, staring at his foot placement to check his mechanics. He knew that tarrying in the open sun wasn't an option, but beyond that, he lacked the energy to analyze his situation further. Desperation was taking hold, the seriousness of his situation was clear to him now, but there was nothing to be done, nothing, except for his robotic walking. Eventually, however, his desperation and anxiety began to fade, replaced by a blank acceptance. This was not a rationally-arrived-at reaction to his predicament, but represented the exhaustion of energy reserves that might have otherwise been allotted to emotional expression. From any objective, and now subjective perspective, he was being transformed into a zombie-like figure without hint of desire or fear. Only his muscular memory remained unaffected, repeating the same sequence of leg and foot movements without conscious knowledge of a purpose.

Barth continued down the trail like this for hours, until sometime in the late afternoon, when, suddenly, a flicker of alertness crossed his face. He raised his head and looked out, expecting there was something to see. The bright, wavy horizon hadn't changed, however, except that it appeared more distorted, the line separating sand and sky now quite indistinct, blurred. Still, he mustered a reserve of energy from some untapped source, focusing on an intuition. There was, at this moment, something out there demanding his attention, something he couldn't detect directly through his senses but which was, Barth was sure, just out of range.

Then it came, almost imperceptibly at first, sporadically, a sound—not recognizable, but something out there which hadn't been present seconds ago. He wasn't hallucinating, he was sure of that. He stopped, removing the distraction of his walking, sharpening his focus on whatever it was he was sensing. Gradually, he detected a steady hum in the distance, as much a vibration he felt in the ground beneath his feet as something he could actually hear. Now he noticed some variation in the sound, directly ahead of him—he knew that much now. The audible oscillations in the signal were consistent with a motor of some kind.

Barth looked due south, following the trail and scanning the landscape, questioning why he hadn't seen some evidence of this phenomenon before detecting it through his hearing. His answer came almost with the thought. Now he could see one small spot of the warped, shimmering horizon moving slightly. It had escaped his attention until now. The spot was becoming darker and larger, advancing at an accelerating pace directly in front of him. Barth spread his legs wide, planting his feet as firmly as possible in the sand, holding his outstretched arms as far as he could reach over his head. He looked straight ahead with a blank, unvarying stare that would not be distracted. Not a show of bravado, or even determination, although his countenance could certainly be mistaken for the latter.

Barth was a blank, empty stick figure, depleted of energy and void of any semblance of emotion. A remaining kernel of rational thought informed his actions and he reflexively conformed to its dictates. No choice was involved. An end to his ordeal in the desert was fast approaching, and it wasn't possible for him to care about the outcome. An end. This was all that mattered in the moment.

No more suffering. Over.

An instant later, the horrible squealing of worn-out drum brakes and the dust trailing out of the cab's wheel wells accompanied the vehicle's appearance in his vision. Definitely not a phantom, although Barth wondered for a split second at the image of the rusting grill and dirty headlights staring at the intruder-obstacle in their path. The truck lurched, then shrugged to a stop, shaking as it did so, thirty feet from him. Its rust and faded blue paint were clearly visible. Barth was able to shake off his stuporous haze momentarily, regaining an awareness of his immediate situation with the remnant of self-consciousness not drained away by the unrelenting heat.

The driver's door swung open and out climbed an old man, a relic likely as old as his truck. He stepped forward while Barth stood still, hardly able to move, now that it wasn't necessary.

"What the hell are you doin' out here?" The driver was as surprised as the struggling survivor.

"I'm here," Barth stammered, knowing his response was inadequate, but unable to add anything, not a word.

"I'm here," he repeated, his voice trailing.

"This way, come with me." The driver sized up the situation, realizing questions were wasted time and effort. He came close, firmly grabbing Barth's right arm and leading him, step by step, to the passenger door, opening it and pushing the stranger into the seat, at which point his head slumped back and his torso went limp. Barth's body assumed command, sinking into the seat's contours.

The road bumps and noise could be felt and heard now. Barth was vaguely aware that he hadn't been sitting here before. He said nothing while surveying the road and the landscape through which he was passing. As far as he could tell it hadn't changed at all except for the fact that his passenger status rendered it much less threatening. When he turned his head he saw the face of the proprietor of the shack where he had gassed up yesterday, now staring directly at him.

"You all right, kid? Take some water."

He handed Barth a plastic canteen. He was only too glad to accept the offer, eagerly guzzling its contents.

"There's plenty, don't worry. You look like death warmed over."

"I feel like it too. I don't think I had much left when you stopped."

"I could see that. What happened to your bike?"

"Somewhere in the canyon, I don't really know. I went off the trail yesterday and started walking this morning. I was beginning to wonder if I'd ever see anyone out here."

"You're lucky. You might get ten people coming up this road in a week."

"Any chance you can help me find my bike and get it to Ridle's Gulch?"

"We'll find your bike later. Ain't nobody gonna bother it, I can tell ya that for sure. But we ain't headed for Ridle's Gulch, not by a long shot. I got work to do, and we'll have to get the bike on the way back. I'll call Hiram Rainwater tonight and let him know, he'll look it over."

"Yeah, thanks. I don't know what's wrong. It looks okay but I can't get it started. Anyway, where are we going?"

Barth didn't think he was being intrusive with his question. He understood that he was a passenger, not setting the itinerary. He was content sitting in the shaded cab, his butt settling in the large indentation in his half of the sweaty vinyl bench seat and a cooling breeze blowing through the open window. Still, even while being grateful to this old coot and willing to go along for the ride, he was curious, to say the least.

"Look, kid, you gotta understand something. I don't need company where I'm headed, and I don't have time to go out of my way and take you back or shuttle you to Ridle's Gulch. On the other hand, I couldn't leave you back there on the road, you'd never make it out here. So I'm stuck with you, and you're stuck with me, like it or not. That's the way it is. If you're sure you can keep your mouth shut and just go along, absolutely sure I mean, we'll get along and you'll get back okay. Otherwise, you have any doubts, just say so, and I'll be glad to stop and let you off. Ridle's Gulch is forty miles up the road. Understand what I'm sayin'?"

The businesslike tone surprised Barth, but who was he to argue?

"Yeah, I understand. Hey, no problem. It's not like I have a choice, is it?"

Barth was beginning to feel nervous about the situation, but knew there wasn't any alternative available to him but to literally ride this out.

"No, you surely don't. But don't worry. You'll be okay. I just can't be too careful and, believe me, if I didn't think I could trust you, I would have let you off a few miles back. I'm not foolin' around, that's all, just want to make myself perfectly clear."

"Oh, no problem here, believe me."

The man had warned him about carrying enough water yesterday, and now was assuring him he had nothing to worry about, so Barth figured, despite his gruff demeanor, whatever the hell was going on, he'd be on his way again if he was patient, and he certainly had time. Still, he couldn't help but wonder what brand of adventure he had committed himself to and why the need for secrecy.

Is this guy smuggling drugs or contraband across the desert? No, I doubt it, neither he nor his truck are exactly inconspicuous, and by the looks of that ramshackle excuse for a gas station it's obvious money isn't exactly a high priority. No, I'll find out soon enough.

"My name's Barth. I'm just riding through on vacation from Kansas City."

Maybe this man had unanswered questions or suspicions about him.

"Gillespie." He looked forward without saying another word. Barth determined this was not a person who enjoyed spontaneous conversation with strangers.

Despite what seemed an interminably long day due to his own ordeal, it wasn't much after five when Gillespie pulled out a GPS from an army surplus canvas bag on the floorboard, certainly an incongruity in this truck. He took a quick look and, apparently satisfied, set it back. Sensing Barth's curiosity, he offered an explanation.

"You never can tell out here. Sometimes the desert'll fool ya and you won't know where you are, even if ya been out here a million times. Even if you turn off at the same place, your tracks will be gone the next time you come out, so you can't depend on that either."

Barth felt reassured that this taciturn old coot had broken his silence and again acknowledged his presence. Wherever it was they were heading, it was evident here was a careful, meticulous soul for whom this excursion held an important purpose, one that, by the luck of his own misadventure, was providing an opportunity for participation. His apprehension was supplanted by intrigue; he could only wonder what the desert held out here that was so compelling.

A few minutes later Gillespie slowed the truck, turning off the road where, sure enough, there was no indication of prior visitation. He steered it carefully down a gentle slope and reached level ground shortly, heading in a straight easterly direction, carefully avoiding the protruding rocks and sudden dips in the terrain. Barth spotted short remnants of tire tracks, no longer than a yard or two, but enough to assure him that Gillespie knew where he was going. Scrub brush and desert flowers were abundant, as well as short cactus plants. Straight ahead he sighted a lone mesa. It became apparent to Barth that their path was oriented to this landmark, still at a distance. Barth directed his attention to the looming natural tower, dark despite the late afternoon sun. From his vantage point it was a dominating presence in the landscape. As they approached it grew even larger, not only because it occupied a greater proportion of their horizon, but because, with the gradual downward sloping of the surrounding land its height was continually magnified.

Another magnificent backdrop for a Technicolor western.

Barth was getting accustomed to Gillespie's preference for silence. He, too, had little use for words now, preoccupied with the awe-inspiring giant of nature standing directly in front of him, in shades of brown at its base turning to reds and even lighter reds and sand as the sun shone off the edge of the leveled top. Gillespie was driving the truck toward a spot directly in the middle of the base, leaving no doubt that this was their destination. He pulled up close to the mesa's edge and stopped, opening the door and turning to Barth.

"You can stay down here if you like, kid, makes no difference to me, but I'm gonna be up there till sometime tomorrow. Once I get up there, that's it," he said, pointing to the summit. Not exactly a friendly invitation, and he still hadn't divulged the purpose of the trip. Barth said nothing in reply. He opened his door and stepped out, noting that he had regained his legs, not entirely, but enough. He figured he really had no choice but to go along. He'd find out soon enough what this taciturn old coot was up to.

"You can make yourself useful by hauling equipment, save me a trip now that you're here. Take the duffel with the shoulder straps, but make damn sure you don't drop it." Barth obliged, pulling out a heavy, jam-packed canvas khaki bag with the legs of a tripod sticking out.

"You sure know how to make someone welcome, that's all I can say."

"Let's get this straight, sonny. I didn't ask you to show up on the road, and you sure didn't seem to care where the hell I was going when I picked you up. I'm not partial to letting fools die in the desert, but I got work to do, and it ain't gonna hurt you one damn bit to take another day or two out of your busy schedule. You and your bike will get back to wherever it is you're heading soon enough, don't worry about that. Just watch your step and you'll get through this."

Barth hadn't intended to trigger this little diatribe from the old man; he only meant to insert a comment regarding his gruff manner of communication.

"Hey, I'm not complaining. I know the deal. I'm better off here than dead on the road, I think. You see me carrying this don't you? All I'm saying is it wouldn't hurt you to be a bit more civil."

"Like I said, follow me."

Gillespie turned directly toward the base and began walking, his backpack tall enough to block the sight of his head. Barth figured he'd made his point. Pressing it further would be useless. He quietly started hiking behind his erstwhile savior. For the first time since leaving Kansas City someone else was setting his agenda and he had no choice but to follow. He'd grown used to making his own schedule and resented this forced interruption. He managed, with some effort, to keep up the brisk pace Gillespie was setting, despite having walked countless miles already this day.

Barth couldn't figure out the nature of this venture, but it was obvious Gillespie had been here before and knew exactly where he was heading. When they reached the nearest point of the mesa, Gillespie stopped for a second, lifting his right foot and placing it firmly on a narrow outcropping about a foot above the desert floor. He shifted his weight forward, boosting himself up on the raised step. At this point Barth realized they were climbing up the face to some unknown level. He detected an ascending line of footholds winding around the side of the tower, at least twenty feet above ground level. Perhaps these were even created by Gillespie. *Is this a geological expedition?* Barth's rudimentary knowledge informed him that gold or silver were highly unlikely to be found in such formations, but why the need for secrecy? He watched Gillespie closely, because he didn't want to fall behind, and to make sure his foot placement mirrored his leader's. In a matter of seconds he realized the path up the side of the tower had no immediate end. He was nervous, looking down at the desert base, now thirty feet below. Leaning in toward the rock wall, he grabbed at handholds when he could find them and paid close attention to his feet. Barth considered Gillespie's offer to let him wait down below, but it was too late to turn back. He needed to stay close, no matter what he thought of this man.

It dawned on Barth that Gillespie must be some sort of nature photographer. That would explain the tripod. The secrecy was for the purpose of ensuring an exclusive market for his photographs, a reasonable precaution. Perhaps he could enjoy this adventure, after all. He shifted his attention back to where it was needed, careful placement of his feet and balancing the pack. The two climbers proceeded slowly, steadily; it was evident they weren't stopping anytime soon. Although he couldn't take time to pause, Barth stole an occasional glimpse outward to enjoy panoramic views of increasingly greater expanses of the earthly landscape to the west. Not a trace of human habitation within sight, not even a visible trace of the dirt trail they had made while getting here. *Perfect for pictures.*

The footholds began to widen, allowing him to place both feet on the same step, relieving the vertigo he was feeling while looking outward. Barth couldn't resist looking in any event. The regularity and number of steps at this height belied any notion that these could have been made by Gillespie. Barth knew that he was trodding on a staircase, painstakingly carved out of the rock walls of the mesa, which had borne the weight of many climbers before him. Now he was asking himself more questions with every step, becoming intrigued with the mystery of the mission, careful to be mindful of his footfalls and the shifting weight of the heavy pack.

What the hell am I carrying, a photography lab?

At this point, high enough to render the truck below an incongruous blue rectangle, Barth was losing his nervousness, even with the edge of the rock ledge a precarious few inches from his right foot. He supposed Gillespie would disclose the secret of their destination to his conscripted pack mule now if he asked, but that wasn't possible; he was too far behind and the climb didn't lend itself to conversation.

Barth could see the edge of the mesa's top, but Gillespie had stopped about thirty feet below, waiting for him to catch up. A minute later they were standing together, Barth one step below. Gillespie pointed to a spot level with his waist to his left.

"Watch it here, make sure you grab something on your side and lean into it until you're almost touching. Look where I put my feet and don't make any mistakes, you got all the grub in your pack and I ain't inclined to starve up here."

This man of few words swung his weight around, keeping his chest close to the rock as he had instructed Barth, and began creeping sideways. Barth's confidence disappeared as he realized he was now a rock climber, not his idea of fun or excitement. He focused his attention on Gillespie's moves as intently as he had ever done with his own while riding. The pair inched slowly in tandem around the side of the rock face. Then the old man stopped, turning his head to his companion.

"Okay, we're here, just keep leaning in until you're standing on the floor. Nothing to it."

Barth was doubtful, and wary, but followed, slowly, watching as Gillespie disappeared from view. He felt a rush of anxiety but kept edging his body along until, suddenly, a whole new image confronted him. To his left was a cavernous opening, extending into the rock as far as he could see, far enough to elude the rays of the afternoon sun, even without the rock overhang on the upper edge. The opening was quite wide, perhaps as much as forty feet, and the floor was remarkably flat, solid rock as far as Barth could tell. The ceiling of the cavern was at least eight feet from the floor at its opening. Gillespie was standing at the edge, his own pack lying on the floor behind him. Barth didn't hesitate in taking the single upward step that propelled him inside this spacious natural sanctuary.

"Wow, this is incredible!" The only words he could muster were woefully inadequate to match the wonder of the site on which he was now standing, surveying an entirely unanticipated landscape. He looked out on the unending vista below and outward, greater than the reach of his eyes.

"This is better than any photograph you could take, now I understand this."

"No, sonny, I don't think you do. The real scenery is inside, back there in the dark. Open your eyes and your ears and you'll get a lesson you won't find in books. Let's get this stuff unpacked first, while we got daylight left, then I'll show you something."

Gillespie's tone was more accommodating than at any time since their meeting.

"Over in the corner there, near the edge, so you don't disturb anything. Just set things out on the ledge and we'll get it straight later."

Barth set his pack down carefully, relieved to get the weight off his back, and looked around, letting his eyes adjust to the shade. He could see scattered piles of stone toward the interior, forming sections of a line, or wall, remnants of a structure with openings and ledges. He heard Gillespie's steps from somewhere in the darkness, then flashes from a light, a lantern. Whatever Gillespie was up to, he was about to find out, but instead of venturing back he decided to stay near the edge, unpacking the bag. He pulled out the tripod, then a small container labeled "camera," then blankets, styrofoam containers, and a metal box of tools constituting the bulk of the weight. A couple of large notebooks emerged from the pack, some cooking utensils tied in a bundle, a large plastic container of unknown fluid, full water bottles, and a clear plastic bag with maps and books. He could see the title of one, *On the Trail of the Lost Anasazi*. He finally knew the secret. This was an ancient dwelling of some sort, and for reasons unknown to him, Gillespie was less than eager to have its location become public. *Treasure? Is this guy a grave robber, looting ancient artifacts for sale?* Whatever was going on, Barth would soon find out. He decided that he had an obligation to this irascible relic to keep his word, even should it prove distasteful to do so.

What it boils down to is, this guy saved my life and he could have left me out there, I owe him that much. Maybe there's a perfectly legit explanation for this.

Gillespie returned from his brief foray into the darkness and surveyed the objects laid out by Barth while unpacking his own rucksack.

"Nothing broke, great. We'll need everything, the two of us."

"Can you tell me now what this is all about?"

"Sure kid. You've heard of the Hohokam people?"

"No, not really."

"Not surprising. Their culture disappeared five hundred years ago, but they lived in Mexico, Arizona, out on the plains, and in this area for fifteen centuries. Some of them lived where you're standin' right now and made their livin' below, when scrub wasn't the only thing growing here. The way I figure, at least four families lived in this cave in the last ten centuries. You've heard of Mesa Verde?"

Barth nodded. The massive cliff dwellings in southern Colorado, he recalled.

"Well, the early cultures, like the Hohokam, lived in houses on the ground, and some lived in caves like this. The houses are long gone, except for holes in the ground, but if you look carefully out there you can see the outlines of irrigation ditches they dug by hand. That's how Hiram and I found this place."

This was the most information provided by this man since they'd been thrown together. Barth guessed that this guy was starting to trust him.

"Here. Take the light and see for yourself what's back there. Just be careful and don't move anything, got that? I'll fix us something to eat."

"Thanks, I won't touch anything."

This guy had saved his life and was entrusting him with something obviously very important. Barth was not about to risk offending him. He walked, then stooped, then crawled to the rear of the cave, barely visible in the remnant of daylight reaching its depths, but easily seen with the aid of the light. His eyes followed the carefully piled flat rocks forming walls that had likely stood for centuries. They were perpendicular to the back wall, setting apart what appeared to be open rooms.

Barth was on his knees, looking into the center space, studying objects he couldn't identify but knew had archaeological significance. A group of undecorated bowls was stacked in the rear corner, upright and appearing to be undisturbed. Next to them was a pile of shells, a mystery in the middle of this desert. Barth crawled to the adjoining alcove to his right and was astounded to see a pair of figurines, possibly made of clay, although he wouldn't touch them. They were light colored, in contrast to the rock floor on which they stood, and, to Barth's untrained eye, represented a form of four-legged animal, now looking straight at the intruder facing them on his hands and knees. Momentarily startled by their presence, he regained his composure, crawling to the other walled-off areas, where groups of similar objects nestled in quiet repose. He was struck by the fact that nothing looked like it had been moved during the uncounted centuries following the domicile's abandonment. Long strands of dried grass were scattered on the floor near the back wall, testimony to the capacity of the land to support agricultural activity during an era long since ended.

In one corner Barth encountered a closed space with walls formed from upright bundles of sticks covered with dried mud. He would later learn that this was called wattle-and-daub construction and that this was a granary, protecting the corn grown below from weather and rodents.

Barth had seen enough to at least know the general nature of Gillespie's interest and decided to return to the opening, hoping his host was still as talkative as he'd been a few minutes earlier. Gillespie, in the meantime, had rearranged the gear and was tending to a pan resting on rocks, heated by a lit sterno can.

"Have a seat and enjoy an elegant repast."

Barth sat opposite Gillespie, the makeshift stove between them, studying his host. Gillespie carefully unwrapped the aluminum foil, removing two oblong, doughy-looking pieces, placing them in the pan. As they warmed, Barth realized he had encountered this appetizing smell before, when he stopped at the Texas-New Mexico border *en route* to Tucumcari.

"What's in the pan?"

"Frybread. You've never had frybread?"

"No."

"Well, it's obvious you haven't done much traveling in these parts. You can't get anywhere near Indian country without seeing this."

"How's it made?"

"Easy. It's just white flour and lard."

"Doesn't strike me as traditional Indian fare."

"Well, it's been traditional since the 1870s. Your government gave it out, the cheapest ingredients possible, to the reservations. It's been around ever since and we can't get rid of it."

"Why do you eat it then?"

"Taste."

Gillespie handed Barth a chunk, and he had to admit, it was delicious, especially at the end of the day he'd been through. He washed it down with a swig from the canteen Gillespie handed him.

"Yeah, I can see getting used to this."

"More like addicted. You go to the reservations, all you see are fat, diabetic Indians who've been eating this all their lives. Frybread and alcohol, the white man's way of getting rid of the Indians he couldn't shoot."

Barth was silent. He didn't know how to respond to the blunt truth of this observation. Anything sounding like agreement, no matter how sincere, might come off as patronizing. Gillespie sensed his unease, quickly filling the void.

"Hey, that's all right. Eat it, enjoy it. I do. Hell, I'm too old to change. Besides, you got to remember, we Indians ain't exactly defenseless. We gave the white man tobacco, after all."

They both managed a laugh. Whatever notion Barth might have had of a Native American in this part of the world, this wasn't it. He hadn't thought of this man's ethnic identity until he had brought it up himself, and it still wasn't obvious, at least from his looks and dress. Also, this man's diction and vocabulary were not what he expected based on his prior encounters with Indians, all confined to television and movie portrayals. This was another in a series of lessons about himself.

From this point their interaction began to get a bit more comfortable. Seeing that Gillespie wasn't quite the irascible curmudgeon of their initial encounter, Barth became less hesitant in asking about his activity in the cave. Gillespie, for his part, saw that he could trust this guy. He seemed genuinely interested in what, for him, was a passion. Gillespie pulled a Tupperware container from one of the packs and removed the top, holding it so that Barth could clearly see a large assortment of arrowheads and a couple of what he correctly guessed were spearheads. Gillespie explained that these were commonly referred to as Clovis points, stones shaped by striking them with other stones, creating indentations called flutes from the induced flaking. The name derived from the fact that a spearhead like those in the container had been found among the skeletal remains of a woolly mammoth near Clovis, New Mexico in the 1930s, although similar points had since been discovered in all 48 contiguous states. Current theory, according to Gillespie, suggested these tools had been brought by Asian hunters across a northern land bridge to North America as many as 13,000 years ago. The hunter-gatherers who lived here would fasten these points to shafts that were propelled by sling-like devices called atlati, sufficiently powerful and accurate to bring down deer, antelope, elk and bighorn sheep. He had discovered the points during his first trip to the cave, a few weeks ago, and brought them with him today to return them to the site where they were found, after studying them at his place, the garage where they had met yesterday.

Barth assumed the role of student while he was getting introduced to an important aspect of American history missing from his textbooks. Relaxed, and seeing he had an attentive audience, Gillespie was becoming animated, eager to convey the rationale for what he regarded as an important mission, his mission. He had become interested, only during his adult life, in the history of his predecessors in the southwest, people like the Anasazi and Hohokam who had migrated from unknown parts of the continent, settling in this area before the Navajo, Zuni or his own tribe, the Hualapai. Gillespie was as absorbed in the study and reconstruction of the history of these early migrants as others were in migrations to the continent by Spanish and Portuguese explorers, or later waves of Irish, Chinese, and East European immigrants. Gillespie saw himself as a searcher for historical antecedents of his own culture, not because it was more important than others, but because it had been neglected and lost, even by Native Americans.

"Why are you doing this by yourself? It seems to me you could be getting some real support, grants, help, you know, so you wouldn't have to be coming here alone to do this."

Barth thought this a natural question, now that it was apparent Gillespie wasn't a grave robber, and wasn't interested in selling artifacts.

Gillespie explained that, in reality, there wasn't much in the way of tangible support for efforts like his, that is, not until the importance of an undiscovered site was well-documented. Only then could you hope to arouse enough interest by the state to get it protected before it was stripped clean by those who made their living selling artifacts to collectors and museums at prices that discouraged anyone desiring to preserve an entire site or collection intact.

"What about the people living on the reservations in the area, aren't they interested in what you're doing?"

"Those reservation trinket traders..."

Gillespie's voice grew louder.

"They think they're doin' me a favor by accepting me as one of them! Hell, what I'm doing is for the REAL Indians, not these guys who don't know anything about their own heritage. They just make it up as they go, copy pottery patterns without any idea what they mean. As long as they stay one step ahead of the tourists, they don't give a damn. The tourists want a taste of genuine Indian culture, these guys are more than willing to give it to them for their dollars. First the Rez, then the frybread, the liquor, then they let us be "authentic." Now you tell me, who's that for, us or them? And these fools, they can't tell the tourist Zuni culture from the real thing, if they ever could. And they don't care, they don't give a goddamn! If these reservation storefront Injuns really cared about themselves, about their connections, I wouldn't be the only one of 'em out here looking for places like this, finding the clues, the real story. Hell, the people who lived where we're sitting are more alive to me than some of the zombies on the Rez. No sir, this place would be swarming with Rez Injuns if it mattered."

Barth was taken aback by this diatribe, by Gillespie's energy, by a point of view he hadn't guessed at, although, sitting in the ancient dwelling with the old guy, he believed the part about the vitality of the cave's last tenants. Gillespie, conscious of the possible impact of his remarks, shifted his tone in an effort to bring both back to the calm they should be enjoying in this setting.

"Hey, don't mind me kid. I just get a hair up my butt about these things once in awhile. We're here, you had a rough day, and life is good, even with its irritations. Just look around you. You don't see no skywalks, like the one my people put in the Grand Canyon."

The tone of the last statement lacked any trace of endorsement.

They were both quiet now, looking out into an endless horizon completely devoid of hints of civilization, past or present. The evening sky was as clear and awe-inspiring as the one Barth had slept under the night before, but without the unanswered question of survival, and with the magical feeling of settling down for the night in this ancient residence. Barth was amazed by the transformation he was enjoying.

As he lay his head down on the rock floor he had a sensation of unusual lightness. Despite the traumatic ordeal of tramping under the hot sun and then, after his rescue, scaling the precarious height of the mesa's carved footpath, there was no feeling of discomfort. On the contrary, when he considered the experience of Gillespie, the dazzling stillness of the expansive night, visible from a vantage point beyond his imagination, and the connecting history of family and people in his lofty sleeping quarters, Barth felt lucky, rich, and contented. In the span of a day he had entered and emerged from a point of physical and emotional despair, through the extreme of draining, life-threatening exhaustion, and the dazed realization of rescue. Finally, through chance circumstances, he'd entered a fascinating, ancient world, thanks to the grizzled savior appearing on his heat-waved horizon. It was, Barth mused, as emotionally complete a day as anyone could expect to experience in a lifetime, missing only one thing he could think of in the moment.

He curled up, pulling the wool Navajo blanket to his neck. It was beginning to feel chilly, but the air was still, no draft could be felt this far back in the cavernous opening. Barth's imagination drifted, conjuring images of men, women and children, families living and sleeping on this floor centuries before him. He was looking out into the same sky, the same wilderness they had seen just before sleep. In vastly different worlds, there was this wondrous overlap, a shared link between him and another moment in the universal timeline.

The smell of coffee was intoxicating to Barth, who'd gone without for a couple days. He sat up, his eyes taking in the rays of sunlight creeping over the desert floor. Gillespie was bent over the makeshift stove, pouring himself a cup.

"You'll have to use a jar for your coffee. I hadn't expected guests. Hot fry-bread will be ready in a few seconds. I don't think you'll be complaining about the menu, considering what you had for breakfast yesterday."

"You got that right. You won't find me complaining about anything now, especially this close to the edge."

Gillespie laughed. It was good to have company, a new experience in his archaeological adventures. Hiram Rainwater always helped him locate these sites, but never accompanied him while he was surveying and cataloging.

Barth was up quickly, refreshed and energized by his sleep in the high, clear air. He stepped to the cave's mouth to take in another view of the area. He still hadn't gotten used to the idea that you could actually be in a place where you could look as far as your eyes could take you in any direction and not detect the presence of anyone else. Unlike yesterday, however, the thought was not accompanied by any hint of distress.

"Okay, kid, no time for sightseeing. The desert ain't goin' nowhere and we got work to do. Have some coffee and frybread and listen up."

Barth was mildly irritated by the authoritarian tone for a brief instant, but he realized the gruff, short command was just Gillespie's interpersonal *modus operandi* and no offense should be taken. Besides, this man had saved his butt and he was gratified at the opportunity to take part in this little adventure. He took a seat near the sterno, enjoying the heat in the cool morning air, grabbing a piece of frybread and gladly accepting the jar of coffee handed to him.

"We've got to make the best of every minute of daylight. What I want you to do is work the camera, starting at the corner of the cave and working your way across the back wall. Take photos of every inch of space on the walls, and every single bone, bowl, tool or whatever you find. Don't move a single thing back there. Get close-ups when you see anything that looks like a design, and watch the shells, the Hohokam were pretty damn good at etching designs in the shells. They used an acid solution they made from fermented saguaro juice, then I imagine they drank whatever was left over."

"What are you going to do?"

"I'll be right behind you, taking notes on everything that has to be described or catalogued. Your photos and my notes should be enough to convince the people who need to be convinced that this place is worth the effort and protection. Anyway, if not, it won't be because we didn't get this thing done right."

Barth had no question about this man's seriousness and adopted his attitude without hesitation. When he finished breakfast Gillespie demonstrated the camera controls. He went to the southwest corner of the cave and got down on his knees, first scanning, and then snapping, overlapping images of the walls and objects. This was slow, methodical, but surprisingly interesting work, especially when he came across evidence of an ancient artist's hand. He became absorbed in his task, carefully checking each image before going on to the next. Not a word was spoken between them, except when Gillespie had Barth show him a few frames, after which he would mumble "Good work," then return to his note-taking. Eventually, Gillespie left Barth alone, absorbed in his own labors.

This was the pattern established early that morning, one they adhered to strictly, without a break, through the daylight hours. Barth occasionally changed his posture, standing when the cave allowed, lying on his back when the available light required. Hours later, satisfied that he had covered every inch of the residence at the rear of the cave, Barth walked to the entrance and took photos of the vistas while Gillespie continued writing notes. Barth decided to relax and sat, dangling his legs over the edge of the cave's mouth, just as he had a few days ago at the Grand Canyon. It seemed longer than a few short days ago that he'd been the passive tourist, absorbing the colors and depths of another of nature's wonders, idly musing over thoughts of Wilbert Rideau and the meanings of freedom.

Gillespie stepped out to the entrance and stood beside Barth, beaming and euphoric, reveling in the knowledge that he'd finished all he had set out to accomplish, thanks to Barth's help. After packing his notebooks with the rest of the gear he invited Barth back to the campfire, not to eat, but to celebrate. He opened an oversize canteen, pouring a clear liquid into his cup and Barth's jar, handing it to him with a warning.

"Watch it, I make a pretty strong mojito!"

"Is this a traditional Indian drink?"

"You are a gringo, aren't you? In case you hadn't noticed, my hair isn't braided and I don't have scalps hanging from my belt. Not yet, anyway. No, this is Cuban, you know, like the cigars. Just drink it, it's good."

Gillespie's laugh told Barth he hadn't been offended, but had taken advantage of Barth's question to make a joke at his expense. The mojito was good, especially after the day's work in the desert air. It was cool and minty, and so sweet Barth couldn't taste the rum that Gillespie indicated was its main ingredient. It slaked his thirst and seemed to put Gillespie in an even better mood than he'd displayed a few minutes ago. Gillespie was relaxed, sitting across from Barth with his back against the cave wall, looking out to the desert in the fading natural light. With the cool night air drifting into their outdoor stage, Barth decided to ask Gillespie about his background, now that it was apparent that the taciturn, gruff recluse of two days ago was a gregarious host and teacher, entertaining his pupil last night with history he couldn't hope to absorb in a classroom.

Perhaps it was the effect of the second mojito, which Gillespie was downing within minutes of the first. Perhaps it was the feeling he derived from a good day's work, finishing his task much sooner than anticipated. Whatever the reason, Gillespie was a more than willing conscript to Barth's invitation to tell his story.

"I grew up a hundred miles from here on the Hualapai reservation, poor as dirt, but I didn't know it. Everybody on the reservation was the same way, you know, except for the traders who come in. We run around the rocks, playing in the desert and watchin' the one TV station, going to the little Navajo school until we're old enough to go to the public junior high, the Rez kids, you know, somehow surviving to high school. One day some lady talks to us Rez kids and says some of us can go to college in the east. I didn't understand why the hell she was talkin' to us, but my mother, she gets on my case real strong, she doesn't let up. She convinces me that I got to go, this is the big break for me. Hiram Rainwater, my good buddy, he and I go together, fly in a plane from Phoenix and next thing you know, we're college students, honest-to-God college students, in Boston, don't you believe! Like nothing you ever saw before, well, maybe you, but Hiram and me are lost there, cold, wet, so crowded. I brought a pair of moccasins my mother made for me. You can imagine, there was no damn place to wear them, all the ground covered with asphalt or concrete, or it's too cold or too wet. They're just like me, they don't belong there, so I hang them on the wall in our apartment. Everyday they remind me and Hiram where our real home is. I count the days until I can put them on my feet again and walk the ground, when they're not just decorations reminding me where I come from."

Gillespie paused to refresh their drinks. He was gently rocking on his earth seat; perhaps the mojitos had loosened him up. Barth wasn't, however, disposed to make any firewater jokes. He didn't have a good gauge of Gillespie's sensibilities in this area, and besides, he was feeling no pain himself. He recalled his own experience with tequila in Elk City. Thankfully, Gillespie wasn't finished.

"We stuck together and somehow survived the first year. We couldn't do the classes, we just didn't have the background. Hiram and I were so far behind in that world we knew we'd never catch up, and I got to tell you, when it's cold and you step in the cold wet stuff every time you walk outside, it gets you down. Anyway, I decided to leave, I had to get the hell out of there, but Hiram, he's different. He has this idea, he's no stupid Indian, he's not gonna get beat by the whitey system, and you know, he's a guy I always looked up to, like a big brother, so I listen, and I stay. We killed ourselves that year, and hated it, but at the end, we were still there. We didn't have any fun, we didn't have any friends, but we survived. We decided we could make it and get our ticket, what we need to get a little respect, a job, all that. We believed it, anyway. I suppose it was worth it. We lived off whitey's money, got our tickets stamped, and the way I see it now, didn't miss anything back on the Rez."

"Sounds like your friend Hiram really made a difference back then."

"And now. Hiram, he's better at socializing, getting out, than me; back then I was too afraid of strangers, they were all strangers to me, and it was still in me what I learned on the Rez growing up, about not trusting the whiteys outside. Didn't bother Hiram, he's smart and easygoing. I would never have survived back then, way up there, without Hiram kicking my butt and reminding me why we were putting up with all that crap. Sometimes they treated us like freaks, you know, the strange red men, like we were a circus act to look at and talk about, I imagine."

Barth couldn't miss the similarities between Gillespie's story and the one he had listened to from Sedley Crump in the plane that night in Oklahoma. This man, however, had left his home, crossed the Mississippi, and returned. And, somehow, he had become the crusty amateur archaeologist who was sharing his frybread and mojitos, as well as his life story.

"What happened after you finished school?"

"When we got out of there and came back, I imagined it would be easier, you know, I'm coming home and all that. It was almost a bigger surprise than when we went east, that's the truth. We weren't really Rez people anymore, we were educated and, you know, in some ways, we were different. It sneaks up on you.

Anyway, Hiram and I come back here, we got work as linemen with SOWEPO, that's Southwest Electric Power, out of Vegas and Lake Havasu City. We were good climbers, that's what mattered, you see what they thought about our engineering degrees. We worked, though, for thirty years we had paychecks every two weeks, and our families were fed, can't complain about that. Hell, all the building in that part of the country, Las Vegas, the crews working for Hiram and myself wired most of that."

"You're married?"

Barth recalled the outpost shack where he had first encountered Gillespie, not a structure that resembled a home, and no sign of anyone else.

"Yeah, I was, twenty-five good years I had with Marilee, two good kids. She passed five years ago, breast cancer."

"Sorry to hear that."

Of course he was, but Barth knew this sounded pretty weak. Nothing adequate to say to that.

They sat silent for a few seconds. Barth stared at the flickering sterno flame while Gillespie looked out at the dark horizon. The moon was a bright half tonight. Gillespie broke the silence.

"Yeah, she was something else. Best part of my life. We really had something together, we did. A real home, kids had everything they could want. She made me proud. She reminded me to be proud of my heritage."

Barth didn't understand Gillespie's reference, but sensed he would find out. He didn't know whether it was the mojitos that allowed him to divulge his story, the atmosphere of this ancient dwelling, or what, but he knew enough to stay out of the way.

"Marilee and me, we were both outsiders, in a way, she grew up in Phoenix, in the city, but she was a proud Hualapai and never forgot it. Maybe being outsiders made us closer, I don't know. Yeah, that's the way I see it. When Hiram and I come back here after college, I had one foot in each culture and I didn't know it. Some of the Rez people weren't shy about letting me know where I fit. When I took the lineman job for SOWEPO, that was more or less it. I decided, make the best of it, get out, see what you can do. Well, I think that was smart, or maybe I was just damn lucky. I probably wouldn't have met Marilee and had the great years and family she gave me. No way."

"You mind telling me how you got from there to here?"

Barth's compulsive desire to find the missing piece couldn't be held in check normally, but certainly not with the addition of a little rum.

"Well, let's see. When the company started building the lines and power station in the sacred Hopi hunting grounds, that's when this started for me. That's when I knew, I'm not part of the Rez, but there's still a lot of it in me. I got plenty pissed when I heard from one of the linemen about the plans, both me and Hiram, but we decided to keep our mouths shut, just play dumb for awhile. When we got enough information, we got together one night and made a list of the elders and the firebrands we knew would take things seriously. Hiram knows an attorney who let us use his office to make calls, just in case. We spent the whole damn night calling everyone we could reach. The next day, we went to work, putting on our best ignorant faces and, you know, the damn fools, they never knew what hit them, it was so fast. All the reporters were out there, the elders, and every screaming hothead in the Rez.

It was magic, it was so damn quick, like Custer at the Little Big Horn, they were dead before they could even fight back. Just like that. Hiram and me, we were scared shitless, hell, we know how these things work. Anyway, we were scared, but we were excited too, we stuck 'em good. Believe it or not, the bastards in the suits dumped their plans right away, hell, they even denied they had any intentions! They brought out their mouthpiece and their map, showed how they planned all along to put the power station and the connecting lines outside the burial grounds. Some people even believed them, but we knew better. Marilee, she knew it too. Hiram and me were up to something and enjoying it too much, so she knew, and you know, she was proud of me, that was the best part. We were a team, you know—she was one hundred percent behind me. When I started getting into all this stuff after that, well, she was with me then, too. All the way."

Gillespie paused, leaning back on his elbows, staring out toward the wilderness. Barth had nothing useful to say. He was as full of emotion as his host, and thought he felt the depth of Gillespie's loss as if it was his own.

"Anyway," Gillespie resumed his monologue, "that's how this started. This is my life now, and when I'm out here, I know Marilee's with me. I'm just as sure of that as I am that people with the same feeling were sitting here a thousand years ago. No doubt about it."

"Incredible. Just incredible."

Barth had nothing of substance to contribute, but felt the need to say something, if only to let Gillespie know he'd been with him the whole time, that his silence couldn't be mistaken for a lack of interest.

"Yeah, well, life goes on. Let's get some sleep. We'll pack in the morning and hit the road. Yeah, I forgot. I tried to call Hiram Rainwater yesterday to see if he could pick up your bike. No luck. Can't get any signal out here in the desert, nothing at all. We'll just have to pick up the bike on the way back and have him look at it. Hiram knows bikes, believe me. He'll get you back on the road, don't worry about that."

"Thanks for trying. I really appreciate that."

"No problem."

Gillespie was another in a succession of very generous people he had met in the last couple weeks. Right now Barth was almost glad he'd gotten himself stranded on the road. He remembered feeling like a hostage with no choice at the time he was rescued and taken here by Gillespie, but those thoughts had been completely and utterly banished, replaced with grateful wonderment at his incredible fortune. Like his other encounters along the way, this was priceless, something that would stick with him long after he had resumed his routine back in Kansas City.

Nothing was said between them after that. The energy had been sapped from both in the telling of Gillespie's story and any chit-chat now would have been superfluous, even sacrilegious. They retired to their respective parcels of bedrock, covering themselves in anticipation of the cool desert night.

With his head on a rock, Barth felt remarkably contented. He had absolutely no sense of discomfort or deprivation. Not at all, when he considered the unusual experience of this man, laying on this same rock floor a few feet away, and the dazzling stillness of the starlit night visible to him, from a vantage point beyond belief. Barth also had the strange sensation of a familiarity with the history of family and people in his sleeping quarters. He felt as lucky and as rich as he could recall at any time in his life. All that was missing …

The morning went by quickly. When Barth awoke, at the break of daylight, the coffee was already made and he could see Gillespie, at the cave's edge, bent down, grasping a long length of nylon rope. Gillespie had carefully replaced everything in the packs they carried up with them and was slowly lowering the entire load down to the bottom of the rock they had so laboriously climbed. This guy was efficient, Barth thought, certainly knew what he was doing.

The two of them relaxed over their coffee for a few minutes, but Gillespie was anxious to break camp and get back. He wanted to start working on the presentation of the site he would use to procure official protection and, he hoped, the funds needed for preservation work. They would drive north first, however, and attempt to retrieve the bike.

With Gillespie in the lead, the two of them, now with much lighter loads, descended the mountain without difficulty. Now and then Barth experienced brief shocks of anxiety while looking down the side of the rock, but by now he was sure what he was feeling was nothing more than cautious confidence or, at least, he was successful in convincing himself this was the correct interpretation. Once reunited with the desert floor, they retrieved the packs and loaded the truck. Gillespie started the truck and they were off. No words were said between them now; there was just the quiet of the desert as it had been when they drove in two days ago. Barth was much more comfortable than he'd been the last time he sat in the passenger's seat, but he couldn't help feeling, just as he had at other points in his journey, a twinge of regret, as sure as the knowledge that this would be a memory, just like Sedley Crump, Bones and Estrella, within the day.

They located the bike less than an hour after returning to the main road and towed it up the hill from which it had fallen, Gillespie driving the truck and Barth holding the bike steady by its bars. With a makeshift ramp constructed from two by sixes, they had little difficulty loading the bike, and were finally off. A cloud of dust followed them, covering the remnants of boot tracks Barth had left behind during his desperate hike beneath the desert sun.

After a quick once-over of Rocinante, Hiram Rainwater stood up, facing Barth and Gillespie, a grim expression firmly planted in his clenched teeth. Barth couldn't imagine what was coming.

"How long you been riding kid?"

"About two weeks now," he admitted, knowing that, under the circumstances, it was best not to exaggerate or embellish the truth. It was obvious from the question that his ignorance was about to be publicly exposed, once again.

"I believe it." The words were half spoken, half laughed. "You see this switch on the bar, next to the front brake?"

"Yeah." Barth was stoic, ready for his lesson.

"That's called the kill switch, what you use to shut off the engine in an emergency, when you lay the bike down and it's still running."

Bike lingo was still a foreign tongue to Barth, but he understood the reference to falling over, as in an accident, rather than the implied intentional maneuver.

"Get on and try the key."

Barth did as he was told, mounting the bike, squeezing the clutch, and switching on the ignition. Nothing.

"Push the kill switch to the right and try again."

He was obviously enjoying this. Again, without a word, Barth followed directions. This time, Rocinante came to life, without any delay, the familiar smooth hum of the engine startling him. Barth looked to Gillespie first, then to his friend. He nodded sheepishly and grinned widely, at himself for his undeniable stupidity and, at the same time, gladly, for the sheer joy of being back in business.

"Stupid, huh?" He couldn't do anything less than admit the obvious.

"Hey, we all been there kid. If this is the dumbest thing you've ever done, you're in better shape than me and Gillespie. Hell, he fell off his rocker years ago."

"Well now, ain't you the voice of sanity, Mr. Rainwater."

Hiram guffawed, loudly, infectiously. Barth and Gillespie joined in, sharing this moment of mirth. After all this, Barth was even glad to have provided the basis for this bit of levity between two long-time buddies. He knew, of course, that he'd be the butt of jokes and stories after his departure, but then, he reasoned, what the hell, nothing wrong with that. Besides, his ignorance was the basis for discovery, after all. If he'd known what he was doing, he would be cruising somewhere in Nevada now or paying the obligatory call on his sister, and the nights in the Anasazi ruins would never have been. Barth determined right then and there that he was going to try his best, at all costs, to maintain his ignorance regarding the mechanical workings of the bike. Sometimes, maybe, ignorance might be bliss.

Kate

No man is an island, entire of itself. — JOHN DONNE

Barth had been on cruise control since leaving Utah, grateful for the peace of mind achieved by rolling down the road, mile after mile, just sun and scenery, an uneventful ride through the mountains and down into flatter regions. He was riding two-lane blacktop consistently now and had the luxury of splitting his focus between the road and his surroundings without worrying about traffic. There simply wasn't any, as it turned out. Routes 6 and 95 were divided into long segments, as much as thirty miles between towns, towns he guessed would not have existed except for the need to stop and gas up. Things were elemental now, wind, light, and a feast for his eyes, no hurry, nothing else to drain his reservoir of attention.

Having survived his "mishap" in the desert, misfortune turning into a once-in-a-lifetime experience, he was determined to "loosen up," to accept things as they happened with the equanimity of a grizzled veteran. Barth was beginning to believe he deserved the accolade, knowing he still had a lot to learn about bikes and riding. Even a skeptic like himself couldn't dismiss the nature and magnitude of his accomplishment, getting this far relatively intact, no matter that hundreds, even thousands, had ridden as far or farther, and as well, or better. Barth was giving himself credit, for once, for letting his irrational impulses gain the upper hand back in Kansas City.

Not all the credit. Rocinante had served him well. A comfortable, dependable, fun and agile rolling mount. He had come to think of the bike, not merely as a well-engineered assembly of high tensile steel and alloy components, but as a responsive grantor of his wishes. It was for these reasons, as well as the ingrained habit of men toward their machines, that Barth referred to the bike in the feminine. Rocinante was more than a conveyance; she was a reliable companion who would do his bidding if he would only meet her minimal maintenance requirements and attend to the lessons she offered in the changing terrain and curves of the road. Rocinante had only been problematic in her performance twice, the first time due to the minor glitch, the loose clutch cable, the second a result of his own ignorance. Barth couldn't ask anything more of a motorcycle than Rocinante had given him. At the thought, Barth gave the grip a hard twist, as he had many times before, and Rocinante, with her understated roar, revved up, carrying her rider a little faster into the highlands of the Monte Cristo Range. Even the lowlands were elevated here, starting at 7,000 feet above sea level and rising from there.

Kate's directions were easy to follow, as it turned out. Barth recalled her description of the house and locale. "Just out of town" were her words. He laughed. Tonopah was half a tank of gas behind him.

I guess it makes sense, people out here use a different scale for describing distances.

He was already fifty miles "out of town," and it had been awhile since he'd seen even a trailer or isolated shack in the distance. He guessed he had encountered four cars and one pickup truck and marveled that he hadn't seen a single bike, especially since this was a great route for unwinding. He would have been more relaxed himself, enjoying the open, sweeping turns and long straight stretches of this desert road, had he not been worrying about missing the turnoff. He was also preoccupied with thoughts about meeting Kate in her corner of the world.

Barth and his sister were not especially close. She was ten years his junior, and Barth had long left home when she was coming of age. In addition, unlike Barth, Kate was precocious and adventurous. Instead of following his course and attending college right away, she'd left town within days of high school graduation, with only a perfunctory goodbye to Mom and Dad, after which the next contact with family was in the form of a card mailed from Amsterdam. Gregory and his parents wondered about her whereabouts for the next couple years, but gradually learned to stop worrying. Worrying, after all, wouldn't have made a difference. Kate demonstrated an independent streak from an early age that rendered her behavior unsurprising, to say the least. She had emerged, following a series of adventures, with a wider experience of the world than her older brother. Then, surprisingly, when their father was in the throes of his last illness, it was she who returned home and assumed responsibility for managing the household. This was the period when Barth, going through his divorce, was emotionally immobilized and incapable of providing meaningful assistance. Kate stayed with her mother for a year following their father's death, making sure she was stable and confident before leaving again, this time heading west, emerging, after another prolonged lack of communication, as a schoolteacher, wife, and mother in the Nevada wilderness. Barth had long ago ceased regarding her as irresponsible and, even with their lack of contact, came to view Kate a bit enviously, with a grudging admiration for the way she had struck out for herself in the world.

The road consisted of packed gravel, two worn ruts leading away from the highway up the side of the mountain, disappearing in a gradual upward spiral. Barth had to concentrate now. Rocinante demonstrated a pronounced tendency to slide sideways on this surface and he was most definitely not a dirt-biker. Memories of his unwanted foray off the trail into the desert sand were fresh enough to evoke a reflexive caution on his part. He dangled both legs off the footpegs in an effort to balance the bike while slowly forging ahead. Kate evidently had no idea what an obstacle this "short side road" posed, insofar as her brother's riding abilities were concerned. He gave the bike more throttle as he gained a little confidence and began making visible progress.

The hillside was patchy with clumps of grass among the scattered rocks and scrub vegetation typical of this altitude. An isolated area, just as Kate had described, also somewhat desolate, lacking the postcard beauty of the New Mexico hills or the canyon area in which he had been stranded. There was no suggestion here of the romance of the Clovis people revealed to Barth by Gillespie. What attraction the area held for his sister, her husband and the children he couldn't imagine, especially considering the years they had been settled here. Barth thought the barren, lonely landscape shared features of the unstimulating region he had, until a few weeks ago, considered to be his home. A place that motivates boredom, maybe escape, but not contentment. Still, he had to allow for the possibility that these impressions wouldn't stand the test of time and experience; he had accumulated ample evidence of the value of openness to other possibilities during his weeks on the road. Besides, despite the lack of closeness in their sibling relationship, Barth knew Kate was a smart, energetic woman, someone who wouldn't stay in one place as a result of habit or inertia. There had to be other reasons for her years out here in the Nevada wilderness.

The road curved upward around the north side of the mountain, hidden from his view, then headed downward, toward a wide, flat area to the west. There was still no sign of habitation other than the ruts in which he was struggling to maintain his balance, slipping and sliding with even slight twists of the throttle. He was forced to maintain a crawling pace now, still dangling his legs off the pegs to keep the bike upright. Barth had a twinge of guilt, forcing Rocinante to make the attempt on terrain for which she was most definitely not designed.

Now he could see a metal pipe snaking its way up the side of the mountain, disappearing beneath the road, with joints at equal intervals allowing it to kink and bend as necessary to reach a destination which, Barth guessed, must also be his. This was likely a water line, there was no way you could dig a well at this altitude. Sure enough, as soon as he rounded the next curve he spotted the house, a small, single-story frame structure set into the west side of the mountain at the end of the pipeline, about thirty feet above him. One switchback and he'd be there. His rear wheel spun and slid in the dry gravel as he turned the bike upward, touching the earth with both legs to maintain balance. Slowly he urged Rocinante up the road until he was within walking distance of the house. He pulled up beside an old, white Toyota pickup with patches of burnt orange, the result of years of desert dust exposure and relentless rust rash spread over most of the sheet metal.

It was a relief to lean the bike on its sidestand and dismount after his ordeal. He felt a layer of sweat on his hands while removing his gloves, a product of the challenging last stretch as much as the heat that had been magnified in his slow crawl up the mountain. As he stood, wiping his hands on his pants and grabbing his bags, the family emerged from the doorway. First Kate, recognizable, although the long brown hair he remembered was cut short, then the two girls, who he'd seen only in photos, then Ron, also known to him through family portraits.

"Merina, Ruth, this is your Uncle Greg from Kansas City."

This was the first time Barth had heard himself referred to as "Uncle." Before now his role had been confined to unseen recipient of thank-you notes for the birthday presents he occasionally remembered to send. The girls, three and five years old, said "Hello, Uncle Greg" in unison, obviously rehearsed, and stood back, hanging onto their father's legs, but clearly smiling. Kate hugged her brother heartily and was surprised that her greeting was returned with as much feeling. Ron waved from his planted spot by the steps, inviting the weary traveler inside to relax.

Together, with Barth and his sister bringing up the rear, the newly-expanded family group climbed the rock steps leading into the house, stepping onto unfinished wood floors matching the siding. The girls were barefoot and Barth, after Ron and Kate, removed his boots at the door. As he entered he could see, to his left, an open walkway to what was obviously a workshop, tools hanging from the walls, large wooden benches and the enticing, exotic scent of freshly cut woods. The room they entered was the largest in the house, furnished with comfortable, worn armchairs, a matching couch against the back wall, and a long wood table abutting the front wall. A ledge stuck out from under the large window with its view of the valley and the western horizon. The late afternoon sun filled the panorama of space and distant mountains.

Ron pulled out a rough, handmade chair from the table and Barth did the same, while Kate left the room, returning with three beers and juice boxes for the girls, who were standing together at the opposite end of the table, clutching its top and staring above its edge with eager curiosity at the welcomed stranger.

"You never said anything about a motorcycle. I couldn't believe my eyes when I saw it was you getting off that bike. You really rode it all the way from KC?"

The tone of incredulity in Kate's voice caught Barth by surprise. He had, he supposed, omitted this detail when he told her he was coming.

"Yeah, I did, believe it or not." Barth responded with a tone of false bravado, as if it was the most natural thing in the world, getting on the bike and riding a couple thousand miles for a visit.

"I'm impressed you made it up the mountain, it's not the easiest thing in the world with the truck." Ron added his note of respect and the three of them laughed together, joined by the two girls, put at ease by their parents' laughter, whatever the reason.

"Actually, I'm impressed that I made it up here. I've been learning as I go, but it's worth it. I should have done this years ago."

"Well, better late than never, Greg. It's incredible, after all these years. I don't know what got into you. When you called, first I thought something's wrong, something terrible. Force of habit with us, you know. I'm just glad you decided to come out here. You know you can stay with us as long as you like."

"Thanks, I really appreciate it. I feel like it's about time I met you, Ron, just to find out what type of guy managed to get Kate's attention long enough to stay in one place, and I should have come out to see the girls a long time ago."

Barth turned as he spoke, looking to his right, where the silent, smiling heads of the girls were perched, together, over the end of the table, still absorbed in what was for them the unusual appearance of a guest in their mountain home. They were wearing matching, floor-length beige cotton dresses covering their legs down to their ankles.

"Look, if you're not too exhausted, why don't you get your things and settle in the back room—Ruth and Merina will show you. I'll put some burritos together and we'll have dinner while you entertain us with the adventures of Greg and his bike. The girls can stay up late."

By now Ruth and Merina knew, whatever was going on, this was special. They followed their newly-found uncle out to his bike, gladly accepting two small bags he handed them from his baggage, and led the way to his room, which was, unmistakably, one of theirs.

Half an hour later the five were around the table again. This time the girls were seated, between Barth and Kate. Before long, they settled into a simple supper, entertained by Barth's condensed descriptions of the people and the land he had seen on the road between Kansas City and their Nevada home.

This was a new feeling for Barth, having the attention of an audience while he was, for the first time in his memory, providing interesting stories based on *his* experiences. He was actually telling *his* stories. Not retelling accounts he'd heard of someone else's adventures, but his own, and telling them any way he wanted. He went back and forth, in no real order, mixing stories of Gillespie and the desert with Sedley Crump and the Oklahoma hills and his night on the

Panhandle plains with the Outcasts. He'd never been much of a storyteller, but then, he never had the raw material at his disposal this journey had provided. As he became more relaxed his hand gestures grew more pronounced, especially as he sensed an absence of boredom in his audience. Although he was certainly aware of the variety and novelty of his road encounters, at this moment, in the telling, Barth knew, as well as he could know anything, that this qualified as one of the most memorable experiences of his lifetime.

Lingering in his descriptions of the characters he had met, their importance to him was undeniable. The fullness of the contact he'd made with other physical and personal worlds was obvious to each listener, even the two girls, and this was true despite the fact that Barth was omitting some aspects of his tale. Out of respect for the sensibilities of the children he made no reference to the aftermath of the gruesome accident he had witnessed in Texas, and, although he mentioned Estrella, he avoided any hint of their relationship, guessing that his sister nonetheless detected a wistful desire in his voice. Ruth and Merina were fascinated with his account of the cave dwelling in the mesa and the idea of people living in this area long before the time span their young imaginations could grasp.

The clearly outlined orange sun was split by the horizon when Barth finished his account of his ramblings, but no one, not even the girls, was exhibiting diminished interest in his stories. It took no great exercise of intellect to draw the conclusion that guests of any kind were scarce here, which was probably the point. He enjoyed spinning his tale, but now it was his turn to ask questions and fill in the gaps of his knowledge of the family's history.

Kate took the lead, telling the story of her sojourn west from their mother's Iowa home. She had gone to San Francisco with no other aim than getting a change of scenery from the Midwest. By her own telling, she led a nomadic existence within the city, taking a series of temporary jobs for the sole purpose of indulging a variety of interests and funding her travels in northern and central California. Kate said she'd done everything and tried everything during this period, but Barth didn't ask for details, figuring he was better off not knowing. She eventually got a job in a Napa Valley winery, becoming a riddler, the person who rotates the racked bottles of champagne while the contents are coming of age. While working there she had met Ron. He was employed as a carpenter, crafting custom cabinetry for the winery and dreaming of the day when he would run his own business. Kate had been the catalyst for his decision to finally take the leap, just as she'd taken the initiative in the development of their relationship and her own return to school to finish the coursework for her teaching certificate. They had uprooted themselves and transformed their lives, abandoning jobs they enjoyed and transplanting themselves to the west Nevada wilderness where they made their home and had been living since.

Merina and Ruth finally wandered outside together, losing interest in the details of the story they couldn't completely understand once Barth had stopped talking. For the first time since Barth had arrived, Ron, content to sit back and listen, began to speak, slowly, in a pronounced southern drawl, taking up where Kate's story left off.

"Kate's the one, you know, that really got things movin', I mean, between us, she sorta pushed me 'long where I wanted to go anyway, gettin' to the place where I could make my furniture, just as I designed, in my own workshop, just like I always wanted. She's the one with the push in her, pushin' herself to finish her college so she could teach and pushin' me to get started here. When we come out here this was just an abandoned shack, no electricity, no water, not liveable, not by a long shot. We just did what we had to do and, sure enough, built us a life out here with the kids. We all did it, but Kate got the ball rollin'. That's a fact."

Ron had said everything he thought necessary to complete the story. Kate sat, quiet and smiling, through his brief summary of their life on the mountain. It was obvious to Barth they were contented with the life they had chosen and made for themselves.

For the next hour the three of them sat, sipping beer and exchanging stories. Kate and Barth recounted the childhoods they hadn't shared except for their parents. Ron described his upbringing in Natchitoches, thirty miles east of the Texas border in Louisiana, a magical land of Creole plantations and oak trees thick with Spanish moss. Like Kate, he'd been eager to leave the world of his childhood when he had the chance, and was quite satisfied with his life out here in the west. Unlike Kate and Barth, neither who spent much time reminiscing about the north Missouri setting of their childhood, Ron was sentimental when he spoke of Louisiana. His hometown was two hundred miles northwest of New Orleans, but he had suffered an acute sense of loss in the aftermath of

Hurricane Katrina, following the exodus and dispersal of its citizenry at the time and wondering whether the heart and soul of Louisiana would ever be restored to its pre-disaster vitality.

"New Orleans has to live, it just has to," he asserted, with a conviction Barth admired. He had never felt the same kind of attachment to place.

Kate emphatically nodded her agreement, and quietly, the three looked out into the darkening sky over the undisturbed peace in the valley below them. Ruth and Merina, in the meantime, returned to the table, each grabbing one of Kate's arms in an unmistaken signal to which their mother willingly responded, following her daughters to a room in the back of the house. Barth and Ron kept their seats without further conversation, enjoying the calm of the settled evening. Barth had been anxious about the family meeting he originally thought of as an overdue necessity, but now, as Kate resumed her seat and nothing was said between them, he realized that another one of the assumptions he packed with him when he set out was utterly wrong. He was still a stranger out here, but he was a welcome stranger, and glad to stay a few days.

A bright sunlight, less filtered in the uncluttered, high mountain altitude, woke him early that morning. He had slept well, even with his feet hanging over the end of the bed, and was ready to explore, despite knowing it must be around seven, if that. Barth could hear the bustle of activity in the house and decided to get up straightaway. He was eager to experience as much of the day out here as possible. Dressing quickly, he stepped out of the room, pausing to look through the open front door. He could see a clouding of dust following the truck as it began rolling down the road, its bed filled with side chairs padded and bound together with twine.

Not sure what was going on, Barth detected two smells reaching him where he stood, one the unmistakable aroma of fresh-brewed coffee and the other, from the opposite direction, he guessed to be freshly-cut wood. He continued standing in the doorway, letting his eyes drink in the undivided expanse of a very blue sky meeting the equally continuous earth halfway. He let himself enjoy the picture book vista while wondering when this too would be segmented, broken up, and filled with high-rise condos, highways and strip malls. Barth guessed he was born a century too late. He would have preferred to live in an era when you could enjoy views like this with no thought that their permanence was in serious jeopardy. He realized, of course, even as the thought came to him, this was a delusion; he'd find other forms of depressing intrusions in his consciousness no matter what period in which he found himself.

I suppose I'll always be a misfit. Might as well get used to it. Stop wasting time ruminating.

The strong coffee aroma again grabbed his attention. He followed the sensuous siren of its smell. Barth realized that he wasn't just reflexively pouring himself a cup. He was absorbing the olfactory stimulation out of choice, just as he might let his eyes linger over a painting on a Nelson Gallery wall on a Sunday afternoon. Only in a setting like this could he know that he actually loved the coffee. It wasn't just the dependence, the morning fix he craved and required, liquid octane he guzzled on his way to something else out of sheer, unvarying habit. Only now, in this lazy morning, could he conclude that this vice was worth the indulgence.

He helped himself to the coffee and sat at the table, taking in the undivided panorama hanging in front of the window, there for his careful study. Any notion that this was a still life, however, was scuttled by the flight path of a diving hawk. It was off at a distance but identifiable, flying in an oblique line to a destination off to his left, disappearing as suddenly as it had appeared.

The sound of hammering interrupted the silence, coming from the workshop Barth had seen on his arrival. This was from the same source as the wood smell. It was high time he investigated.

Wood clamps, hand saws, augurs, bits, and tools he couldn't identify hung from their assigned places on the back wall. Sawn boards of various widths, lengths, colors and grains were stacked in open racks, and Ron, bent over the long oak bench filling the center of the room, was gently tapping two pieces together, absorbed in the task, although aware of Barth's presence.

"Just trying to get these chairs finished. Kate took half of them into town and I've got to finish the set this week."

"Don't let me interrupt anything. I'm glad to watch, this looks interesting, seeing a craftsman at work."

"Well, come over to this side, you'll get a closer look."

Ron guessed that Barth's interest was genuine, not merely polite. He took the two pieces apart and applied wood glue before slipping them back together, taking time to explain the advantages of the mortise and tenon joint to his audience. After placing a clamp on the joint he set it aside to dry and picked up a two-foot oak plank, which he proceeded to cut, positioning it on the router to give it a uniform edge. Barth was content to take a seat and watch while Ron returned his focus to the work. Ron was tall and lanky, with short-cut hair, and was dressed in a casual and conservative manner that would not attract attention in a crowd. He was not unfriendly, merely quietspoken and intent on his craft—watching him it was apparent that the term work did not apply.

Barth surveyed the room again, noting the presence of a computer in a corner with the image of a blueprint showing brightly on the screen. He could see parts of chairs, cabinets and what he guessed were tables, in various states of completion, all in variations of a simple, unadorned style typical of the arts and crafts school and the Stickley furniture of a century past.

"How did you get started in this business?"

"Well, that's easy. My father worked in a sawmill and brought home odd pieces of wood when I was a kid, cut them up in the backyard and made chairs and what-not for the neighbors. He was good enough, neighbors would ask him to make tables, cabinets, sometimes chairs, just out of the odd pieces, you know, but he made 'em look good, even when the wood didn't match. Taught me to use hand tools, how to pick out a good piece of wood, things like that. Came in handy, I tell ya, when I decided to get out of there. I was sixteen, just left, that's all. I sure didn't know what I was doin' then, just pure ignorance, that was me, but you know how it is, some kids, you can't tell 'em nothin.'"

This was more than Barth expected from Ron, based on his taciturn nature thus far.

"So, how'd you end up out here?"

"Well, lessee now. I just decided to head out, west, and kept on goin' till I finally ended up in Frisco. I was lucky, though. Never had any problem finding work there, all I had to do was find a wood shop, or the milling room of a lumberyard. I'd convince them I knew what I was doin', no problem there. I kept goin' from one shop to another, movin' up to the best shop in Sausalito. That's where I met Kate. She was working for the winery then, doing her riddlin' and ordering and designing cabinets, and I ended up getting the job, and we ended up gettin' hitched."

Barth suspected important details were missing from this Cliff's notes account of Ron's life from high school dropout to husband, but appreciated being let in this far.

"How'd you end up here?"

"Katie, all Katie. She sorta pushed me, convinced me I was good enough. 'You should have your own business,' she kept tellin' me, 'make your own decisions.' I thought my work was good enough, tell you the truth, but I never thought seriously about workin' for myself until she convinced me. She set up all the business stuff, the books, takin' orders, deliveries, all that, and all I have to do is what I do best, take the wood and turn it into things useful and pleasin' to the eyes. We decided the city wasn't anyplace to be raisin' kids, and we found this place through friends."

"Looks like you've made a nice home for yourselves. How do the girls like it, I mean, don't they ever miss friends out here?"

"Yeah, especially in summer, but they've grown up here, they're used to it mostly. They see their friends at school and when Kate goes to town, like this morning, when she takes an order of furniture into Beatty and picks up groceries. There might be a time when we have to rethink this for the girls, we both know that, hell, they might get the same bug I got in Louisiana and take off, you never know about kids."

"I guess not." They laughed together.

Barth was content to hang out for the next couple days while Ruth and Merina grew accustomed to his presence, walking down the trail with him and pointing out wildflowers, lizards and rocks he would have missed. He in turn told them about Kansas City, about things they might find interesting, things they wouldn't see out here, like the Missouri River, barbecue joints and the zoo. Ruth couldn't understand much of what her uncle was talking about, but followed Merina's lead, trying her best to listen intently to words and the intonations signifying enthusiasm on his part. Content wasn't really that important under the circumstances; the three of them, or four, when Kate or Ron took time to join them, were enjoying the quiet of midsummer on the mountainside.

Except for a trip to Beatty, during which Barth accompanied his sister to make a delivery of finished chairs and an armoire, they stayed on the mountain, and Rocinante occupied the same spot she'd been left in when he arrived. The trip into town provided another chance for Barth to talk to his sister, but the town itself was nothing special, basically another example of the gas and restaurant pit stops Barth had passed through on his way out here. The family home, on the other hand, even in its isolation, was an invigorating place.

By his third day, between walking the trail, pitching in with the housework, and dawdling in the shop while Ron was going about his business, Barth had become absorbed in even the most mundane aspects of living in the desert home. He was fascinated with the way Ron and Kate, and even, to a lesser extent, Ruth and Merina, assumed responsibility for the necessary tasks comprising family life, and the manner in which they were accomplished, with no specific roles assigned to each member, except, of course, for the woodworking and Kate's seasonal school teaching. Merina would, without prompting, and with Ruth tagging along, pick up the dishes from the table or separate the recyclables for the trash. In the evening one of them might pick out a book for Kate or Ron to read aloud, and Merina would sit next to the reading parent, pointing out words she knew or wanted to learn. Ruth and Merina were also adept at finding their own entertainment in and out of the house, requiring little supervision. It didn't escape Barth's notice that he observed no traces of boredom. At times long silences occurred, but no one ever seemed the least bothered or compelled to initiate conversation. This was an adjustment for Barth. He was used to spending most of his non-working time alone, but he was always uncomfortable with extended silences, compulsively filling the background air with music or sitting on his couch and flicking through the hundred cable channels available to him, demonstrating an attention span short enough to seriously limit opportunities for contemplation. Life with Kate and the family was full of such opportunities, if he chose to take them, just as the long stretches on the road with Rocinante were a breeding ground for reflection.

Barth announced he would be leaving tomorrow, concluding that the amount of time he had spent here was just about right, enough so that Kate and her family had a chance to think of him as someone other than a postcard stranger, enough for him to establish a real connection with the sister he hadn't known. The apprehension he felt earlier, when this was an obligatory stop, one he couldn't avoid, had evaporated in the dry desert heat. All the same, this seemed like a good time to go. He mapped out a route taking him into California through Death Valley, figuring this was an available experience he should have in what would likely be a once-in-a-lifetime trip. After that he'd head north and west by a route he would choose later, the only requirement that he end up in San Francisco for a few days of fun in the big city.

The last day on the mountain passed quickly, and quietly, with no hint in the actions of Kate, Ron, the girls, or their guest, that it held any special significance. The girls, exhibiting an interest in Rocinante not as strong as that of Matias, took turns sitting on the bike, then sat together on the seat while they were photographed by Kate. Other combinations of family members were duly memorialized that afternoon, but there was no sign of sadness. Merina and Ruth were furnished with a bucket of soapy water, sponges and a hose and made a hilarious attempt to wash the bike, the first time the layers of dirt had been threatened since Matias's efforts a thousand miles back. Perhaps as much as fifty percent of the accumulated grunge was removed in this manner, much of it finding its way to the girls' dresses, but the efforts were much appreciated by the adults, especially for the entertainment value.

In the late afternoon Ron retired to the kitchen to prepare supper while Barth, Kate and the girls took one last walk down the trail. The mood was light as Ruth and Merina ran ahead and the pair of older siblings rambled in their parallel ruts. Barth made sure there was no ambiguity regarding his feelings.

"This whole trip has been worth it, you know, just seeing you settled into your life out here, making a life I think most people just dream about."

"Well, Greg, that's good to hear, we're happy out here most of the time. I think you could do the same for yourself if you wanted."

"I don't know, sometimes I think, maybe it's too late for me to think seriously about any big changes. I wouldn't have the slightest idea where to begin. Besides, whatever you might think, my life isn't anything to complain about."

Kate turned her head sideways and her eyes met his, accompanied by a slight smile that communicated a questioning of her brother's last assertion.

"Well, great, if that's true. At least you've been moving. I'm still surprised you did this."

"Yeah, I am too."

Laughing in agreement, they walked on, changing the subject to a chronicling of the childrens' most recent learning experiences, formal and otherwise.

Barth shared his last supper with the family on a rough wood table in back of the house, above the roof line, looking to the unobstructed western horizon he'd grown accustomed to during the last three days. Ron prepared a simple but exotic dinner of rice and beans, generously seasoned with cayenne pepper, along with baked catfish he'd purchased during one of the family's rare trips to Las Vegas. The meal, inspired by his Cajun background, included Nevada red wine, a commodity beyond Barth's imagining until that moment and, despite any violation of culinary protocol, an addition that complemented the other tastes and smells perfectly. Whether it was the food, the setting, or the presence of their guest, Ruth and Merina sensed the special nature of the occasion. No one took any notice, however, when they left the table together, heading toward the house. A few minutes later they returned, Merina's hands carefully cradling a small accordion she brought to her father. It wasn't an elaborate instrument, but had a distinctive red silhouette painted on the top wood panel—as it turned out, a crayfish, or crawfish, or, in Ron's drawl, "what we call a crawdaddy." It was a vital survivor of his childhood, and it was apparent from the girls' expectant look that a performance was forthcoming.

Ron happily accepted the sacred offering, slipping his hands into its worn leather straps, drawing them apart, and pressing the bellows into his service. Magically, a course of airborne notes coalesced in a stream of zydeco rhythms familiar to Kate and the girls, riveting Barth's attention. Ron was playing with a joy and vibrancy conveying, as words could not, the love of the Louisiana of his youth, of a proud heritage handed down by his own father, who had played the same instrument and had a firsthand knowledge of the real giants, names like Clifton Chenier and Boozoo Chavis. Ruth and Merina jumped and turned in their own version of dancing while Kate began clapping. Barth, caught up in the joy of the moment, was stomping his feet. He was unexpectedly swept into the slipstream of another culture and its music, an echo of the magic of the mariachi band in Tucumcari.

For Barth, in this instant, everything was coming together, the physical energy of the shared Cajun rhythms, the mountain air setting, the buzz from the wine, the family setting. This was it, or at least close enough for him.

Ron played a few more of the girls' favorites, songs he'd heard himself for the first time when he was Ruth's age. When he finished he handed the accordion to Merina who, with proper respect, held it snugly in her arms and headed toward the house, Ruth in tow.

The act of playing the music of his soul had an energizing effect on Ron, who spontaneously gave Barth a brief discourse on the subject of zydeco, explaining its basis, originally with the fiddle as its mainstay, in southwestern Louisiana, long before its acceptance in New Orleans. This tangent led to teenage memories of New Orleans, damned by his neighbors as a den of iniquity but enjoyed by himself as the garden of earthly delights. Barth joined in, describing an incident that occurred during his graduate school days. A bunch of his fellow students had driven to the Big Easy for a convention, and he still retained a vague memory of sitting on a bench one hot afternoon in Jackson Square. He had ingested unknown quantities of cold Dixie beer and raw oysters, indulging in an unusual degree of daring, or foolishness, for the serious student he was at the time. Even in his retelling, Barth recalled the nausea and dizziness he had suffered, but now with self-deprecating laughter.

"Kate, has Ron ever shown you around the French Quarter?"

A short pause, then Ron answered.

"No, not yet. We been to Natchitoches, but no closer. It's too hard, still. I hope Kate and the girls see it like I can imagine it, the real New Orleans."

They sat quietly for another minute or two, then Ron got up, gathered a few dishes, and excused himself to put the girls to bed.

"I envy someone who has a hometown he still feels that strongly about."

Barth's envy was real.

"Yeah, Marceline wasn't hell, but I wouldn't go back to visit. I haven't been anywhere near the Midwest since I left for California."

"Mom took a long time getting over you leaving her."

"It wasn't like I was abandoning her. I stayed a year in that damn house while you were who knows where, calling once every few months to check in and keep your guilt under control. I mean, just because I happened to be there when Dad died and you had more important things to do, I didn't think I had to be the dutiful daughter the rest of my life. You get out in the world, doing whatever it was you were doing, it's time for me to have a life too."

The outburst caught Barth off guard.

"Hey, I'm not complaining. You know as well as I do I was in no shape then to be of help to anyone, including myself."

"Yeah, I guess I know."

Kate paused at the reminder that her brother, maddeningly unavailable at the time, had been experiencing his own version of hell.

"I didn't realize then what you were going through and all I could think of, was 'Where the hell are you?' I guess I expected you to come and take charge and as soon as the funeral's over, you disappear. I was scared, I had no idea how to deal with the situation. You were always the one who knew what to do when things got crazy. There were times when I was ready to collapse and it would have been nice to have some help."

"You're right, Kate, I know, you're right. I didn't want to go anywhere near that one-horse town again, and right then, I couldn't be of any use to anybody. I should have done a lot more, I know that. I made my escape and I was afraid, maybe I'd get sucked back into that crap and never get out again."

Barth knew her sizing up was right on target and made no effort at denial. He was surprised, however, at the idea of Kate ever being scared; he had never imagined her except with a supreme self-confidence. She was the intrepid explorer. He was also disoriented at hearing her characterization of him as the one who could always cope with difficulties. She was talking about a person he didn't know.

"Well, it's ancient history now. I had to get out of there too, even if I wasn't like you, I didn't know what I wanted and what I had to do to get there. It took me longer to figure out my life, taking detours, side roads, experimenting and hoping I'd find out what I wanted. You know, Greg, I always envied you back then. I was jealous because I couldn't be sure of what I wanted. But now, I'm glad you did what you wanted and you're happy where you are."

Barth could only wonder, *Where in hell did this come from*? He was incredulous; he couldn't believe he'd given anyone the impression he was satisfied with the life he had chosen for himself.

He recalled his first memorable lesson in idolization and misperception, occurring before Kate was even born. His uncle, a big baseball fan, had driven him to Kansas City to see the Athletics in old Municipal Stadium, as it turned out, the year before the As left town for Oakland. The As were mediocre, at best, and Charley O. Finley, their flamboyant owner, tried every gimmick he could think of, yellow baseballs and rabbits springing out of the ground to deliver fresh balls, to maintain fan interest, all to no avail. On that particular night, however, there was a reason to be there that even Gregory, still too young for Little League, understood. The Yankees were in town, and with them the Mick, the great larger-than-life Mickey Mantle. It was the thrill of young Gregory's life to sit with his uncle off by first base, breathing the same air as the great one, and the fact that Mantle did not hit a home run, that he whiffed in three at-bats, never mattered. He cherished that night, holding on to its memory as affirmation that he, Gregory Barth, must be special, certainly, because he had seen the Mick. Only years later, sometime in his teens, did he learn about some of Mantle's more human qualities, the foibles and faults of his hero with feet of clay. Eventually, of course, Barth grew to be more tolerant of perceived faults in himself as well as others, just as he developed a healthy skepticism toward the canonization of human beings. Despite this, he had never seriously questioned the image of Kate he firmly held while their lives were safely distant.

"Kate, I think maybe we have to do a little re-educating. I always thought of you as the independent upstart kid who could handle anything and, as for me, I don't know where in hell you got your ideas. I can't remember the last time I knew for certain what I wanted. Maybe taking this trip, I don't know, even then, it was just knowing I had to do something, and that's a lot for me. I guess ten years difference, not much chance to get to know each other."

"Hell, Greg, you're the psychologist."

They laughed loudly, with a heartiness in their reactions that cast their long-held misunderstandings into the trash heap of useless assumptions. Pausing, they smiled at each other. Barth was about to make some comment about the relief he was feeling when Kate, ignoring protocol, upped the ante.

"Tell me, Greg, how's your love life?"

Barth was blindsided by the question, although it wasn't out of character for her to be blunt and to the point. He knew it was no use avoiding her, even if this wasn't a subject he was eager to discuss. But, then… Maybe it was the cumulative impact of the wine, the food, the effect of Ron's open longing for his lost Louisiana, or maybe the knowledge that this was it, the last night he'd have a chance to commune directly with the sister he'd just begun to know. Whatever the reasons, he found himself willing, even desiring, to invite his sister into the memorable detour of nights and miles past.

Taking a few seconds to summarize his situation in Kansas City—after all, that was all that was required—he began telling his sister about Estrella and Tucumcari, the details fresh in his mind. Kate seemed surprised, but didn't interrupt him. Barth found it was not only easier than he thought discussing the matter, he actually wanted to tell somebody, and Kate was perfect for the role of listener. Barth left out little in his account, and what he did leave out, Kate was more than up to the task of filling in. As she was listening it became obvious this wasn't just another experience for her brother. It wasn't yet ended for him; he was still grappling with its impact. Kate couldn't recall her older brother ever being so lost in a subject before.

"This woman really put her brand on you. I'm surprised you could leave."

"Yeah, well, two different worlds, just too different. We had to be realistic. The longer I stayed, the worse it would have been. Estrella knew it too. She has her life there, she made it, and there's just too much for her to give up. We never got that far anyway, and that's probably for the best."

Barth wondered whether he sounded convincing.

"Well, what you've just described to me doesn't sound like a one-night stand, not by a long shot. You ever think you could settle down with someone again?"

"I suppose it's within the realm of possibility, but now, I'm not holding my breath. Anyway, it happened, I'm glad it happened, no regrets, but that's it. Time to move on."

"If you say so."

Kate wasn't sure she believed her brother, but saw no point in pressing the issue. Greg had come a long way since she'd had any interaction with him, and he sure didn't need her advice, not even her opinion. Besides, she was satisfied with the contact they'd made in a few days, more substantial than at any time in their lives. She could see her brother's life was hardly free from worry and sensed the anxiety he was experiencing, the uncertainty that was the driving force behind his westward ride. She was glad to be the beneficiary of her brother's discomfort, and was surprised he could communicate these aspects of his life to her, even indirectly. This was not the big brother she'd hardly known in years past, an image she had created, but, instead, a much more human version. Even the saga of his involvement with the woman, Estrella, which Kate knew to be incomplete in important ways, was comforting to her. Greg was able to take chances after all, and if things didn't have a storybook ending, well, he was showing a capacity to make himself vulnerable, and that was something. They were brother and sister after all.

The two of them sat together, silently studying the orange glow of the western horizon. Barth was playing with the thought that he was beginning to enjoy silences like these during the last couple weeks, silences which seemed strange at first, causing him to feel that he must attempt to fill them, with what, he didn't know, since he had no ready access to television or radio. At any rate, the important things between him and his sister had either been said or, at some point in the last few days, understood. For his part, Barth understood that the worries he had years ago for his wandering sister could be put to rest. She had emerged from the years of nomadic existence and made a life any sensible person might envy. Kate, on the other hand, had feelings of admiration for her brother because he was wandering, because she could see an ability to question himself she hadn't guessed at before.

They savored these realizations in silence for the better part of an hour, at the same time attempting to cope with the adjustments they'd be making in a few hours when Barth would be leaving.

"Make sure you keep hydrated while you're riding through Death Valley tomorrow. It's not called that for nothing."

"I'll be fine. I couldn't be this close and not go through it. I'm not sure how many more of these trips I'll ever take."

"Well, I'm glad you took this one. We're all glad you came out here. Still, take it easy tomorrow. People do get stranded out there. You can take my cell phone if you like. Just mail it to me later."

"No thanks. I've got this far without any civilization crutches, I'm not going back there until this trip ends."

"I think I understand. I'd tell you not to do anything foolish, but if you listened to that advice we'd still be strangers."

"Yeah, you can't underestimate the value of foolishness. I'm learning that."

As Barth lay in bed he was conscious of a mild disquiet he attributed to the prospect of the next turn in his adventures when he left in the morning for California. In the silence of the mountain he was aware of the faint light of tonight's moon sprinkling the valley outside his bedroom window. The unblemished view to the north wasn't so different than the one he had enjoyed a few nights ago from the mouth of the mesa cave dwelling with Gillespie. During both nights he had been a resting, comfortable guest in the dwellings of families who had studied the same skies a thousand years apart. Parents, children, friends, relatives, all serving their roles in the chain of communities linking civilizations through centuries. Barth had imagined the family inhabiting the cave dwelling which was his resting place then. Now he had an opportunity during the last three days to see this family firsthand, talk with them, eat with them and, finally, to be a part, a small part, perhaps, of this unit. Even as a peripheral member Barth felt a developing sense of belonging, a level of comfort and welcome he couldn't have anticipated as he was nursing Rocinante up the rock-strewn road. Seeing Kate, Ron, and his two nieces running around their home, he felt his own role changing, slowly, imperceptibly, from visitor to a connected part of this group. In this short time he had grown comfortable, to a degree which surprised him.

Barth's thoughts drifted to fresh memories of another family—Estrella, Matias and Graciela. He wondered what today had been like for them, what ordinary activities occupied their hours. Then, he had been an observer, not part of their world, even after what had happened.

In the still quiet his mind was drifting, uninterrupted, and this series of thoughts, and the feelings they evoked, added a layer of consciousness to his sense of place. It was, after all, his sense of being out of place, somehow dislocated in the world in which he lived, the world he'd made for himself, or, perhaps, the world he had let grow around him, while standing still, that had propelled him on this mad, crazy trip in the first place. Alone with these thoughts, staring out into the barely visible contours of the mountains, miles away, Barth was confident of a glint of recognition, a tie to these worlds, which he couldn't articulate.

He reflected on the frank exchange between himself and Kate, their clashing perceptions of the past and the consequences for both. It was a relief that they had been able to acknowledge, if not accept, differences separating them, unnecessarily, as it turned out.

There were other differences that had been unknown to him. He was completely surprised at Kate's image of him. Barth never thought of himself as the stable, responsible sibling, not at all. It came as a shock that he'd been viewed that way, at least until the crisis that unfolded as his marriage collapsed, followed by his father's death. His unavailability at the time, perhaps understandable, had nevertheless haunted him, undermining his own sense of adequacy. He understood Kate's resentment, but had no idea, until this very evening, that Kate's sense of competence and independence had been fostered and reinforced by her experience as a caretaker. She learned she was capable of jumping into the breach and getting the job done, even well done, and the crisis had been, in the long run, beneficial, providing confidence for her subsequent forays into life. Barth wondered whether, years from now, he'd reflect on this quiet night and be glad for the discontent that brought him here.

Just then he heard the creaking of a door and muffled footsteps outside his room. A few seconds later the sound of water running from the kitchen faucet reached his ears, followed by a short silence and the patter of small feet. Barth lay back on the bed, looked beyond his own feet to the unchanging darkness beyond the window, and fell asleep.

Barth bent to his knees, saying a tearful goodbye to the nieces he'd only known until the last three days by their telephone voices. Merina and Ruth hugged their Uncle Greg, spotting his cheeks with wet kisses, eager to show how much his visit had affected them. They were both beaming as they backed up, hugging Ron's legs while Barth mounted Rocinante. His desire was to get the bike started and going, not drawing out the leaving any longer than necessary. Just as he was pulling in the clutch and extending his right thumb to press the starter button, Kate ran over, grabbing his arm.

"Listen, Greg, I know you're not the sentimental type, but just so you know, it's been really great to see you. I feel like I know my big brother a little."

"Well, I finally see that my wild woman sister has found herself."

"You know, you might not really need to keep traveling all over this country to find yourself."

"Thank you, Zen Mistress Kate. I think I'll be okay." She bent over to kiss him and stepped back while he started up and edged away, heading slowly down the gravel road.

California Drifting

Oh, Mama, can this really be the end? To be stuck in San Francisco with the Elsewhere Blues Again. — A NOD TO BOB DYLAN

"All alone? Just pick up your phone!"

Barth sat on the single rickety wood chair in this walk-in closet, watching the ad inviting him to talk with, for the sum of four dollars per minute, any of the buxom lasses with nice asses displayed on the TV sitting on the dresser. The mild misery he'd been feeling since his walk was only reinforced by the obvious message.

You're such a loser, you're primed to be duped by this scam, he thought, continuing to stare at the screen. San Francisco was a major disappointment.

What a difference a few days had made in his attitude.

He'd left Kate's mountain home riding at a leisurely pace, luxuriating in the satisfaction derived from visiting his long-lost sister and her family. His understanding of her sense of place and contentment made a deep impression on Barth. In some ways a stark contrast to his nagging doubts regarding the pattern that was his life, he gained a measure of insight he could never have hoped for in their previous long-distance contacts. All this would have been missed had he not acted on the urge to go, in a manner directly contradicting everything characteristic of him in his prior existence.

Barth stopped at Beatty, the last chance to gas up in Nevada. No sense in tempting fate any more than necessary in this heat. He decided that he'd also avoid the manmade risks here, namely the one-armed bandits of the Stagecoach Inn—from what he could see, an establishment that had seen better days. He could gamble any time he wanted on the ersatz "boats" back in Kansas City and had never indulged even an idle curiosity. If he was going to be idle now it might as well be out on the asphalt, gambling on which set of sights the route he chose would reveal. 374 was a narrower road, but still paved, offering grand scenery of its own, including an opportunity to turn off and see the ghost of Rhyolite, an abandoned Nevada mining town. He passed, as he did the chance to take the route to Titus Canyon. Reportedly spectacular, but, weighing the matter, it wasn't worth twenty-five miles of dirt road. This was ideal territory for a dual-sport bike, but he'd given Rocinante enough undeserved abuse on rough roads.

Barth relaxed while crossing the border into California, taking in the changing vistas and distant hamlets in this sparsely populated region. He took note of the bikes heading in each direction—single riders like himself, couples riding two-up on luxury touring rigs, and groups of riders, dressed and packed for serious cross-country mileage. Their license plates, from all regions of the country, informed him that he wasn't the only pilgrim on the road. Twice he was passed by packs of California cruisers whose gear and passengers recalled the Okie Outcasts.

Heading into Death Valley he recalled the tale of the wagon train of 49ers heading out here that had given the place its name after taking a wrong turn. Those pioneers had come with a sense of purpose, perhaps desperation, seeking a plot of ground they could call home, where they could build their lives. Barth wondered what they would have thought of Neal Cassady's cruising through here, getting his "kicks," or his own self-indulgent motives, lacking any question of elemental survival.

As long as he kept moving he shouldn't have any problem cruising until he reached Ballarat, another ghost town in the Panamint Mountains, where he'd be within walking distance of more dramatic landscapes. After the Grand Canyon, Zion and Bryce Canyon, Barth could have been excused for declining the opportunity to take in more of nature's wonders, but those sights were a few days behind him. He kept reminding himself the odds he'd ever do anything this foolish again, bringing his middle-aged body out here, were slim. The next time he saw this country, it might be through tinted windows in an air-conditioned tour bus, a thought that was momentarily depressing. The sensation of movement that came with riding was wholly stripped away in the confines of a four-wheeled glass-enclosed cage. Barth's whole persona had begun to change in this regard; basking in the steady breezes he had become accustomed to on the road, he was acquiring a belief in movement itself. Along with this had come a need to actually feel himself moving, an impossibility in the confines of a four-wheeled vehicle.

What the hell, I've been telling people for years they need to change, make changes, go from point A to point B, advising them, this is how you can do it, try this, try that, see how this feels, these are all trips from one place to another, you know, 'better to burn out than rust out,' all that crap. For once, before you leave this mortal coil, move yourself. Take your own advice for a change. That's right, that's exactly right, a change, hell, it probably doesn't matter if it's wrong, whatever wrong means. Die with your boots on, old fart.

Barth laughed at this melodramatic embellishment of his latest installment of soul-searching, but the feel of a sudden gust of cooling air on his neck and up through his helmet was confirmation that he was, after all, on the right track. The biking experience, he'd come to realize a few hundred miles ago, provided a great balance, allowing him, on his own, unable to talk or be distracted by others' conversation, to take a good long look at himself and indulge in these philosophical meanderings. On the other hand, the wind, rain, road conditions, curves and traffic precluded any prolonged disengagement from the world outside him, to say nothing of the constantly changing vistas, all his for the looking.

Will any of this have an impact once I get back to Kansas City, or will I merge with the rush hour traffic on I-435 and forget all this, or worse, laugh it off as my mid-life crisis?

Officially riding in California, Barth made a snap decision to turn south on the east side of the valley, leaving more time to take it in. He wasn't far from Furnace Creek, headquarters for the park and tourist center. He'd stop and reconnoiter, get a bite, stretch his legs, and decide what constituted a "must-see" for this afternoon. Descending rapidly now, in a downward dive from the heights of the border mountains into the valley, he was effortlessly gaining speed and enjoying the mild sweeping curves, surveying the wide, flat bed of the sand desert separating him from the mountains on the other side. Some were high enough to show snow caps even in late July. It must have compounded the misery of the 1860s wagon-borne traveler to see them while suffering in 100-plus degree heat, knowing relief was a mirage at their walking pace. His own mild discomfort, with the wind whipping through his jacket, was nothing. For Barth, the Joshua trees, providing little shade with their bunches of Yucca-like leaves, were exotic, holding no sinister warnings.

The Furnace Creek Ranch was a surprise—rooms, cabins, groceries, a saloon, four-star hotel, Mexican restaurant, pizza pub, café, even an 18-hole golf course. Tall, spindly palm trees, obviously transplants, fronted the stucco and tile-roofed inn. Not what Barth expected. Death Valley wasn't as desolate as the Utah desert in which he'd been stranded, and here he had a chance to gas up and stretch his legs. The heat, however, was insufferable, enough to spur him onward, back to the road. First, he managed to get the lay of the land from a group of bikers riding out from Los Angeles. They were solicitous in their welcome, especially when they found out how far he'd ridden, and recommended he ride twenty-five miles further south to get the best look at the Valley from Dante's View. None of them appeared to have doubts about Barth's abilities as they were describing the twisting road he'd be taking to the summit.

Other riders were veering from side to side, recklessly crossing the centerline, attempting to maintain a line through Zabriskie Point while gaining altitude. The thinning air induced a playful, almost careless attitude. Barth found himself exaggerating leans in the non-stop chain of tight switchbacks. Like a master yachtsman, he was practicing his tacking, using the changes of direction to maintain the course unobtainable by a straight path.

I-435 was never this much fun.

He dismounted at Dante's View, where the valley floor was more than a mile beneath his feet. Badwater Basin, directly below him, was in fact the lowest point in the Western Hemisphere, if he was interested. White, swirling cloud-like formations were visible above the desert floor. Across the wide expanse of the valley he had a clear view of the Panamint Range and, beyond, peaks of the Sierra Nevada. As he studied the far mountains, Barth could see twisted, broken strata of rock formations, aftereffects of earthquakes in the area millions of years before his appearance on this earth. The infamous heat of Death Valley, which

Barth had sampled at Furnace Creek, was a product of the abnormal depth of the valley, up to 280 feet below sea level and, therefore, closer to the earth's molten core. Barth again found himself in awe of the sheer power and magnitude of natural forces.

It occurred to him, as he stood breathing the mountain air, that Maryann and Herschel, riding cross-country in their Beemer sidecar rig, must have already made it to Kansas City. If they had taken 35 from Oklahoma City they would have passed directly through the Kansas Flint Hills. What did they think of that flavor of nature, was their reaction anything akin to what he was experiencing here overlooking Death Valley? *Surely not*, he guessed, *but who knows?*

When he left he doubled back through Furnace Creek, giddy from the combination of thin air and the thrill of weaving his way down the mountain road through the surreal topography. He crossed the white salt flats of the valley to Panamint Springs, stopping again, this time to rehydrate. Barth was looking forward to the hustle and bustle of San Francisco. Despite the appreciation he had acquired for the wilderness and solitude, he was ready for change. *Time to head north.*

He was wiping the accumulated dirt and grime off his face shield, ready to hit the road, when a loud, rumbling "Vrr..rroo..OOM," accompanied by a trailing cloud of dust, wheeled into the lot and, to Barth's dismay, pulled up alongside him. The noise was irritating, to say the least, and the fact that the rider had come up so close was also annoying. *He has the whole damn lot practically to himself!* His bike was a gleaming white cruiser, bathed in a sea of sparkling chrome, with extended front forks, slash-cut wide-open pipes, studded black leather saddlebags, a matching wide fringed seat, and a custom flame paint job covering the tank and fenders that alone likely cost its owner more than Barth had paid for Rocinante. As far as Barth could tell, dirt and rain had never come in contact with a square millimeter of the bike's surface, not counting the tires.

Barth was eager to pull out in the wake of this rude interruption, but rider etiquette required at least a brief exchange of pleasantries. The biker dismounted and, to Barth's seeing, was a perfect complement to his ride. Black leather chaps, matching boots, torso covered by a denim shirt with missing sleeves, and a black leather vest sporting the embroidered image of a mountain on the back encircled by the legend "Valley Deserters-California." A local, no doubt, which explained the pristine look of the bike. He wasn't wearing a helmet and his long gray hair was bound together behind his neck with a simple leather band. He had a well-trimmed wisp of a black beard, what would be referred to as a "soul patch" in Kansas City. Tanned biceps were decorated with ancient tattoos and mottoes not legible to Barth, who had no interest at this moment.

Barth was still seated as the stranger approached, extending a half-gloved hand and a loud, hearty, "Heya, dude, where ya travelin' from?"

Barth's resistance wavered. *This guy means no harm. Loosen up.*

He took the outstretched hand, receiving a firm, hearty grip in return.

"Kansas City. Just trying to see some of the country, wander around for a few weeks."

"Fantastic, man. I wish I could ride like that, but this area is a great place for riding every day. You do what you can."

Barth was puzzled by the remark. If he, the archetypal biker gringo, could get off his sedentary ass and come this far, he couldn't understand why anyone who claimed to have the desire couldn't do likewise. If the guy had been one of his clients he would have, diplomatically, told him he was full of crap, but no such confrontation was called for.

"Yeah, well, I've never done anything like this before, so I'm sure anybody can if they really want to. Just takes time and desire, that's all, at least that's all I started out with."

Barth never would have seen himself as an inspirational model, certainly not when it came to the subject of motorcycle adventure.

"Oh yeah, I got the desire, got that in spades, my problem is, I just don't have the body to go with it, not since Nam."

Barth hadn't noticed before now, but he could see this guy's uncovered left forearm, bent upward in a grotesque frozen angle, shriveled, and held in position by atrophied musculature. He didn't know what to say.

"Well, that's a long time ago." The rider sensed Barth's discomfort. He was probably used to it, and quickly attempted to put him at ease.

He introduced himself as Clem Jarvis, a former Los Angeles resident who had moved out here years ago for the sole purpose of indulging his dream of riding the road, even with his significant restrictions. He had joined the army as a kid, lying about his age at a time when no one was looking too closely, only to find himself, less than a year later, enduring a long series of skin grafts and rehab to repair a shattered arm and hip. A dose of Khe Sanh shrapnel irrevocably changed the course of his life in ways that could never have been predicted at the time.

Barth's demeanor changed dramatically in the span of a few seconds. His best quality, being a good listener, one that served him in good stead with friends and clients alike, now made its appearance. At the same time, it became apparent to Clem that here was someone interested in his story. Deciding he was in no hurry after all, Barth dismounted, extending an invitation to go inside for a beer.

Settled in a booth with a view of the lot and their bikes, Barth listened while this guy filled in the details of his story.

Clement Jarvis was a street-smart kid whose blue-collar parents never pushed him in school, believing it didn't matter anyway. His decision to enlist was, as he saw it then, the best available choice. He had escaped his neighborhood, had the promise, if he stayed, of acquiring some sort of job skill, and, in the meantime, a guaranteed three meals a day. This was no small enticement, even at the price of being an infantry grunt and serving a tour in the great unknown of Southeast Asia.

While he and his wrecked body were being patched together at the L.A. Veterans Hospital, his survival instinct kicked in and, deprived of physical tools, he decided to make something of his situation. In the period of his confinement, on his own initiative, he completed the requirements for his G.E.D., an accomplishment beyond his imagining at the time, the first real achievement in his life. Determined, and convinced he had nothing to lose, he took advantage of his disability status and enrolled at Orange County Community College, where he was exposed to kids who expected more out of life and where, he learned, he could succeed, at least in this respect. His social life, nothing special to begin with, was a victim of his disfigurement, but Clem Jarvis, with his first taste of success in a different world, harnessed the energy and attention he would otherwise have devoted to who-knows-what.

From that point on, he never looked back and rarely spent time on regrets, escaping the fate that the weight and direction of his background had ordained for him. Clement Jarvis eventually became a high school English teacher, enjoying a long career trying to interest kids, his kids, in something, anything, in his personal crusade to make a difference in lives besides his own. He had never married, but again, if he had regrets, they weren't evident to his friends, students and colleagues. Finally, at the end of a long career, Clem retired, more than comfortable with his teaching pension and disability payments, to the mountains, here in Panamint Springs, where he could indulge his personal passions, catching up on his reading and riding his motorcycle.

Barth absorbed Clem's story with the same level of interest with which he had enjoyed the privilege of being let in to glimpse the lives of Mabel Cavanaugh, Sedley Crump, Estrella and Gillespie. The exuberant greeting extended by Clem in the parking lot, he knew, wasn't feigned, but the product of this guy's determined optimism and genuine respect for the long distance bikers regularly passing through the Valley. Barth learned, to his dismay, that the crippling injuries Clem sustained on that foreign battlefield years ago made rides any longer than ten or twenty miles a pain-filled ordeal. As it was, Clem had very limited use of his left arm and hand. When they returned to their waiting bikes he showed Barth the engineering feat that enabled him to ride, moving the clutch mechanism over to the right grip, making it possible for Clem to operate both the clutch and brake with his good hand.

Ingenuity, determination, and optimism, this guy has a healthy supply.

"You know, when I was a kid, I loved motorcycles, all of 'em, but I couldn't afford one, not even a damn scooter. Now, money's no problem, but hell, I can't really ride, not like you guys."

For the first time during their meeting Barth sensed a twinge of regret in Clem, and he himself felt a pang of guilt.

"Hey, it's all right, you know. I get to see the riders like you out here everyday, it's like I get to travel to all these places, and that's plenty."

Plenty, maybe, Barth thought, but he knew it wasn't enough, and he wasn't about to condescend to throwing back some transparent platitude.

"Yeah, I know I'm spoiled. I guess it takes someone like you to remind me."

"Hey, that's my function, don't ya understand? Don't waste any time worrying about me, kid, you ride your ride, maybe give me a thought sometime when you're sweeping through a wild curve, scraping your pegs. Lean into it for both of us."

Barth laughed with Clem. It was funny, being referred to as 'kid.' Clem could have been his older brother.

"Yes, I can do that. I promise you, I'll do that. If you dream about riding in San Francisco in the next couple days, you'll know where it came from."

"I'll look forward to it, dude. Well, time for you to get movin'. Rubber side down. It wouldn't hurt to wash your bike, you know, show it some respect."

"Yes, I'll do that too." Barth laughed again, stepping forward, this time making sure to take Clem's hand with the same enthusiasm with which it was offered.

Barth donned his helmet and gloves while Clem took a rag from his vest pocket and began rubbing a spot on his bike's tank where there was, from Barth's vantage point, an imaginary smudge. Likely he spent as much time with his bike as Barth did with Rocinante.

Barth nodded to Clem and, as the salutation was returned, let the clutch out and slipped back onto the road.

It was good, once again having the luxury of being alone with his thoughts, but Barth had no desire to maintain this state of affairs as a permanent condition. He could aspire to create a rewarding life entirely independently, like Sedley Crump, but he recalled the man's admission of occasional loneliness. His brush with love, as he thought of his time in Tucumcari with Estrella, had left a reservoir of still-unresolved feelings he was at a loss to interpret in ways that made sense. Nine days and eight hundred miles ago, Tucumcari still had a hold on him. Finally, it occurred to him that his own largely unplanned mobility had allowed him to observe the nature of different sources of stability in the lives of Sedley Crump, Estrella, and Kate. Even Gillespie was anchored, so to speak, to his cultural history, certainly in his vision and determination to labor in its service. These people were anchored, he thought, or, at least, seemed satisfied with their anchors. He himself had plenty of anchors in his life, but they felt like dead weights, not sources of contentment, that was the difference.

There was, Barth assumed, something to be learned from this, but, for the moment, he shoved this insight-in-the-making aside, preferring instead to indulge less taxing and more hedonistic demands on his consciousness, the passing views from the road. With good weather, clear visibility and stretches of good, straight roads, his riding skills had progressed to the point of being nearly automatic, allowing him a degree of relaxation he couldn't have enjoyed that first day heading south in Missouri. There would be time in the evening for the heady work of reconstructing and interpreting any meaning and significance attached to his stay with Kate and her family.

In another day he'd be riding into the Bay area, a destination chosen at the outset of the journey for its guarantee that he'd have at least one fun stop along the way. *No demands, no obligations, just a few days' relaxation on the coast, wandering the streets, coffee houses, restaurants, cruising the Embarcadero. What could be easier?*

Barth was riding in the unknown middle California, not the California of vacation postcards, but the state of brightly-colored, beckoning labels pasted on the ends of wooden crates in which the region's produce was shipped. This was the home of migrant farmworkers and fruit and vegetable growers, suppliers of his salads and avocados. Vast farms, in the middle of summer, the topography not really so different from its counterpart in Nebraska or Iowa. Just the difference in crops, with a longer growing season, distinguished the regions.

He had a vague sense, from his internalized map, of heading north, a very real sensation to him, although he couldn't verify it directly through his senses. He had to rely, instead, on road signs designating routes and directions. Barth was conscious of the fact that, except for the initial stretch between Kansas City and Joplin, it had been mostly west, west, and west.

The knowledge that he was heading north, toward his final destination, Seattle, triggered a nostalgia for the road behind him. Not for any particular experience along the way. It was just that the change in direction marked a final, if long, section of the ride, and the thought of Seattle, in turn, was a reminder that he'd have to either sell or ship Rocinante before catching a flight home. This idea, sensible to him when he set out from Kansas City, now evoked revulsion, a damning self-condemnation. Rocinante, after all, had gone through so much with him, had made his vision of this once-in-a-lifetime ride possible, and had never let him down, not once. Irrational, yes, Barth knew this, but he couldn't suppress the thought that this beautiful whirring assemblage of well-designed parts had shown more fidelity to him than he had experienced, or given, in many important relationships in his life.

This is stupid, hell yes, I know she's a machine, yeah, but I can do this, I'll figure it out later, of course I will.

Having temporarily dispelled the notion of himself as traitor, he again attempted to relax. Barth knew, of course, that these ruminations about Seattle and Rocinante were basically tangents, smoke screens for the source of anxiety that would crop up in his thoughts during the next few days. The coming crisis, one he could see clearly, but not avoid, or defuse, concerned the endpoint of his journey. Once arrived, or soon afterward, he'd have to confront a series of questions about the nature of the whole adventure.

What use is this to me?

Has this made any real difference?

Where the hell do I go from here?

The gravity of these questions, and their answers, couldn't be denied. Barth found the prospect of dealing with them to be daunting and, he was sure, exhausting.

Then, out of nowhere, he found himself on the crest of a steep dip in the road, with a sharp turn to the right at its bottom. Instantly, Barth transferred his weight to the footpegs, lifting his butt off the seat, tightening his hold on the grips to maintain his line, assessing the slope of the decline, the degree of his turn, and preparing for a quick countersteer and weight shift.

Bike, rider and thought moved in perfect concordance. A slight lift off the road, straight and true touchdown on the downhill slope, an automatic lean to the right, well within the turn's radius, and just as quickly, resumption of an upright rolling position, settling back into the straightaway.

Immediately, Barth was filled with the satisfying, incontrovertible pride of the craftsman, the accomplished rider, acting reflexively, without hesitation, thought, or doubt. He took a full breath and sat back, looking ahead. This was some sort of divine intervention. Drawn back, jerked back, fiercely and immediately to the here and now, his perspective was dramatically altered in the seconds required to execute the maneuver.

Barth rejected the anxiety and preoccupation of a moment ago. He had, in effect, left it sitting behind him at the top of the hill, like ballast cast overboard to right the ship. *Enough introspection, enough for now, enough for many miles,* he hoped.

If I ever do something like this again, I'm riding with Dave. I'll twist his arm, whatever it takes.

Barth concluded that, under such circumstances, opportunities to wallow in unproductive meanderings would be minimized.

He rolled into the town of Porterville in the late afternoon, as the sun was poised to make its descent behind the surrounding hills. With little effort, he located a small, cheap, family-run motel and, after buying take-out barbecue, settled in for an evening of prone contemplation and cable TV. Barth thought he was a prime candidate for sleep and one-way entertainment. By this time, however, he'd undergone a change.

Sitting on the bed, he flicked on the remote and began surfing, ready to enjoy a relaxing evening and treat himself to an old movie. Eventually, finding nothing to his liking, he became bored and restless, a feeling quite foreign to him during the last two weeks.

Have I really changed that much?

Barth, a self-professed news junkie, had been out of touch with the rest of the world, his focus directed almost exclusively to his immediate surroundings while riding and the characters and scenery he encountered between stretches of road. He had stolen glances at newspaper headlines at rest stops and restaurants along the way, but without the constant companion of radio, he hadn't adhered to his ritual of turning on the news and, surprising to him, wasn't missing this component of his life. He didn't miss the morning paper, looking through the usual magazines and journals, or setting his alarm at bedtime. He did miss friends and colleagues, most of all when he had the feeling they'd enjoy the succession of spectacular panoramas or the unbelievable stories he had to tell them. Unbelievable, he knew, because they'd be coming from him.

Sitting here, in this comfortable room, with his dinner and TV, he was the mirror image of the Gregory Barth lounging in his Kansas City home weeks ago. He wasn't rejecting his prior life, but the intervening experience had conveyed to him, as nothing else could, the message that so-called vital elements of his existence could be jettisoned without an ounce of loss or regret. None at all. Sedley and Bones, Turner and Ina, Estrella and Matias, Gillespie, Kate and all the others along the way, these were encounters with an impact. He thought of

Mabel Cavanaugh, back in her room, typing away, with no time for chit-chat or social amenities, the garbage of life thrown out the window. For a second Barth believed he knew her a little better. This ordinary night, in this ordinary room, was somehow transformed, against a dramatically different background, into an extraordinary insight.

Even after the day's ride, all he needed was food in his belly, a good shower, and he was ready to explore, at least get a look at this place, an ordinary burgh to its inhabitants, perhaps, but a place he wouldn't pass through again. He owed it to himself to at least take a quick ride, increasing his odds of seeing something or meeting someone worth the effort. He saddled Rocinante once again and headed toward the town's main drag, then began riding slowly, deliberately, in the local traffic, with the frequent starts and stops he'd forgotten as a highway rider. He was a cruiser now, not headed anywhere.

Eventually, after a few back-and-forth passes in the center of town, the idea of exploring lost its luster. The storefronts and the mall weren't particularly inviting, he'd already eaten, and nothing was beckoning to him. Barth knew he was missing something here, but decided he lacked the determination required to find it. Besides, maybe that was the point. His most memorable experiences thus far seemed to occur when he wasn't expecting anything. This was just an ordinary interlude, he reckoned, and there was nothing wrong with that.

With that thought, Barth returned to the motel and, following his reasoning, had a very ordinary end to his day, getting a good night's sleep and slowly, methodically, packing his things and preparing himself the next morning for the ride to San Francisco. His excitement quotient would undoubtedly increase in the city.

Before leaving Porterville, he stopped at a diner for a late breakfast and an opportunity to review his plan for the day's ride. On an impulse, he decided to check on things back at the office. There wasn't a compelling reason—Barth was sure things were under control and, besides, he knew Dave was more than capable of handling anything that could come up. Still, he was feeling an inexplicable need to get in touch with the home base. Thanks to his decision to leave his cell phone, one he was now beginning to regret, it was necessary to get a fistful of quarters and patiently pump them into the diner's public telephone.

"Our office hours are between nine and twelve and one to six Monday through Friday. If you wish to…"

Eleanor's voice, even recorded, was reassuring. He'd been out long enough to become dislocated, forgetting the time difference, knowledge of no use to him until this moment. Barth was struck with the disappointment he was feeling at the failure to make the connection. He punched the code to retrieve his messages, deleting the usual solicitations and meeting reminders, finally getting a welcome, familiar voice.

"Hey, wild man, guess you're enjoying the scenery. Just wanted to let you know everything's under control here, so don't waste your time worrying, have fun. Adios." Dave's voice brought a laugh, and a jolting reminder of obligations.

Exactly why he was concerned, after all the miles and days between himself and Kansas City, he couldn't say. He convinced himself there was nothing to this. *Time to get rolling*, riding to awaiting adventure in the Bay area.

"Come, hear Uncle John's band…."

The prospect of being in this city conjured up invigorating associations of an era long gone. Barth believed he could find some vestige of what he romanticized as a wonderful, vibrant interlude, the Summer of Love, etched in his memory. Of course, he hadn't been a participant. This hardly mattered at the moment he was wheeling through the northward traffic. After all, Rocinante wasn't an accidental name.

San Francisco, in his original plan, would provide a few days' respite in a stimulating and exotic setting after hundreds of miles riding in the desert and farm country of central California. Seattle was on his itinerary because it seemed a fitting place to end a long trip west and because he'd never been to that part of the country, but San Francisco was included on the assumption of its guaranteed fun value. It had never occurred to Barth but that the time spent in the Bay area would be the most enjoyable chapter of his westward travels. The variety of people and cultures in this seaside metropolis held promise for adventures that might not be expected on the two thousand miles of prologue since Kansas City. This feeling was reinforced, if not heightened, as he was wheeling north on 101 through the thick urban sprawl of San Jose, leaving Palo Alto and San Mateo behind him, obtaining his first clear view of the Bay itself, off to his right near Coyote Point. A few minutes later he was able to leave the highway traffic at Bayshore Boulevard, connecting to Hillside Boulevard and then to Mission Street, where he experienced a glint of recognition. The city traffic, despite its slower pace, wasn't noticeably more hospitable than the bumper-to-bumper commuter lanes on the freeway. Barth found himself momentarily nostalgic about the easy cruising in Death Valley.

Much to his disappointment, the funky ethnicity and relaxed atmosphere of the Mission Street area had disappeared since his last visit, during his college years. The comfortable Victorian slums of that era had been transformed to bright, neatly-trimmed painted ladies hugging the curbs on both sides of the street, proud testimony to the gradual but determined gentrification that had gained a firm grip on this edge of the city. The street people, vividly recalled from his youth, were nowhere in sight. Apartments had been converted to up-scale residences or bed and breakfast establishments, but Barth had no desire to stay in the sterile tourist mecca supplanting what he remembered as a noisy, lively neighborhood. This wasn't the reason for coming to San Francisco. Disappointed, he decided to keep riding, making a swing through downtown to the Embarcadero while considering his next move.

Times change, places change, after all, why should I be surprised?

As he turned north on Market Street toward the piers, he yanked the zipper up on his collar to keep the chilling wind off his neck. The dry desert air of Nevada and Death Valley was a distant memory, even on a July afternoon. Navigating through traffic, the buses, trolleys and jaywalkers in the business district required all his attention. Riding became an ordeal to be dispensed with at the earliest opportunity, as soon as he could locate sleeping quarters. Barth tested his patience in the congestion of the Embarcadero and made a sharp turn just before getting to Fisherman's Wharf, realizing that taking this tourist-jammed route was a mistake. Slowly, he worked his way back to Market Street, not bothering to chance a glance at the Bay or the Oakland Bridge lest he become an accident statistic in the city traffic.

Barth's luck held, and he managed to find a small, decrepit hotel in the middle of Chinatown with space in the alley behind it for Rocinante. He hadn't been particular about accommodations to this point and certainly wasn't about to change his tastes now. After all, a week ago he'd spent his nights sleeping in the desert and on the rock floor of the mesa cave with no ill effects. All he needed was a bed and shower, and besides, here in Chinatown, he was in the city, close enough to walk to Columbus Avenue, Union Square, even to the bay itself, and he could use the exercise. The daytime temperatures were unseasonably high, but this was slight discomfort compared to his recent desert experience, and, in any event, didn't inhibit his explorations.

During the next few days Barth walked up and down the length of the Embarcadero, sitting on the piers and taking in the passing ships and the outline of Alcatraz. At these moments, Otis Redding would come back to him, singing "Sittin' here restin' my bones, and this loneliness won't leave me alone, sittin' on the dock of the bay, wastin' time, wastin' time." Barth had nothing against wasting time, but his growing loneliness was another matter. Watching other tourists crowd the shops and Ghirardelli Square at night was hardly a cure. He'd go up to the base of the bridge and sit with homeless transients who gathered there at sunset, walk along the shore in the direction of the Presidio, then set off for the long uphill walk toward Chinatown, wandering in the Haight-Ashbury neighborhood and sightseeing on Columbus Ave., now with more than its share of upscale coffee shops and bistro-style restaurants. Attempting to relive his youth, he found himself sitting between the stacks at City Lights at night, browsing through books and periodicals that never made it inland to Kansas City. When he would finally retire to his downscale cubbyhole, Chinatown was still bustling and noisy with the latest edition of tourists and stragglers. There certainly was no lack of activity.

It all seemed out of place to Barth, or rather, he seemed out of place—remarkably, surprisingly, out of place. Nothing held his attention for any length of time, and he quickly became bored with sights and places in which he could never imagine having this reaction. Gradually, the reason became apparent. Since entering the city he hadn't had anything remotely resembling real contact with anybody, not even an extended conversation. That was fine in Porterville, he had no such expectations there, and besides, he had just come off three days with Kate and her family. Here, he believed that prolonged solitude or a sense of aloneness would be impossible. Even his natural introversion hadn't gotten in the way of incredible, unexpected encounters on the road, but during the days and nights here he hadn't connected with anyone. This result could be chalked up as just another in the succession of surprises in his adventures, but not a pleasant surprise. Barth wanted more, expected more, out of this destination—whether he had a right to was irrelevant. He hadn't experienced this degree of restless dissatisfaction since that last weekend, so long ago, back in Kansas City. He now knew why he'd been disappointed by the failure to connect with someone when he called the office from Porterville, but he hadn't tried again.

Barth lay prostrate on the old iron-framed bed, immersed in a feeling he hadn't experienced at any time during his journey, something close to despair. He had shut off the window unit and thrown open the sash, an act which magnified the enervating effect of the atypical sweltering heat, but somehow diminished his loneliness, if only because he could hear the bustle of the street below. He felt foolish for expecting to find some sort of connection here and was assessing the accumulated disappointments of the last days. This wasn't what he expected in San Francisco, not the immediate heat, an aberration, and not the feeling he had now, the lone transient, passing through, with no contact here and none anticipated. He couldn't explain the change that had overcome him since arriving here. After all, less than a week ago he'd been lying alone on a sand and rock bed, stranded and truly isolated, and he had somehow managed to conjure up a feeling of connectedness in the cool desert night. Here, in the midst of this unending sea of humanity, he was alone, detached, even as he could hear the bustle of street life outside his window. There was such a thing as too much solitude.

Right now, if my life ended in this fleabag hotel, no one would give a damn, hell, no one would even know until checkout time, and then I'd just be a pain in the ass to deal with to free the room up. Excess baggage, that's it.

Barth sensed that his mood had gone over the melodramatic edge, that something might come up, even here, to change it without warning, but this awareness had no immediate impact. He was feeling as old and dissipated as his surroundings. After all he had seen and experienced, it had come down to this.

Stretching his arm out to the bedside table, he grabbed for his cigarettes. He'd resumed smoking to blunt some of the edginess he was feeling, an effort to fill a void, to dull the awareness of being alone since leaving Nevada. He moved to the old chair, turning on the TV set for nothing more than background noise in a feeble attempt to distract himself.

The irony of his acute sense of isolation in the midst of the density of non-English speakers within earshot of his room might have otherwise induced laughter in the man who had acquired, almost by necessity, the ability to laugh at himself. At this point, however, all he could think of was the sense of utter failure to achieve anything of significance, as he saw it, after traveling halfway across the country. The energy that had propelled him out of Kansas City weeks ago was gone. At this moment there wasn't anything of value he could describe in return for his efforts. These feelings were magnified by the contradiction of romantic notions he still held to while wheeling the bike into the city of the Summer of Love. Even the remnants of his fantasy, in the Columbus Avenue area, still anchored by the stubborn presence of the City Lights Bookstore, had disappointed. Why he had expected the scene to be populated by other than upscale coffee shops and boutique restaurants, he couldn't recall. The closest opportunity for making a human connection here had been extended by the panhandlers, homeless and prostitutes in Union Square, at a price, of course. In the most densely populated section of this huge, sprawling city, Barth couldn't help but conclude that he had felt much less alone, less disconnected, in Red Feather, with Bones and the Okie Outcasts in the Texas high country, or Tucumcari, or even during the night spent stranded in the Utah desert. *Especially Tucumcari.*

The ad for telephone intimacy appearing on the TV screen caught his attention.

Right now even contact with these boiler-room whores is starting to look good. He turned off the offending box and resumed occupation of the bed, alone again with his ruminations.

Barth recalled the time with his sister, with Ron and the kids, how settled and contented they seemed with the ordinary challenges of family life and the demands of life on the mountain. Like Sed, like Estrella, there was a solid feeling about them. They seemed to be almost natural outgrowths of their surroundings, and, like Gillespie in the desert, each exhibited a respectful, custodial attitude toward their individual worlds. Barth couldn't imagine feeling a similar sense of place toward what he still regarded as his home. As far as he could figure, his attachment to the part of the Midwest in which he'd spent the greater part of his life was based on not much more than inertia. It occurred to him this was a general rule to which these individuals were notable exceptions.

This sense of isolation and lack of personal achievement was heightened by the realization that, at this point in his journey, he was no longer on his way out, but, given the time allotted, was somewhere on the way back, officially once he reached Seattle, now not much more than a day's ride, two at the most. If this was true, if he was, indeed, on his way home, what was he headed for, he thought, but more of the same? Barth had a sense of dread as the thought intruded and stuck. In another week he'd be back in his glass-walled box, answering mail and phone calls, writing reports and seeing the same clients. Except for Karen Leffler, who, he imagined, had made a clean break.

What's the point of it all?

Barth turned on his side, facing the blank wall, a move underscoring his isolation. Emotional fatigue was consuming him. He was aware of the irrational degree of his depression, simultaneously experiencing a glimmer of hope in the form of the idea that, maybe with some sleep, he could ride out this storm and re-establish equilibrium. He'd been surprised before in the course of his travels, why couldn't lightning strike again? The thought took some of the edge off his gloomy outlook, and, just before falling off to sleep, the vividly-recalled sensation of Estrella's warm hold on his body asserted itself into his consciousness. This was real, after all, something that couldn't be glossed over, a resilient contradiction of his present state. The brief, but intense connection forged with this woman in a few days' time hadn't diminished appreciably with the growing distance between them. Slowly, a reappraisal of the bounty of his adventure was taking place, coming from a source Barth couldn't fathom or, in any event, lacked the energy to explore. Whatever the reason, his body gradually yielded to the physical and emotional demands for rest.

The bustle outside woke Barth from what must have been a sound sleep. He had a vague recollection of his emotional state at the time he sacked out, but everything from then on was a blank. He'd gotten used to waking in the early morning hours during the last three weeks, but this was the first time he'd been awakened by the sounds of a large city coming to life. Another reminder of the place from which he had come at the beginning of his journey, the city to which he'd be returning in a few short days. A look out the window, however, was enough to render further comparison something akin to ridiculous.

Grant Street was a bustle of human activity, a narrow-walled city canyon filled with pedestrians hauling sacks and boxes of goods for the sidewalk stalls, and bumper-to-bumper traffic crawling along at the same speed. Much too early for the tourist crowds, the Asian faces and the vague din of languages beyond his comprehension underscored the sleepy observation that no, this wasn't Kansas City. Here before his eyes and ears was a subculture, the product of the collision of worlds, an accommodation of convenience refusing to surrender its original roots. Barth was the outsider here, a transient occupant of a temporary flop-house bed, acutely aware of his visitor status. San Francisco, for all its charms, was less hospitable and welcoming than the Nevada desert in which he'd spent an uncertain evening. Even the bums in Union Square ignored him when he ran out of cigarettes and change. The fierce cool winds that had greeted him on his arrival were the perfect symbol for his reception in this town, and Barth, whether fairly or not, decided that this leg of the trip may have been a mistake after all.

Slowly, as if pushed, he rolled out of bed, stumbling into his socks and pants, shuffling over to the sink, where he splashed cold water over his face. At this moment, staring blankly in the mirror, Barth couldn't think of a convincing reason to get up, other than habit. That would have to be enough today.

Leaving the hotel and walking down the street, Barth surveyed the maze of narrow storefronts opening to cavernous interiors, with aisles separated by glass and wood counters packed to capacity. Merchants hawking the usual oriental trinkets for the tourists, carved toys selling for a nominal price, as well as elaborate carved jade and ivory pieces and room-filling ceramic vases decorated with dragons and flowers. Antique cinnabar lacquer boxes and delicately-painted Chinese landscapes on multi-textured linens and handmade paper for wealthy connoisseurs. Interspersed among these, but no less crowded, were hardware stores and herbal medicine bazaars catering to the locals, he presumed, alongside the usual array of exotic restaurants of all sizes and price ranges. In the noisy bustle of the early morning, before tourist hordes ascended to this section of Grant Street, Barth's status as a transient and stranger was felt more acutely than during the evenings, when the regular invasion of visitors was at its peak.

Barth decided to head over to MotoJava, a biker joint on Bryant Street, once he had put himself together and managed some breakfast. He'd gotten a tip that the work there was decent and reasonable and decided to get an oil change and a new set of plugs while considering the route he would take out of the city. Once he hit the road and regained the sensation of rolling over asphalt and leaning his bike and body into curves he was sure he would regain his emotional equilibrium.

Maybe that's it… All I really need is to get rolling again. If it doesn't work here, change the scenery, simple as that.

Laughter… Here, in a few short weeks, he had somehow been transformed from the sedentary soul inhabiting a succession of four-walled cells to the freedom rider requiring a fix of windblown oxygen. He had become a Harley ad, or maybe a Honda ad.

Barth was on his second cup of coffee, walking around the shop among metal carcasses of bikes old and newer, the staccato sound of pneumatic tools punctuating the language of gearheads immersed in their respective views of nirvana. The smell of discarded oil mixed well with the aroma of brewed arabica, a soothing combination in this setting. Carburetors were being rejetted, front forks extended, and bars were being raised for custom cruisers, but, alas, Rocinante was being treated to a mundane oil change and cable adjustment, a tightening of the pesky clutch mechanism Sed had worked on in Red Feather. Barth may have put in his miles, perhaps he had a greater breadth of experience than the local riders loitering around the MotoJava lot, but he was not yet a member of this branch of the fraternity, at least in his thinking. He shared with them only the fact that occasionally all of them engaged in brief bouts of two-wheeled travel. Barth was an outsider, even here, but like Bones and Turner and the other Okie Outcasts, the bikers, in effect, accepted him, inasmuch as they seemed not to take any special notice of his presence. As far as they knew, he was another two-wheeled traveling vagabond, and that was enough. *Harleys, Yamahas, Beemers, Ducatis, what's the difference? We're all in the same fraternity*—that was the unspoken creed. *Everything else is just a matter of taste, that's all.* There was likely as much variety in this slice of humanity as any other.

These ruminations were interrupted when the mechanic who was working on his bike called him over from the parcel of floor space on which Rocinante was perched, balanced off the floor on the centerstand.

"The bike looks fine, everything seems ready, but if you haven't had a valve adjustment lately, you should consider it."

Barth scratched his head for a second, quickly calculating the approximate mileage since he set off last month.

"You might be okay, but sooner or later you need to check the valve clearances and any wear in the valve seats."

Sounded reasonable to Barth, especially considering his complete ignorance of the terms. He was sure he couldn't distinguish between a valve seat and the one on which he sat. Still, his predilection was to be safe rather than sorry and find himself stuck out on the road. Memories of being stranded in the desert were still fresh. He listened as the mechanic, who introduced himself as Terry, attempted to explain the motor's mysteries to him. Barth readily assented after being informed that the job would take no more than an hour. As much as he wanted to get out of this city, he reckoned this was a small price to pay for road reassurance.

"Micha, you got a second, I want you to come over and look at this man's bike."

A tall, lanky middle-aged man in grease-stained bib overalls and hair spiraling toward space in every direction walked over to them.

"Micha, this is Mr. Barth. This is your kind of bike, look at it and see if it needs a valve job. He'll take good care of you." With a nod to Barth, Terry walked off to tend to other business.

The mechanic quickly surveyed the bike, until his gaze fixed on the rear fender and the tag. When he spoke, it was with a thick east European accent.

"Missoori, that is a long way, huh?"

"About fifteen hundred miles as the crow flies." Barth realized the likelihood that this man understood the expression was small, but refrained from any attempt at clarification. Micha forced his hand, however, and Barth had to explain that he had, in fact, put nearly twice that mileage on the bike since leaving Kansas City. The mechanic started peppering Barth with questions about the places he'd seen during the last few weeks. He was cataloging Barth's responses into familiar and foreign categories through looks of recognition as he listened to the pronunciation of place names. He was obviously more intent on absorbing details of this stranger's travels than information regarding the running condition of his bike.

"You see here, nobody travels so far, even me." Micha threw his right hand out in a sweeping gesture, pointing a finger at the rear fenders of the bikes lined up against the opposite wall. Barth got the point-only clean bikes sporting California plates were visible, an observation that had escaped him. This guy Micha seemed interested in Barth's travels, more so than anyone he had met since Herschel and Maryann. He asked general questions about the terrain and the people Barth had encountered for a couple minutes, then caught himself, turning his attention back to Rocinante.

"This bike, it is a good one for travel, you know it is made near the part of the world where I come. Very dependable, I think, I also think a valve job is good after so many miles. I have two bikes to finish and I can do this bike tomorrow morning first."

Barth was eager and ready to leave this city after the disappointment of the last few days, and all his gear was packed, ready to ride. This was not welcome news. Still, after debating the idea of riding out now and taking his chances, he reluctantly concluded it was better to err on the side of caution. His internalized organizer reminded him he had no appointments to keep, that there was no reason to fret over the unexpected delay.

"All right, then, if you can definitely take care of this tomorrow morning. Do you know any places I can walk to that aren't expensive for the night?" He could have returned to his Chinatown digs, but didn't want to chance reviving the associations he had with that place. Barth figured this guy had to know more about the South Beach area than he could find out by wandering the neighborhood.

"Look, Mr. Barth, I tell you what, you wait for me to finish and you come with me, no problem. We fix you up and you go tomorrow morning, no problem."

Barth was taken aback by this out-of-the-blue offer to help him look, but his experience with Sedley Crump and Bones had opened him to the possibilities of unexpected hospitality. He accepted, thankfully, and without hesitation.

When Micha finished, they left the shop, late in the afternoon, a cool wind greeting them on the street. Barth had expected to be riding as a passenger on Micha's bike, but learned to his surprise that the mechanic owned no motorized vehicles.

"Too expensive, anyway, I can ride any bike I want at the shop, even yours."

Both laughed at the joke and walked to what turned out to be the nearest BART stop, under Market Street. Barth then learned that by "We" Micha had meant an invitation to stay with him and his wife that evening in their apartment. He was glad to accept the stranger's generosity and relieved that he wouldn't be alone tonight. They were headed across the bay to Micha's place in Oakland. He had telephoned ahead to warn his wife of the guest he was bringing for dinner.

It was a nice change to sit as a passenger, letting someone else worry about destinations, directions, and driving. The look of the commuters seated around him reminded Barth of the life he'd left behind, strangers unengaged with strangers sitting next to them, no different than his drives to and from the office on the freeway. Micha Nonoka, his last name a corruption of Nienkievicz, wasn't part of this picture. If his accent wasn't conspicuous, even in this multicultural city, the loud voice which carried it couldn't be missed, and the speaker couldn't care less. He continued the questioning he'd begun in the garage, fascinated by the smallest details in Barth's account of his travels. It was obvious that Micha had more than a passing knowledge of the geography of his adopted country. What he wanted from Barth was a fleshing-out of the skeleton, stories of the characters populating the changing scenery, descriptions which would make his vision of the country the rider had passed through more vivid, more real. At the same time, the intensity of Micha's interest, and the obvious fact that here was another character whose story could not fail to entertain, if not stimulate him, had the effect of reviving Barth. He was shedding the feelings of uselessness and depression that had engulfed him just a few hours ago. At least temporarily, he was experiencing a feeling of re-attachment to the human race. For the first time, the stop in San Francisco seemed like a good idea.

Barth prodded and persuaded Micha to talk about his own travels and arrival in the Bay area, a story he knew would be more interesting than his own.

Micha, his first name was actually Mieczyslav, was a teenager just graduated from an engineering course in his hometown of Gdansk when offered the opportunity, with six classmates, to work on a commercial fishing ship, the Archangel. A chance to see some of the world, to escape the drab, confining atmosphere of communist Poland in those days, was an offer young men without obligations or other favorable prospects wouldn't turn down. It turned out to be hard work, however, lacking any excitement, with long stretches at sea during which the men had no one else for company but themselves. On those occasions when they stopped at foreign ports, moreover, they weren't allowed to leave the ship except with one other shipmate, a rule imposed to reduce the likelihood of group escape attempts. Neither Micha nor his hometown friends, who had become a close knit group in the course of the long voyage, initially entertained any such ideas, but, eventually, the promise of freedom and adventure which had served as the impetus for signing on had turned to boredom, confinement and repression easily matching that they had left behind.

After traveling halfway around the world, they stopped for a few days in Vladivostok, a Russian port in the Pacific, for a complete unloading of the ship's hold and minor repairs. Here they were allowed to leave the ship as a group, presumably the danger of going AWOL was virtually nonexistent. They spent money freely while offship, on all those things which young men on their own would be expected to lavish their attention. Their appetites temporarily sated, they returned to the Archangel the first evening with bodies and spirits spent and numb. Nevertheless, with the resilience of youth, they managed to re-group by noon the next day and return to their dockside explorations with a new reservoir of energy. On this day, however, while eating lunch at a Chinese restaurant, they received disturbing news from an expatriate Polish waiter. Recognizing the sailors as homeland boys, he communicated the news from Poland, that Jaruszelski had declared martial law following the latest demands from Solidarity, the labor union openly opposed to the communist puppet regime. He showed them a week-old paper in their language he carried with him, stuffed in his jacket. The news was sanitized, of course, with Jaruszelski cast in the role of savior, clamping down for the safety of the citizenry, threatened by a few hooligans. Micha and his shipmates, however, had long ago acquired the ability to decipher the headlines, and it was obvious that things were bad back home, even dangerous. It was also apparent to them, as they were sipping their tea, they themselves might have been among the hunted hooligans. They could see clearly the grim resignation and forced compliance of their mothers and fathers, sisters and brothers, enforced by conscripted Polish surrogates for the same Russians who were patrolling these streets and guarding the Archangel.

Their brief interlude of joking and relaxation ended abruptly, without further discussion. Habit dictated a complete refrain from conversation that could be remotely construed as political in unfamiliar surroundings and, the communal mood having changed, they ceased attempts at talk, finishing their meal in silence. Their silence, in fact, became the basis for a strengthened bond among them once they returned to their routine on the Archangel, now headed northeast to the fishing grounds off the Aleutian Islands and the Alaskan coast. The somber faces of the young men, continuing to execute their shipboard duties with reliability and thoroughness that didn't arouse suspicion, were no longer the faces of children. They masked a shared fierce anger and newfound conviction, never verbalized, and a resolution that they, young men with their lives ahead of them, would not tolerate their imprisonment, either at home or on the Archangel, indefinitely.

Micha paused for a second, and Barth immediately turned in his seat, directly facing the storyteller. He had to hear every detail of this dangerous adventure.
"What did you guys decide to do then?"
Micha, convinced Barth was interested, resumed his account with the energy with which he had begun a few minutes earlier.

The opportunity the seamen were looking for came sooner than expected, when one of them became violently ill with an undiagnosed stomach ailment beyond the treatment skills of the ship's medical aide. A medical assistance boat was summoned from Anchorage by radio to pick up the patient, and Micha's group knew the time was ripe. This was it. For the first time since leaving Vladivostok, words were spoken between them and there was no dissent, no hesitation. Four of them, including Micha, would have been expected to be on deck anyway to assist in bringing the boat alongside, but the others, usually working below decks, would have to remain inconspicuous in the background. All were wearing street clothes underneath their rain gear, and all of them stole occasional glances at the windows in the bridge, attempting to gauge the direction of the captain's attention. It was, of course, understood that he was armed and authorized to shoot anyone attempting to desert the ship, but this was hardly a deterrent for these desperate men.

As soon as the small American cruiser pulled alongside, ropes were thrown down from the rails of the Archangel and the docking of the boats was quickly effected. The patient, bundled up and strapped to an aluminum gurney, was lowered over the side by the ropes, including one held by Micha. A few words in Russian were exchanged between the medical aide of the Archangel and his counterpart on the American cruiser. Then came the command, spoken in English by one of the American seamen, to pull away.

In a split second, with precise coordination that belied the fact that there had been little planning and no practice, Micha and his mates made their move. Instead of pulling up the ropes tied to the rails of the Archangel, they jumped over the side, sliding down, onto the steel deck of the smaller ship, just starting to pull away. The others had not hesitated either, jumping out of the Archangel's shadows, grabbing the ropes with gloved hands and flinging themselves overboard. One of the jumpers sustained a broken ankle for his troubles, but this was lost to anyone's attention in the ensuing chaos.

The American ship was pulling steadily away while Micha was shouting, as loudly as he could, words he'd been rehearsing since the plan had been hatched—"We want freedom, please, we are Poles, we want freedom, please!" Repeating the phrase over and over, he fixed his attention on two American seamen who had hauled the sick patient aboard just moments before. The other men instinctively fell in behind him and knelt on the deck, reinforcing Micha's plea and underscoring the fact that they represented no threat of danger.

In the meantime, a group of hands gathered on the starboard side of the Archangel, but in the commotion did nothing as the cruiser was pulling away but look on, perhaps enviously, though none could acknowledge such feelings openly. The captain, aware of a disturbance, then, finally, realizing what was happening, emerged from the bridge and began climbing down the metal staircase. His pistol was drawn, but by then even he knew it was too late. It was over. All he could do under the circumstances was launch a useless protest requiring mounds of paperwork and possibly subjecting him to suspicion or discipline. There was absolutely no question of pursuit—the American ship was already well on its way out of international waters. Micha and his mates were silent, staring at the Archangel as it became less real to them, now an image receding into the distance as they headed steadily toward the coast. For a change, they believed, the coast of a land with real opportunities. They were safe, and they knew it.

Micha paused here, catching his breath as the train jerked to a stop and a group of passengers crowded in front of them, waiting for the doors to open. Barth had been caught up in the telling of this story, the most interesting event in his San Francisco stay thus far. Ordinarily he would have been attentive to his new surroundings, soaking in his impressions of the riders and trying to divine the exact locations of each stop. He had done neither: he was intent on following every detail of Micha's history. Fearing the pause signaled an end to his account, and certain there was more to know about this life, Barth urged him on.

"Well, you escaped, fantastic, what happened after that?"

Micha obliged the eager listener, the best audience he could recall, other than his wife.

In the days that followed, events occurred with a dizzying speed for the Polish seamen, now instant celebrities in the Anchorage community. They were taken to a local jail, only because no one knew what to do with them, while local and federal bureaucrats sorted things out. It was determined that these men were seeking, and entitled to, political asylum, a popular decision in the wake of the news of the repression of the Jaruszelski regime. After a photo of the group appeared on the front page of the *Anchorage Daily News*, the authorities were deluged with offers from locals for help, including lodging and employment. As soon as it became apparent that these intruders were exactly as described— innocent, desperate seamen—they were placed in homes of volunteer families contacted through local Catholic charities, under the reasoning that, at least in this aspect of their lives, there would be some pre-existing bonds between hosts and guests. They were quickly, with little difficulty, absorbed in the community, most of them having some sort of training making them easily employable. Micha found work at a small engine repair shop, quickly proving his usefulness, even making the transition from metric tools and measurements with little difficulty. He soon established a reputation for competence at fixing everything from snowblowers to small tractors and ATVs and was able, almost immediately, to earn a living at a level undreamed of in his homeland.

At the same time, the family he lived with provided a conduit for his integration in the Anchorage community, to an extent that he rarely felt lonely, although thoughts of his family, which he couldn't contact, were never far from his consciousness. He eventually established his own residence in a small downtown apartment, but maintained contact with the family that had taken him in, especially the older daughter, Jennifer, who had taken it upon herself to assist Micha in negotiating the obstacles of everyday life in this country. It was she who christened him with the name by which he was still known, primarily because Miecszyslav was not a moniker that rolled off the tongue in any reliably understood manner, and Micha had no objection. In the course of time, the relationship blossomed into a romance, and, without objection from her parents, they were married and set up house together in the apartment.

Within a year of Micha's arrival on the Alaska shore, the meeting that precipitated the couple's next move took place. A vacationing rider having trouble with his German-made touring bike was referred to Micha for consultation. Micha, familiar with the workings of this particular model from the experience of his youth, diagnosed and fixed the problem, a minor glitch in the air intake, without difficulty. The rider, impressed with his work, introduced himself as the business manager of a bike shop in San Francisco on vacation in Alaska. After a short discussion, during which he determined that the demonstration of mechanical skills he had witnessed was not an aberration, he offered Micha a job, at a salary nearly twice what he was making in Anchorage. Micha took the man's card and thanked him, but didn't seriously contemplate acceptance until he relayed the story to Jennifer that evening.

To his surprise, she urged him to contact the stranger and discuss the offer in more detail. Micha by that time had no urge to relocate. He'd seen his quota of the world, but for Jennifer, it was a different matter. She had lived in Anchorage all her life and, while the idea was not an obsession, she had imagined life in a metropolitan area somewhere in the lower forty-eight. This was, for her, like the jump from the Archangel that had brought Micha into her life, an opportunity she couldn't turn down. The job was discussed, arrangements were made, and the move quickly completed.

That, basically, was Micha Nonoka's story, except for the birth of their first child, a few months following their arrival in the Bay area.

"Off here!" Micha barked the command, standing, as the train pulled to a stop. Barth jumped, stepping off quickly, stretching his steps to keep pace with Micha, who wasn't waiting. The pair weaved their way through the slow-moving crowd and up the flights of steps, re-entering the outside world in an old downtown section of Oakland—that was all that Barth could tell. Micha slowed to a good walking speed once they hit the sidewalk and the two continued down the street, side by side.

The mixture of nationalities and cultures was striking compared to the South Beach area, evidenced by the faces, dress and accents in the radar of Barth's senses. This feeling was heightened, of course, by his escort, oblivious to his surroundings as he negotiated a path through the moving crowds. At the first corner they stepped around a makeshift line of Hispanic men handling building materials being passed from an open truck at curbside through the side door of an office building. The scene would have been familiar to Barth in Kansas City and, he guessed, in every major metropolis in North America. Now, however, the sight and the sounds of their speech triggered another memory. He thought of the men he had worked with while building Graciela's house. That now seemed a world away.

Micha uttered not a word while leading his guest on a route obviously committed to memory. After four or five blocks of shops and storefronts he turned into an uncluttered alleyway too narrow for motorized traffic, except for the motor scooters and bicycles leaning against brick walls with doors and windows opening directly into their path. They walked about fifty feet when Micha stopped, extracting a key from his jacket and unlocking an old wooden, windowless door, gesturing to Barth to follow. They entered the rear of an older apartment building, ascending a short flight of stairs and walking down a dark, narrow hallway between four apartments, then descended a matching stairway to the building's main entrance, with a metal and glass door beyond which were revealed well-trimmed hedges and a narrow walkway leading to a street. Micha unlocked a mailbox on the wall and removed a rolled up newspaper, smiling as he glanced at it. "This way," he nodded. Barth followed him up a narrow stairway, past the first landing, turning down the hallway once they'd reached the third floor.

At the second door on the left Micha stopped, giving it a hard, deliberate three-knock, eliciting a clear, unaccented "I'm coming." The door opened and Jennifer, a slender woman in her forties, dressed in jeans and a long-sleeved white cotton blouse, ushered her husband in with a kiss on the cheek and grasped Barth's extended hand.

"Micha says you're from Kansas City. That's a whole lot of riding."

"Yeah, well, from what I've been hearing, Micha is the real traveler. I appreciate the invitation."

"Sit down and make yourself at home, Mr. Barth."

"Greg, please, and thanks."

Micha ducked into the kitchen, reappearing with three glasses filled with a clear liquid he called slivovitz, explaining that this was plum brandy. He toasted his guest's success in his journey and Barth in turn congratulated both Jennifer and Micha for what he could guess was a comfortable life for the two transplants. The clean, neatly organized apartment was filled with evidence of a settled, comfortable existence. There were family photos on nearly every ledge and flat surface, including many of Micha and Jennifer with their children, the son who had arrived shortly following their own arrival in the Bay area and a daughter, perhaps ten years younger. School memorabilia documenting the kids' academic careers was proudly displayed in a glass cabinet between the living area and the kitchen, and photos of in-laws, parents, and grandparents were prominent, some with backgrounds suggesting Alaska to Barth and some with clothing variations undoubtedly from Micha's Polish hometown. Barth eagerly inquired after the details of particular photos. Jennifer's responses cemented the image of a struggling, but happy family unit with its share of successes and a determination to deepen its roots in the place they called home. Gradually, Barth came to understand why Micha, having traveled much of the world, deeply interested in the parts of this country he hadn't seen, had no burning desire to be a traveler or visitor at this stage of his life, not even to own his own vehicle. As he sat with the couple at their melamite kitchen table that evening, sipping slivovitz, consuming large helpings of steaming pasta seasoned with paprika, trading stories from their respective histories, he began to acquire a glimmer of understanding of a general contentment he'd seen elsewhere in the past month. Sedley Crump, Bones, Estrella, Kate—these people had shown some of this same, not idealized, but real satisfaction with their status in the cosmos. No affectations, no Pollyannish aphorisms to tide them over, just a determined, decided take on the sum totals of their lives.

Jennifer cleared the table and Micha retrieved a couple items from a bookcase near the front door, an atlas and the paper he'd brought with him. He sat for a second, glancing over the front page of the Polish-language newspaper, then tossed it into a nearby chair and opened the atlas on the table so it could be seen by Jennifer and his guest. Now he asked Barth to recapitulate his journey, demanding that he point out towns, cities, natural attractions and stories along his route. Barth was still unused to the interest shown by others in his travels, but he felt obliged, and embellished his adventures to an extent his hosts would find entertaining. As it turned out, this wasn't necessary. Even Barth, while recounting his stories, knew that, for once, he had something to talk about in his own life worth listening to. Micha and Jennifer eagerly demanded details from their guest to make the successive images and descriptions more vivid. Describe the colors of the sky over the mesas in Tucumcari, how does a single black man survive in rural Oklahoma, did you see a Saguaro cactus in the desert, why does Gillespie explore the Utah ruins, and where are you going now?

Barth patiently responded to each inquiry, again realizing as he did so that he had experienced adventures at least as exciting and stimulating as anything he'd done prior to the morning when he left Kansas City. It was as if his life had begun that morning, and now he imagined that, years from now, when he was rocking in his chair on the porch of a nursing home, he'd be boring other residents with constant repetition of his present adventures, not with tales from his professional life. This might be the only part of his life with entertainment value. He hoped not, but this was a start.

"Mr. Barth, you have traveled a long way for a vacation and education," observed Micha. "Well, you and Jennifer have traveled and seen quite a bit of the world," he replied.

"Yes, of course, but it is different for us, our traveling is for our lives, our necessity, you understand."

"I understand. But my traveling, this is also for my life, and my necessity."

"Ah yes, you are right, I understand this, you are right."

Jennifer raised her glass at Micha's remark and the other two joined in, clinking them together as she punctuated the thought.

"To all the travelers, may they find their destinations."

"Or at least get moving." Barth couldn't resist the urge.

The three of them laughed aloud.

When Micha tapped Barth on the shoulder the next morning it was still dark. Barth was well rested, however, and rolled over, sitting on the sofa and stretching his arms. The company, food and slivovitz of the last evening had hastened a deep, restful sleep, in contrast to his lonely experience in the Grant Street hotel.

The members of the Nienkievicz family were already in motion. Jennifer was tending to their daughter and preparing for the school day, while Micha was at the table, reading the Polish-language newspaper. He was absorbed in its contents, but after a few seconds motioned his guest to join him, pouring a strong-smelling cup of coffee.

"We'll eat at MotoJava, they have good rolls and coffee, this is just to get started."

"Sure." Barth sipped the hot coffee, as strong-tasting as advertised by its smell. He retrieved his boots and socks and began the methodical, overlearned process of shodding his feet for a day's ride.

Jennifer emerged from a bedroom, preceded by her daughter, in her early teens, who she introduced as Sheila. She seemed little interested in this middle-aged stranger and was blithely unimpressed with his status as a bike rider from Missouri. They said their good-byes and Jennifer ushered her daughter out to walk to the local school bus stop. Micha was eager to go, and the two of them left the apartment, now with dawn breaking, retracing the route to MotoJava. For a brief moment, Barth had the sensation of rejoining the morning exodus of humanity to its workplace assignments. He couldn't explain why, but the feeling was strangely comforting.

Riders were already gathered in the coffee shop area, none giving the impression of having appointments or jobs waiting for them in the immediate future. From what Barth could observe, the mechanics in the garage were already busy. Micha excused himself to work on Rocinante and Barth found a table by a window where he could enjoy a second cup of coffee. From where he sat he couldn't see Micha but was content to loiter with the present members of this loosely defined biker community. He began looking over his maps to make decisions regarding the itinerary for the next few days. He still intended to head for Seattle, the final destination hadn't changed, but he had to decide which route to take through northern California and whether to head in the direction of Mt. Hood once he reached Oregon, sometime this evening, he reckoned.

He had a number of available choices—the ocean route along Highway 1, through the Napa Valley and north on 5 in central California to Mt. Shasta, or even into northeastern California, entering Oregon's less-populous eastern regions. The latter choice, lacking the tourist aura of Death Valley and the traffic density of San Francisco and the coast, seemed a good bet, offering a welcome change from what Barth had come to see as a mistake, heading into the Bay area. If not for the chance meeting with Micha and his family, reviving his otherwise tired spirits in this city, coming here would have to be judged a disappointment.

He was again infected with the urge he had acquired, the urge to move, and, following this urge, Barth walked to the front counter and paid his bill in advance, figuring he'd cut a couple minutes from his departure time.

With nothing else to do until his bike was ready, Barth resumed his seat and began reminiscing about his trip, even with a few days and hundreds of miles between him and Seattle. He was conscious of the fact that the "end" was in sight, at least since leaving Nevada, but he hadn't spent much time thinking about this other than his Chinatown hotel ruminations. The encounter with Micha had restored some balance in his outlook. Barth realized that long periods without contact, even here, could have an impact on his sense of well-being. He might occasionally experience bouts of loneliness in the desert or even during a long day's ride, but in those situations he had no realistic expectations of the person-to-person adventures that had come, unexpectedly. Here, the lack of any comparable experience, until yesterday's meeting with Micha, was disappointing, to say the least. He had anticipated so much more.

All in all, he concluded, the journey was worth it-the miles, the characters, the three-dimensional *National Geographic* vistas, the thrill of two-wheeled travel and the sense of mastery he had acquired in the process. In his summing up he found himself incredulous at the thought of the cast of characters he had encountered. From Sedley Crump to Micha, all of them unforgettable, even Kate, who, it turns out, he hadn't really known before now. And, of course, Estrella.

He had no idea how all that was behind would affect him after his return to Kansas City. It would, he knew that; perhaps in a newfound confidence to stray from his humdrum routine, perhaps in subtle ways he couldn't imagine while sitting here, sipping his coffee.

Barth stood up and started wandering through the labyrinth of motorcycles backed up against the ancient brick and mortared walls, each waiting its turn for professional attention or retrieval and return to its owner's garage. In all his travels, Barth had yet to view any collection of bikes in an inner sanctum like this. The riders here, as far as he could tell, comprised a cross-section of two-wheeled subcultures. There were the cruiser bikers, with their choppers, the speed-crazed wannabes with hot-colored crotch rockets, vintage enthusiasts with belted leather jackets sporting stitched-on marque logos, some of them completely foreign to Barth, names like Moto Guzzi, Husqvarna, Zundapp, Norton, Indian. He guessed he might not be the only rookie here, the one who couldn't tell one make from another. In the vernacular of the species, the men, and they were, by and large, male, were gearheads. These riders, whatever their choice of wheels, all had in common a singular passion for riding, whether around town, a short jaunt across the bridge into Marin County, or farther, through the Napa Valley or south, along the coast, to Carmel or Big Sur. It was evident they held a matching reverence for their bikes.

Barth was enthralled as he inched his way through the concrete and brick caverns, eyeing the aesthetic and mechanical masterpieces, rubber-tired thoroughbreds in their stalls. On the walls hung stamped tin signs and posters, advertising makes and races from decades past, some in foreign languages, exemplars of painstaking artistry in a variety of colors and styles. His college German was sufficiently intact to translate the phrase "Das Schnellste Motorrad Der Welte," printed in the art deco slipstream of a 1930s racer. The bright red, white and green of the letters in "Meccanica Ducati" beneath a sleek streak of spoked wings was a reminder that the sensuousness of Italian design was pervasive.

As if to punctuate this thought, his eyes caught the sight of a sleek bright red Ducati sportbike being pushed out from the back by a shapely woman, obviously its owner, clad from her neck to the tip of her boots in matching red leather, scuff marks and dulled kneeguards attesting to her status as an experienced rider. In silent, stealthy unison, the men, standing or kneeling next to their bikes, and those sitting and sipping their lattes with backs pushing their chairs up on hind legs, snuck admiring glances at this rapture-inducing vision. Barth was not immune to the magical draw created by her appearance, following her with a focused gaze until she disappeared outside the main entrance.

Behind him he heard Micha's voice utter a hearty "Halloo," getting his attention and beckoning him to come back. He walked over to the space where the mechanic was kneeling, facing the bike and gripping a wrench, torquing a bolt on the engine block. The wrench slipped out of his hand, clanging on the floor and eliciting a loud "Shee-it" from Micha.

Barth could not suppress a laugh. The sound of the epithet in a thick European accent gutted it of any force-it was merely funny in its distorted translation. Micha looked at him, glaring, then laughing himself, all in the span of the seconds it took until he realized that the source of Barth's mirth had nothing to do with the dropped wrench. They laughed together in their shared awareness of the problem of cross-cultural cursing.

"She is all ready to go, you will have no trouble at all." Barth wondered whether the gender reference to Rocinante was something universal, or just another idiom Micha had picked up in the course of his linguistic acculturation.

"You know if I do I'll be calling and expecting you to come to Seattle and fix the bike."

"No problem. Trust me." They laughed together this time. Barth took hold of the grips, pushing Rocinante out the garage entrance. Micha followed him to the street.

The problem of parting again. Something he never could have imagined the morning he impatiently rushed to put Kansas City behind him, having to learn how to say good-byes to all these people whose lives intersected with his for brief interludes. All, including Micha, excepting Kate, who he would never see again. Barth could never be accused of maudlin or sentimental tendencies, but these were not easy times for him, especially now, as he contemplated the approaching end of his road wanderings. Back in Missouri, there would be no more such good-byes.

"See you in Kansas City, friend." Barth knew he wouldn't.

"Shu-wer." Micha knew he wouldn't.

They laughed together, one final laugh, and Barth pulled the clutch lever, pressed the starter, and turned into the morning Bryant Street traffic.

That settles it. Oregon, here I come.

Night Vision

This is your gift to me, one endless night. — JIMMIE DALE GILMORE

The decision to set off for Eugene late in the day, through the mountains, in this weather, was one Barth now regarded as evidence of arrogance, if not idiocy.

I should know better by now.

The thought intruded into his consciousness repeatedly with the pounding, wind-driven rain. While adapting to the dryness and heat of the southwest, including the ride through Death Valley, he'd forgotten the misery experienced his first day out, three weeks ago, soaked to the skin and freezing outside Joplin.

This part of the riding experience could be described with no better word than ordeal, attempting to maintain a line on the slick road while gusting winds were conspiring to push him off the shoulder or in the path of oncoming traffic. It was a constant struggle, shifting his weight and concentrating the sum of his energies on the one and only present goal, going forward. The thought of stopping had been dismissed half an hour ago with the realization that the narrow road offered no safety in the darkness. The only realistic alternative was to keep moving, despite the fact that Rocinante's headlight didn't provide a significant margin of error. Unrelenting vigilance was an absolute requirement for survival under these conditions. The effort was sapping Barth's strength, stretching his endurance to its limit while he scanned the road for a sign, a light, anything with a hint or promise of rest that could sustain him for the next mile. Adding to this was the bone-chilling cold and wetness, now penetrating so deeply his muscles were tensing, making him less sure of his ability to react quickly when conditions demanded. With all his riding during these weeks, he was lacking any semblance of confidence in the present moment. He knew enough to realize how precarious his situation had become. He also knew his prior escapes were no grounds for conclusions regarding the ending of this immediate adventure. His lack of planning was once again apparent, resulting in this midnight ride in the middle of nowhere in the worst of conditions.

The sudden appearance of a sharp left-hand turn in the darkness forced him to lean, pushing the bars quickly to avoid veering off the road into the trees. With what could now be regarded as a well-honed reflex, Barth managed to right the bike just short of the road's shoulder, slowing down while regaining the center of the lane. Had he attempted this maneuver four weeks ago, he would have found himself off the bike, somewhere in the woods off the rain-slick road.

"Dammit," he yelled, his only recourse, utterly useless. He took his left hand off the clutch, wiping his visor with his forearm, an effort that didn't noticeably improve his view of the road. He wanted to slow down, would have liked to get down to fifty, a speed which would provide more control in these conditions and the added benefit of reducing the probability of serious injury if he went off the road or was thrown from the bike. This was, however, not an option on this road. A speeding car wouldn't be able to avoid rear-ending him on the downside of a hill. Barth was trapped, and he knew it, swearing to himself at the realization. In times like the present he would occasionally entertain the idea that this trip had been a reckless, stupid venture, but these thoughts were fleeting, dismissed in the immediacy of conditions that quickly redirected his energies to the road's non-stop demands.

The tall firs lining the route blotted out the scenery he couldn't, in any event, detect in the darkness, heightening his sense of isolation. He couldn't see the treetops bending to the fierce, unrelenting wind, but the howling gusts, a shrieking presence, left no doubt, the threat of impending disaster was real. The layers of plastic and foam protecting his head from the elements didn't insulate him from these sounds, adding to the anxiety he was feeling about conditions he couldn't see and the slippery pavement he knew was right under him, waiting for a misstep. The sound of raindrops on his helmet and the muffled whirring of the engine were his companions in the moment—comforting, despite the circumstances, if only because they were dependable.

I could have been sleeping in Mt. Hood right now, he thought.

Armweary, it was becoming an effort to maintain a constant tension on the throttle, but Barth still had reserves of adrenalin he could summon, making these small and vital adjustments as demanded. He was scared, but his body, showing its accumulated experience, was adapting, shifting automatically into the turns and relaxing on the short stretches of straightaway occasionally encountered in this hilly country. Barth could have chosen Highway 5, the shorter, direct, and more traveled route, and likely he'd be sleeping in a warm, comfortable bed now, but he didn't dwell on this rumination for more than a few seconds, dismissing it as useless. This mental ability had been honed to an impressive degree while riding, and was serving him well at the moment. The road would let him know when there was an opportunity for reflection, productive or otherwise.

In the meantime, focus on the road, keep the centerline in sight, speed steady, foot and hand ready to brake, look for debris, dips, bumps, anything requiring quick maneuvering. Scared, yes, scared, oh yeah, … but I can do this.

The miles passed, gradually but certainly, in this manner, with an occasional car from the opposite direction lighting the road before him for a few brief seconds. Vehicles approaching him from behind in this drenching rain were invariably traveling faster and passing him, providing taillights he could follow for short intervals. Barth was tired, to be sure, weary, but confidence was gradually returning, even in his worn state. He knew that the mere tolling of miles increased the probability of his inevitable encounter with an outpost of civilization. He was shivering, cold, and thoroughly soaked, but he could consider these sensations later, as they disappeared in the middle of a hot shower.

"Boy, this is not Tucumcari," he yelled, laughing out loud, another portent of survival. In the last weeks he had acquired the ability to laugh, yell, even scream out loud while riding, losing his suburban life inhibitions, at least in this single respect. His internal conversations were occasionally carried on with audible subtitles, one of the unequivocal benefits of the freedom of the road. Such behavior would have warranted his own diagnosis of some species of psychosis, Barth thought, but now he was living by a new set of rules.

"Who the hell cares?" he yelled, loudly, for emphasis, and for the secondary purpose of keeping himself awake. He laughed again, wondering whether these important lessons were included in motorcycle training courses.

Three cars passed heading south, more vehicles than he had encountered at one time in the last two hours. Looks of incredulity were visible on the faces of each of the drivers. At the same instant he observed a wider sky made possible by a straight stretch of road. His calculations informed him that the two observations were signs of an approaching town. His map, taped to the tank and less than 20 inches from his eyes, was useless in the dark. He'd forgotten the names of the next possible stops in the midst of his rain-soaked ordeal, but this information was irrelevant, even useless. The road would reveal everything soon enough, he only had to keep moving.

The road was flattening out and the woods on either side becoming less dense, increasing visibility to a degree making it possible for Barth to relax, allowing him to sit back in his seat while scanning a more open horizon, including the dark outline of what looked like a mountain range in the distance. Off to his right, he detected what he believed to be the silhouette of a junked car in a small clearing, another hopeful sign. Barth's fear and anxiety, the most prominent of his visceral reactions to his riding conditions only minutes ago, began to subside, replaced with excitement and anticipation of the discovery of the first sign of a port in this storm, a prospect now appearing imminent. His newfound confidence prompted a roll on the throttle and an acceleration of bike and pulse rate.

The changing terrain was now more forgiving. He was entertaining a belief that, within the hour, he'd be lying in a dry and comfortable bed, well beyond the gripping tension and rigors of the elements he had endured without letup during this leg of his journey. Flickering lights were detected off in the distance; hopefully, these were from something other than oncoming traffic. Barth could feel the tension draining from his muscles and the return of fatigue. He was also basking in the thought, now almost a surety, that within a day, two at the outside, he would reach Seattle, end of the road, and could take well-deserved satisfaction in the realization of something that, by any standard, internal or superimposed, he could forevermore consider a genuine, valued achievement, something to be embellished and bragged about when he finally took his seat in life's rocking chair. Even as he had this thought, however, within striking distance of the finish line in his rolling marathon, Barth was unsettled, not able to completely savor the anticipation of the once only dreamed-of objective.

"Goodnight," he muttered to the woman behind the counter, turning to the door. He had no reserve energies for niceties at this point, and he surmised the proprietor, disturbed from a sound sleep at this hour, had even less interest in engaging in conversation with this soaked, tired specimen whose sanity was in doubt.

The cabin that was this night's residence was cramped, with barely room to walk around the small single bed. The heavy coats of varnish on the pine walls served notice that this wasn't the Marriott. This was, however, home for the night—warm, dry, and with no hint of the road outside, save for the muted patter of the rain on the window. Barth dropped his case on the floor, pulled a wooden stool from a corner, and sat down to begin stripping off the rain-soaked clothes clinging to his body like a second skin. Too tired to care, he dropped each item in its turn on a pile next to the door, until, cold and naked, he flopped on the bed, giving up conscious control at the earliest possible moment and collapsing into an instant, deep sleep.

Some time later, he awoke, shivering, aware that a light, from the lamp next to the bed, was still on, and that he hadn't covered himself. He reached over to switch off the light and pulled on the blanket, slipping his aching legs into the comfort of a woolen cocoon. Now, at last, Barth thought, a sense of real comfort and safety that reminded him of Tucumcari, an observation he instantly recognized, even in his somnolent state, as anything but random. The ordeal of this night's ride, the unrelenting stress of the cold, rain, and darkness, could now be contrasted with the luxury of his warm surroundings. Nonetheless, Barth was experiencing a tension, bordering on anxiety, accompanied by a growing awareness of its source. Here, in the vortex of protection he'd desperately been seeking, Barth had a sense of incompleteness, a vivid recollection of the consuming warmth and acceptance, even love, he'd felt during those desert nights. Visions of Estrella first intruded, then dominated, his thoughts, engulfing Barth in a disorienting cascade of emotions and images temporarily blunting the accumulated exhaustion of the road. The raw, basic comfort he longed for so desperately while navigating the rain and wind in the mountain roads a few short hours ago now seemed to be surprisingly elusive.

The tension and anxiety Barth was feeling was the product of a new revelation, one that had somehow crystallized at this late, lonely hour. Barth felt, or knew, that the brief, intense experience with Estrella had grown in him, gradually, imperceptibly, perhaps, but not to be denied. He sat up, facing the window, looking out at the night, mulling over this realization and the feelings that impelled him to explore the part of him the rain and his weariness had, finally, been unable to suppress. In his dark surroundings, silent save for the muffled sounds of the continuing storm, Barth wondered at the surprise he was feeling, for perhaps the first time in this long journey, a surprise coming, not from events as they were experienced, not from his immediate interactions with the characters he encountered, but from his inner rumblings, now freed for exposure and analysis. Here, on the brink of success, the completion of his journey, he was in the grip of a growing anxiety, an acute fear that shook him, every last fiber of sore, aching muscle. He sat there, still, for five, maybe ten minutes, then, finally, succumbing again to the inevitable demands of his wracked body, and the possibility, at long last, of a deep, satisfying sleep.

What is going on here?, he wondered, waking a few hours later and slowly reconstructing the events of the evening and the restless ramblings preceding sleep. The psychic meanderings of the last few hours had consumed as much energy as the survival ride of the previous night, with a final destination unclear to him as he stared out the window.

Something was very different now, that much he knew.

The rain was still tapping relentlessly on the cabin window, exclamation points for a dreary day, at least it would seem that way, but Barth was somewhere else and his personal scenery bore no resemblance to the Oregon high country where his odyssey had taken its latest turn. Energized by the lukewarm shower and thankful for the single cup of weak coffee, compliments of the electric coffeemaker next to the sink, he began fumbling energetically through the side case containing his clothes.

He was focused like a laser in his search for what, at another time, had been nothing more than a casual afterthought, a memento of an experience yet to be interpreted. The contents of his rolled up jeans revealed nothing, to his surprise, and now the search assumed an importance and demand on his energies that had been uncharacteristic of any single action or experience of the last month. He hadn't counted on this hitch, this suddenly horrific obstacle, and, for a moment, the easygoing demeanor that had been cultivated and nourished during the last weeks vanished. A quick look through the tank bag was just as unproductive, but the building frustration of the last few minutes provided Barth a message as clear and unambiguous as any of the revelations of the road.

Where the hell did I put it?

Barth began fumbling, randomly, wildly, through the items spread out on top of the dresser. As he did so, he realized he was absorbed with a sense of certainty very much like that he had felt, strange and foreign to himself, on that hot morning in Missouri when he made the first turn of his westward journey. Just as then, the weather had no discernible impact on his mood; he was driven by a force that couldn't be affected by something as trivial or temporary as his immediate surroundings. The present obstacle was, in a sense, also trivial, he knew, but no less frustrating in the moment. He was at once impelled to continue his frantic and futile search, but another course presented itself in the next second.

He attempted some semblance of restoration of a relaxed state by repeating the overlearned ritual of packing the side cases, converting this mundane activity into a form of methodical meditation. Perhaps he could calm himself through this self-imposed ruse and "collect" his feelings, so to speak, although, even as he experienced this train of thought, he managed a silent laugh. He had, after all, already collected his feelings, at least the feelings that mattered, and had no desire to direct his energies elsewhere. Nevertheless, he was able to go through the well-rehearsed steps—crushable, cushioning clothing in the bottom, and so forth, with the map, marked with today's route, the flashlight, and the extra water bottle, in the most accessible area at the top of the case. Completing this ritual provided a sense of mastery and competence all out of proportion to the complexity of the task, but for Barth it had assumed an importance because it was indisputable evidence of his capacity to enter a new world and, as necessary, learn the small elements comprising this different means of existence. He didn't deceive himself into any self-definition as expert, but he knew, by now, that he could get by, and that certainly was something.

Finished with his packing, he set the cases on the floor next to the cabin door and grabbed his jacket. Barth was in no hurry to set off, although he didn't regard the rain, at this point in his travels, as a significant impediment. Rather, he decided to attempt to relax for a moment, regain his composure, and stay with the preoccupying thoughts of the last hours, immersing himself temporarily in the calm and quiet of the atmosphere that allowed, even invited, this luxury. Slipping his arms in the sleeves, he opened the door and felt the coolness of the rain-soaked hills. He sat on the rusting metal chair on the porch and looked out, at nothing in particular, still absorbed in the thoughts of the morning. Unlike most such mornings during the last couple weeks, however, Barth was not in the here-and-now of his expedition to wherever, but was musing over the definitive quality of the desire that now engulfed him. The contrast between the plan-as-you-go, meandering nature of his travels and the compelling immediacy of his present state was unsettling and undeniable, a magnetic north that would not, in the end, be deflected.

He looked out at his bike, parked five feet from the door, absorbing the sight of the raindrops plopping on the vinyl seat, beading and rolling off in a mesmerizing rhythm. No letup was in sight, as far as he could tell. He stood up, stepping to the bike to retrieve the raingear he had stowed under the seat, many miles ago. Might as well head out, he told himself, his preoccupation notwithstanding, and start moving in the only manner presently available to him.

Unhooking the seat, he reached for the gear packed in the rear compartment, the bright yellow matching overpants and raincoat he had stuffed there outside Tucumcari. He turned and walked back to the cabin, entered, and sat on the corner of the bed while pulling on the pants, then stood in front of the mirror and pulled the jacket over his head. Reflexively placing his hands in the pockets to push the jacket down, his right hand grasped an object with an instantly familiar feel, jolting him into a sudden state of excitement. Barth sighed audibly and emphatically, removing what he already knew to be the substitute object of his desire. The crushed, until now forgotten, but intact yellow matchbook with its simple, bright red printing was resting in his hand, the focus of his gaze and full attention, paper proxy for the feelings consuming him during the last few hours. The sudden rush of adrenalin he was feeling told him as much about his immediate course of action as any volume of spoken insightful analysis could have accomplished. No convincing was needed. The prize he held in his hand was both sign and direction, and Barth, the eternal skeptic who was constitutionally incapable of any act that could be remotely construed as superstitious, now wholeheartedly accepted the significance of the message. He recognized this sign as the material embodiment of his desire, and he was primed to receive the "message," without qualification.

He sat for a minute or two, excited and absorbed in his revelation. This was, he thought, the first time in the last month he'd experienced the feeling that he had a definite, clear destination, that he was no longer the *ad hoc* wanderer. It occurred to him that the lack of structure that was the most deliberate aspect of his recent adventures was no more or less the source of his rootless soul than the predictable nature of the life he'd been living for as long as he could recall.

"Soul," he remarked, "not a part of my vocabulary," yet he didn't reject the word that had not quite eluded the radar-censor of his internal dialogue. Instead, he stood up and moved to the other side of the bed, next to the nightstand, his course of action clear and his lack of hesitation notable, even to himself. He picked up the receiver and began the tedious and irritating process of dialing, the act itself proof of the necessity, even under these heightened, almost ecstatic circumstances, of bending his will to the strictures of another world. Forcing a patience which wouldn't have required much effort a few short hours ago, he methodically pressed each key with the degree of care a safebreaker devotes to each number in the sequence required to open a vault holding anticipated riches. Barth was amazed at his ability to exercise some semblance of control even as he did so.

It now occurred to him that, had he been in a rational state of mind, he could have obtained the number an hour ago through directory assistance. It was dumbfounding, the degree to which his overwhelming desire had blocked the routes to his common sense. He laughed at himself, again, a habit he had acquired in the last four weeks. Finally, after what seemed to be an eternity, he waited, listening to the first of the repeated tones as he glanced at his watch…

"Yes, this should be okay."

"Tucumcari Truck Stop, Hello?" The quickness of the response and the instant recognition of its voice, unanticipated in the midst of the frustrations of the last few minutes, jolted Barth, immediately bringing a smile to his face for no one to see.

"Hey, this is the Kansas City Biker Boy Message Service," he announced, clearly and loudly enough to overcome any technical glitches in the transmission, "…and I have a message for Estrella, Dancing Queen of the Desert." The quick, unrestrained laughter in his ear immediately communicated recognition and warmth.

"I was thinking about you last night, the night before, the last few days…"

"And you knew you couldn't live without me, that's why you called?"

"Well, I know how strange this is," he hesitated, … "I really want to hear your voice again, I just really need to talk to you."

"What is it you want to talk about? You know it's the middle of breakfast here, my Biker Boy, I got business to do."

Her tone was now somewhat brusque, somewhat kidding, but she was genuinely surprised and her response was meant, as much as anything, to elicit, in as little time as possible, the answer to her question, a question which didn't betray the depth of the sudden anxiety she was experiencing.

Barth did not miss her use of the possessive in the reference to him, a seemingly insignificant, but unexpected adjective that startled and excited him, no matter what her intention.

"I'm sorry, Estrella, I wasn't thinking, I just had to tell you how much I've missed you and that's the thing right now, do you miss me at all?" He sighed, quickly resuming, reacting to what he assumed was her impatience.

"I know this seems really strange, I know it is, Estrella, but this is what I had to do, I don't know what else to do, I had to tell you, I want to know… can you say anything to me?"

His bumbling, crudely phrased statements and questions were voiced in an unmistakable desperation she couldn't miss.

The feeling she had experienced when he left, how was it he had been so expressive and intense with her and then shut himself down, as she saw it, and leave, just leave? Now her questions from that other morning made perfect sense. What had been a striking, unsettling interlude for her, she realized, had been the same for her Gregory. Even the self-professed drifter, it seemed, could feel a tie, a connection.

"Where are you?"

"Somewhere in the Cascade Mountains, near Eugene… Oregon, as far as I can tell."

"What made you call me?"

"Look, Estrella. I gotta know, do you miss me?" Now it was Barth's turn to press for a response.

"You call me, just like that, you think I can stop everything here, just like that, and answer this question?"

Her voice was raised and demanding, masking the anxiety she was feeling as it became clear that it was her Gregory again speaking to her, not the biker boy who had amused her for awhile before leaving.

"How can I answer you?" She waited, for what seemed an eternity.

"Tell me you want to see me, it's as simple as that, just say that to me Estrella, and your biker boy will be on the road. That's all I need." "I mean it," he added. Given their history, or lack of it, the extra emphasis in his bumbling, inarticulate plea was demanded.

"Look, don't fool around, if you really want to be with me, then come, but if you just want to see me and take off, I don't need that." Now she was forcing his hand, calling his bluff, and, she fervently hoped, not driving him away. She sensed the intensity in his voice—it was a match for what she was feeling. In these few seconds she was allowing herself to become vulnerable once again.

"I'm not fooling around, this is it, I'M COMING, you hear that?" "I LOVE YOU."

Barth was surprised at the force in his voice.

"I love you, Gregory, I do," she responded, amazed at the sound of the words leaving her lips, just as she was stunned, elated, by his. A sense of relief overcame her with the realization that mutual, open expression of feelings, though much delayed, had finally occurred. She understood, absolutely, what it meant that he had made this call.

"Hey, what about Seattle, you said nothin' was gonna stop you from Seattle?" she added, lowering the intensity of their exchange only slightly.

Without blinking, Barth chucked the planned ending of his wandering itinerary.

"Seattle can wait."

Martin Zehr is a psychologist with the Marion Bloch Neuroscience Institute in Kansas City, Missouri. He is a member of the Mark Twain Circle of America and his motorcycle travels have earned him membership in the Iron Butt Association, requiring the completion of a 1,000-mile ride in 24 hours, and recognition as an Honorary Newfoundlander. He lives in Kansas City with his wife, Susan, and their occasional rescue dogs.

74037210R00176

Made in the USA
Columbia, SC
23 July 2017